03/16

05/12/19

WITHDRAWN

Books should be returned or renewed by the last
date above. Renew by phone **03000 41 31 31** or
online *www.kent.gov.uk/libs*

Libraries Registration & Archives

TEN
DAYS

Also by Gillian Slovo

Fiction
An Honourable Man
Black Orchids
Ice Road
Red Dust
The Betrayal
Close Call
Catnap
Façade
Ties of Blood
Death Comes Staccato
Death by Analysis
Morbid Symptoms

Non-fiction
The General (with Ahmed Errichadi)
Every Secret Thing

Plays
The Riots
Guantanamo – Honor Bound to Defend Freedom
(with Victoria Brittain)

TEN
DAYS

GILLIAN
SLOVO

CANONGATE
Edinburgh · London

Published in Great Britain in 2016 by Canongate Books Ltd,
14 High Street, Edinburgh EH1 1TE

www.canongate.tv

1

British Library Cataloguing-in-Publication Data
A catalogue record for this book is available on
request from the British Library

ISBN 978 1 78211 638 7
Export ISBN 978 1 78211 639 4

Typeset in Palatino by Palimpsest Book Production Ltd,
Falkirk, Stirlingshire

Printed and bound in Great Britain by Clays Ltd, St Ives plc.

To Robyn,
for her calm persistence, courage under fire,
and fierce plotting brain.

Thursday

4 a.m.

The beating of a helicopter swooping low over the Lovelace estate must have been what first shook Cathy from sleep, but what had brought her to consciousness was the much softer click of a door. She stretched an arm out and across the bed. The sheet was warm and she could still feel the imprint of Banji's body on it, but he had gone.

She'd fetch him back, she decided, pulling on her dressing gown and making her way down the corridor to the front door. By the time she reached it, he had already crossed the landing and was nearly at the walkway.

'Banji.'

He stopped and turned.

A tall man, toned by the gym, there was something about the way he stood there under the dark rotating blades of the helicopter that made her doubt that it was him. But as the helicopter flew away he seemed to return to the skin of the man she knew. He yawned and smiled, and said, 'It's early.' And yawned again. 'Go back to bed.'

'I will if you will.'

He shook his head. 'Better not.' He was speaking so softly she could barely make out what he was saying. 'I've got a lot on.'

'Lyndall was expecting to see you at breakfast. She'll be disappointed.' Even in the dim light she could see how his expression softened at the mention of her daughter. 'Come on,' she said. 'Come back to bed.'

'Nah.' He gestured with his arm – half a wave and half a waving of her off. 'You're all right. I'll catch her later.' A decisive turn and he strode off down the walkway.

Biting back her disappointment, she crossed the landing and went to stand at the edge of the balcony so she could see over the low wall. From there she followed his progress for as long as she could. Which wasn't long: he was moving at such a pace his brown skin had soon faded into the night.

It was hot there but so much hotter inside; she stayed where she was, looking out on the concrete and steel of the Lovelace buildings and the web of walkways that connected them.

The estate was the last stand of a twentieth-century modernist dream which years of neglect had turned into a dangerous nightmare of piss-stained crevices. It was scheduled for demolition and boards were beginning to take the place of windows and front doors, while neighbourliness was being replaced by long farewells or midnight flits.

She looked out at the separate blocks, each on different levels, which were joined by the spiralling walkways stretching to left and right. Usually so noisy, the estate was now subdued. With every door closed and every window dark, she might almost be able to hear the Lovelace residents breathing in their sleep.

As she stood there, a neon bulb winked out on the walkway opposite. Another that the council would not bother replacing; darkness was heralding the end of the Lovelace. Sighing, she went back inside.

She was halfway to bed when she heard a footfall. Cheered by the prospect of Banji's return, she hurried into the lounge, dodging the clutter of furniture (two comfy sofas and too many over-cushioned old chairs that she was always promising Lyndall she would prune), to reach the flat line-up of steel windows that faced out onto the estate. She was just in time to catch sight of a shadow flitting by.

Too slight a figure to be Banji. Must be Jayden, who lived with his mother at the other end of the landing. On his way, she guessed, to help out in the market.

PRIVATE AND CONFIDENTIAL
FOR INQUIRY USE ONLY

Submission to the internal inquiry of the Metropolitan Police into Operation Bedrock

Submission 987/S/1–15: photographic evidence produced by Air Support Unit 27AWZ pertaining to surveillance prior to the outbreak of the disturbances

location: Lovelace estate

subject: routine surveillance

This evidence was collected at 4:01:23 on ███ ████ ████ when Air Support Unit 27AWZ, India 95, passed over the Lovelace estate in Rockham.

In response to an ongoing request by ████████████ 27AWZ carried out a routine passing surveillance on the estate.

As the ASU passed over Flat 45, Lovelace Block 3, a man, IC3, emerged. Camera facilities were employed to photograph this man, later identified to be the man known as Banji. He turned to address someone (not visible) who stood in the open doorway of Flat 45. The conversation was brief. The man then proceeded unaccompanied down the runway and towards the south-western exit of the Lovelace estate.

A female figure, IC1, stepped out from Flat 45 and watched as the man departed.

The ASU did not continue its surveillance.

4.15 a.m.

Peter Whiteley was just about to leave the bedroom when he heard Frances sigh. He turned to look at the bed. She was lying perfectly still, and although he thought that the sheet, which was all that was covering her, might have shifted, it was too dark to be sure.

Another, quieter sigh, but still no movement. She must be sighing in her sleep.

The burble of a police radio told him that they were gearing up for his arrival. He left the bedroom and made his way downstairs.

The kitchen was even hotter than the bedroom. Not that this stopped Patsy from springing out of her basket at first sight of him and bouncing over, her rasping tongue making a tour of his face. 'Only time you're friendly to me,' he said, feigning affection by stroking her silken back, 'is when there's no one else to feed you.' Her answer was one last slurp of his lips before she raced across the kitchen to stand by her bowl so she could wolf down what he put there in less time than it took him to fill the kettle.

He called out, softly, through the open window. 'You there?'

The officer, who must have been perched on the stone bench just below the window, popped into view: 'Morning, sir.'

'Good morning.' Peter lifted his gaze to the dark sky. 'Or almost.'

'I'll fetch your driver, shall I?'

'Tell him half an hour.'

Peter unbolted the kitchen door (strange the habit that had them locking the door at night despite the fact that the windows were open and the house guarded back and front) and stepped out.

Dark and a smell like dry bracken. So dark he could only just make out the cluster of bushes that, once full and green, were now wilting into the cracked soil. He went a few steps further into the garden, feeling the warmth of the spiky grass on his bare feet and the dust that each one of his steps stirred up. The night seemed to

6

press down on him, the air heavier and much hotter than any English night should be. He could just make out the shadowed outline of the beech at the bottom of the garden, with its uneven cankered trunk standing stark against the blackened sky. An ancient tree: he hoped it would find a way to pull in moisture from the thickened air.

It was so quiet that he heard the kettle clicking off. He made his way back into the kitchen, leaving the door ajar.

'Help yourself.' He fetched down two mugs. 'One for me as well. No sugar.'

4.20 a.m.

The instant that Joshua Yares woke, he got straight out of a bed that looked as if it had barely been slept in. He nevertheless pulled tight the light-blue sheets, smartening up corners that were already well tucked in, before fetching the neatly folded counterpane from the chair and smoothing it over the top.

He stepped back to survey the result, approaching the bed again to flatten a faint wrinkle on the top left-hand corner. Once it was all perfectly smooth and flat, he took hold of the sweat pants and a T-shirt he had laid out the night before and, having dressed, laced up his running trainers.

Taking the narrow stairs two at a time, he was soon out on the street. A few paces jogged before he began to run in earnest.

He liked running, especially when nobody was about. And although he'd slowed considerably since his record-breaking days, he still ran with the strength and agility of a much younger man.

He pushed his torso forward as if in a race, and then, feet pounding the pavement and sweat beading his forehead (no one being about), he vaulted the gate to the park and set off across the high grass, hearing it crackle as he mowed it down.

4.22 a.m.

Peter was sweating as he stepped into the shower.

He closed his eyes, tilted back his head and let the water wash over him. Might as well enjoy it now, because if this awful drought persisted showers would soon be replaced by queuing at standpipes and water trucks for rationed water.

But this was England: the drought could surely not persist. As a matter of fact, he'd yesterday heard a weatherman predicting an imminent reversion to the grey disappointment of an average summer. That would please the PM: one less crisis to fend off in these dismal times.

He dried himself vigorously before tossing down the towel.

Thirty years married and Frances was still offended by this habit. But he couldn't rid himself of the superstition that the ritual brought him luck, and luck in great quantities is what he needed now. Courage, he told himself, and made to leave. In turning away, however, he caught a glimpse of himself in the mirror. I look washed out, he thought, despite the sun. He sucked in his stomach and flashed himself a smile. He smoothed down hair that was only beginning to grey. Better.

Now for the finishing touches.

He pulled open the cedar doors of his dressing-room wardrobes and surveyed the rows of suits and shirts and ties. Not the fawn linen. Too flash for the House. Same for the beige. Not the dark blue either – he'd overused it recently – and certainly not the grey, which always seemed too lightweight. Black then, with a white shirt, and the mauve tie for a dash of colour.

It was an ensemble that, even as he put it on, felt heavy for a day that was going to break all records. But when it was this hot in the House, permission to remove outer garments was frequently granted and, having learnt the hard way how badly the thick dark hair of his forearms played on television, he knew better than to give in to the temptation of a short-sleeved shirt.

He sucked in his paunch before taking another glance, this time in the full-length mirror. Shoelaces tied; shirt tucked; trousers pulled up; flies zipped; socks smooth. Frances had trained him to carry out this check first thing and sporadically throughout the day. It was part of the game that politicians, even serious ones, had to play: cutting their cloth in obeisance to a world that judged them by standards they themselves would balk at. Another smile – looking good – before he went back downstairs.

There was a mug of thick dark tea waiting for him. He took a sip and grimaced. Nobody in sight, so he spooned in a couple of sugars. A few more gulps before he set the cup aside. He stretched up for Patsy's lead while simultaneously holding out his other arm to ward her off: stray pieces of her brown and blonde hair on his suit would give the wrong impression.

'Round the block,' he said to her and to the policeman who, hearing him moving about the kitchen, had reappeared.

4.25 a.m.

Cathy's galley kitchen was a wreck despite last night's dinner having only been a takeaway. She managed to throw the cartons away, pile up the dirty dishes and pass a cloth over the melamine surfaces before the kettle boiled. She'd do the rest later; now she was desperate for a cuppa.

She opened the cupboard, gazing for a moment at the cluster of teapots before closing the cupboard and grabbing a mug that she rinsed out before making tea from a bag.

She took the mug down the narrow corridor. She went quietly so as not to wake Lyndall, but as she drew abreast of her daughter's bedroom she was seized by an impulse to go in.

Don't, she told herself. And then she did.

It was sweltering in there and Lyndall, who still slept with a night light on, had pushed off her top sheet to lie uncovered in her shortie-pyjamas. In the faint yellow glow from the floor, she looked uncharacteristically pale and deathly still. Cathy couldn't even see if she was breathing.

She tiptoed across the room. Still no sign of life. Knowing that she shouldn't, she lowered her hand to Lyndall's forehead.

'Geroff, Mum.' Lyndall pulled up her sheet and turned with it to face the wall.

Embarrassed, Cathy went back to bed.

4.35 a.m.

When Peter came out of the house, one of the two waiting officers spoke softly into his radio while the other moved aside to let him pass. He opened the gate at the end of the path and let Patsy bounce through, even though this was against the rules, Patsy's therapist having apparently decided that Patsy took Charles's absences at school to mean that he was a discard and she the favoured child, which was why she kept trying to bite Charles when he came home. So now, apparently, they had to re-educate the dog into knowing her place in the family hierarchy, which meant never letting her lead the way.

'Dog therapist!' He might have said the words out loud, although the officers did not react.

They were good, this current team of SO1, the specialist protection branch, adept at keeping a low profile. He could hear them, a few steps back, their regular padding a companionable sound in this soft, dark night while Patsy sniffed the ground.

There was no light from any of the houses that stood back behind front gardens, just the shadows of the trees that lined this gracious street. Walking here he felt a sense of belonging and, yes, he was not ashamed to admit it, of comfort, especially when compared to the streets on which he had been dragged up.

Despite his irritation about this enforced walk, he did enjoy the quiet of the empty mornings. To move for once unbothered by what other people saw and thought and said – this was insomnia's reward. Not that it was the smoothest of walks. The dog, having been fed, reverted to her usual irritating habit of setting off at such a brisk pace that she pulled him along (lucky there was nobody about to see or, worse, sneak a picture of him) until he grew accustomed to her pace, at which point she slowed right down so she could sniff at each and every tree they passed. She must have sensed that he was in a hurry because now she really took her time; they were halfway down the next block before she made her choice.

She stopped and squatted. He looked away (another of the bloody psychologist's instructions) while she did her business and then, feeling a tug on the lead, reached into his pocket.

Damn – he'd forgotten to bring a bag. He couldn't leave the pavement fouled; he'd have to go back. He glanced in irritation at his watch.

'Here you are, sir.'

'Thank you.' He took the outstretched bag, wondering as he did what Joshua Yares, such a stickler for the rules, would think of that.

He scooped up the dog mess and, holding it at arm's length, turned. 'Your Commissioner's first day.'

The officers nodded, all three of them simultaneously, although none of them smiled. They didn't like Yares any more than Peter did.

5.15 a.m.

Forty-five minutes to the second and the new Metropolitan Police Commissioner Joshua Yares was back at his front door. He was sweating hard and, better still, had run out of his mind the worries that beset him before the start of any task.

No matter that he had landed the big one – chief of the Met – he was not going to expend energy worrying about the way they'd got rid of his predecessor or about the extent of the mess they were expecting him to clear up. Far better to begin with a clear head and an expectation that things would go right. And if they didn't? Well, then he would deal with each problem strictly in the order in which it arose.

He buffed his trainers against the doormat, watching the dust rise, and then he took them off and strode upstairs to shower, fast, as he did everything, while still taking care to systematically wash and dry himself.

And now the moment that had been so long in its anticipation.

He put on a gleaming pair of white briefs that he had removed from their packaging the night before. Then the socks, black and new as well, and a crisp white shirt – he'd ironed it twice to make sure – and after that the black trousers that he'd had specially fitted to suit his athletic frame. He knotted the black tie but, seeing it marginally off kilter, redid the knot before fitting it snugly, but not too tightly, under his collar. And finally two items that set the seal on his newfound status: his tunic and his cap.

The black tunic – also especially fitted – with its gorget patches and ceremonial aiguillettes that passed from the pocket to the top button sat nicely across his broad shoulders. He fastened the buttons, starting from the bottom and ending at the point parallel with his jacket where the black and grey striped bar of his Queen's Medal and the red, blue and white bars of the two Jubilees were lined up. Such a pleasure to see them there, especially since he had every

11

expectation that, come the new year, they would be trumped by the yellow and brown of a K.

He smoothed his jacket down. It looked clean and pressed and right.

And finally, not that he needed it just then, his cap. This, with a crown above the Bath Star and its wreath-enclosed tipstaves, and the oak leaves that ran along both the inner and outer edges of the peak, would tell even the most casual onlooker that he was the most senior policeman in the land. He placed it carefully, using the mirror to ensure that the peak sat along the line of his forehead. He closed his eyes and felt along the cap, and then, with eyes still closed, took it off, breathed in and out, before replacing the cap. Eyes open. It was perfectly aligned. Now he'd be able to do it like this every time, even in a hurry.

He took off the cap and was about to make his way downstairs when something else occurred. Yes, why not? He went over to the wall behind his bed and, leaning across, lifted off the framed photograph that, taken on the occasion of the Queen's Diamond Jubilee, had him beside the Queen. It would go nicely in his new office. With photograph and cap in hand, he made his way downstairs.

5.25: he clicked on the radio and remained standing as he ate his usual breakfast of two slices of wholemeal toast (both with marmalade) and a percolated coffee to which he added just the tiniest dash of milk.

He was just putting his plate in the dishwasher when the item he'd been half expecting came on.

'Today,' he heard, '*is the new Commissioner of the Metropolitan Police Joshua Yares's first day.*'

He straightened up and smiled.

'*To give the background to the appointment which saw the Prime Minister and Home Secretary involved in a public spat, we go to our home affairs correspondent . . .*'

5.35 a.m.

As his Jaguar drifted through the deserted streets, in the wake of an unmarked Rover, Peter sat back and listened to the news.

'*Following reports of corruption at the heart of the Met,*' he heard, '*and the unexpected resignation of the last Commissioner, the new man, Joshua*

12

Yares, *whose nickname of "The Wall" is said to derive from his refusal to accept lower standards, was the Prime Minister's choice.'*

Now the test of whether they were going to fall into the trap that he had set for them.

'In a recent interview,' he heard, *'the Home Secretary, Peter Whiteley, suggested that Yares's well-documented friendship with the Prime Minister might put the independence of the Met at risk. In expressing his disgruntlement, and in such a forthright manner, the Home Secretary gave grist to the rumours that there has been a rift between the two politicians and that he is about to launch a leadership challenge – something that many in the Party have long anticipated.'*

Yes – he smiled – they'd taken the bait.

Clever Frances: it had been her idea for Peter to go public with his defeat over the new appointment. That the Prime Minister had overruled his Home Secretary had increased the Party faithful's dissatisfaction with their leader's rising control-freakery, which, according to the latest poll, was also beginning to annoy the electorate.

'That's the news this morning. Now let's see what the weather has in store for us.'

No prizes for guessing that what the weather had in store was hot, even hotter or the hottest day since records began. 'Switch it off,' he said.

When his driver obeyed, he settled himself into the silence, ignoring the pile of red boxes and early editions beside him and blurring his vision so that the flashing past of dim street lights and the night buses carrying a cargo of workers on their way to wake the city did not intrude. He yawned.

He was able to function on little sleep, and pretty well, but on the rare occasions when it was possible just to be, and not to act, this same weariness would wash over him. He could feel it in his bones, as if he had just run the marathon, although the truth was he couldn't remember the last time he'd done any exercise. The swimming pool at Chequers two weekends ago might have been his chance – especially in the heat – but the hosepipe ban and the resulting surface of green slime that no amount of straining seemed to shift had put him off. Another yawn. The strain of preparing to launch a leadership challenge – even though he was convinced that it had to be done – was telling on him.

'Tired, sir?'

Although he pretended he hadn't heard the question, it did break his reverie.

He glanced at the boxes, thinking of the heap of briefing and official papers they contained. He'd gone through the lot the previous evening: glancing at the 'to see'; reading more carefully through the summaries of the 'to decide' papers and then deciding; and after that he had spent some considerable time pondering the ones that had been specially marked as having potential presentational problems. These – the problems that the press might seize on – he couldn't risk. Not now when the stakes were about to go sky high.

This thought carried him back to Yares, whose appointment the Prime Minister had bludgeoned through. Why had such an adept politician, whose deviousness included giving his ministers their heads (along with rope to hang themselves), interfered in Peter's choice? Sure, Yares looked good on paper, but the other candidate, Anil Chahda, was already Deputy Commissioner. Having served under the last bod, Chahda knew the ropes, and given he was also Britain's highest-ranking ethnic officer his promotion would have been a coup not only for Peter but also for the whole government. Never mind that Chahda was the kind of policeman that a Home Secretary could do business with.

Yet the PM had been so intent on seeing Yares in the job he'd left Peter with no choice other than to concede. It was all too odd. The Prime Minister was far too ruthless to do anything for the sake of friendship, so his actions could not be explained by his connection to Yares.

Something else was going on, although Peter couldn't figure out what. He must set somebody to solving the mystery, somebody he could trust, which thought sunk him into the soup of wondering, at this, the most decisive moment of his career, who he could and couldn't trust. This led him in turn on to the things he knew and the things he didn't know, and then to facts and figures and questions he hadn't answered, and questions he might be asked at the dispatch box, all of them piling up one against the other, so that it was as if he were being sucked under a particularly boggy marsh, the gluey waters closing over his head about to suffocate him and . . .

'In the marsh,' he heard.

He came to with a start. 'I beg your pardon?'

'Your offices in Marsham Street? Is that where you want to go?'

He glanced at his watch: 5.53.

He could picture the fuss that would ensue if he pitched up at Marsham Street at such an early hour. Private secretaries, diary secretaries, and their secretaries, researchers and the tea makers who lubricated them all would be rousted from their beds and made to taxi in, and all because their Secretary of State was having trouble sleeping. Not the kind of reputation he wanted and, anyway, he needed time to think and calm to do it in. Where better than in his office behind the Speaker's Chair? 'If you wouldn't mind dropping me at the House.'

'Of course, sir.'

'St Stephen's entrance.'

He caught the surprised flicker of the driver's eyes.

'I like to, every now and then,' he said. Because it reminded him, although he didn't say this, of his first time walking in as an MP. And of the time before as well, the very first in his life, when he was the boy on a school trip who'd said out loud what he was thinking – that one day he would belong to this place – and then had to endure the mocking hilarity of his peers. 'Is that a problem?'

'I'm fond of St Stephen's myself,' the driver said. 'We all are. But it only opens at eight.'

'Drop me by Carriage Gates, then. I'll walk the rest of the way.'

5.57 a.m.

The car carrying Met Commissioner Joshua Yares swept round Parliament Square and before it turned into Bridge Street Joshua's gaze was snagged by the sight of a Jaguar that had stopped by Carriage Gates. That any car had been allowed to stop there rather than being waved away or through was what first attracted his attention, but what kept him looking was the sight of the door of the Jaguar being opened by a waiting policeman to allow the disgorgement of the portly figure of Home Secretary Peter Whiteley.

'Strange.'

'It's early,' the driver said. 'And he is the Home Secretary. They wouldn't normally stop there.'

'Hmm.' No point in telling his driver that the oddity Joshua had been pondering was not this random act of hubris but the sight of Peter Whiteley choosing to walk anywhere and so early. Wonder what he's up to, he thought, as his car rounded the corner and Big Ben began to toll the hour.

6 a.m.

'It's 6 o'clock, and, as the countdown for next year's election begins, the heat-wave continues.'

As if anybody needed to be told that the temperature and humidity were breaking all records and had been for weeks. Cathy flung herself across the bed, banging on the radio to cut it off.

She was boiling. Picking up the sheet she had thrown to the floor, she wrapped it round herself and went over to the window.

Just as she thought: the bloody radiator was on. Those bastards in the housing department. They'd promised they'd solve the problem – the way they'd talked had led her to believe they had already solved the problem – but for the fifth day in a row the central boiler, which barely functioned in winter, had switched the whole estate on at five. The crazy logic of a council: too mean to hire a proper engineer to fix the glitch but prepared to pay the enormous electricity bills that would fall to them when the Lovelace came down.

It's like a microcosm for the world, she thought: burning before final destruction.

A shower. Cold. That's what was required.

She prolonged the shower's beneficial effects by letting the water evaporate as she moved into the lounge.

With its heaters blaring, this room was also unbearably hot. If they don't fix it soon, she thought, I'll pull the radiators off the wall: that'd force their hands.

Catching the fury behind that intention, she thought maybe Lyndall was right: maybe they should cut their losses and move before the estate breathed its last.

The bedroom had to be cooler than this. She made her way back and, having opened the curtains, settled herself on top of the bed. And there she lay, letting her thoughts drift as she watched the night edged out by a bloodied dawn that washed the dirty white walls with pink. Soon after, bands of crimson and purple and deep dark red began to streak the sky in defiance of the rising sun.

Such a ferocious sight. Red sky in the morning: an omen.

For days now she'd had a feeling of something not being right. It wasn't just Banji's recent reappearance, or the impending closure of the estate; it was a feeling that something awful was about to happen. To her. To Lyndall. Or to somebody they knew. Banji perhaps.

She seemed to see again that vision of him, dwarfed by the helicopter, and then the lonely slope of his back as he had walked away.

She should have kept him with her, should not have let him go.

A crazy thought. She couldn't have stopped him. Never could.

It's the heat, she thought, it's playing with my mind. Except this was not the first time that a similar foreboding had gripped her. She'd felt it just before her father had died, for example, or when . . .

No, she would not think of it. She reached out and switched on the radio.

'It's 6. 15,' she heard, '*and the temperature in London continues to climb.*'

1.45 p.m.

All Joshua had to do was ask for coffee and it would be instantly supplied. But hours of speed-reading through seemingly unending piles of urgent for-his-eyes-only documents made him want a short break, and, as well, it would be good for him to be sighted by some of the thousands who worked in the building, especially on his first day.

He made his way down the corridor, reaching the lift just as the door began to glide shut. The policeman inside the lift jabbed at a button and the door slid open.

'That's all right, officer. I'll take the stairs.' As Joshua turned away, he took with him a frozen image of the man's rictus grin.

He pushed through the swing doors and made his way down, two steps at a time, to the senior canteen on the third floor.

It was a quiet room, and luxurious, its windows lining the whole of one wall to look out on the Thames, and with plush tables and chairs that wouldn't have been out of place in a five-star restaurant. Another of his predecessor's extravagances, although, from what he'd read that morning, a comparatively small one. Even so, given the dire state of the Met's finances, it would have to go.

No need, anyway, for silver service, especially when all you were after was a coffee. 'No, thanks,' he told the waiter who was bent on ushering him to the Commissioner's special table, 'I'll get it myself.'

There was a queue by the takeaway counter, which evaporated at his approach. 'Go ahead,' he said to an officer who should have been in front of him, but she smiled and slunk away.

'Coffee,' he said. 'Strong and black,' and when the woman behind the counter reached for a cup from above the coffee machine, he added, 'Takeaway.'

'We can easily fetch the cup, sir. When you're done.'

'I've no doubt that you can. But why should you have to? A paper cup will do.'

18

Although she had a state-of-the-art espresso machine, the coffee she poured into the Styrofoam cup smelt stale. Still, she made it strong to suit his taste.

'Thanks. How much is that?'

'Oh no, sir, you don't need to pay.'

'Yes,' he said, thinking that this was another thing he was going to have to change, 'yes, I do.'

Turning to leave, he saw his deputy, Anil Chahda, sitting at a corner table with what looked to be half of the senior management team. They were clearly well settled in, the table littered with empty plates.

By the way they were sitting and not talking, he knew they must have been watching him. Probably thought he should have lunched with them. And also bought them lunch.

Well, they needed to start thinking differently.

He nodded in response to Chahda's dipped head.

One of the group, a man he didn't recognise, perhaps someone on secondment, lifted up his cup and called, 'Why not come and join us, sir?'

It was a friendly gesture, especially from a group who must have expected him to have them in first thing – something that he had decided against doing.

He knew he should go over now. But his pile of reading beckoned, and he could do without the discomfort of sitting amongst them and not giving away his plan to prune the team.

'I must get back,' he said.

Silence – although he could feel all eyes on him – as he made his way across the room. He pushed the door.

'Stuck-up twat,' he heard as he went out.

If that was the best they could come up with, they wouldn't be giving him any trouble. Smiling, he held his cup aloft as he climbed the stairs, two at a time again, and soon was back in the cool solitude of his grand domain.

2 p.m.

After Cathy got off the bus, she felt the sun so hot she knew it would soon burn through the white cheesecloth of her loose shirt. She pulled up her collar to protect the back of her neck and walked down Rockham High Street, feeling the hem of her long skirt fluttering against her ankles and hearing her sandals slapping against the pavement.

Every door on the High Street was open and every shopkeeper out on the pavement on boxes or fold-out chairs, and although they were normally a garrulous bunch they now sat silently, as if the humidity and the traffic fumes had drained them of all life.

Her route took her past Rockham police station, a fortified brick one-storey in the midst of run-down shops. They'd tried to pretty it up by grassing the front and then ruined the effect by planting an oversize 'Welcome to Rockham Police Station' noticeboard on the lawn. Now a couple of workmen were levering out this board while a third was up a ladder manoeuvring a CCTV camera. The sight perplexed her. Were they shutting the police station, as it was rumoured they planned eventually to do, even before the Lovelace had come down?

'That's it.' The men prised the sign from its chained surrounds. They dropped it in the midst of glass that, once a protection against the elements, was now littering the lawn. That's when Cathy saw that someone had graffitied on the sign, so that it now read: 'Welcome to Wreck'em Police Station'.

'Witty,' Cathy said.

'Think so, do you?' One of the men shot her a dirty look.

There was a new sign on the edge of the lawn near Cathy, which the men went to fetch. It was clearly very heavy. As they turned, one of them stumbled. The sign teetered. Without thinking, Cathy put out a hand to stop it falling.

'Keep off,' one of the men yelled. Seeing how she jumped, he lowered his voice. 'Didn't mean to frighten you. It's this paint, you see. It's AI – Anti Interference. Dyes your hand.' He used a forearm to wipe away the perspiration that, having collected on his forehead, was beginning to drip down. 'Not that you'd know you'd been marked, not until they flash you with an infrared gun and your hand lights up like it's Christmas. Sticks to your skin for a week – fuck knows what chemicals have ate into you in the meantime. No washing it off neither. That's why we're wearing gloves in this fucking heat.'

'What happens if somebody touches it by mistake?'

20

'No chance of that. We're gonna glass it in and then embed the post in concrete – the lawn is history. And after that we'll fence the lot in.'

'That's overkill, isn't it?'

'You think so? It's the badlands around here, and from what we've heard it's only going to get badder.' He grimaced. 'Now, if you don't mind, we have to get on.'

She left them to it, walking along the High Street until she turned off to go down the market. There the ice was melting almost as fast as the fishmongers could lay it down, so that water was dripping off the trays onto the pavement and into the gutters, flavouring the air with the stink of fish. Careful to hold her skirt up, she stepped onto the pavement and kept going, passing a pound shop, one of three along the parade. She stopped by a display of plastic boxes of various sizes, and mops and brooms that had spilt out onto the pavement and almost into the road.

'Jayden?'

Jayden, who had been picking up the fallen brooms, looked up. A taciturn boy, he nodded to her.

'You were out early this morning.'

He shrugged and said something that sounded like 'I dunno.'

'Not at school?'

He shook his head and didn't speak, but whether this was because he was truanting and didn't want to say so, or because he couldn't summon up the energy for an explanation, she couldn't tell.

'Come and have some cake with us after your tea.'

'Okay,' he said. And gave a little smile. Which she knew was the best she was going to get out of him.

She moved on only to stop again at the last shop in the run. It wasn't her favourite, but it was the cheapest. She reached over the display of peppers and okra and tomatoes to the plantain at the back. She had just picked up a piece when a voice sounded in her ear: 'That plantain's tired.'

She looked up and straight into the sun, so that all she first saw against the dazzle was a dark shape. She took a step back, blinked and her vision cleared: 'Banji. You scared me.'

He smiled and his eyes crinkled. Which she'd always liked. She smiled back.

He took the plantain she'd been reaching for, turning it over to expose a bruised underside. 'If you have to shop here, you've got to shop clever.' He put the piece back and picked through the pile. 'This one's fresher.'

As she took it from him, his other hand touched and held hers.

'You're so cool,' she said.

'I was born cool.' He smiled again.

They stood for a moment not speaking, and she thought how mismatched they – a stout white woman and a tall black man, standing close – must look, and then she thought that she should take back her hand.

She didn't want to.

'How was Lindi this morning?' he said.

'Disappointed you weren't there. And stroppy as hell.'

'Can't imagine where she gets that from.' Another smile as he increased his pressure on her hand.

She looked down at his long brown fingers with their broad square-cut nails and the back of his hand with its raised veins. She saw her own hand in his, plump and white, as he continued, gently, to squeeze it.

It was fifteen years since he'd left, and his going had been so brutal and so final she'd neither expected to see him again nor hoped that she might. But now she found herself in the grip of some of the feelings she had thought long gone. He's playing me, she told herself. And said, 'Where did you go this morning?', although she knew he wouldn't like the question.

He took his hand away so abruptly that she was pulled forwards.

'What the hell?' She backed away from him. 'Why do you always have to be so difficult?'

Not often that she shouted at him, and now she saw, in his rapid blinking, how she had taken him by surprise. Good, she thought.

'Hey.' He reached out to tap her, gently, on the nose. 'I didn't mean to unbalance you.'

If he thought he could win her over so easily, he better think again. She turned her wrist to look at her watch and, although she had nowhere to be, said, 'I'm late.' Plantain in hand, she went into the shop.

There was a queue by the till. She wandered through the narrow aisles, giving herself space in which to cool down and Banji time to make good his escape. But when at last she re-emerged, she found that he had waited for her.

'I'm sorry.' He was looking down at her, twitching his nose in that other way she had also always found appealing. 'I was out of line.'

She couldn't remember him ever apologising. Despite herself, she softened. Said, 'And I overreacted. The heat's doing me in.' She even thought of stretching up to kiss him.

But his attention had already moved off. 'Trouble,' he said.

She followed his gaze and saw Ruben, who, six feet three and broad with it, his head covered even in this extreme heat by a hoodie, was cutting a swathe down the middle of the market as only Ruben ever did. He walked as if he was completely alone in an empty space, windmilling his arms to accompany words that seemed to burst from him. 'Option,' Cathy heard. 'Action. Traction. Mischief.' To punctuate the last, he slapped open palms against his chest so hard it sounded like a gun going off.

'He must be off his meds,' Banji said.

'He won't hurt anybody. Not unless he feels threatened.'

'No, but he might hurt himself. And . . . Oh shit.'

Banji had already seen what Cathy only now noticed – two uniformed policemen making straight for Ruben. She knew most of Rockham's bobbies, but she had not seen these two before. And Ruben did not take to strangers.

'If they try and stop him . . .' Banji began.

She didn't stick around to hear what he was going to say. 'Come on,' she called as she began to run.

By the time she reached Ruben, a group of onlookers, mostly young men who, for want of something better to do, hung around the market, had also been drawn to the scene. She could feel the heat coming off them, and she knew this wasn't just down to the weather.

As a member of the police community liaison committee, she'd clocked the recent rise in confrontations between the police and Rockham's youth, a result of the Clean-Up-Rockham campaign that the new borough commander had set in motion. It was a grand-sounding initiative that so far seemed to consist primarily of an escalation in stop and searches, with a corresponding rise in allegations of harassment. With the imminent closure of the estate upping the tension, the last thing they needed was another incident, especially one involving Ruben, who was a kind of Lovelace mascot. She pushed her way to the front.

'I'm asking you nicely, sir,' the older of the two policeman, a sergeant, was saying to Ruben. 'Lift your hood away.'

'Action,' Ruben said. 'Mischief.' He windmilled his arms close to the policeman's face.

'Careful,' the policeman said. 'Hit me and there'll be trouble.'

'Action.' Ruben sped up the agitation of his arms.

The policeman held his ground. 'Under Section 60 of the Public Order Act, I am authorised to request that you remove your face covering. All you have to do, sir, is take it down and then, all things being well, we can go on our way.'

'Mischief,' Ruben said, and again, 'mischief.'

'Let him alone,' came a shout from inside the crowd, and from someone else, 'He's not doing any harm,' while the crowd moved closer.

'Do what you've been trained to do,' the sergeant told his junior.

'Assistance required,' the constable said into his radio as he turned to face the gathering. He was young, and new, and the hand that held the radio was trembling.

Not so his sergeant. A big man, and sure of his authority, he stepped close enough to Ruben for their noses to be almost touching.

'Action,' Ruben said. 'Traction.' He flicked both hands at the policeman as if trying to shoo away an insect.

'No need to take the piss.' The sergeant moved closer.

'Don't touch me.' Ruben backed off until he ended up jammed against a stall.

'Leave him alone!' The cry was taken up by other members of the now growing crowd.

'Sarge.' This from the young constable.

But the sergeant was not prepared to listen either to his junior's appeal or to the rumblings of the crowd. 'Your choice,' he said, and might have laid hands on Ruben had not someone darted from the crowd to interpose himself between the two.

'Hold on, officer.' It was Reverend Pius Batcher of the local Methodists and a fellow member of the liaison committee. Normally a soft-spoken man, Pius now used a voice built up by years in the pulpit: 'You're new to the area, so allow me to introduce you to Ruben, a member of my congregation. Ruben wouldn't hurt a fly. Not unless you invade his personal space.'

'I wouldn't care if he was the Archbishop himself,' the policeman said, 'I would still ask him to remove his hood.'

'Which he will do, officer. In good time.' Pius smiled as he saw the policeman taking in his dog collar. 'I'll stand here,' he said, 'while Marcus there,' he nodded his head at the dreadlocked third member of their small committee, who must have arrived with him, 'asks these concerned members of our community to back away. Meanwhile, Cathy here,' he inclined his head in her direction, 'will help Ruben.'

What the crowd would not do for the rookie they did for Marcus, stepping back when he asked them to. Not far, though. They kept pressure on the policeman, who called out, 'Sarge.'

The sergeant looked towards his young constable. He frowned and seemed about to turn away when the young policeman said softly, 'There's a lot of them.'

In that moment, before the sergeant could do anything worse, Cathy said to Ruben, 'You know me, Ruben, don't you?'

Ruben had lowered his head and was looking at his shoes. He did not look up.

'And you know I'd never do anything to hurt you?'

At least this time he nodded.

'What they need you to do is pull back your hood. Only for a moment. They want to see your face. Do you understand?'

Another, reluctant, nod.

'OK, then. I'm going to help you.' She moved just one step closer. 'The first thing I'm going to do is to put my hand on your arm.' She reached out her arm: 'Here goes.'

He jerked away, his head shaking wildly while his arms, which he'd crossed and folded around himself so that each hand was holding on to the opposite forearm, were likewise shaking. She knew that he was holding on to himself, not so much as protection from her but to stop

25

himself from hurting her. Seeing the effort this was costing him, she took a step back. As she did, she saw, out of the corner of her eye, how the sergeant mirrored her movement by coming closer. If she didn't manage to get Ruben's cooperation, and soon, the sergeant would take over, with unpredictable consequences.

She said, 'Ruben.' Commanding him but without raising her voice. He lifted his head.

'I know you don't want to hurt me,' she said. 'And,' hoping it was true, 'I know you won't. I'm going to try again.'

She reached out, and to her relief this time he let her rest it on his velveteen sleeve. His arm was shaking, and his eyes had filled with tears. He was clearly struggling with himself, but he did, at least, let her hand be.

'I'm going to leave my hand there and come closer.' She moved in on him, keeping her voice low, making sure to clearly enunciate her intentions. 'And now, what I'm going to do, is stand in front of you, and reach up, and move your hood back. Because I'm standing here, only me and the policeman will be able to see your face. Will you let me do that?'

He looked at her. Blankly.

'Will you?'

His shook himself, as if coming back to himself. And nodded. Almost imperceptibly, but it was consent.

'Okay, then.' Without taking her eyes off him, Cathy called, 'Officer, please join us.'

She had been so concentrated on making the small space they occupied safe for Ruben that all thoughts and all sounds had faded. Now she felt rather than heard the sergeant closing in.

'I'm going to take down his hood,' she said. 'Please don't touch him.'

She took the policeman's silence as consent. She stretched up her arm, 'No one but us can see,' and nudged the hood off Ruben's bald head.

He let out a strangled cry, and both his hands shot up to cover his face.

'I'm sorry, ma'am, I have to have a proper look.'

She almost had to stand on tiptoes to take hold of Ruben's hands and pry them away.

'Reaction,' Ruben whispered. He was still trembling.

'Satisfied?' Cathy didn't wait for the policeman's reply. 'You did great,' she said, letting go of Ruben's hands. 'You can put back your hood.'

He pulled his hood over his head so roughly that it covered his eyes. 'Action,' he said. His voice was louder now than it had been before. 'Traction.' And his arms wilder.

'It's okay.' Out of the corner of her eye she saw the sergeant's confirming nod. 'You can go.'

Ruben took a step forward and seemed to stumble. It happened sometimes – his legs just gave out on him.

She resisted the impulse to help. She got out of his way so he could stretch both arms out as if the air would support them. Then at last, with his head hung low, he shambled away, a wounded bear in search of his cave. 'Option,' he muttered. 'Action.' His face was crumpled in distress. 'Traction. Mischief.'

'Show's over.' The younger policeman now tried to exert an authority that had so far eluded him.

The onlookers did not move on. They looked at him and his colleague. And did not speak.

'Move along.' His quivering Adam's apple indicated that he had a lot to learn before he could exert authority over such a disaffected bunch. Which was probably fortunate, Cathy thought: a more experienced officer might have gone in harder, with unpredictable consequences.

'If there's trouble,' Marcus told the crowd, 'it'll be us that suffers for it. Ruben is safe. Let's go back to our lives.' At which the crowd did begin to disperse.

'Well then,' this from the young policeman.

'Break it up,' the sergeant told the air.

As Pius began to tell the sergeant what he should have done, their voices faded from Cathy's consciousness. Her first sensation had been relief that Ruben was safe. But now something else was bothering her. Something out of kilter. Something missing.

Someone.

Banji.

Where had he got to? Out of the corner of her eye she saw the sergeant stalk off. 'Have you seen Banji?'

'He's over there.' Marcus pointed to the far end of the market where Banji was still standing.

He didn't notice her looking. He was too busy watching Ruben.

'How come he didn't help?'

She must have spoken the thought aloud, because Marcus came back with, 'That coconut. He thinks only of his own skin.'

Knowing that there was little love lost between the two men, she didn't reply. Besides, she couldn't help thinking that Marcus was right: Banji had been the first to spot trouble looming, and yet when she had gone to help, he had abandoned her.

Again.

As he had done early this morning.

And fifteen years ago.

She sighed.

'Something troubling you?' This from Pius.

'Nothing I can't handle,' she said, hoping it was the truth.

8.30 p.m.

Mr Hashi had asked Jayden to come early, which meant he'd had to skip school, and then Mr Hashi had also asked him to stay on late. Okay by Jayden. He needed to earn enough to see them through until his mother's next disability payment.

He carried the last of the plastic bins inside, stacking them below the left side shelf as Mr Hashi had taught him to do. He stretched up on tiptoes, removing the long hook from where it hung and, taking it outside, used it to pull the shutter down. He left just enough space for him to duck under and then, once inside, closed the gap and bolted the shutter. He put the hook back, pulled up the counter, walked through, slammed the till drawer as he passed and opened the door behind the counter to call, 'Mr Hashi.'

No answer. He tried again: 'Mr Hashi.'

'Come up, Jay Don.' This was the way Mr Hashi always pronounced his name. 'We have *lahoh* for you.'

He glanced back at the wall clock: 8.40. Lyndall's mum would be wondering where he'd got to. So would his mum if, that is, she knew what the time was. But he was hungry, and Mr Hashi always acted hurt if Jayden said no to his invitations. 'I'm coming.' He pulled the door shut behind him.

Darkness and something wrong with the wiring, which meant there was no point trying to find the light switch. As he made his way up the steep stairs, he took care to steer dead centre so he wouldn't bang into any of the goods that lined both edges. As he neared the flat that Mr Hashi shared with his mother, the smell of cardamom and cinnamon and the incense that they always had burning grew more pungent.

The door he knocked on was immediately opened. 'Come in, Jay Don.' As hot as it was, Mr Hashi was wearing that same dark-blue jumper he never seemed to take off. He stepped aside to let Jayden into

29

a small room whose piles of cushions and thick carpeting made everything much hotter than it already was outside.

Mr Hashi's mother was sitting on her usual cushion in a corner. Jayden went over to stand in front of her and bow, as Mr Hashi had taught him to do. When she said, 'Salaam Alaikum,' he answered, 'Wa-Alaikum-Salaam,' as he'd also been taught, although it always felt a bit strange having to twist his tongue around the words.

'Are you feeling better?' he asked, at which she, who didn't have a word of English but who could tell his question was kindly meant, stretched her grin even wider so he got a glimpse of her few remaining teeth where they stuck out of her gums.

'Sit, sit,' Mr Hashi urged him. 'You are our guest.'

One half of the room was the women's section. Crossing into the other half, Jayden lowered himself down. When first he'd been invited in, he'd thought the lack of furniture strange; now he liked the cushions. They were much more comfortable than anything they had at home.

'Is your mum okay?' Mr Hashi had needed him early so he could take his mother to the hospital.

'She is old.' Mr Hashi gave a resigned shrug. He turned to the stove, picked up the silver teapot and poured from it into a glass cup. He added milk and a spoon of sugar, and then he put the cup on a silver tray on which was already laid a plate piled high with the flat pancake bread that Jayden had learnt to love and, beside it, a bowl of honey.

'The till drawer was open, Mr Hashi,' Jayden said. 'You got to get it fixed.'

'True. I got to.' Mr Hashi put the tray down on the small metallic side table beside Jayden. 'Now worry about yourself, growing boy, Jay Don. And eat. My mother baked the biscuits you like. She will be most disappointed if you don't have at least five.'

9 p.m.

Cathy and Lyndall had opened every door and every window and still the place was too hot, so they had moved out onto the landing. As had most of the estate. Conversation, laughter and the sounds of quarrelling rose up into the sticky air to the accompaniment of the heavy base beat blasting out of one of the flats. Arthur from next door had fallen asleep in his rickety deckchair, his mouth slack, his snores beating out their own rhythm against the general racket, and nothing, not even the giggling kids who were running up and jumping over his outstretched legs, occasionally delivering a mistaken backward kick, disturbed him.

'Shift up.' Cathy used a foot to nudge Lyndall, who was sprawled out on sofa cushions. 'And take this, will you?' She passed down the plate she'd just fetched from the kitchen.

'Mmm.' The cake was a soggy mess surrounded by a sticky puddle of icing. 'That looks . . . umm . . . good?'

'No need to lie.' Cathy lowered herself down 'It's my worst ever. Chocolate wasn't the best choice in this weather, especially with the fridge on the blink. But it's Jayden's favourite, and it may taste better than it looks.'

'And Jayden is where exactly?'

'He's never been the most punctual of boys. Give him a knock, will you?'

Lyndall, who was in one of her more cooperative moods, sprung up, her gazelle legs making short shrift of the distance between their front door and Jayden's. She beat a tattoo against the board that had been nailed in over a broken pane. No answer. She knocked again, and harder. A long pause before the door opened a crack. Lyndall spoke into it, and whoever was behind the crack said something before banging the door shut.

Lyndall shrugged and came back. Standing in front of Cathy, she lowered her head and raised her shoulders in a perfect imitation of Jayden's mother's slump: 'She doesn't know.' She also had Jayden's mother's monotone pitch perfect. 'Never sees him. Doesn't know what he's up to,' and now an escalation in pitch, 'doesn't care. He should be protecting her, but he's a bastard. Like his father. End of.' Lyndall smiled. Having ditched Jayden's mother's sour expression, she now looked so pretty, especially given that the lowering sun added a golden lustre to her coffee-coloured skin. 'Who's Jayden meant to be protecting her from?'

'Her enemies, I guess.' Cathy sighed. 'Of which she makes many. She's going to be at the bottom of every list when they close the Lovelace.' She sighed again. 'Poor Jayden.'

'At least he knows who his bastard of a father is.'

'Lyndall!' Cathy had to shield her eyes against the lowering sun in order to see her daughter. 'You promised.'

'Yeah, okay.' Lyndall's hands raised high in mock surrender. 'I won't ask for another week.' She dropped her hands, slapping them for emphasis against her bare legs. She gave a quick smile, her way of showing that she didn't bear a grudge, before she walked the few paces to the low wall that overlooked the estate.

The sun was just now dipping behind the furthest building, and the black of the intertwining walkways had taken on a silver sheen. 'There's another meeting at the centre,' Lyndall said.

'I didn't hear of any meeting.' Cathy went over to stand next to Lyndall. She saw the doors to the community centre open and a handful of people filing in. 'I wonder what it's about.'

'Scouts against the Bomb? Mothers for Rap?' Lyndall smiled. 'Oh no, if that had been it, you'd be there, wouldn't you, Mum? How about Rastafarians for a Better Quality of Puff?'

Next to the community centre was another low-brick building that had started out life as a launderette. After it closed, a series of deluded optimists had tried and failed to turn it variously into a functioning chippie, a newsagent and, for a few mad months, a soft furnishings shop. Each reinvention had failed more spectacularly than the previous one. Now, with the Lovelace coming down, the council had given up trying to rent the space and had, instead, boarded up the building, but badly, so someone soon prised open a hole big enough for a person to get in and out. As they stood looking down, a woman climbed through this hole.

'Hold on to your wallets,' Lyndall said. The woman straightened up, tugged down her tiny skirt, put the sunglasses that had been embedded in her straw-coloured hair on her nose and then, teetering on high heels, sashayed in a generally forward direction. 'The pop-up brothel's on the move.'

'Just because she uses,' Cathy said, 'doesn't make her a prostitute.'

'Oh, Mum,' Lyndall said. 'You're such an innocent.'

'Well, it doesn't.'

'Yeah, yeah, and you're the one who landed us in an estate named after a porn star and didn't even realise it.'

'I keep telling you, Richard Lovelace was a seventeenth-century poet.'

'So you do,' Lyndall said, 'and I bet you also think the mistresses he writes about are all allegories.' But she said it without much emphasis, because her attention had been caught by something else. 'Looks like Ruben's off on one,' she said.

As the tottering woman neared the edge of a building, Ruben had rounded the corner. He was holding something that, when Cathy looked harder, turned out to be a long stick. Coming abreast of the woman, he lifted the stick. She held up two fingers and flicked them, then kept on going. It was a gesture that, if Ruben saw it, he ignored. He thwacked the stick down against his palm. His lips were moving, although he was too far away for Cathy to hear what he was saying, as he continued, rhythmically, to hit his palm.

'I better go down,' she said.

'No need.' This from Lyndall, whose eyes were keener than her mother's. 'Banji's on the case.'

Cathy saw that Lyndall was right and that Banji had also rounded the corner. As Ruben made slow progress, Banji made no effort to catch up with him, instead matching his pace to the other man's so he wouldn't be seen. At one point Ruben wheeled round to stand stock-still, peering into the rapidly descending dark as if he knew someone was following him. But by then Banji had melted back against a wall so Ruben didn't spot him.

Banji's such a contradiction, Cathy thought: first he steers clear of any involvement, and then, just as I decide he's a complete waste of space, here he is, quite clearly following Ruben to make sure he stays safe.

The door to the community centre was still open. When Ruben came abreast of it he stopped. Banji stopped behind him. Someone must have been standing near the door because, although Cathy couldn't make out who it was, they came to the threshold and spoke to Ruben, who raised his stick arm. The someone must have talked some more because although Ruben kept the arm up he neither stepped away nor raised it further.

'Must be somebody who knows him.' Cathy felt herself relax.

The door was opened wider, and Ruben stepped in.

'They'll talk him down,' Cathy said. 'They'll keep him safe. I'm going to make some tea.'

9.10 p.m.

There was so much to catch up with and so much to put right that Joshua Yares would have stayed on if Downing Street hadn't called. It was for the best: if he'd kept going, others in the senior management team might have felt obliged to do the same. Probably wiser not to stretch their patience so early on.

The secretary who'd called had made it clear that this was a private visit, so Joshua circled round to Horse Guards Parade in order to go in through the back.

'The Prime Minister's expecting you, sir.' A man led him up the narrow service stairs to the third-floor flat and rapped smartly on the door. Without waiting for a response, he opened the door, saying, 'Please do go in. And help yourself to a drink. The PM will be with you in a jiffy,' before he went away.

Joshua hadn't been in the living room for a while, and now he admired afresh how successful Marianne had been in her project to stamp out all the tasteful traces of the previous occupants. The room was in fact such a riot of colour the tabloids had nicknamed it Dizzy Street.

None of this was much to Joshua's taste, but when Marianne was in residence there was a crazy logic that seemed to work. Now, however, everything looked to be out of place and clashing with everything else. Marianne must be in the country, leaving the room to the mercy of the whirlwind that was Teddy, who was bound to be the source of the loud rock music issuing from deeper in the flat.

Joshua was hot and thirsty from his walk. He poured himself a soda water.

'That all you want?'

He turned. 'Prime Minister.'

'No need to stand on ceremony, Josh. Here we can still be friends. Fix me a malt, will you? No ice.' The Prime Minister had always been a vigorous man and, although he looked exhausted, he strode rather than walked across the room, and when he opened the door to shout, 'Turn that racket down. And come and say hello to Joshua,' his voice was loud enough to penetrate the music, which was immediately cut off.

'That God for that.' Taking the glass from Joshua, the PM went over to one of the sofas, plopped himself down into its bright-cushioned embrace and took such a big swig that he almost downed the lot.

'Bad day?'

'Not much fun. Bit of a pattern at the moment. I wake, see the blue sky, remember the latest guestimate of how much water there is in our reservoirs and decide, yet again, that somebody up there has it in for me.' He drank what remained of his glass before putting it down with a bang.

'Another?'

'Better not.' He stretched out his long legs and sighed. 'It's frenetic at the moment. Marianne's right to have made good her escape. She sends her love by the way.'

'And mine to her.' With Marianne away, Joshua couldn't help wondering why this sudden summons to the private residence. And on his first day as Commissioner.

'You must have heard Whiteley using your appointment to attack me?'

Could this be the reason? But surely the Prime Minister knew that, now he was in post, there was no way that Joshua could get involved in a squabble between politicians, especially in the same party, even if it did seem to be about him. Joshua gave a noncommittal nod.

'The ungrateful bastard is after my job. Didn't think he'd dare. Frances, his Lady Macbeth of a wife, sweats politics – if, that is, she ever sweats. I can't help admiring her even though she's dangerous. She was born to it. But he had to fight hard to get where he is, and he got there with my help. I thought he was genuinely interested in public service. And loyal.'

There was a time when Joshua could have pointed out that a series of disastrous polls might have something to do with Whiteley's new-found disloyalty, but he must now be more circumspect. He was saved anyway from replying because the door was flung open to reveal the Prime Minister's son, Teddy, who was dressed in a pair of frayed cut-off shorts and no top, so that his sharp ribs seemed to stick out through his pale-white skin.

'Hello, Joshua,' he said, and immediately turned away.

'Teddy!'

He turned back. 'Sorry.' He put a hearty fakery into his voice as he repeated his greeting, 'Hello, Joshua,' adding, 'enjoying the new job, are we?'

'Too early to say.' Although Teddy's tone had made it clear that he was only doing what his father expected of him, and with ill grace, Joshua couldn't help smiling. Not easy to live under the spotlight in Downing Street when you were seventeen, especially when you were pitching for edgy eccentricity, as Teddy obviously was. And despite the pimples, and the louche posture, and the drawled disinterest, Joshua could still see remnants of the enthusiastic young boy he had always warmed to. 'How are things with you?'

'Fucking awful, actually. Nothing but revision, and in this heat. Which, speaking of. Must get back to it.'

He made to leave but stopped when his father said, 'You remember I'm off tomorrow?'

'Sure do.' It was said breezily enough and yet, Joshua thought, there was also something sad in Teddy's tone. What was Marianne doing in the country when Teddy was about to sit exams, he wondered, a thought reinforced by the PM's next statement.

'If you want Mum back while I'm gone, you only have to say.'

'Kind of you,' another effete drawl, 'but you'll soon be,' he made speech marks with his hand, '*home*. What more could I possibly need? You go and have a good time, why don't you? I hope the glad-handing of a president does the trick with your disastrous polls.'

The Prime Minister seemed to flinch, and yet when he said, 'Try and get a bit of air when I'm away,' he sounded calm.

'Will do.'

'But for pity's sake dress properly when you go out.'

'What's the matter, pater?' Teddy smiled. 'Do you think my ugly mug will impact your popularity?' He winked at Joshua and exited, closing the door firmly behind him.

'He's impossible.' The Prime Minister sighed. 'I'm sorry.'

'Not to worry.'

Should he say something or should he keep his mouth shut?

Of course he should say something: he was after all the boy's god-father. 'He has got very thin,' he said.

'Has he?' The PM's frown displayed more uncertainty than disagreement – an odd thing to see in a man who was usually so bullishly confident. He swallowed. He leant forward and swallowed again. But if he had been about to say something, a loud knock on the door stopped him. He leant back. 'Come.'

A man poked his head around the door. 'Sorry to disturb, Prime Minister, but you wanted to know when they arrived?'

'Thank you. I'll be down in a moment.' The door closed, and when the Prime Minister looked at Joshua, Joshua thought he must have imagined that earlier uncertainty. 'Duty calls. I'm truly grateful for your coming at such short notice. Before you go, there is something I need to ask you.'

10 p.m.

The cake had tipped the kitchen from messy into a disaster zone, and she was trying to clear it when she heard Lyndall calling, 'Mum.'

If she'd told Lyndall once, she'd told her a thousand times: come into the same room as me if you want to speak to me.

'Mum.'

She ran a pan under the tap, seeing how thick was the crust of congealed food on it.

'Mum.'

'I'm in the kitchen.'

'Mum, hurry.' There was now no mistaking the urgency in Lyndall's voice. It got Cathy to the balcony in seconds.

She saw Lyndall at the balcony edge. Not just her but a whole line-up of neighbours were also looking down as the dark sky flashed blue.

'What's going on?' When she went to join them, she saw that the flashing lights were coming from a bevy of police cars. She counted four outside the community centre and one on its way to join them.

'They drove up,' Lyndall said. 'All of them at once. And then all the police rushed in.'

The sound of more sirens rent the air. 'I better get down.'

'I'll come with you.'

'No, don't.' Her voice was firm enough to show that there would be no gainsaying her. 'Stay here.'

As she got to the bottom of the last gangway, four more police cars screeched to a halt and eight more police officers rushed into the centre.

Something really serious. She ran the last few yards only to find her path blocked by a policewoman. 'You can't go in.'

'I'm a member of the police liaison committee. You will let me,' she said with an authority that came as a complete surprise to her, and to her greater surprise it worked.

She pushed the door open and stepped in.

She could hear the sounds of raised voices and of banging, but there was no one in the darkened entrance hall. She felt along the wall until she had located the light switch, which she flicked on. Nothing. The bulb must have blown.

More shouting: was that Banji's voice rising above the others?

She knew the centre well enough to feel her way through the dark towards the assembly room that was at the back. More shouting. Something happening which, despite the massive police presence, had not been resolved.

'Get the fuck off him,' she heard.

Was that Banji's voice?

'Can't you see you're hurting him?'

It was Banji.

She pushed through the double doors.

Afterwards she was sorry that she had, because the memory of what she saw would never leave her.

At first she couldn't make sense of it, because the images she absorbed were so fractured. She saw the room – big and square and windowless. It wasn't just hot, it was so steaming hot and it stank of mould and damp and sweat that seemed to be coming off the walls. Pushed up against one of these walls were two armchairs whose floral cushioning had been yellowed by age and overuse. Above the chairs, a series of posters, stuck up more to hide the damp stains on the wall than to tell the community how to combat STDs, when the local MP had his surgery and why breastfeeding was best. And near these sofas . . .

'Let me go to him,' she heard.

She saw Banji face down on the floor, his hands cuffed behind his back. He was still struggling to free himself. He was shouting so loudly that she could hear what he was saying above the din that issued from the corner where a group of people, also all shouting, were penned in by policemen with batons extended. 'You're supposed to be the good guys,' he was shouting. 'You're the police. The representatives of the law. You're meant to help. Can't you see how you're hurting him?'

Her gaze moved off Banji and to the middle of the room.

And there was the sight she must have been avoiding, because it was the sight she should immediately have taken in.

A mass of uniforms. Police in a scrum. And the ball that they were struggling for was Ruben.

He was on his stomach, also handcuffed, but in his case two policemen were holding down each arm, while three others had laid themselves across his legs, as a sixth, who had strapped Ruben's legs below the knee, was tightening a further strap around his calves.

Ruben's leg twitched, as if he were trying to kick out or to stop the strap biting in. His head shifted a fraction to the side, only to be wrenched back by one of the policemen.

'Don't move,' all the officers seemed to be yelling at once. 'Don't move.'

He had stopped moving. Couldn't. Not with so many of them on him.

But their blood was up. 'Don't move,' one of them yelled, as he pressed down on Ruben's head.

Poor Ruben, he must be terrified. She had to do something.

'One more step.' Where had he come from, this policeman whose face reared so close to hers? 'And you'll also be downed.' He pushed her back, and when she half fell, he held her up and pushed her again until she found herself backed against the wall, with his hand holding her there. 'Calm down,' he said, while turning to his officers and gesturing with the other hand at Banji: 'Get that man out of here.'

As the din in the room continued unabated, two of the officers linked an arm under each of Banji's arms and hauled him up. 'Come on, son.'

With huge effort, Banji wrenched himself forward, breaking their lock. She thought he was going to run. He didn't. He stood stock-still and yelled, 'Look what you've done.'

His shouting ricocheted around the room, silencing all the others.

And again: 'Look what you've done!'

Only one sound now: a guttural exhalation from the centre of the room.

And then, when everybody seemed to hold their breath, there was no longer anything to hear.

'You've killed him. You were called to help and you've killed him.'

The officer who'd been pinning Cathy back let go of her. He strode over to Ruben's prone body, kneeling down, lowering his head until his ear was adjacent to Ruben's mouth. 'Quiet.'

No need for that command. The dreadful silence that had descended was never going to lift.

The policeman raised his head to say, calmly, 'Call an ambulance.' And calmly again, 'Get off,' to the officers who were pressing down on Ruben. 'Turn him over.' They pushed the prone body. His head lolled back; they all heard it crack. 'Careful, for fuck's sake. And take off those restraints.'

They managed to roll Ruben over.

As much as she wanted to, Cathy could not bring herself to avert her gaze. She saw Ruben. His skin was grey. His mouth open. Slack. Blood. From where? She couldn't see, and now she couldn't see anything much else except the sergeant who, having straddled Ruben, was breathing rhythmically into his mouth between compressions on his chest.

She watched, but even though she willed him on and told herself that they would soon hear Ruben coughing, something in her already knew it wasn't going to happen.

It was too late.

Ruben had gone.

Friday

5.30 a.m.

When Cathy heard the front door closing, she stormed out into the hall: 'Where the hell have you been?'

Lyndall, who'd been intent on laying her keys softly down on the table, jumped.

'I asked you a question. Where have you been?'

'But I left a note.'

'Yes, and I saw your bed was empty long before I found your note. Why did you sneak out like that?'

'I wrote you I was with Jayden.'

'Jayden's turned into a bodyguard, has he?' She heard her voice rising.

'We weren't in danger, Mum. It was getting light.'

'Getting light! Getting light! You think that's going to keep you safe from . . .' And now she heard a voice inside telling her to stop it. 'From . . .'

'I'm sorry, Mum. I heard you up and down all night, so when I saw you were sleeping, I didn't want to wake you.'

Hearing how shaky Lyndall sounded, Cathy calmed down. And it was true, she had had a terrible night. Every time she'd closed her eyes she'd been assailed by images – of Ruben's head lolling back, or of his slack body being worked on by the paramedics, or of that sheet covering a face that no longer looked like his.

'It's not your morning to be at work,' Lyndall said. 'Why don't you go back to bed?'

'I can't. Ruben's parents need support. And we have to discuss how we're going to deal with this.'

'Go and have a shower, then. I'll make breakfast. In times of stress you need to eat,' said with such sweet sincerity that it drove off the last of Cathy's aggravation.

She touched her daughter gently on the cheek. 'Who's the mother here, missie?'

43

'Well, I am the better cook.'

'That's not hard, is it? Tea would be lovely.'

'Don't worry, Mum, don't sweat it. Go take that shower.'

6 a.m.

If this bloody heat goes on much longer, Peter thought, I'll have to take up residence in the shower. Trying to ignore the dark pooling under his arms, he looked down at the list Patricia had drawn up for him.

As ever, she'd done a thorough job, but knowing how the slightest miscalculation might galvanise the other side or, worse, open the way for a compromise candidate to steal his prize, he was going to check it again. He considered phoning Patricia and asking her to do it with him. But no: she worked so hard. Leave her to her beauty sleep.

She'd divided their MPs into three categories: unquestionably for him, unquestionably against him, and a middle group – by far the largest – of the undecided or the unknown. These were the ones he and his team needed to work on. And all before the recess. It was going to be a tough nine days.

He looked down at the separate columns. There were names of MPs with whom he'd grown up politically, or bonded with on his first day in the House, or plotted with or against, as well as names of MPs who had driven him mad or to laughter, or those whose late-night camaraderie helped him bear the frustrations of political life – all of them now reduced to three categories: for, against or unknown.

That it should come to this.

The prospect of what he knew he had to do, and not the heat, was what was making him sweat. Now it drove him from his desk.

The milky light of dawn had hardened – soon the relentless sun would burn off any nuance. Then the green-carpeted corridors would be full of the people who oiled the wheels of Parliament. But for this moment the House was empty. Nowhere to go and nobody to talk to. He would take a stroll, he thought, before going back to stare at that blasted list.

He walked along the Lower Ministers' corridor and pushed through the double doors of the Chamber, going round the Speaker's Chair and into the Chamber proper. Odd to be there when those green benches were empty of the members and the hubbub they created. Odd also to have come this way by the opposition benches. He looked over the line to where he usually sat and thought that if things went well, he'd soon be two paces to the right, directly behind the dispatch box. And responsible for everything. A shiver of anticipation ran down his spine.

I'll wash my face, he thought, and then get on. Leaving the Chamber, he made his way to the nearest toilet, going straight over to a basin. He switched on the tap and, lowering his head, splashed his face with water before running his wrists under the tap, sighing with the relief of it.

He was about to splash his face again when he heard a sound. Someone groaning? He switched off the tap.

Nothing.

Must have been the antique plumbing system, protesting at this early use. He turned on the tap again and cupped his hands. He was in the process of lowering his head when someone – it was a human sound, not mechanical – groaned again.

'Are you all right?'

No answer. But he hadn't imagined the sound. It had come from one of the stalls.

He walked along the line-up, gingerly pushing each door in turn. They swung open, empty, until the last, which, although it wasn't locked, resisted his push. He pressed against it harder.

'Watch it, you bastard. That's my leg.'

He knew that voice. He craned his head around the door to see Albion Hind, member for one of the Midlands constituencies. Albion was half on and half off the lavatory, and his eyes were shut.

'Albion, it's Peter.' At least the man's trousers were still up.

Albion groaned.

'Are you ill?'

A ginger opening of one eye. 'Do I look ill?'

Never the most picturesque of men, Albion looked not so much ill as really awful. His nose was habitually bulbous and reddened from drink, and that long strand of greasy hair that had flopped away from the bald patch it was meant to conceal didn't help. All as usual. What was new, however, particularly so early in the morning, was the mess of gravy or dark vomit that stained his shirt.

A revolting sight. Peter was half tempted to back off, close the door and leave Albion to his own devices. 'Let's get you out of here,' he said.

'You and whose army?' Albion's eyelids shuttered down.

'Shift.' Peter pushed at the door.

Albion groaned, but he did inch away from the door, allowing Peter to widen the gap and squeeze in. Not much room to manoeuvre, but he eventually managed to bend over the fallen man. He was assailed by the mix of stale tobacco, soured alcohol and vomit so toxic that it took an effort of will not to rear away. He concentrated on breathing exclusively through his mouth. 'Lift your arms.' He pushed his own arms under Albion's, linking them at the other's back, and then, saying, 'Upsy', he hauled Albion to his feet.

'I want to stay here,' Albion groaned.

'To be spotted by the other side? Or, worse, by a bastard from the lobby? I think not.'

He turned them both round, using a knee to push Albion, and that way manoeuvred the other man, crab-like, out of the stall and over to a wall. 'Stay here.'

When he let go, Albion slid all the way down to the floor. No point in picking him up. 'I'll fetch help,' he said.

'Kind of you.'

'Oh well.' He was glad that he had bothered.

'Never figured you for a kind man.'

Just like bloody Albion, adding a sting to his gratitude. Should have let him stew in his own festered failure.

Which thought seemed to transmit itself to Albion. 'You can't know what it's like.' He was clearly on the brink of tears. The weight of his eyelids seemed too much to bear. They closed while he was saying something that sounded like 'votes for sale', although Peter, who now wanted more than anything to get away, couldn't be sure.

He found a doorkeeper who agreed to deposit Albion in a nearby hotel. Something at least accomplished. It was harder to shake off his feelings of pity for Albion, who, once a high-flyer, had sunk so low.

There but for the grace of God, he thought, and then he told himself that this was nonsense. Albion's many vices were what had done for him; Peter's would not. Of this he would make sure. He went back to his office, intent on ridding himself of clothes that must now reek of Albion Hind's failure.

He pushed the door so hard that it banged back against the wall, and when he did, he saw how a slim, dark figure who had been standing by his desk jumped.

'What the . . .' His vision cleared. 'Oh, it's you, Patricia.'

The sight of her always set his pulse racing. She was a gorgeous-looking young woman, and she knew it, donning a succession of bright colours like this sleeveless yellow summer frock that showed off her bronzed skin to its best advantage. He wanted to compliment her on it but no need: she'd clocked his appreciative regard and it made her smile.

'I was thinking of ringing you,' he said.

'Your wife beat you to it.'

'My wife?'

'Your mobile's off.'

He took it from his pocket – 'Oh yes, so it is' – and switched it on, and as it loaded he saw three missed calls from Frances. 'Did she say what she wanted?'

'To tell you that the PM's going to be on at 7.15.'

Of course he was. Trying to steal Peter's thunder.

'She thinks they might be planning to ambush him with his latest legalise drugs obsession. She says you should hear it live in case you're rung for comment.' Patricia indicated a folder she must just have placed on his desk. 'I've digested the salient facts. The Dutch example's telling. And the rake-offs of the Colorado and Washington dispensaries should cause some alarm.'

First Frances and now Patricia: his women were certainly coming through for him. 'That's extremely helpful.' He cleared his throat. 'But now I think I'd better ring . . .'

'. . . your wife. Yes, Home Secretary. I'll leave you to it.' She was smiling as she passed him by.

The scent she gave off was redolent of spring flowers that would long ago have wilted in this heat. Hope she didn't think the stench that must be coming off him was his. 'Oh, and Patricia?'

'Yes?' The way she looked at him: she was such a coquette!

'Might be worth turning your keen eye on our new Commissioner. Background. Connections. That type of thing.'

'Of course.' She was all business. 'Anything in particular?'

'Not sure. He was vetted, naturally, but I think there might have been something missed. Sniff around: see, for starters, if you can find anything about his relationship with the PM. Something peculiar there which might be . . .' – how should he put it – 'be . . .'

'Helpful,' she said. 'Of course.' She slipped out of the room, softly, as she always did.

10 a.m.

The heavy tread that Joshua Yares had been keeping half an ear out for caused him to raise his head. 'Anil? Would you mind stepping in for a moment?'

'Of course.' Deputy Commissioner Anil Chahda, highest-ranking ethnic officer in the British police, retraced his steps and walked into Joshua's office. 'How can I help?'

Joshua gestured at the sofas that stood at one end of his vast office.

Chahda was broad with a bullish head, wide shoulders and a stocky frame, and when he sat down on the sofa he seemed to take up the whole of it.

'How can I be of assistance?'

'I gather there's been a death?' Joshua paused, expecting a response, but when nothing came he said, 'In Rockham.'

'Ah,' an intake of breath. 'That death. Unfortunate. Male. IC3. Record of mental instability – officers have been called to his home on several previous occasions. On this occasion a member of the public reported that the man was wielding a weapon in a public place.'

'I understand that sections in the community dispute this version. They say the man posed no danger and that the police were not in fact called?'

'I can't answer to that, sir.' Chahda shrugged. 'I'm merely reporting what the IPCC has said.'

'And I have also been told that there was an earlier incident involving this same man and an officer?'

'You're ahead of me on that as well, sir. All I have been told is that the officers who attended called for back-up after the man became violent. It took eight officers to restrain him – others held back members of the public who had become emotional – and in the course of this the prisoner developed breathing difficulties. The officer in charge, who has had advanced CPR training, did his best to revive him, unfortunately without success. There'll be a post mortem of course. It is always possible that a pre-existing condition might have provoked his collapse. At the moment, however, it's probably sensible to assume that the cause of death will be related to positional asphyxia.'

'The officers involved have written up their reports?'

'Naturally.'

'And I assume their bodycams will confirm their written statements?'

'The IPCC has all the footage, sir. They'll match the reports with it. Although it is worth saying that several of the bodycams were malfunctioning, and, as well, in moments of such confusion the footage does not always illuminate.'

All of which was true. Why, then, did it sound like a series of excuses?

'Check that they covered the earlier incident as well, will you? And pull the records of all the officers involved. I'd like to know if any of them have been subject to any disciplinary action for misconduct. Just in case.'

'Certainly, sir. If you think that's necessary.' The edge to Chahda's voice might have indicated that he wasn't best pleased by Joshua's interference, but his smile belied this.

'I gather Chief Superintendent Gaby Wright is in charge there?'

'She is. A recent appointment as Acting Commander.'

'I had a look at her stats. I see there's been a spike in Section 60 stops since she took over?'

'That's correct and in my opinion unavoidable. The Lovelace has never been easy to police, and word of its closure has been met by a rise in antisocial behaviour and crime. If I was in CS Wright's shoes, I would have done the same thing. She's a good officer. Tough but fair.'

'No doubt. But given the circumstances, don't you think it might be worth her going a bit easier?'

'It might, sir, if she had the numbers. A visible presence on the street would ease things. But she doesn't have the officers. I put a report on your desk about this.' Chahda glanced at the high pile of buff folders – priority reading for the new Commissioner. 'In it, CS Wright makes a special-case argument for more resources. She needs greater visibility and the ability to intervene to head off trouble. Without that, she's had to resort to the increased use of Section 60.'

'I see.' Must read faster, he thought, knowing, though, that if he did, he would find a score of other such requests from other boroughs.

'I spoke to her this morning, and she has done everything I would have wanted her to. The emergency services have been instructed to attend flashpoints in Rockham only after due authorisation; officers of the TSG will keep a low profile so as not to aggravate the situation; there will be no independent contractors in the Lovelace monitoring tagged offenders; and there is a stay on the execution of arrest warrants in Rockham until further notice. Local officers have also been instructed to display special sensitivity when addressing the question.'

'Sounds competent.'

'She is a good officer, sir. I'm confident that everything will go smoothly.' A pause before: 'Is there anything else, sir?'

You had to admire the man: he was thorough and to the point. 'There is something,' Joshua said. 'Get somebody to pull out the records of any stops under Section 4 of the RTA 1988 in the central London area for me. Any incident reported in the last three weeks.'

'May I ask why?'

'Something I need to check. If you wouldn't mind?'

'Of course. I'll see it done.'

'Thanks, Anil. And there are also a couple more things. Set up a press conference to brief on the Rockham incident – the bare bones of what happened, the fact that the IPCC will now be in charge of the investigation.'

'Yes, sir. I can certainly do that.'

'Thank you.' He glanced down at his diary. 'I've got a brief window at 1.15, shall we set it for then?'

'You will be doing the briefing yourself, sir?'

'I think that's best, don't you? First week and all that – give the public an opportunity to get to know their new Commissioner. I trust that's not a problem?'

'No, sir, it's not a problem. I'll set it in motion for 1315 hours.' A pause and then: 'You mentioned two matters?'

'Yes, I did. Given this is early days for us, I want to make sure that you are aware that incidents like the one in Rockham should be reported to me as soon as they occur. I have no intention of interfering in the chain of command, but I do expect to be kept informed.'

'Of course you do, sir.' Chahda nodded to reinforce this affirmation. 'A report of the Rockham death is highlighted in the summary of yesterday's events. It is on its way to you. But I will certainly take note that you wish for more immediate notification.'

As ever, a model response. 'Thanks, Anil.' Joshua couldn't help feeling that his determination to take control of the job might have made him slightly overdo his domination of his deputy. 'That will be all.'

1 p.m.

Cathy was about to head up the gangway when she saw the fox. It was a big one and decrepit, its fur matted and its tail a ragged thing.

There were many foxes that haunted the estate – more of them recently since the Lovelace had begun to stink of blocked drains and rotting rubbish, and especially in this heat – but she had only ever spotted them at night or in the early morning, and then just out of the corner of her eye. But this one was limping forward in the full light of day, and when its path crossed with hers it did not run away. She stopped and it did too. She looked at it and it held her gaze. Its legs, she saw, were shaking. She shut her eyes.

When she opened them again, the fox had gone. Too fast a disappearance, surely, given how sick it had seemed?

She'd not had enough sleep; she shook herself into motion.

The door to Ruben's parents' place was ajar. She gave the bell a quick press to warn them that she was there, and then she walked in and down the corridor.

For the second time that day, she couldn't help but be struck by the pictures of Ruben that lined the walls. They brought such a lump to her throat that she quickened her pace. But there was no escape. The living room, which she soon reached, was also dominated by a large full-colour portrait of Ruben that hung above the mantelpiece. It was Ruben on one of his better days, lit by an open smile.

Despite the room containing a vast array of objects – plastic flowers, china shepherdesses, a large red plastic heart, a sign that flashed the word 'smile' in neon, as well as many gilt-framed photos of the wider family – Cathy's gaze kept being pulled back to this portrait. And every time she looked at him, and he seemed to look back, that same thought occurred: that she did not know what she would do if Lyndall were to die, never mind in such a terrible way.

'Mrs Mason, you're back, and with provisions for us all.' Ruben's mother's face was blotched by tears, but her voice was strong and she even managed a smile. 'Here, let me unburden you.' She took the bulging carrier bags from Cathy and passed them to another woman. 'There are plates in the kitchen,' and to Cathy: 'We were looking at the albums. Come, join us.'

The room was crowded – relatives, friends and neighbours rallying as word of what had happened spread. There were many, including the Reverend Pius and Marcus, she knew well, but there were also many with whom she had only a nodding acquaintance and some she had never met. They were united by what had happened, and as the crowd parted to let the two women through, Cathy was greeted by a smile here and an embrace there.

Such a warm inclusivity in this most terrible of times. Yet in the midst of it, Ruben's father, who was standing at the other end of the room, looked very much alone.

'The police didn't bother to tell us he was gone.' He had been saying this when Cathy had first arrived early that morning, and he was still saying it. 'Our friends had to bear that strain. Nobody else cares. His death didn't merit more than a small mention, and only in one news-paper.'

Reverend Pius shifted to one side to make room for Cathy on the black settee that was jammed against a heater. Just as in Cathy's flat, the heater was on and the room was boiling. No one seemed to notice, or if they did they didn't seem to care.

'When we went to the police station to ask them what had happened, they didn't even offer to seat us,' Ruben's father continued. 'We can't say nothing, they told us, except that someone phoned them to complain about Ruben's behaviour. We told them: that cannot be. Everybody knew Ruben. Nobody would have rung the police, not without first asking us. All the man reply is: you have to speak to the IPCC. He wouldn't come out from behind his bulletproof glass and look us in the eye and speak to us, human being to human being. We are the ones who have suffered such great loss, but he was the one to feel unsafe.'

'Come now, Bernard.' Ruben's mother patted the place beside her. 'Come, look.'

Her husband came to the settee, but as she turned the page of the album, he wasn't really looking. She stopped and reached up to take his hand and squeeze it. He squeezed hers back. A beat as they looked at each other, and then she dropped her hand and turned another page.

'He was such a happy child.' She pointed at a photograph of the young Ruben, circa five years old. He was kneeling on a patch of grass, holding a football and smiling up into the lens. 'Always wanting to know everything. Full of love.' She blinked back tears and carried on scrolling through a detailed record of the growing boy.

It was hard not to be drawn into the pleasure that she took in each of the images of her son, her fingers occasionally dropping to the page to stroke his face. It was even harder not to see her agony and the adjustment demanded of her to come to terms with what had happened. Her tenses continually had to be fast-forwarded into a present in which she could not yet bring herself to believe. 'This friend,' she pointed to a photo of Ruben with another boy, 'is a favourite who he sees . . .' a pause, '*saw* almost every week. He is here now.' She pointed to a youngish man who was sitting, solitary, on a hard chair. Noticing her pointing finger, he dropped his head and covered his eyes with a hand. 'He's a good boy,' she said, before going back to the album. She sped up, pages turning almost carelessly, creating a flickering blur out of Ruben's childhood until at last she stopped.

It was a photo of an adolescent Ruben. Facing the camera. No smile or other welcome. A blank and uncompromising stare.

Ruben's mother's eyes had filled with tears. 'He lost his bearings,' she said. 'All of a sudden he went somewhere in his head and we found we could not follow where.' She turned another page. 'We were visitors only on occasion.' And there was the adult Ruben, the one Cathy had known and the one above the mantelpiece, and he was smiling. 'Sometimes, with the medication, then he would come back to us.'

'To us, perhaps, but not to himself.' This from Ruben's father. 'He said what the doctor gave him put him in the grave,' that last word reverberating in a room that fell silent.

'Come, Bernard.' She patted the space beside her. 'Come sit.'

He was a vigorous man, in his sixties, muscled from many years labouring in a packing house. But now, as he lowered himself onto the settee, he looked much older and also much more frail. 'My son was never violent,' he said. 'He never raised a serious hand. Neither against his mother or me. Or any other human being.'

'He did get frightened.' This from his wife. 'If you touched him wrong.'

'He was a good boy.' His voice once more filled the room. 'And he was a good man. He was my light.'

1.15 p.m.

'Home Secretary?' Peter's Parliamentary Private Secretary, who had slid into the office noiselessly as he always did, gave one of his self-deprecatory little coughs.

'Yes?' He still had much to do, and Frances, who hated to be kept waiting, was imminently due. 'What is it?'

'Commissioner Yares phoned.'

'He did, did he?' He nodded to Patricia to make sure she was paying attention. 'And what did he want?'

'To tell you that there has been a death in Rockham.'

'I'm sorry to hear it.' But why – is what he didn't say – am I being interrupted by this news? 'Another knifing?'

'No, an accident. The police were involved.'

'I see.'

'I would have kept this for my end-of-day summary rather than bother you with it now, but Mr Parsons, the Member, as I'm sure you are aware, whose constituency includes Rockham, has advised us he has asked the Speaker's permission to raise a question abut the incident.'

'Has he indeed?' And Joshua Yares had thought to warn him. Perhaps he was trying, harder than Peter had anticipated, to be cooperative.

'The Commissioner will be briefing the press. He wanted you to know that as well.'

Perhaps not so much cooperative as dotting the i's and crossing his t's, something for which he was a stickler, especially when it came to covering his own back.

'Oh, and your wife is waiting in the lobby.'

'Good God, man, why didn't you say so?' He was already on his feet and slinging on his jacket, saying to Patricia, 'We'll have to go on with this when I get back.'

Another little cough. 'You have an appointment with the Taiwanese ambassador, Home Secretary, on your return from lunch.'

So he did. Nothing to be done save for: 'Let's finish up in the lift,' and then to his PPS: 'You'll look into the Rockham business?'

'Yes, Home Secretary. There'll be a report in your box tonight.'

1.16 p.m.

A quick glance at the mirror to check everything was where it ought to be and then Joshua Yares strode through the door and into the claustrophobic room with its duck-egg soundproofed walls and grey blinds that shut out even the slightest hint of daylight. Lucky it was air-conditioned or keeping his jacket on would have been nigh impossible.

Chahda and the head press bod were already at the table that had been raised onto a podium in front of a backdrop of Met logos. As the cameras flashed – so many of them, he knew, because the press were also using this first appearance to build up a store of stock photos – he seated himself between the two.

His statement, on one single piece of paper, was there neatly in front of him, but it was worth giving the photographers, and the TV cameras at the back, a little more time to satisfy their cravings. As he sat, unsmiling, and the cameras flashed, the head of press leant over to whisper, 'Should I set up a confab with the CRA?'

He shook his head: 'Not for this one.' There would be plenty of other occasions for him to get to know those members of the Crime Reporters Association to whom the Met would entrust sensitive information, and he didn't want them to think he was making capital out of a tragedy. 'Shall we begin?'

'Absolutely, sir. Ladies and gentlemen.' The press man's raised voice had produced an immediate hush. 'Our new Commissioner of the Metropolis, Commissioner Joshua Yares, will read a short statement. There will be no questions at this time,' and then turning to Joshua: 'Commissioner?'

'Thank you, Mark.' A quick glance at the paper and he had memorised what was written there. He looked up. 'And thank you all for coming. It is my sad duty to inform you that yesterday in Rockham, in response to a call from the public, police officers attended a community centre

56

on the Lovelace estate. When a man in his early thirties became violent, the Rockham officers took measures to restrain him. Unfortunately, the man developed breathing difficulties. Officers gave him CPR until an ambulance arrived to take the man to hospital. He was pronounced dead on arrival. At a request from the man's parents, we will not, at present, be releasing the man's details. My office is liaising with the parents, and I would ask you, on their behalf, that once their son's name is released you give them the privacy they will need to come to terms with their loss. As in every case where a death occurs in police presence, the Independent Police Complaints Commission has been put in charge of the investigation. Any further questions should be addressed to them. Thank you. That is all.'

He was already on his feet and beginning the short walk away as questions were fired at him, such as: 'Do you think this is a bad omen?' and 'How's the first day otherwise?' and that one he knew would be inevitable: 'Will you comment on the rumour that the Home Secretary is less than delighted at your appointment?' All of which he ignored, taking care to keep his expression neutral without discounting the gravity of the news he had delivered, and then at last he was out and he could let his breath go.

1.20 p.m.
There was quite a bustle in the atrium – more visitors than usual crowding around the front desk – so Peter leant his head in so as to hear what Patricia was telling him. While listening to what she had to say, he also looked to where Frances was standing at the centre of a circle of his staff. She had on her beige frock with pink trimming that toned perfectly with her peach complexion and wavy blonde hair. She was so attractive, he thought, a judgement with which the men fawning on her were bound to concur. One of them said something in response to which she threw back her head, elongating her neck, and laughed, and although he wasn't close enough to see them, he knew she must be treating the men to a flash of those perfect white teeth. He felt such pride watching her, and another feeling that he was almost ashamed to name. He knew it, however, for what it was: a slight jealousy that she was so at home in this world that, despite

his high status, sometimes made him feel like an outsider, and a fat one at that.

'What I'm trying to say, Minister . . .' Patricia must have registered his inattention. She raised her voice to pull him back.

'Not now,' he said.

Frances had already turned her head to look at him. She frowned.

Could he have done something to annoy her? But, no, she was smiling again as she said something to the men, who responded by parting to let her through. He must have imagined it.

But he soon realised that she really was annoyed. Not that she said as much. But by her turning away of her cheek when he had gone to peck it once they were outside, and by her brisk nod at his driver and his bodyguards, and by the way she sat beside him in the car, poker straight, and pushed an errant blonde hair firmly back into place, he could tell that something was bothering her.

'Dog been playing up?'

'Why would she be?' Her tone was pinched. She was definitely annoyed.

Perhaps she was feeling unacknowledged.

'I tried to ring you back this morning,' he said, 'but you didn't answer.'

She shrugged.

Yes, that was most likely it. And he had been remiss. 'Would I be right in thinking you had something to do with the *Today* item?'

'Nobody tells *Today* what to run.' Her voice was clipped. 'Except perhaps the DG – and it's doubtful, even in his case, that he can.'

'Well, thank you for your efforts in the aftermath.'

Her nod was curt, giving nothing away.

Oh, Lord – looked to be a day of sulks. All he needed.

'I think I struck the right balance between giving the PM support and also representing the mainstream view of the Party,' he tried. 'Don't you?'

'Yes, Peter.' She sounded dutiful. And clearly bored.

He looked away and in doing so caught his driver's eye. He pressed a button and the glass screen that divided front from back went gliding up.

'There's been an incident involving the police in Rockham,' he said, 'resulting in the death of a member of the public. Timothy Parsons is planning to ask a question in the House.'

'That dreadful man.' He had hoped that her annoyance, whatever its cause, might fade in the face of the thing that really engaged her – the intricacies of politics – and so it proved. 'Bitter as well: resents the fact that he was passed over in the last reshuffle. Not that he deserved another chance after the mess he made in Transport. And now he's asking questions to catch you out – and from our side of the House.'

'It is odd, especially since he's not exactly known for his social conscience. Rumour is he does his best to steer clear of surgeries: too many needy people.'

Frances frowned. Good – a sign she had her thinking cap on. 'The PM has Parsons up to it,' she said. 'Despite the reshuffle, Parsons remains his man.'

She was, as ever, right. Parsons' name had been top of the list of those who would never in a million years vote for Peter. 'But why would the PM set his dogs on this death?'

'He has gone out on a limb on the drugs issue,' Frances said, 'throwing the party into uproar. The opposition are jumping on the bandwagon, quoting police resistance to the measure. So if he can provoke the country into concern about the police, he thinks he might be able to turn the tide. He can't do it himself, so he's recruited Parsons.'

Which put a new complexion on Yares's phone call: 'Of course that must be it. How clever of you.'

She smiled. Not so much the ice queen now. 'We should talk about the lunch. Our table is close to some fairly influential Party funders. We will not be sitting with them, I've made sure of that. We don't want to give too much away until we are sure we have all our ducks in a row. All we need at the moment is to meet and greet, with a word or two in relevant ears. I'll make the running. You follow.'

'Don't I always, darling?'

Too frivolous. She turned her head and looked at him. Sharply.

Knowing that it always took her a while to come out of one of her glooms, he should have been more careful. 'I depend on you,' he said.

'Do you?'

That acid tone again.

Irritation rising, he thought, that's it, I give up. She, of all people, should know how burdened he was by work and responsibility. She certainly did know that the Home Office was the most perilous of all the great ministries of state, never mind the dangers attached to trying to unseat his Leader. And yet here she was playing her own petulant games. He had no patience for it. Not any more. If she wanted to tell him what was bothering her, she should come out with it. In the meantime, he would hold his tongue. He turned his head away from her to look out of the window.

Uniform blue sky. Women in skimpy clothes lying on brown grass. Roses that had flowered and withered before their time. Bloody heat. He found himself wishing for the end of summer even before the real summer was properly underway.

'Are you having an affair?'

'What?' Of all the things that might be bothering her, this was one that had never occurred to him. 'An affair?' Ridiculous echo. Must do better.

'Just answer the question, Peter.'

'I will. If that's what you want. But before I do, do you happen to have a suggestion as to who I might be having this supposed affair with?'

'As a matter of fact, I do. I'd say it was your Special Adviser.'

'With Patricia?' Incredulity hyped up his voice.

She was in contrast very calm: 'Do you have another Special Adviser?' When he didn't say anything, she continued: 'I thought not. So, Peter, tell me, are you having an affair with your Special Adviser, Patricia Diaz?'

'Is that why you phoned Patricia this morning? Were you checking up on me?'

He caught his driver's eye again. He hoped the soundproofing worked, especially when Frances raised her voice to say, 'Answer the question. Are you and Patricia Diaz having an affair?'

'No.' He lowered his voice. 'We are not.'

'Is that the truth?' She was looking at him fiercely, as only Frances could.

'Yes, it is the truth. Cross my heart and hope to die.' He did it. He crossed his heart. 'There. Does that satisfy?'

He could see, by the softening of her expression, that it did.

He reached across for her hand. Thank goodness she gave it to him. 'Whatever made you think I was having an affair?'

'Oh, I don't know. Your early rising. Your late returns. The way she looked at me when you both stepped out of the lift.'

'The way she looked at *you*.' Echo again, but needs must. 'Come on, darling, that's absurd. As for the hours I keep: the House is your second home and has been for most of your life. You know how extreme the demands are, especially when one becomes a minister, never mind a secretary of state.'

'Yes, I do know. And I also know many MPs play away from home. Daddy led the hunt, if you remember.'

Not that he or, come to that, most of the country could forget. Her father (thankfully now deceased) had been a notorious philanderer. His womanising, played out in public, had caused his wife, and his four daughters, awful misery.

'I would never do that to you.'

'You had better not.'

He squeezed her hand. 'I need you, Frances, by my side. I wouldn't do anything to jeopardise that.'

'Wouldn't you?'

So plaintively asked, her question both warmed and annoyed him. 'You have to trust me.'

'I do. I will. But if you betray my trust . . .'

She didn't complete her threat because by then they had arrived.

3 p.m.

The Lovelace was subdued. Doors open and people outside on the landings to escape the heat, but even the smallest of children, who couldn't know what had happened, didn't seem to have the heart to play. As for the adults, what conversation there was, was carried out in voices too soft to be overheard.

If it had been me, Cathy couldn't help thinking, if it had been me. She kept checking her watch, wondering whether Lyndall should already have arrived home from school, and this despite that she knew it was too early. If it had been me . . .

She kept an eye out for the fox, but even that proved no distraction. Had it been real? And if it was, had it been sick? Or worse, rabid? Perhaps she should go home and phone the RSPCA.

She didn't feel like going home. With the meeting due at her place later, she needed provisions. She counted the change in her purse: if she was careful, she could manage.

It was so humid that her skin was moist with perspiration and her throat raw. She needed water and she needed it now. Since she was just then passing the local Londis, she stepped in.

It was a small outlet, run by one of the Somalian newcomers to the area whose daughter went to school with Lyndall, and it was usually a relaxed place. But what she heard when she stepped in was a voice raised in anger.

'What the fuck do you mean you can't?'

She knew that voice and the man who, with his back to her, banged a fist against the counter: 'You've got no right to refuse.'

'Banji?'

He whirled round, looked at her and then looked right past her.

'Banji. It's Cathy.'

'You think I'm such a fucking muppet I don't know who you are?' He turned back to the counter behind which Mrs Sharif was standing. 'Just sell me a can – I've got the money – and I'll get out of your fucking way.'

Mrs Sharif shook her head.

He slammed both hands down on the counter and pushed on them: he was about to vault over. And would have done so had not Cathy run up to grab him by the arm and pull him away from the counter.

'What the fuck?'

She could smell his breath, sour and stale. 'Mrs Sharif can't sell you alcohol.'

'Why the fuck not?'

'Because she hasn't got a licence.'

'Oh.' Fury mutating into something closer to confusion. 'Hasn't she?'

She could see Mrs Sharif inching along the counter. She was heading for the telephone at its far end.

The last thing anybody needed was more police. 'Come on.' She tugged at Banji's arm. 'Come, let's get some air,' and to Mrs Sharif: 'Don't worry. I'll make sure he doesn't come back.'

He let her lead him out of the shop, but once they were outside he shook her off. 'Call this air?' He seemed unsteady on his feet.

'Are you drunk?' But he'd given up all intoxicants. Or at least he'd told her that he had. 'Are you?'

'Are you?' he said in imitation of her voice.

Walk away, she told herself, and not for the first time.

She did not walk away.

He looked awful. His trousers and dirty white T-shirt were what he had been wearing yesterday, and they were both now so crumpled he must have slept in them. Or not slept at all, which was probably the case: the whites of his eyes were pink.

'What happened?' The last she'd seen of him he'd been let off by the police with a caution.

The fury seemed to drain out of him then. In its place: a misery that crumpled his expression as he said, 'They killed him.'

'Yes.' She felt herself relax. 'They did.'

'And I didn't stop them.'

She reached out a consoling hand.

He jumped as if her touch could burn. 'I was watching out for him.'

'You did what you could.'

'Well, it wasn't fucking good enough, was it?' His face was screwed up in rage, an unaccustomed sight coming as it did from a man whose manner these days was a non-committal containment that made him seem almost devoid of emotion.

Not so in the past. Then he had been quick to anger. And then he had also drunk a lot and taken other things besides.

'I lost my phone,' he said.

'What?'

'Are you deaf or what? I lost my fucking phone.'

Okay, she thought, so he lost his phone. She took hers out of her pocket. 'You can use mine.'

'No.' He shook his head. Violently. 'What if she rung back and you answered?'

She must be his wife – his ex-wife. That he'd had an acrimonious break-up was one of the few personal details he had let slip.

'You could number guard it,' she said.

He backed away even further. 'You don't understand.' He'd raised his voice again – 'Nobody does' – and hardened as he glared at her. 'I'm all alone.'

Such accusatory self-pity, as if he was so much worse off than everybody else. 'Oh, for goodness sake,' she heard herself saying. 'Use my phone. Or don't. Just do me a favour and stop whining.'

There: the end of tiptoeing around him in case something she did made him leave her. Let him go if he wanted to. It would be better if he did. She looked at him, straight, waiting for his bite-back.

He threw his head back and laughed. Long and hard, and he kept his balance while he was doing it. He isn't drunk, she thought.

A memory of that previous night: Banji held down and unable to get the police to hear what he was telling them – that they were killing Ruben. It must have been unbearable. 'I'm sorry,' she said. 'I shouldn't have spoken to you like that.'

He took her by surprise again. He reached out and touched a gentle finger against her lips. 'Don't be sorry. Be feisty. It suits you, Cathy Mason.'

So many lightning changes of mood: a dance she couldn't follow.

But then Banji was a man who never would be followed. 'Catch you later,' he said. 'Something I have to do,' and he walked away.

10 p.m.

'It's late,' the Reverend Pius said. 'And we've had a productive meeting. We are agreed. We'll set off from the Lovelace tomorrow at three, and others will join us outside the police station. We'll support the family while they seek an explanation from the police about their actions in relation to Ruben. Once they've been given that, we will disperse. Thanks, everybody, for attending and to Cathy for opening her home to us.' He stretched and tried to conceal a yawn that anyway sounded out.

No wonder he was tired: he'd had to work hard to contain the rage that had at moments threatened to burst out.

'That was well chaired,' Marcus said.

Cathy nodded her agreement, although she was distracted. One final look around the room as the crowd that had packed her living room thinned confirmed it. 'Banji wasn't here,' she said.

'Were you expecting him?'

'After last night? Yes, of course.'

'Well, you know what Banji's like.' Marcus got to his feet and also yawned. 'They seek him here, they seek him there, the Lovelace seeks him everywhere.'

He said it so sweetly it made her laugh, but still: 'You've never liked him, have you?'

'I don't like him.' Marcus shrugged. 'I don't dislike him. I don't know him. Does anybody?'

Yes, she nearly said. I do. But then she thought back to the way Banji had behaved that afternoon, and then to their more distant past, and she realised that she never had been able to predict what he would do.

'You better come.' Pius, who had left the room, suddenly re-appeared.

'Why?'

'It's your daughter.' Before she had time to press him, he was gone.

She went after him as fast as she could, weaving her way past knots of people still picking over what had been discussed. She had to stop herself from knocking some of them to the ground. It was a short distance to the hall, but it seemed to take an age to get there. Then she found her progress even more impeded. People were moving forward but so slowly. She could not understand it. She stood on her tiptoes and looked over their heads to see that the crowd, instead of dispersing, was standing just outside the door.

What had this to do with Lyndall? She'd been in and out during the meeting – bored, Cathy had assumed.

'Excuse me.' One last push and she was over the threshold.

'Look.'

Pius was smiling, and when she looked to the place he was pointing at, she understood why.

The night was aglow. Not with a fire that burnt – that had been her first thought – but with a soft, shimmering light. It was like looking at a cluster of stars, except this light came not from the sky but from down below.

'Your daughter and her friend did this.'

So that's why Lyndall and Jayden had been out so early. They must have gone to the wholesalers to buy tealights, which, in their glass containers, they had placed at regular intervals across the Lovelace. Down one of the gangways the river of light went and up another, as if following a route. And, yes, that's what they were doing. The kids had marked out Ruben's last walk with light and, yes again, her eyes confirmed it because there, in front of the community centre, was a great cluster, so many of them that it was from here that the impression of burning had come. A great flowing mass of light.

She looked and she looked. Her vision seemed to blur.

'Magnificent.' Pius's voice in her ear. 'And to think they keep lecturing us that we have a problem with our youth.'

She nodded but could not speak.

Lyndall must be here somewhere. She had to find her. She scanned the crowd and sure enough there was her daughter standing next to Jayden.

She could not speak, but she could do something better. She clasped her hands together and she put them over her heart and lowered her head and held it there, not in prayer but in appreciation of the great gift that they had been given.

Saturday

8 a.m.

With his wife and daughters away for the weekend, Chief Inspector Billy Ridgerton, cadre-trained in public order critical incidents, had done a fellow officer a favour by agreeing to take his place on call.

Last time he'd volunteered, there'd been major and almost simultaneous ructions in four different locations. He couldn't be that unlucky again. To reinforce this conviction he'd got up late – late for him, that is – and made himself a cup of instant coffee that he drank standing up.

The sun had yet to round the building, and for one glorious moment, as clouds swept across the sky, it looked as if the heatwave might be about to break. An illusion: the clouds soon dissolved, leaving a sky so blue it was clear they were in for another scorcher. He'd promised Angie he'd have a go at the unruly hedge that was strangely flourishing in the heat. Better start before it got too hot. But first he should check the available intel, just in case his services were going to be required.

There were the usual football fixtures, all of which looked to be, in policing terms, well under control. There were also a couple of fairs in London's parks which, barring the spontaneous immolation of a bouncy castle, shouldn't cause much trouble, and a vintage car race that might at worst lead to a bit of a traffic build-up. The only item of concern was the vigil that was due in Rockham.

Billy already knew of the death – an awful misfortune and one every copper dreaded – and he was familiar enough with Rockham to know that when things got hairy there, they really got hairy. Before he set to on the hedge, he decided to check if there were any issues by phoning the station and asking to speak to Rockham's Commander, CS Gaby Wright.

'She's up north at a conference,' he was told. 'Policing for change or some such bollocks.'

'Okay, so are there any issues?'

71

'Issues?' The sergeant sounded clueless: he must have been an acting, and a new one at that.

'Any likelihood of things going pear-shaped?' How much more clearly did Billy need to put it? 'Any reason for me to get my kit? Come over? Lend a hand?'

'Hold on a mo.' Maybe he was a pretender rather than an acting, because he now covered the phone rather than putting Billy on hold, so that Billy could hear a muffled conversation, the bozo who'd answered consulting one of his colleagues and then at last coming back to say, 'We've done a risk assessment and there's no reason to be concerned.'

There was always a reason in Rockham, but it wasn't Billy's job to point this out. He'd asked and they'd answered, and they'd ring if things started to go wrong. Shoving his mobile into a pocket, he went to the shed to fetch the clippers and a spade – he needed also to pull out all those bastard shoots which were coming up through the dried-up lawn – and then he set to dealing with the hedge.

11 a.m.

'Excellent choice.' Peter made his way to the back of the garden to where Frances was sitting in the shade of the oak. 'It's far too stuffy inside.' He leant over to kiss Frances. The dog, who had been lying under her chair, barked and would have nipped his leg had he not jumped smartly back. 'What's got into her?'

'She's hot like the rest of us.' Frances laid the stack of Saturday papers she'd been leafing through onto the table. 'How was Cabinet?'

'Bloody.' He sat down heavily in one of the wrought-iron chairs, nodding his thanks as Frances poured him a tumbler of iced tea. 'Coventry wouldn't be nearly far enough for them; they'd have sent me to Timbuktu if they could.' He drank the tea in one and stretched out his glass for a refill. 'The full Cabinet and not a single person as much as glanced my way. And when it was over, they evaporated faster than the clouds.'

'I wouldn't worry.' Frances dropped ice from an ice bucket into his glass: 'They're only trying to figure out when to jump.'

'Perhaps that's it.' He put his glass back on the table, and in doing so displaced one of the newspapers. 'Oh. There's my mobile. I wondered where it had got to.' Despite the cooling effect of Frances's iced tea, he was still desperately hot. He undid his laces and removed his shoes, checking that Patsy was out of biting distance before peeling off his socks. Such a relief. He stretched out his legs, feeling the dry grass prickle the soles of his feet. 'The PM was off to the summit as soon as it was over. He made a point of saying that. Three times in fact. I guess he thinks that the sight of him grinning in a sea of world leaders will give him a boost.'

'Too late for that. He's already haemorrhaged too much support.'

'I expect you're right. I couldn't help feeling sorry for him, though. At one point when he passed a note to the Foreign Secretary, his hands were visibly trembling.'

When Frances did not reply, he looked across at her. Her gaze, he saw, was focused on his feet, or more accurately on his white socks, yellowed by perspiration, that he had taken off. Although her face was partly shaded by the oak, he wondered whether that was distaste in her expression. But, no, he must have been mistaken. When she raised her head, her blue eyes were clear and calm, and she was smiling as she said, 'The PM's lost it.'

'So it seems.' Politics was such a cruel game. 'And so quickly. I can't help wondering why.'

'Who knows. Maybe it's his bitch of a wife' – the two women never had much liked each other – 'or his errant son. But it doesn't matter why. The truth is that he is simply not up to the job. His spell in Number 10 has finished him.'

As it could finish me, he thought, and not for the first time.

'Without someone new at the helm,' Frances said, 'the election is as good as lost.'

Right again. The PM knew it, the pollsters knew it, and the Party knew it. Most important of all, the hacks had started to say it out loud.

But it was one thing to accept that change was due and another to be the one to wield the knife. The PM, as ineffective as he was, was also liked by the Party; the person who deposed him could end up bearing the brunt of any backlash.

All very well for Frances to urge him on: she didn't have to put up with the side glances when they thought you weren't looking and, worse, vicious stage whispers they meant you to overhear. And what made her so sure he was going to win?

They'd been married so long she read his thoughts. 'You won't fail,' she said. 'They won't let you. They can't. You're the only viable candidate.'

'But people hate disloyalty. Now I've fired the starting gun, I could be trampled in the stampede.'

'What people really hate, Peter, and here I am talking about MPs, is losing their seats.' Her raised voice woke the dog, who looked up, accusingly, at Peter. 'But this isn't just about our MPs. It's about the whole Party. It's about the whole Country.'

The way she capitalised the Country – and made it sound right – made him think, as he often did, that she should have been the politician. She would have made a good enforcer: a fabulous whip.

'If the opposition win the election,' she was saying, 'they'll wreck everything you and the Party, and yes, let's give him credit where it's due, the PM, have worked so hard to achieve. Someone has to stop the rot. We can.'

He noted her use of the collective noun – another of her habits that could annoy. Yes, he'd be the first to admit that they were a team, and a good one. But he was Home Secretary and potential new Leader of her precious Country, and she was just his wife.

He was overcome, suddenly, by the most terrible fatigue.

It's the humidity, he thought, which had climbed even higher since the episode of the phantom clouds. The air was now so thick he was almost tempted to try to grab hold of it and squeeze it out. Water, that's what he craved. Not to drink but to immerse himself in. If only there had been a nearby stretch of water into which he could throw himself and for one glorious moment expunge the memory of the PM's trembling hands and the prospect of the fight to come. He let the imaginary water wash over him, and soon it was almost as if he really was floating down a river in a different country where life moves at a slower pace, with the sound of the cicadas' rubbing feet creating a reassuring background thrum . . .

'Third time this morning; you'd better answer it.'

He snapped his eyes open. The sound he had taken for cicadas was his phone vibrating on the metal table. When he reached for it, he registered the caller's name. 'Yes?'

A reply so indistinct he had to strain to hear it.

'This is a terrible line.'

Another soft sentence.

'I still can't hear you.'

Some more words, just as soft but also blurred, as if her mouth was latched on to her phone. He gave her a moment, straining to make sense of what she was saying, before cutting her short: 'You're still inaudible. Later.' He hung up and tossed the phone onto the table. 'Silly girl.'

'What did she want?'

'She's looking into Yares's connection to the PM. There's something between the two, I am convinced of it. Patricia seems to think she's found that something, but I could make neither head nor tail of what she was saying. Turns out she was in a pub surrounded by police officers. Doesn't she know how leaky they are?'

'She's young.' Frances's tone was even and even disinterested. Must have got over her uncharacteristic fit of jealousy. 'But at least she's keen.'

'Keen, yes. A little too much so at times.' He yawned, stretched up his arms and yawned again. 'The Cabinet took it out of me. And if you don't mind, darling, I've still got some catching up to do before I can take a well-earned snooze.' He got to his feet. He really was exhausted.

Such an effort even to make it to the house in this heat.

He was halfway there when she called him. 'You forgot this.'

She was holding up his mobile.

He shook his head. 'Don't need it,' and turned away. But almost immediately he turned back again. 'Oh,' a long sigh, 'I guess I had better take it. There's a meeting I have to go to later this afternoon; they said they'll text me when they've fixed the venue.'

3 p.m.

A handful of Lovelace residents had gathered outside Ruben's parents' flat. Not enough people so far for the many posters Lyndall and her troupe had made. Cathy was holding a clump by their sticks, so as not to damage the photos of Ruben mounted on their tops, and hoping the demonstration wouldn't stay this small.

Lyndall was a few feet away with more posters. Jayden was by her side. The two were chattering madly as they had been since early morning.

The last few days seemed to have brought them closer, Cathy thought, seeing how carefree Jayden, who usually wore a worried frown, looked. He had been dealt such a difficult hand yet show him the smallest kindness and he changed. The kind shopkeeper who kept him in work always said so, and there was more proof in the way that in Lyndall's company he seemed to act like a normal kid. A pity that their friendship was unlikely to outlast the closing of the Lovelace. Not because they didn't like each other – which they clearly did – but because their different financial circumstances meant they would end up living miles apart.

'Here they are.'

Reverend Pius led the way out of the flat, closely followed by Ruben's parents. As the two walked hand in hand, heads held high, nodding in acknowledgement of each member of the waiting group, Cathy was once more struck by their grace, especially when, coming abreast of Lyndall and Jayden, they stopped. No words were spoken, but Ruben's mother reached out to touch each of the youngsters gently on the forehead: an acknowledgement and a blessing for the river of light they had created.

'Shall we?' Pius led the way down the gangway.

They followed, mostly in single file, tracing the route of the previous night's candle path. Doors kept opening as they progressed down the different levels, more residents coming out to join them, so that by the time they reached ground level a handful had turned into a respectable bunch, with all the posters now held aloft, and when they came abreast of the community centre, they numbered, by Cathy's reckoning, about sixty. And this was only the beginning. She needn't have worried: more would join them once they were outside the police station.

The community centre was closed, as it had been since Ruben's death. Police tape barred an entrance that was now banked by flowers. There were no police guarding the flowers, which, given the ill feeling towards the force, was probably wise. And there would have been no need: the flowers were untouched.

The crowd stood silent as Ruben's parents stooped down to read the cards that people had left. They walked slowly along the line, picking up each in turn, giving them equal attention. That done, Ruben's mother laid her own tribute – a single poppy – on top.

She stayed like that for a moment, her head bent, her hand resting on the poppy. 'He loves red poppies,' she said to the air.

'Come.' Pius helped her up and then, linking his arm to hers and to her husband's, led the way out of the Lovelace and into a market that was already packing up. As the now sizeable crowd walked between the stalls, traders stood by: an honour guard paying tribute to a man who had once been their familiar.

4 p.m.
Peter came to with a start.

The room was dark, curtains drawn, and it took him a moment to work out where he was. Hearing movement in the bathroom, he realised that he must have dozed off. He felt the air wonderfully cool. How long had he been asleep?

'How long have I been sleeping?' he called.

The bathroom door opened, light framing the glorious vision of Patricia, whose skin, still wet from her shower, glistened a golden brown in the light. 'Not long.' She stretched up her arms and yawned.

She was so lovely. Desire rose up in him. Again. He patted the bed. 'Come here.'

'I'm wet.'

'For me, I hope.' Another pat. 'Come on. Come here.'

She took her time, walking slowly towards the bed, smiling as he followed her every step. He was practically drooling when she slid in beside him.

If only, he thought. He laid a hand on her stomach and with the other pulled the sheet over her. 'Come closer.' He felt the brush of her breasts against his chest. He wanted her. So much. If only he could stop the clock and stay, here, in this room.

But . . . he lifted himself up, reaching for his watch.

'Oh no you don't.' She wrenched the watch out of his grasp and threw it across the room.

He winced as it hit the wall. 'Do you mind? That's a Hublot.'

'Should be strong enough to survive, then, shouldn't it?'

He made to go and fetch it back, but before he could she straddled him, pinning him down by his hands, kneeling on all fours and grinning.

She's so pretty, he thought, and so damn irreverent. At least in bed.

She lowered her head close enough for him to feel her hair brush against his neck. She whispered one word, 'Stay,' in his ear.

How he would have liked to stay. But one couldn't run away from time, especially when it was blinking in neon green from the bedside table. 'I can't.'

When he thought he felt her stiffen, he prayed that she wasn't going to make a fuss. But being with Frances, the mistress of the sudden freeze, had made him oversensitive. Instead of sinking into the sullen silence that was Frances's intimate, Patricia laughed out loud. 'Big talker.' She kissed him, passionately, on the lips. 'Until the next time.' She shifted off him so he could get out of bed.

A shower to get rid, not of her but of the smell of her (so light and flowery, he thought, which he loved).

When he was with her and naked, his only thoughts were of her. Now, as the water flowed, what dominated was the memory of the lie he'd told his wife. Not something he was proud of. But her question had come so out of the blue he'd panicked, and once his denial had been released, it created its own momentum. To undo it now would be tricky.

Because her father had betrayed her mother in such an appallingly public manner, Frances was particularly touchy. She'd never understand that what he had with Patricia in no way affected his feelings for her. She was his wife, his counsel and the mother of his child: he wasn't going to leave her. So why would he cause her pain for something that fulfilled a need but which was otherwise unimportant?

What was it that had even made her ask, he wondered. Had someone talked? It couldn't be. If she had been sure of her facts, she would have pressed him harder.

'Why are you taking so long?'

Patricia. He must go to her. He rubbed himself briskly with a towel. Despite his exertions, his sleep and a fairly hot shower, he was still feeling cool. A place that got the temperature right was a rarity; pity the need to protect himself from prying eyes meant that the next time they'd have to use a different hotel.

He came out of the bathroom to find her still in bed. She was lying on her back, sheet discarded, arms behind her head, stark naked and looking straight at him.

'What a wanton child you are.'

'Child?' She wrinkled her nose.

'Temptress, then.' She was that as well, and irresistible. He went over to the bed and kissed her. 'I wish I could stay.'

'I know.' The arms that had gone round his neck gave a quick squeeze before letting go.

He collected his clothes from the various points on the carpet where he had shed them. 'If you don't mind, I'll go first.'

She nodded.

Strange the transition between the intimacy of bed and the clothes that called up the outside world. Her eyes stayed fixed on him as he dressed. It made him feel a little awkward, so he averted his gaze until he had finished and was putting on his tie.

He looked around him. Something missing.

'Your watch.'

He fetched it from the place where it had fallen onto the thick pile carpet. He held it to his ear. Foolish. It was a Hublot. He wasn't ever going to hear it ticking. He strapped it on.

She was still watching him and it was still unnerving. Something he had done? 'I'm sorry,' he said.

'What for?' Her tone was light.

'The way I spoke to you when you called.'

She shrugged.

'I was with my wife.'

He caught an involuntary narrowing of her hazel eyes. Understandable. If he put himself in her shoes, he could see it was difficult for her as well.

I'll make it up to her, he thought. Buy her something. Fully dressed now, and conscious that his driver would be waiting in the lobby, he went over to the bed.

She smiled up at him.

Let the driver wait. He leant over to kiss her. Showing her, without words, how much he thought of her. He felt her melting in his arms.

How he wanted to stay.

'They'll be waiting for you downstairs,' she said. 'You'd better go.'

Such a sweet girl. And so considerate. He sighed and straightened up. 'By the way,' he said. 'Did you really uncover something between the PM and Commissioner Yares or was that just your excuse for ringing?'

'Both,' she said. 'Did you know that Yares is Teddy's godfather?'

He nodded. 'He has some long-standing connection to the PM's wife – I think their parents may have known each other – which he declared in his application in tedious detail. The man's such a stickler, he's a bore.' He pulled the knot of his tie tight. 'Peculiar decision to choose a godfather who's a Jew, but I suppose there's less of the God about most of us these days, and that includes the PM. The public doesn't seem to care. Anything else?'

'I'm working on it.' She had on her serious assistant's expression. 'I've got some leads. That's what I was doing in that pub.'

'You're a marvel. Do your best, will you?'

'Yes, Peter.' She so rarely used his Christian name. 'I'll do my best.'

4.40 p.m.

The demonstrators had set up camp on the pavement opposite the police station and a few hundred yards down from it. The police had closed Rockham train station and the road leading to it, and diverted southward-bound traffic through a one-way system and away from the police station, which was therefore isolated and easier to guard with a small number of officers. Normally they would have set up this diversion at the large junction at Rockhill Park, but this time, for some reason that no one could understand, they let traffic pass the park, only afterwards diverting it via the smaller Blackrod Road. As a result, the High Street to the north of the police station was soon crammed with cars trying to U-turn their way back to the diversion. To deal with the logjam, a patrol car parked nearby to disgorge two uniformed officers who proceeded to direct the traffic back.

For their part, the demonstrators did as they always did: they spilt out into the road to stop traffic from the south passing by. The police's answer to this – again as per usual – was to create a makeshift roadblock in the south so that the demonstrators now had full possession of the area a few hundred yards from the police station in what was a kind of informal, if unpoliced, kettle.

So far so routine. An hour and a half after they had first arrived, everything was still calm. The day continued ferociously hot. A whipround raised money for a stack of collective water, which they stored in a couple of polystyrene boxes packed with ice. An enterprising ice-cream seller parked near the southernmost perimeter of the demonstration, from which position he did a roaring trade. Ice creams passed amongst the crowd, some of it gifted good-naturedly to the officers who were working valiantly in that heat to turn away traffic from the northern boundary of the enclosure. With the sun beating down, it felt more like a summer party than a protest, especially when someone used a beach umbrella to create a shaded sanctuary for babies and those who could least tolerate the heat.

They stood chatting and holding up their placards, waiting to see whether anybody would come out and talk to them. At 3.30 p.m., when no officer appeared, Ruben's parents, accompanied by the Reverend Pius, had made their way into the police station. Their intention was to ask the police for their version of what had happened, something that had not so far been shared with the parents.

When the three did not return, the assumption was that they were talking to the powers that be. And so the demonstrators waited for them to reappear, and as they waited, the demonstration grew.

And then at last: 'There they are.' Marcus, who stood shoulders above most people, was pointing over the heads of the crowd and towards the police station. The crowd turned, almost as one, to see Pius and Ruben's parents coming out.

Marcus pushed his way to the front. 'Doesn't look good,' he muttered to Cathy, who had also noticed the downward cast of Ruben's mother's head and the negative shaking of Pius's. The three were in fact walking slowly, as if reluctant to rejoin the demonstration, or, Cathy suddenly realised, as if they wanted a conversation in private, something that must also have struck Marcus, who whispered, 'Let's meet them by the roadblock,' in her ear.

PRIVATE AND CONFIDENTIAL
FOR INQUIRY USE ONLY

Submission to the internal inquiry of the Metropolitan Police into Operation Bedrock

Submission 573/A/1: photographic evidence gathered by ASU 27AWZ between 16:43 and 16:51 on ███████████████

location: the area immediately adjacent to Rockham police station

subject: demonstration

At 16:43 hours, Air Support Unit 27AWZ, call sign India 95, passed over Rockham High Street, where a crowd had gathered. On instructions from the rear police officer, the pilot circled the area while the police observer operated video camera facilities and recorded still images. The attached images, date and time stamped, were captured during the period of surveillance and selected at the request of the Chairman of the internal inquiry. The complete series of surveillance pictures are attached as an appendix.

Camera still 0578/19413

time stamp: 16:49:10

A crowd estimated at approximately one hundred stands two hundred yards to the south of Rockham police station. They have filled the pavement and spilt into the road. A young man, IC3, with long dreadlocks, who with others has climbed the wall behind the pavement, points in a northerly direction towards a police roadblock manned by two uniformed officers. A patrol car is visible, parked in a side street to the south of this roadblock.

Camera stills 0578/19414–9

time stamp: 16:49:15 – 16:50:55 inclusive

Just north of Rockham police station, officers direct southward-bound traffic, which had gone beyond the diversion, back towards Blackrod

Road. A line of traffic has built up. Several vehicles are in the process of turning round, with the result that both sides of the north-leading road are blocked.

Camera still 0578/19421

time stamp: 16:51:10

Five adults, three IC3 males, one IC1 female and one IC3 female, stand on the verge by the northern roadblock. They appear to be locked in conversation.

4.51 p.m.

'All this time?' Despite her effort to appear calm, Cathy couldn't keep the disbelief from her voice.

'For most of it,' Pius said. 'At first they asked us to wait outside, but when we pointed out that this would enrage the crowd they told us we could take a seat.'

'"Pull up a pew, Reverend," is what the policeman said' – this from Ruben's father – 'As if this was some kind of a joke.'

'We sat for gone an hour,' Pius continued, 'until at last a sergeant came out – not one any of us have met before. He said there was nothing more they could do because the matter was now in the hands of the IPCC. We asked them how we could contact the IPCC on a Saturday, and they said it was not their business.'

'They were rude.' Again from Ruben's father. 'They kill our son and then they are rude.'

'We told them that wasn't good enough,' Pius said. 'We asked to speak to Chief Superintendent Wright. They said she wasn't there. So we asked for her second-in-command.'

'He also wasn't there.'

'They told us they would request a visit to the family home by a senior officer, after consultation with the IPCC. We said we needed one now and here. We waited some more, and then a moment ago they came to tell us that they had just sent a car for a superintendent who is acting up as a chief superintendent. They reckoned it will take an hour to fetch him.'

'But we've been here since three and it's nearly five,' Marcus said. 'The crowd from the football will soon be coming down the High Street. Are they trying to provoke us?'

'Truth is,' Pius said, 'and it pains me to say this – I don't think they know what they're doing. We told them we needed to be gone by dusk – that we had children with us – and that we didn't want anything to go awry. All they would say was that they'd do their best.'

'Rude. And they the ones killed our son.' Ruben's father's raised voice attracted the attention of several members of the crowd.

Ruben's mother went to stand in front of her husband. 'Whosoever shall compel thee to go a mile, go with him twain.' Although her voice was soft, she held him with a hard gaze. 'Our son was never violent. We don't want trouble.'

'And we won't have it.' Stepping in between them, Pius put one arm around each of Ruben's parents. 'Come. Let us go and tell the others, and then we will wait, calmly and patiently, for an officer to be brought to us.'

Submission to the internal inquiry of the Metropolitan Police into Operation Bedrock

Submission 573/A/2: photographic evidence gathered by ASU 27AWZ, India 95, at 17:03 hours on ██████████████

Camera still 0578/194139

time stamp: 17:03:07

location: 200 yards south of Rockham police station

subject: demonstration

A man, IC3, stands in front of the crowd, speaking into a bullhorn. Several members of the crowd have their hands up, perhaps remonstrating against what is being said.

Camera stills 0578/194140–19507 appended in annex/4 show build-up of numbers in the demonstration.

Submission to the internal inquiry of the Metropolitan Police into Operation Bedrock

Submission 573/A/3: photographic evidence gathered by ASU 27AWZ, call sign India 95, pertaining to the incident involving police vehicle IRV 02 PFD

location: Rockham High Street south of Rockham police station

subject: demonstration

Camera still 0578/19508

time stamp: 17:44:59

Incident Response Vehicle number 02 PFD, travels down Rockham High Street, heading north.

(Note to Inquiry. At 17:52:00 Air Support Unit 27AWZ radioed base to warn that the IRV appears to be heading straight towards the demonstration. Subsequent inquiry ascertained that IRV 02 PFD was responding to a report of a TWOC incident.)

Camera still 0578/19509

time stamp: 17:45:16

location: Rockham High Street south of Rockham police station

subject: demonstration

IRV number 02 PFD mounts the pavement to pass the roadblock.

5.45 p.m.

They heard the siren long before they saw the car. It was background noise that everybody assumed would fade. But instead the noise increased in intensity and duration until:

'What the fuck?'

Someone on the southern edge of the crowd pointed to the police car that, unable to press forward because of the roadblock, had mounted the pavement and was heading straight for the demonstrators.

'Stop.'

The car kept coming.

'Stop.'

The car blasted out a series of warning siren bursts as if expecting that the people in its path could somehow disappear. A child's buggy, complete with screaming infant, was carried overhead to safety as others scrambled out of the way.

The pressure of people still around the car had forced it to slow down, but it did not stop even when one of the policemen from the northern end of the roadblock starting running towards it. A demonstrator, who had been standing outside the fruit and veg shop, picked up a tomato and threw it at the patrol car. 'Stop. You're going to hurt somebody.'

The tomato struck the windscreen and burst, as the cry 'Stop!' was taken up by many voices. And still the car kept going.

'Stop!' People closest to the shop reached into boxes that lined the pavement, grabbing anything to hand, so that tomatoes and carrots and purple plums and avocados went flying through the air, some of them landing on the car and others splattering in the road. And then at last, the car, its driver possibly having spotted his fellow officer running towards him, applied his brakes so that by the time the policeman had arrived and banged on a side window, the car had come to a complete halt. The driver's side window slid down allowing the out-of-breath policeman to speak, briefly, to his fellows inside.

89

The window closed. The policeman stepped away. The car got moving again, backing up the way it had come, and although it clipped the side of the ice-cream van as it went, it did not stop but instead, siren wailing, reversed down the pavement until it could turn and speed away.

Submission to the internal inquiry of the Metropolitan Police into Operation Bedrock

Submission 573/A/4: further photographic evidence gathered by Air Support Unit 27AWZ, call sign India 95, pertaining to the incident involving IRV 02 PFD

Camera stills 0578/19510

time stamp: 17:48:31

location: perimeter of southern roadblock

subject: collision

IRV 02 PFD clips the front side driver's bumper of a parked van.

Camera stills 0578/19511

time stamp: 17:49:56

location: perimeter of southern roadblock

subject: collision

IRV 02 PFD reversing away as the van driver steps out.

Submission 573/A/5: photographic evidence gathered by Air Support Unit 27AWZ, call sign India 95, between 18:29 and 18:46 hours on ██████████████, pertaining to the appearance of Chief Inspector Raj Privadi

Camera still 0578/19536

time stamp: 18:29:33

location: 200 yards south of Rockham police station

subject: arrival of senior officer

Newly arrived police vehicle IRV 01 HDR is stopped by northern road-block. A uniformed police officer who has come out of the car is walking through the block towards the demonstration. The crowd is now estimated at approximately one hundred and fifty persons.

Camera stills 0578/19537–41

time stamp: 18:30:51–18:40:12

location: 200 yards south of Rockham police station

subject: communication between senior officer and representatives of the demonstrators

Officer attempts to address the demonstrators but appears to be rebuffed. Officer walks back behind the roadblock and into Rockham police station.

Submission 573/A/6: photographic evidence gathered by Air Support Unit 27AWZ, call sign India 95, between 18:40 and 18:46 hours on ██████████████ pertaining to the appearance of the bus ARL VLW 96 on the scene

Camera still 0578/19627

time stamp: 18:40:03

location: northerly roadblock

92

subject: movement of traffic

Bus ARL VLW 96 stationary at the northern roadblock. The driver is out of his cab and talking to one of the police officers whose hand is in the air and twisted to one side as if describing to the driver the process by which he can turn round in the road. Beyond the roadblock the line of traffic is blocking the bus's exit.

Camera still 0578/19628

time stamp: 18:45:12

location: northerly roadblock

subject: movement of traffic

In trying to turn, the bus has mounted the pavement and is facing a wall. Passengers disgorge from the stationary bus while those who have already descended are being ushered through the roadblock. Several of them have turned towards the crowd.

Note: This is the last of the series. At 18:46:15 27AWZ returned to base to refuel.

8.15 p.m.

They had been waiting for almost five hours, and they were still waiting. And as they waited, the demonstration had grown.

Half an hour previously, a patrol car, blues and twos flashing, had stopped by the southern roadblock to disgorge a chief inspector. Here, it appeared, was the promised senior officer. But he only had to show his face and he was met by derision. 'They're using you for your black face,' someone shouted, while someone else demanded to know why the policeman would do the white man's dirty work, and soon the cry 'House nigger! House nigger!' drove him into the police station.

And still they stood and still they waited.

As the sun dipped it also dazzled, turning the northern sky yellow. The day's last hurrah and the crowd grew. Threads of pinks and oranges began to trail through the sky and intensified as the sun slipped down. By 8.20, the police station was washed in crimson.

Such a glorious sight and yet it felt menacing, reminding Cathy of the recent sunrise and the foreboding which had then possessed her. That was the day that Ruben had been killed. And now?

She looked around her, registering how the crowd had changed. Whereas most of the early demonstrators had been Lovelace residents or members of Ruben's extended family, the new arrivals were not so easily recognisable. They were younger and more energetic and, she thought, and hoped she was mistaken in this, spoiling for a fight.

'They are not going to send anybody to speak to us,' Ruben's mother said. 'There is nothing to be gained by staying.'

Pius and Marcus agreed. They had made their point. They must now regroup.

'Let's see the family safe indoors,' Pius said.

It had been a while since Lyndall had been around. 'You go ahead,' Cathy said. 'I need to find Lyndall.'

94

The crowd was much more densely packed; she looked this way and that.

'Would you like us to wait for you?'

She took in the exhaustion on Ruben's mother's face and the anger on his father's. 'No. Don't wait.'

She'd find Lyndall and then they'd both get out of there.

She started at the southern border of the enclosure. No Lyndall, nor Jayden either, just curious people heading down the High Street to check out what was going on. More of them were coming: the whole area would soon be densely packed.

A drum began to beat.

The sound seemed to pass right through her, intensifying her awareness of her thumping heart. The fear that she had tried to tell herself was only her imagination reared up, and once it came it would not go. She felt it hammering at her throat, taking away her breath as she walked. Faster and faster she went until she was almost running.

She called out 'Lyndall?' as she darted in and out of the knots of people who had gathered together: 'Lyndall?'

She pushed on, heading for the northern roadblock: 'Lyndall?' Lyndall would never hear her mobile in this crowd. 'Lyndall?'

Someone she passed heard her cry and took it up: 'Lyndall!' Others joined in so that soon the air was vibrating with the calling of her daughter's name: 'Lyndall! Lyndall! Lyndall!' the drum now also pounding out the syllables: 'Lyn-dall! Lyn-dall! Lyn-dall!'

She told herself that she had felt like this before when Lyndall had been late. Nothing had happened then. Nothing was going to happen now.

'Lyn-dall! Lyn-dall! Lyn-dall!'

Someone grasped hold of her. She turned to face them.

'What the hell's wrong with you?' Lyndall was so red with mortification that her face almost matched the colour of the setting sun. 'I was here. I've been here all the time. You're such a panicker.'

'Come on. We're off.'

'I'm not going. It's fine. He'll look after me.' She indicated the man beside her.

So caught up had Cathy been in the relief of finding Lyndall, she hadn't noticed Banji there. Although perhaps she hadn't noticed him because he looked nothing like himself. The distress she had seen in him that previous day seemed now to have pulled down his brow and pinched in his face. The irises of his eyes that were yesterday pink had darkened to a bloodshot red; below them the skin had blackened with fatigue.

She had seen how upset he was and yet had failed to seek him out. Cruel of her. She reached out to touch him.

Without even looking at her, he shifted out of reach. His focus was on the northern roadblock. 'Where did they go?'

They? She looked to the point where the two policeman had been turning the traffic back and saw that, although the patrol car was still in the side street and beside it the abandoned bus, the two officers had vanished.

'Maybe they've gone to move the roadblock back.'

It was as if she wasn't there.

'There's enough of them.' He was talking to himself.

She looked again, this time beyond the roadblock. She saw that where there had recently been three officers in the vicinity of the police station there were now at least twenty. No casual collection this: they were standing in lines as still as sentries.

'Has someone turned them to stone?' Lyndall's joke foundered under the uneasy crack of her voice.

'It's going to kick off,' Banji said. 'They'll make sure of that.'

She wasn't sure whether the 'they' he was referring to was the police or the group of young men who had also sidled into view. They were not luxuriating in the warm evening; they were moving with a serious intention that soon displayed itself. They went over to the unguarded panda car, stopping within ten yards of it.

'They'll do something.' Banji was now clearly talking about the police. 'Even if they don't have the right protective kit. They have to do something.'

The battering ram of young men seemed to agree. They looked expectantly at the police lines.

The police in the lines looked back. And did not move.

Later, when Cathy thought about how it had begun, it came to her as a series of freeze frames.

First off a fluid moment: one of the youths separated himself from his group and strolled over to the shop whose boxes were still laid out on the pavement. He picked up a box, returned to his starting point, put down the box, took out a cabbage, backed off a few yards and then began to run.

Freeze frame: the man in full stride, his arm stretched back behind him.

The cabbage arcs up on a high trajectory towards the car.

The cabbage hits the front windscreen, which cracks.

Those two sides – the group of youths and the police – face each other.

Freeze frame.

And then double time.

The box of cabbages became a focal point, a stopping place for grabbing arms that reached in, withdrew and threw, until the air was thick with flying cabbages. They hit the car and dented it as, attracted by the noise, more members of the crowd started running towards the commotion.

The police did not react.

The first of the group were already advancing on the dented car. Someone tried to pull open a front door. When that didn't work, someone else placed his elbow against the cracked glass on the driver's side and jerked it back. The glass caved in. He inserted his hand through the gap, pulled up the lock and opened the door. Someone pushed him aside and dived into the car, soon to re-emerge, triumphantly, with a trophy. A CS canister. The sight produced a long drawn-out cheer.

And still the police did not move.

We should go, Cathy thought, but somehow couldn't tear herself away.

More of the youths were in the car, ripping it to pieces. One of their number must have released the handbrake. A shout went up: 'Roll it.' The men in the car scrambled out as a handful of other youths got behind it and, at the shout of 'One, two, three, push', pushed. The car edged forward.

'One, two, three push.'

This time, before the 'push', Cathy was certain that she saw the young men stop and look at the police line, as if, she was later to decide, daring the police to react.

The police did not react.

'One, two, three . . .' There must have been a slope in the road because this time on the third 'push' the car rolled forward and did not stop until it hit the kerb. It mounted the kerb before slipping back. It was now directly in front of the vegetable shop.

A man, the owner, came out of his shop, his hands up as if to wave the car away. He shouted 'Help!' at the watching lines of police. 'Come help me.'

No reaction.

As the youths lined themselves up behind the car, readying themselves for a last push, the shopkeeper and his sons, who had also dashed out, planted themselves at the car's front end. They laid their hands on the battered bonnet and pushed. The car seesawed backwards and forwards for a moment in a contest that the shopkeeper was bound to lose save that several of the youths pushing at its rear voluntarily gave up, while a couple of the others were physically wrenched away by Banji.

'One, two, three push.' The people at the car's front end were now in the majority, and the car rolled backwards, coming to a halt in the middle of the road.

Such an odd sight. A battered patrol car, isolated as a row of police just looked on. It was a trophy that the crowd began to circle. Round and round they went, banging hands against open mouths and whooping.

A voice yelling in Cathy's ear: 'They're going to torch it.' Lyndall's voice. 'Hurry up, Mum. We have to leave.'

Hand in hand they began to run, pushing against a tide of excited incomers. A 'whoosh'. They stopped and turned. Just in time to see a thin jet of fire flare from the open petrol cap of the police car. And then, as the people around it stepped away, the car exploded.

A collective howl, exultation and rage mixed, rose up into the night and although some of the crowd now retreated from the burning car they were soon replaced by others who, drawn to the blaze, joined the whooping dance around the flames, while a small subgroup split off from this crowd to run over to the bus and around it until they had disappeared from sight.

The bus began to rock, imperceptibly at first, so that Cathy thought she might be imagining the movement, but then she realised that they were pushing it from the side, forwards and back, slowly at first but then gathering speed, a huge red pendulum whose main arc was forwards and towards the street, until, one more heave, and the bus tipped over. Spotlit by the burning car, it arced down, gathering speed as it neared the ground, and then it was down, splinters of broken glass flying out, to the sound of cheers and breaking metal, the bulk of the crowd racing for it.

'Come on. Quick. Let's get out of here before they set the bus on fire.'

8.25 p.m.

The untidiness of the hedge was history. Or at least it would be once Billy had bagged up the last of the cuttings.

It had taken longer than he'd expected. Hours in fact, although he had had a break to watch the match and the post-match commentary, which he'd bookended with an extended snooze.

A rare treat to spend a Saturday without demands and he'd milked it – not that he didn't miss the girls but they'd be back, at which point Angie would be over the moon about his good work.

Just one more bag to fill and then, he thought, a pizza and a low-alcohol beer. Perhaps two. He'd earned them. As he began to sweep along the pavement, he felt his phone buzz. He pulled it out and clicked it on: 'Yup?'

'Billy? It's Mike.'

Mike was not part of that weekend's command complex, so this must be a social call. Billy felt himself relax. 'What's up?'

'A bus on fire in Rockham.'

'Oh yeah? Course there is. Pull the other one.'

'This isn't a wind-up,' Mike said. 'I'm on the ground. The station's under siege and there's hardly any Level 2 here. They're going through the call list – you'll be hearing from them soon – but I thought I'd give you a heads-up so you can organise your kit.'

Without thinking about it, Billy had straightened up, and when he asked, 'How bad?' he sounded extremely calm.

'Really bad. And it's only going to get worse.'

9.15 p.m.

Jayden had dreamt this same dream, and on more than one occasion. He and Lyndall walking down an unfamiliar street. Him reaching out for her, like she (he was never in any doubt about this in the dream) wanted him to do. But as their fingers touched, a hot wind, no, not a wind, a tornado ripped them from each other, and he was sucked up into the twisting centre, powerless as she seemed to shrink, or else he was being blown further and further away from her – he couldn't tell which it was. He only knew that he could no longer make her face out in a gathered crowd.

And now he found himself living this dream even though the street they were on was Rockham's main thoroughfare and they had been torn asunder not by a wind but by the force of the rampaging crowd. Her hand reached out for his, but he was jammed so tight that he had been lifted off the ground, with the thrust of the group carrying him away from her.

He saw her mouth open. He knew she must be calling to him, but he couldn't hear what she was saying, and soon he couldn't see her either. He struggled to free himself and eventually managed to tunnel his way out of this cyclone of people, many more of whom were heading in the opposite direction. He lowered his head and barrelled against this oncoming tide, back to the place where they'd been parted. But she was long gone.

He thought he heard her name, not once but many times. He scanned the crowd as that implausible cry 'Lyn-dall, Lyn-dall', which his imagination must have summoned up, mocked him. He tried to jump up, the better to see where she might have gone, but that set the people around him jumping, the action spreading through the crowd so that all he could now see was a myriad of bobbing heads. He felt a terrible sense of failure: he had not kept her safe.

A bang, and the tide turned, and he with it, all of them running at the noise that was the bursting into flames of a squad car. Then he saw Lyndall, lit up by the flash of the explosion. She was safe. With her mother at her side.

He could have reached them, he should have, but something, perhaps the way they stood, so close to each other, held him back.

She was safe. That's all that mattered. He saw them turning away. Like he should too. Get back to his own mother.

The fire around the police car had helped clear the path, especially now that some of the crowd were making for the bus. He could easily have gone and caught up with Lyndall. And yet knowing she was safe had released him.

To what?

To be here. In this moment. With all these people. Some of whom he knew. Some of whom he didn't. All of them flushed by the heat, and the fires, and not knowing what was going to come next, and, yes, now he felt it flooding through him he could name it for himself: exhilaration.

His life upturned. His early rises to open and clean the shop and buy the breakfast and bring it back and leave it for his mother who, despite how hard he shook her, never would get up. And then the trudge to school, and he always on the late register, and those mouths that spoke at him words he was too tired to take much notice of, detentions handed out which he had to miss because it was time to get back to work again.

All those people – his teachers, his boss, the social workers. These people who were always telling him who he was and what he had to do. They were nowhere here. Fuck them. Fuck their rules. Fuck their prohibitions. The things they told him he couldn't do. The things they told him he couldn't have.

They were nowhere here. Those people who always told him what he was allowed.

The police, yes, he could see them, were there, but they just stood and looked. And here he was with all the others. He could do what they were doing, he could pick up a brick, look there was one, he felt its rough edges in his hand, and he could surge on and into one of the broken shops.

'Let's get 'em' – that chorus rising and he joining it – 'Let's get 'em', and he didn't care who it was they were going to get, he just wanted to act, to be carried along by the crowd and to do what they were going to do. And already there was the sound of breaking glass, and shadows were flitting in and out of shops that had been blasted open, and people coming out, not just the young and not just men but all kinds of people, holding things they'd grabbed, and he too, all he had to do was move with the tide and he could have some of what they were having, things he'd only ever dreamt of owning: trainers, not the old sad ones he wore, but the ones other kids flaunted, the confident boys who stood out. He didn't even have to break in or anything – he let drop the brick he was holding – it was already done. All he had to do was follow. And now, before it all disappeared.

'Come on.' He was talking to himself and to the night: 'Come on,' urging himself forwards, laughing even, oh how much he wanted to do something, anything, without first having to think of the consequences. To be in the now, like he never was.

Because. He stopped. The crowd surging past.

Because.

If he got caught.

If he didn't make it home.

If he wasn't there to buy the breakfast.

If he didn't put it on the table.

If all those ifs came to pass.

She wouldn't manage. Not if he wasn't there.

'Come on.' They were calling to each other, and they were still coming on.

All of them but him.

He dropped his head and turned away.

9.55 p.m.

The table was groaning with Frances's splendid food and lit by candles to soften the velvet night. Around the table were close friends, all of whom were supportive of his leadership bid. Not that it had even been broached: they knew, without Peter having to say as much, that what he needed more than anything was a break from the relentless pressure.

So they gave it to him, following his lead in keeping the conversation light.

Oh, the joy of relaxing with people who understood and who, even more importantly, were not going to sell his every unguarded word to the tabloids.

He kept their glasses topped up with a particularly subtle Gigondas rosé, which had gone down very nicely. If the heatwave continued, which the weathermen were now saying was a distinct possibility, he would have to organise another couple of cases. He reached for the bottle.

'Here, let me.' Frances's hand covered his before slipping under it to take the bottle. She got to her feet and began doing the rounds of the table, and by the time she'd reached him, the bottle was empty. He twisted round: there were two upturned empties in the ice bucket and that was it.

He made to rise, but Frances now laid her hands on his shoulders. 'Don't worry, darling, I'll fetch more.' For a moment she stayed where she was and, although it was hot, he felt his tight shoulders relaxing under the pressure of her kneading fingers. He let out a long sigh of contentment.

'Me next' – this from one of their guests.

Frances laughed, removed her hands and, having guaranteed 'I'll be back', made her way through the garden and to the kitchen.

'A marvellous woman. You lucky man.'

A chorus of agreement circled the table while Peter thought about his luck. He reached for his glass and drained it of its last few drops. More soon to come.

Not, however, that soon. The conversation moved through the greatest gaffes ever committed in public, and then, raucously, in private, and still Frances did not return. There were bottles in the wine fridge: he knew because he'd put them there. He turned to look through the darkness and towards the house.

The kitchen was lit up, so he could see her clearly. She was standing with her back to him. She wasn't moving – not bringing out dessert, then – and she wasn't anywhere near the wine fridge. What on earth? He was about to go and check on her, but when she turned to look his

way he saw that there was a simple enough explanation for her immo-
bility: she was on the phone. He could see her nodding as she held it
to her ear. Someone must have phoned, although he hadn't heard the
ringing, which, given they'd rigged up an amplification system, was
odd.

She seemed to be staring straight at him, although since she was in
the light and he in the dark he knew that she wouldn't be able to see
him. Perhaps she was just glaring in that way of hers in order to transmit
to whoever was on the other end that they needed to stop talking and
hang up. Which is exactly what happened. Her hand moved the phone
down to the counter.

She'd be back soon. He turned to their guests. And heard her calling.
'Peter.' She'd stepped out of the kitchen, phone in hand. 'You had better
take this.'

He glanced at his watch. Nearly ten. It must be important or Frances
would have given the caller short shrift. He sighed and pushed himself
to his feet. 'Duty calls.' He took a step forward, only to trip over the
blasted dog, who was always underfoot.

'Steady.' As the dog yelped, one of the guests reached out a hand to
stop Peter falling. 'Better have some coffee, old boy.'

To prove that he wasn't really drunk, he walked in a deliberate
straight line to the kitchen, where Frances stood, phone still in hand.
'It's the Commissioner,' she said. 'Something about Rockham.'

'Covering his arse, I bet.' Peter reached for the phone.

But Frances kept hold of it for a moment. 'If it's serious, take it seriously. With the PM at the summit, this is your chance. The Party already
knows what you're capable of; if you play this right, you can also show
the Country.'

'Indeed.' He took the phone from her. 'Home Secretary here,' sitting
down as he listened to what Joshua Yares had to say. In the background,
Frances busied herself making coffee.

11 p.m.
The Lovelace rang out with shouts and the pounding of feet, people
running either towards or away from the trouble.

'Jayden's not back.' As Lyndall turned away from the balcony's edge, her eyes filled with tears. 'Something must have happened. I've got to go and get him.'

'I'm sorry, darling, I can't let you.'

'You know what Jayden's like: he always wants to please. They'll make him do things and they won't keep him safe. Please – I have to find him.'

'You're a mixed-race kid in what is effectively a race riot. If the police pick you up – and in that circumstance they'll go for anybody they can get – you'll be in trouble.'

'I don't care.'

'Well, I do.'

Lyndall bunched her fist and hissed out one word – 'Hypocrite' – through tight lips.

'I beg your pardon?'

'You must have lectured me a million times on how we are only strong if we band together. And now, when one of the vulnerable that you're always on about is in trouble, all that matters to you is that your daughter is safe.'

It was a speech delivered on such a stream of righteous indignation that it almost made Cathy laugh. Except this was no laughing matter. 'You're my daughter and you're only fourteen. It's my job to keep you safe.'

'And Jayden is my friend. It's my job to keep him safe.'

'I'm sorry, but the answer is still no.' Cathy held up a hand to stop a fresh onslaught: 'How about if I went?'

'He doesn't trust you like he trusts me.'

'That's as may be but, bottom line, I don't care how many times you ask me, I will not let you out in it. But I can go. If you'd like me to?'

Lyndall gave an almost imperceptible nod.

'Okay, but only if you promise to stay put.'

Another, slightly more emphatic, nod.

'You also need to promise that you will not come looking for either of us. Do you promise that?'

And a third.

'I want to hear you say it.'

'Yes, Mum, I promise.' Such a small voice – it told Cathy that, despite her bravado, Lyndall might be relieved not to have to head back out onto the streets. Hardly surprising. It had been scary enough when they pushed their way out of the melee; it was bound to be even scarier now.

'Okay. I'll go and see if I can find him. Meanwhile, you need to get inside and stay inside. Any trouble, any at all, even if you think it may just be your imagination, ring me. If I don't answer – it'll probably be too noisy for me to hear my mobile – ring Pius. Do you understand?'

'Yes, Mum. I understand. And,' when Lyndall kissed her on the cheek, Cathy realised that her daughter was almost as tall as her, 'thanks, Mum. Please be careful.' She went into the flat and closed the door.

Submission to the internal inquiry of the Metropolitan Police into Operation Bedrock

Submission 601/b/1: written submission by Chief Inspector William (Billy) Ridgerton

I was the cadre trained in public order critical incidence on call on the weekend of the Rockham disturbances.

I arrived at the scene at 2235 hours. There were two cordons, one with unprotected police officers and no disorder whatsoever to the south. To the north was a large barricade with members of the public throwing missiles, including petrol bombs. The crowd numbered in the region of three hundred, with a nucleus of the crowd causing problems and a high proportion of onlookers.

I located a chief inspector based in Rockham who filled me in as to the outbreak of the disturbances. I then contacted Silver in Littleworth and informed them that I was faced with three immediate tasks: protection and security of the station; the creation of a reactionary gap in which my officers could work to alleviate the pressure to the north and, if possible, arrest troublemakers; and the creation of a sterile corridor for the LFB and LAS to advance, since by this point fires were being set.

We were light on resources, especially protected officers. Initially I had at my command a coterie of TSG officers and some Level 2 trained officers seconded for aid. I had urgent need of more shield-trained officers and I informed Silver of this. I also informed Silver that I had two to three PSUs who had been in the front line for three hours and who needed to be relieved.

By 2300 hours, having taken stock of the situation, I and my men pushed forwards.

11.05 p.m.

They had set up Gold Command on the fourth floor.

A line of seated officers was monitoring the bank of screens, their computers providing the sound, as they communicated with Silver in Littleworth and Bronze on the ground. In the middle of the room there was a projected map of Rockham complete with the position of rioters, onlookers and emergency services. It was such a rapidly changing scenario it soon took on the look of a fast-forwarded weather map except that reports coming in made it clear that the clouds hanging over Rockham would soon be the smoke of burning buildings rather than that morning's mysterious promise of rain.

Joshua stood to one side as Anil Chahda took charge. As he watched his deputy calmly issuing orders, his respect for Chahda increased. Having previously seemed stolid, Chahda was now showing how fast, and how effectively, he could move when he had to. Which is more than could be said for those in charge of Rockham police station.

'What on earth did they think they were doing leaving a patrol car and a bus exposed?'

'I expect it's down to inexperience on the ground, sir,' Chahda said. 'Gaby Wright was unfortunately away. She's on her way back and her task, and ours, is to take control. You agree that arrests are not an immediate priority?'

'Yes. Not enough men on the ground. They can always organise CCTV grabs afterwards. For the moment, let's just concentrate on making sure that nobody gets killed.'

'Yes, sir.' Anil smiled, which was not a sight Joshua had ever seen before.

What a mess, and before Joshua had even completed a week in post. By the looks of it even Billy Ridgerton, as capable as he undoubtedly was, would have to work a miracle to stop the trouble with the scarce resources available to him. Wouldn't be easy, either, to give him more, what with it being Saturday and so many of the men having opted to take their annual leave during this hot spell.

'Don't let me get in your way, Anil. Carry on.'

'Thanks, sir.' Anil Chahda half turned away but then froze. 'Uh oh. What's he doing here?'

'He' was Home Secretary Peter Whiteley, who was just then coming through the door.

Damn. They had rioting in Rockham and every indication that it was about to spread. All they needed now was a Home Secretary who, knowing him, was trying to steal a march on his PM and the Mayor by acting the strong man.

'We need to deal with this. Come with me.' Joshua made his way over to the door, with Chahda at his heels. 'Home Secretary, this is a surprise.' To Peter Whiteley's bodyguards who were standing to attention, he added, 'That's fine, men, relax,' and then, 'How can I help you, Home Secretary?'

'I've come to see how I can help you.' Peter Whiteley lurched forward.

Was he drunk? 'Thank you, Home Secretary, but as I'm sure you can see,' Joshua's gesture embraced all the officers working quietly at their desks, 'we're on it.'

'Anything you need.' Another lurch: he must be drunk. 'Permission to use Section 44 for example.'

Oh great. In a situation when they didn't even have enough officers on the ground to contain the trouble, never mind arrest any of the troublemakers, this idiot was suggesting that they use the blanket provisions of the Terrorism Act. And with the Rockham nick under siege, where did he think they were going to put the people they arrested?

Smile, Joshua told himself, and speak. 'Thank you for that, Home Secretary, but our immediate priority must be to stop the disruption at the same time as we make sure to keep our officers and the public safe.'

'Well, how about I get on to the networks? Tell them to apply ACCOLC? Call gapping?'

'Thank you again, but at this moment there are no reports that the networks are overloaded.' With great effort, Joshua kept calm. Not for much longer, though. If Peter Whiteley did not take the hint, Joshua would have to tell him, and in no uncertain terms, that political interference in operational policing – albeit under the guise of offering help – would not be tolerated.

'We cannot have anarchy on our streets,' Peter Whiteley said. 'Anything you need. Anything.'

Out of the corner of his eye, Joshua watched one of the officers handing Chahda a piece of paper: must be important or the officer wouldn't have come over, not with Whiteley there, this thought confirmed by the sight of Chahda blanching.

'Problem?'

Chahda nodded and said softly in Joshua's ear, 'The disturbance is now within two miles of a highly flammable solvent recycling facility. We'll have to redistribute our men.'

'What's that?' As Peter Whiteley raised his voice, he couldn't stop himself from doing another little lurch forward. 'What's that?' Not just drunk but a hysteric. And a dangerous one. Now was the time to evict him.

'We should brief you, Home Secretary, and thoroughly. Anil, if you wouldn't mind taking the Home Secretary to our spill-out operations room where he will be more comfortable.' He pointed to the door with such authority that Peter Whiteley obediently turned towards it. 'I'll take over temporary command while you're gone.'

'Yes, sir.' Chahda didn't like it, but he must have realised that if he didn't get this bloody politician out of Joshua's hair he'd be having to cope with the consequences of the Metropolitan Commissioner of Police tearing a strip off his Home Secretary in front of the whole of Gold Command. The Mayor would love that. So would the PM. And the tabloids would have a field day when it leaked out, which these things always did.

As the Home Secretary's embarrassed protection squad followed Whiteley and Chahda, Joshua made his way to the communications officer. 'Transmit to Silver and Bronze the following communication as an instruction,' he said, handing over the note on which he'd scrawled some sentences. 'Send this first. Then contact India 95 and tell them we need thermal imaging and fast. We've got to work out how many people are in the area in case we have to evacuate.' As the officer set to, he added, 'Put it on loudspeaker, will you?'

Which is how he was able to hear Billy Ridgerton responding to the news with a loud 'You've got to be fucking joking.'

11.15 p.m.
A solvent recycling centre in a built-up area: what muppet had thought that wouldn't be a problem? And how come it hadn't been on any of the maps Billy had checked, just in case, earlier that day? Must be a recent act of moronic incompetence and one that had been shuffled out of sight by some pen-pusher.

No time to give vent to his fury. He had instead now to tell men who were already exhausted by the pressure on them and the heat that he was going to further deplete their numbers by dispatching some of them to a factory some peaceful two miles away. They weren't going to like it.

'Shift, sir.' Tony, Billy's minder, pushed him to one side at the same time as he lifted his short shield over Billy's head. A piece of something hard, clearly aimed at Billy, bounced off the shield and hit Tony on the cheek. It was a bit of paving stone, sharp at one end. Blood trickled down Tony's cheek.

'You okay?'

'Fine and dandy, sir.' Tony wiped the blood clear of his eye. It was the third hit he had taken for Billy that evening, and it wasn't going to be the last.

Four paces ahead, a line of officers was trying to claim ground so as to push on to the junction at Rockhall Park and clear a route for the LFB and LAS, who were champing at the bit behind them.

'This is diabolical,' Tony said. They had policed some bad disturbances together – not least the recent G8 where all hell had broken loose – but this was no anti-capitalist riot like G8. It was a full-blown attack on the police, with burning and pillaging as a side order to this main event. That much had been clear from the moment they'd pitched up to be met by a hail of bottles, broken paving stones and even petrol bombs. No wonder some of his men were only too eager to lash out. He'd had to stop a few so far, and he knew he'd have to stop more before the night was out.

He couldn't really blame them. They all shared the same frustration.

They couldn't push forward fast enough because some of the rioters had had the bright idea of copycatting the G8 maniacs by chaining shopping trolleys together to form a barricade and, would you believe it, the clippers strong enough to cut through were missing from the inventory. Added to that was the heat: although their arm and leg guards offered much-needed protection, they also dramatically increased the wearer's body temperature. And should they manage to push close enough to the fires to do any good, he would have to worry about their body armour melting, and the nightmare injuries that could arise. He'd already lost one officer. She'd started to fit – badly – and had to be bodily passed back along the police lines until they could get her to an ambulance.

Not a pretty sight to see one of his officers manhandled, even by her own, but this was another thing he couldn't afford to dwell on. There were so many other people to be fearful for: the members of the public who were caught up in the middle of the disturbance and, even worse, those who might soon be trapped in burning premises; or the likelihood that where petrol bombs and paving stones led, firearms might follow; or that omnipresent terror that one of his men could be separated from the main group and torn to pieces by the mob, something that he was in no doubt could happen if he didn't manage to keep them all together. Plus there was the worry about the finger-wagging and worse that would follow should one of his hard-pressed men hurt one of the rioters. And while he was weighing up all these possibilities, he had Silver, and now Gold, shouting instructions through his earpiece, along with an urgent need to come up with tactics that would take them in the right direction of a desirable endgame. If all this wasn't bad enough, India 95 was relaying sightings of the build-up of disturbance in nearby boroughs, which raised the nerve-wracking possibility that one riot might join up with another. And now he had orders to send men two miles away. Not just any men: his bravest and his best.

'Run over to that shop there.' Although he was so dry it felt as if he'd been knifed in the throat, he could only make himself heard by bellowing in his runner's ear. 'Fetch water for the men. Tell them we'll pay later: sign a chit for whatever they ask, but don't come back without water.'

'Yes, sir.' Good man, he was off in a trice.

'Come on.' This to Tony. 'We're going forward.' With Tony's shield covering him, they ran together to the lines ahead and pushed through to the front. 'You four.' He had to wallop them on the back in quick succession in order to get their attention. 'Step out.'

By the time they reached the back lines, the runner had returned with water. One of the men punched through the plastic to pull out a bottle, practically ripping off its top with his teeth to get to the liquid, and soon all the others were doing likewise.

'Take water forward to the men and quickly. Not just this. Much more.'

'No need, sir,' the runner pointed ahead to where members of the public, bottles and crates of water in hand, were snaking through the barrage to reach his men and hand the water over.

'See. Not everybody hates us,' the runner yelled in Billy's ear.

No, Billy thought, only the ones who really want to kill us.

Pushing the thought aside, he told the four men that Gold had ordered that they go and organise the possible defence of a solvent reprocessing plant.

'Are they nuts?' one of the men said. 'There's nowhere near enough of us as it is.' Despite this statement, Billy caught the glimmer of relief crossing the man's face. Understandable: if a senior officer was to come along and tell Billy to get the hell out of here, and that's an order, he'd be gone like a shot. But that wasn't going to happen. Instead, he must now make less-experienced officers, some of whom showed every sign of wanting to freeze under the onslaught, push forward.

'Madness,' he said.

But only to himself.

11.20 p.m.

'Madness' was the light-hearted descriptor that passed from mouth to mouth on the High Street as Cathy made her way along it: 'Madness'.

Instead of the shortcut through the market, she had gone the long way round, approaching the police station from the south. When she saw what was happening, she was glad that she had.

They had blocked the road further up so that there was no longer any traffic. A good thing too. The pavement and street were crammed with people either escaping the trouble to the north, heading straight for it, or just loitering about swapping the stories they'd heard. 'They ran over a baby in a buggy' was one and 'they beat up a teenage girl because she was slow to move' another. Despite these apocryphal tales, the people in this part of the High Street seemed pretty relaxed. A troupe of drummers had settled at the pavement's edge and were beating out a rhythm. Another group had laid blankets on the pavement and were sharing a picnic as a familiar figure who bore the nickname Alf-the-Armageddonist scattered his handwritten leaflets warning of the imminent end of world.

No sign of Jayden. As Cathy pushed northwards, she kept bumping into people she knew, some of whom she hadn't seen for quite a while. All around her, other members of the crowd were exchanging greetings and catching up with each other. So much cheerful normality, it was like being at a carnival except without the usual police presence because the police were concentrated further down the road.

First off there was a queue of stationary fire engines and ambulances, waiting for she knew not what. Beyond them were the dark forms of police lines pushing against a barrier she couldn't yet see except when something flared on its way down. Flaming bottles filled with petrol: were they, she wondered, the source of the smell that was stronger as she moved closer to the trouble?

'Lyndall's not still out in this, is she?' Reverend Pius, who was pushing a young woman in a wheelchair, came up to Cathy.

'No, she's at home,' Cathy said. 'Did you get Ruben's parents back safely?'

'Yes. Poor things. They were terribly distressed at the way their vigil has been hijacked. None of this,' he pointed back towards the police station, 'is what they would have wanted. What any of us would have wanted. I don't know what the police were thinking of, not containing what was a peaceful demonstration. And because they didn't, we've now got anarchy. They're breaking into shops further up. I even saw some of them in a McDonald's cooking chips. Can you believe it? I mean, if you're going to loot, loot; don't stop and make yourself something to eat.' He said this with a smile, which was almost immediately wiped off. 'Seriously, though, this is the last thing we need. Marcus is out there trying to talk sense into them, but you know what an optimist Marcus is. It's already gone too far for sense, and it hasn't even peaked. I'd go home if I were you.'

'I'm looking for Jayden. Have you seen him?'

'At the demonstration, yes. Not since.' Pius sighed. 'I hope you find him soon. He should be indoors. We all should. I'm only out because Marsha here,' he glanced down at the woman he was pushing, 'has run out of some of her medication. I said I'd escort her to the all-night pharmacy. Otherwise I would come with you.'

'It's fine.' Cathy smiled. 'I'm fine,' and smiled again, although the truth was she really did not feel fine.

Jayden was not in the section of the High Street that was still peaceful. He could be somewhere in the area ahead where the trouble was. The smell of burning was even stronger. She thought about turning back, but the prospect of Lyndall's reaction if she failed to even venture into the territory where Jayden might be trapped drove her forward.

She threaded her way past the fire engines and ambulances, whose crews were standing by their vehicles and staring into the place where she was headed.

'You sure you want to go there, love?'

No. She wasn't sure. But she had to.

Soon she was close enough to see that in front of the ordinary bobbies was a line of riot police. They were like medieval warriors in their black body armour, blue steel helmets and transparent visors, and their high transparent shields.

The crowd was thicker now. On the sidelines: sightseers. In the road: a gang of youths. There were, by her estimation, about thirty of them and they were working, wordlessly, as one. First, they picked up objects – stones, and what looked like pieces of paving, and bottles that were piled up by the roadside. Then they formed a ragged line before running, again as one and full pelt, at the police, throwing their missiles and still running, stopping just short of touching distance of the police. Then they stood, closer than they had been before, jeering.

It was a ritualised encounter in which the police also played their part. Their first move was to make a protective wall of shields. After the missiles had landed, they banged these shields on the ground in a stunning cacophony of restrained aggression. Then, at a word from one of their number, they lifted their shields and marched forward in straight lines, driving the young men back.

The men armed themselves again, ready for the next onslaught. The police stepped back to their original position.

An eerie sight, almost hypnotic. She was tempted to keep watching. But Jayden would never have joined these hooded and handkerchiefed youths. She must get on.

There was no way of passing in front of the police station without risking injury. She turned down a side road that led around the back.

How strange. The road she had slipped into curved away from the High Street before doubling back to meet it further on. Because of this it should have been a shortcut to further trouble, but instead it was quiet. She passed a group of riot police guarding the back of the station. Beyond this line, and inside the gates, was a crowd of more policemen in ordinary uniforms. Caged, she guessed, and forbidden to go out. They watched in silence as she walked by.

Soon she was beyond the police station and in a road devoid of rioters or police. Or anybody else for that matter. As if a bomb had landed, she thought.

There must have been people here once, because they'd dug up and removed the paving stones. Since there was no traffic, she walked down the middle of the road. It was strangely quiet, so much so that she could hear the padding of her own footsteps. Could the battle she'd just witnessed have come to an abrupt end?

Wishful thinking. As she walked on, sounds began to intrude. There was the loud buzzing of a helicopter passing overhead. Then voices, jagged in the night. She rounded the curve of the road, knowing that she would soon be back on the High Street. The shouting had increased in volume, but now there was a different sound, like the tearing of something metallic. Were they pulling down the railings, she wondered.

If that was what they were doing, it was going to get very bad indeed. As an inner voice instructed her to turn round, go back, her feet kept on, taking her closer to the crossroads.

She had forgotten that this corner of the High Street had a wider pavement on which was sited a set of high, bright-green metallic lockers bearing the legend: 'You order at home, we deliver here'. It was new to the area.

It no longer looked new. A group of young men had seen to that by using crowbars to wrench open the lockers and pull out the contents. She made to cross the road to avoid them, but before she could one of the men must have sensed that she was there. He turned abruptly, crowbar raised. He had a blue spotted bandana tied around the back of his head in such a way that it covered the whole area of his face below eyes that glared at her.

Is this how it was going to end? Downed by someone not much older than her daughter? She should run.

If she ran, he would catch her. She stood her ground.

His hand dropped. He reached into the drawer he had just opened and pulled something out. He thrust it her way. 'Fancy this?'

She looked down at a square parcel made of cardboard. A book, she guessed. She shook her head: no.

He shrugged and let the parcel drop before applying himself to opening the next.

'You know they've got CCTV on that building over there,' she said. 'And it's pointed at you.'

He indicated his bandana. 'We'll hit the camera next. Bastards, watching us like we're animals in the zoo. They deserve everything we're gonna give them.'

She was on the brink of telling him that what he was doing was going to harm his community not the police, but Pius was right: this had all gone too far for reason. She turned away.

In that moment, everything changed. A man came running from the north. Abreast of them, he yelled, 'They've torched the fabric shop. The building's going to go up and there's people still in the flats.'

When Lyndall was younger, Cathy used to play a game which they had called 'Would you?' A repetitive game. Mother to daughter: 'Would you eat green vegetables if you were starving?' Or: 'Would you take a spider out of the bath if no one else was around?' Daughter to mother: 'Would you stop trying to make me eat cabbage if I was allergic to it?'

Or: 'Would you run into a burning building to save me?' Answers in order: 'No', 'No,' 'But you aren't,' and 'Yes, of course, darling, I would do anything to save you.' And now, as she ran down the road with the men who had been attacking the storage lockers, Cathy was contemplating going into a burning building to save not her daughter but some strangers who might not even be in there.

Not that the building was yet burning. The shop beside and below it was: smoke poured through the front where the glass was already smashed. Above and to the side of the shop front was a set of flats. A side door would have given them access, but it was closed and locked.

A man was already trying to kick it down. He kicked. It shuddered but did not break. He kicked again. Another man was jabbing at the intercom even though a wire trailing down from its base suggested that none of the doorbells had worked for some time.

'Move.' Two of Cathy's companions yanked the men from the doorway before going to work on it. They hit at the gap between door and doorjamb, opening up spaces top and bottom. As the helicopter hovered, drowning out all other sound, the men inserted their crowbars into the spaces they had created. That done, they beckoned two of their fellows forward and together all four pushed against the lever of the crowbars. The door did not budge. More gesticulation and the four dropped their crowbars, moved away from the door, held hands and ran at it, and kicked. They did this three times until at last the door caved in.

They went into the building, Cathy following. There was smoke visibly leaking through the edges of a blocked-up door that must once have led into the shop. Someone was taking charge, pointing each of them to different floors. Cathy was allocated the first floor along with the man who had tried to present her with the book. As she made for the stairs, he took the bandanna off his face and tied it around hers.

'What about you?' She was shouting over the noise of the helicopter.

'I'm cool,' came his reply. 'Come on now, lady, let's roll.'

There were two flats on the first floor. Cathy banged on the door nearest to the stairs. No answer. The man pushed her out of the way and kicked the door. Either he was a pro or else the door was not as robust as the one downstairs, because it crashed open. In they went, running from room to room. The place looked like it had been hurriedly abandoned with half-filled cups and unwashed plates littering a kitchen counter. Great: whoever had been here had gone.

The smoke was thicker now and darker than it had been. Her eyes were smarting and her throat felt as if somebody was sticking it with pins. She ran to the second flat and banged on that door. Waited. And banged again.

'They're gone.' With every breath, more smoke was clogging her lungs. 'Let's get out of here.'

He shook his head, pushed her out of the way and launched himself, shoulder-first, at the door. Which fell. He was there and then he was gone, running into the flat. The smoke was now so thick it was as if it had swallowed him. She called out as she came to what must be the living room. He was next to her and she hadn't seen him. 'Go to the left,' he shouted in her ear, pushing her in that direction, 'I'll go right.'

She went left and found herself in a small room. It wasn't yet as badly affected as the rest of the flat, so she was able to see, through the smoke that was drifting in, the outline of a single bed and a chest of drawers – the only furniture there. She heard him calling, 'Nobody here.'

They'd done their best. They could leave. They had to before the fire felled them.

She was on her way out when a movement at the peripheral edge of her vision brought her to a halt. She turned.

In the short space of time that she'd been in the room, it had got worse. A blanket of grey fog was beginning to obscure her vision; she must have mistaken it for movement. Nobody there.

A cough.

Someone. But where?

Under the bed?

'Help! Here!' Her shouting made her cough. She doubled over, calling, 'Here!' as loudly as she could.

He was already in the room. She felt him pass her by. He must be going to the bed. She heard a creaking of metal. 'Give me a hand.'

She stumbled over to his side. Crouched. Two figures under the tilted bed. She could just make out their shapes: a woman and a small child who were cowering against the wall.

She stretched out a hand.

The woman pulled her child closer and inched away.

The bandanna. It must be scaring her. Cathy ripped it off. 'Fire,' she gasped. 'Come.'

This time when Cathy reached for the child, the woman handed her over before scrambling out herself.

'We've got to get out of here.' Grabbing the child, the man made for the door.

Cathy was about to follow him when the woman said something she didn't understand.

'We've got to go,' Cathy said.

The woman turned away.

'We have to.'

The woman darted off and across the room to the chest of drawers. She snatched a gilt-framed photograph and a pack of baby's nappies that had been on top.

'Come on.' Smoke so black and thick it felt as if they might have to carve a passage through it.

The man and child had disappeared. She made herself retrace in her mind the route in, the number of steps through the flat, counting them back, as with one arm around the woman's shoulders she stretched the other out in front, feeling for the gap where the door should be. Her mind told her that this was a small flat: how hard could it be to get out? But her perception told a different story: it was as if the smoke, black now, had become the room and it was infinite. She had no idea which way to go.

Time slowed. Somebody breathing heavily. A distraction. She wished they would stop – until it occurred to her that what she was hearing were her own laboured breaths. She took a deep breath in. It almost choked her. She started panting, trying that way to expel the smoke from her lungs. 'Where's the door?'

No answer.

'Door,' Cathy bellowed as if, even without English, the woman would understand.

She could feel the shaking of the woman's head.

What if they were going the wrong way? That's it. The door must be behind them. She made to turn.

The woman grabbed hold of her wrist. It was her place: she would know the way out. Except the woman then seemed to be frozen and trying to keep Cathy with her.

'Come on.' It would soon be too late. Which way to go?

A memory flashed through her mind like smoke. Something she needed to remember. She tried with all her might to pull it to her.

She saw Ruben walking with his arms outstretched. That was it: that's what she needed to do.

She reached out her arms, first in a straight line and then, as she went forward, the woman still holding on to her wrist, she widened them. One hit what felt at first like a wall, but when she ran her hand down she found that it was grooved. An architrave: they must be at the door. She took a step forward. An indent underfoot. A mat. They were on the landing. Which meant that the stairs were to the left.

Or were they to the right?

'Where are the stairs?' She couldn't see the woman any more, could only feel her face and the tears that were rolling down. 'The stairs!'

No response.

Left, she thought, they must be on the left. She turned left.

A hand pulled her. Not the woman's this time. The man's. His face jammed close to hers. She could smell his sweat and it smelt of fear and smoke. The woman grabbed hold of him, running her hands down his arms, and then she began to wail.

'Come on,' he was shouting at them both.

The woman was shaking now, so hard Cathy could feel the tremors passing through herself.

'Her baby! She thinks you've lost her baby.'

'She's safe. She's outside.'

The woman wailed even louder.

Cathy folded her arms, one over the other, to make a cradle. Standing tight against the woman, she raised the arms to rock them back and forth, touching the woman's head to show the motion, back and forth, back and forth, before taking the woman's arm and pointing it in the direction – right – of the stairs.

The woman's cries ceased.

'Let's go.' The man turned. 'Hold on to my shoulders.'

121

Cathy placed both hands on his shoulders and the woman did likewise to hers, and then the man led them across the corridor and down the stairs.

How he led them out she would never know. The air was so thick, a wall of black smoke that, bending low as he told them to do, they had to push against. Each step took an age; each breath felt like it could be her last. Give up, a voice kept telling her, give up. The only thing that stopped her from listening to that voice was the woman's hand on her shoulder and an overwhelming need whose name was Lyndall. Give up, she thought again, and then another sound: the heavy burr of a helicopter passing overhead.

They were out. The air she gulped made her dizzy. She dropped to her knees. Gasping. One thought: that she should be left there to do nothing else but breathe.

'Get up.' Hands got hold of her and hauled her, scraping her skin, across the ground.

She wanted to get away from those hands. 'Let go.' A voice that sounded nothing like hers. 'Let go.'

At last they did let go.

She was no longer moving, or being moved – was just lying there. The relief of it. She lay still, summoning up the strength to open her eyes. When she found it, she saw that either the night had clouded over or else something had happened to her vision. She tasted grit and ash. Felt something pushing at her lips.

Why wouldn't they let her alone? She moved her head away. They pulled it back.

'Drink.' One hard finger on each side of her jaw forced her mouth open.

They poured in a deep slug of brackish-tasting water. She coughed and the water was regurgitated.

'Sit her up.'

Hands looped under her arms and hauled her up.

Sitting, her breath came easier. This time when the bottle touched her lips, she took it for herself.

'Take it easy: sip it.'

Despite that what she wanted to do was gulp it down, she sipped it. This time the water stayed down. When she'd had enough, she upturned what remained over her head, and the smoke that had filmed her vision dissolved.

'You okay, love?'

She nodded. And heard a shout. 'There she goes.'

Heads turned towards the building. Hers as well.

She saw the downstairs shop ablaze, and she saw flames licking out of the upper floors. The building was groaning, cracks and crashes coming from deep within it as ceilings fell down onto floors and floors collapsed through to floors below.

To think that she might have been in there.

Above, the helicopter kept circling, its spotlight picking through the crowd that was beginning to edge away from the blazing building. Except, she saw, for a handful of youths who were going forward, intent on offering something to the fire. Something tawny.

A fox. Must be the one whose path had crossed with hers. Then it had been sick; now it must be dead, because it made no effort to get away, neither when the hands held it up nor when they thrust it away.

And then there was a dead fox flying though the air and landing in the building that was to be its funeral pyre.

Sunday

1.30 a.m.

Even before Peter had put his key in the lock, he heard the sound of rioting. When he made his way into the living room, he found Frances on the sofa, the dog at her side, both of them gazing at the blaring television.

'Shocking, isn't it?' He kissed her on the forehead.

She looked up. 'How was it?'

'It was worth doing,' he yawned. 'I know you were concerned – and perhaps you were right, I was a little in my cups – but there's nothing like having to control chaos to sober up a man. I spent some time in New Scotland Yard – got a full briefing from the Deputy Commissioner – and then I went to the office and concentrated on clearing the decks. If this continues – and the police opinion is that it will – I'm going to be busy.'

'Yes, darling. I'm sure you will be.' She kept her eyes on the television.

Perhaps some remnant of her earlier anger was still lurking. He leant down to tap the dog on its nose. 'Budge up.'

The dog shot him a dirty look, but it did let him take its place. 'Sorry to have deserted you mid supper.'

'Don't worry, Peter. I understand.' She was still concentrated on the flickering images of a burning building.

'Did they stay long?'

'Quite a while. We came in to see what was going on and then found we couldn't tear ourselves away. As a matter of fact,' she glanced at her wristwatch, 'the last of them only left fifteen minutes ago.' A pause and then: 'Would you like a nightcap?'

An unexpected suggestion, especially when she'd been so sniffy about his earlier drinking. He looked at where she was sitting, out of range and still concentrated on the television. He said, 'Good idea.'

She went over to the drinks cabinet. 'Cognac?'

'Why not?'

She poured a small drop into one belled glass and considerably more into a second, which she then handed to him. She came back to sit beside him, and for a while they just sat there, swirling their glasses and warming them in their hands. She was closer now, although her gaze still kept straying to the scenes unfolding and endlessly repeating on the television.

'Ghastly, isn't it?'

'Yes,' she nodded, 'ghastly.' A pause as she took a small sip of cognac. 'And mesmerising.'

His cognac smelt of figs and cinnamon, and it tasted of slightly salty caramel as it slipped down the back of his throat. 'Horrifying would be a more appropriate descriptor.'

'Yes, it is horrifying. But you know,' now she did look up, 'I've been sitting here for hours, watching, and the more I watched, the more I began to think that there must be something wonderful about throwing caution to the wind, like they have, and just acting.' She must have seen his objections welling because she went on, hurriedly, 'Not that I'm for a moment condoning the destruction – nothing like that. But every now and then I see people, obviously poor and presumably without prospects, caught up in the middle of this awful riot. And they look happy. No, not just happy. They look jubilant.'

'Of course they do. They're bent on destruction.'

'Are they really?' Her tone was so flattened there was no way of knowing whether she'd taken offence (that he'd seen fit to lecture her?) or was being sarcastic (telling him, once again, that she was the one who had taught him the basics of politics?) or was merely disappointed (that he would not empathise with her childish excitement?). The last, he decided, when she put down her glass and got to her feet. 'I'm off to bed.'

'I wish I could join you. But I better get back to the office. Plan for COBRA. I only dropped in to pick up a change of clothes. I'll do some tidying up in the kitchen before I go.'

'No need.' One pat on the skirt of her frock and the dog was at her side. 'I've done most of it already,' and then, and with the dog close on her heel, she left the room.

PRIVATE AND CONFIDENTIAL
FOR INQUIRY USE ONLY

Submission to the internal inquiry of the Metropolitan Police into Operation Bedrock

Submission 9992/D/23–D/45: photographic evidence gathered by Air Support Unit 27AWZ, call sign India 95, between 03:00 and 03:13 hours on ███████████████

Camera stills 0678/D23–D45

location: Rockham police station and Rockham High Street

subject: day two disturbances

Supplemental photographic evidence captured by 27AWZ in the vicinity of:

(a) Rockham police station
(b) Rockham High Street: 20–50 metres north of the police station
(c) Rockham High Street: 150 metres north of the police station

The attached photographs catalogue the spread of disturbances in the immediate surrounds of the Rockham police station.

Numbers D23–D29 indicate the pressure on the Level 2 trained officers safeguarding the police station.

Numbers D30–D39 catalogue the advance of the eight officers led by Bronze Leader Chief Inspector B. Ridgerton as they push northwards along Rockham High Street.

Numbers D40–D45 show the fire in the commercial/residential premises (known in the area as Budget Stores) 150 metres north of the police station on Rockham High Street. These photographs include the location of three LFB appliances as they await clearance of the area (see images D30–D39) in order to gain access to the fires set in the roads and to the burning building.

3.15 a.m.

Rockham had once been Billy's beat. Poor as it undoubtedly was, he'd come across a lot of good people here. At this point, however, as pillaging took the place of protest, he was beginning to hate the whole borough and all who sailed in her. Without exception.

'Don't you even think of sleeping,' the sergeant in front of Billy grasped one of his drooping constables by the shoulder, 'or I'll lay you out myself.' His fingers must have passed through padding and into bone, and dug in hard, because the constable tried to shake him off, thus shaking himself back into the moment. Now the sergeant strode behind the line of six constables, walloping each on the helmet as he passed. 'Hold the line,' his voice loud enough to penetrate the pandemonium, 'hold the fucking line.' His shouting was designed as a counter to the people who were banging and throwing things and blowing on car horns, creating a racket so deafening it was enough to disorient the strongest man. This, combined with the fear they must all be experiencing, could produce a kind of tunnel vision in which their hearing would also close down. Their sergeant's voice, to which they were so acclimatised, was there to break through this, which it clearly did. Their muscle memories kicking in, the men lined up closer to each other.

'You're doing a great job. Keep formation.' He'd been shouting for so long his voice was breaking, but now he somehow managed to raise it to another level: 'Keep together. Here they come. Shields high.'

They lifted their shields and held them high as a line of youth ran at them, stopping within hailing distance and letting loose a barrage of splintered paving stones that, lit by the starburst of a flaring fire-work, soon came raining down. A second pack of rioters – they were beginning to organise themselves – followed, also throwing their makeshift missiles. And then came one of those now familiar pauses that punctuated this ritual: attack, counter-attack and retreat having

130

gone on for hours, leaving both sides exhausted. They used this moment before re-armament and re-repulsion to try to out-eyeball each other.

Into the hiatus the sergeant yelled, 'Sit rep on the left,' to stop his men being hypnotised by the other side, and, sure enough, the descriptions of the looting taking place down the side street furnished by the officer on the left was enough to pull them out of any such possible trance. The sergeant transmitted the information back to Billy, who nodded and waved a hand to indicate that they should move towards the line of youths already in the process of re-forming.

'Forward on my count,' the sergeant called. 'One, two, and together: charge.'

They were members of the Met's Territorial Support Group, the toughest of the tough, bulked out by the gym and protein shakes, and they were a ferocious sight, especially when on the move. 'Charge!' their sergeant ordered, and they charged, one of their number bawling out, '*Semper Paratus*,' which he must have lifted off the Manchester TAU, and then repetitively '*Semper Paratus*' until his comrades took up the cry, changing it to '*Semper fucking Paratus*' as, with all the courage of this slogan, they charged forward, scattering the opposition.

Not that they'd be gone for long. They were guerrilla fighters, albeit in expensive tracksuits and branded trainers, whose only objective was to ruck with Billy's men. His men, on the other hand, who would have been capable of controlling a much bigger crowd if members of that crowd had stayed together, were slowed down by their cumbersome kit and the need to protect each other and the public. They must be itching to lay hands on the yobs, but to do so was to risk isolation. And woe betide any man who found himself alone in this mob.

'Stop,' Billy called, his instruction passed on by the sergeant's 'Halt, halt,' to which the men responded by wheeling to a halt and at their sergeant's yelled 'Regroup', re-forming themselves into a line.

They'd gained another ten yards and even this was dangerous.

Their safest bet would have been to consolidate their position at the earlier crossroads rather than trying to force forward to the next. But because fires were being set, they had to forge ahead. To add to their difficulties, an orgiastic bout of thievery seemed to have taken hold of the whole community. Only five minutes previously, Billy had spotted an apparently respectable middle-aged couple pushing a trolley piled so high with nappies and powdered baby milk they could have kept a Romanian orphanage going for a month. He had watched them coming close: close enough to clock him. Their panic at the sight of him almost made him laugh. But it didn't take them long to figure out what he already knew – that there was no way he could expose himself, or abandon his men, by nicking them – and so, as they slowly trundled away, they were the ones to be laughing.

Too dumb to see the blinking of an overhead CCTV camera. That would soon have them laughing on the other side of their faces.

CCTV was all very well, but still it rankled not to catch people in the act. But Billy needed the men to push on while keeping them and the 'innocent' safe. It was a job made more difficult by the ever-present plague of sightseers. Women, some with babes in arms, would you believe, were laughing and cheering and pointing as if this was a circus they had paid to see, even though, Billy knew, should the criminals decide to turn on the onlookers, as they might easily do, these 'decent' people of Rockham would be the first to expect protection from his men.

They were unlikely to get it. Having left a contingent of officers outside the police station, and dispatched another to ring-fence the solvent factory, this group of constables and their sergeant were the only mobile and kitted-out representatives of law and order in a three-mile crime scene of arson, robbery and riot. What they were doing, and the length of time they would most likely have to keep on doing it, required almost superhuman effort.

They were a long way off from being able to establish order. The red in the air indicated premises ablaze – and the police were nowhere near. The clang of pipes dragged against corrugated iron was a signal to other looters to come and help lever security gates off shop entrances – and the police weren't there either. And although a section of his precious TSG had control of the perimeter of the solvent factory, if any of these young animals got wind of this strategic target, that too would soon be lost.

'Billy,' a voice sounded in his ear. 'Are you still there?'

Where the fuck else was there for him to go? 'Yes,' he said, 'I'm here.'

'There are fresh messages coming through on the FWIN. You need to hear them.'

3.19 a.m.

If an outsider had happened to drop in to the Scotland Yard operations room on that early morning, they would have been forgiven for mistaking the quiet for nothing of much importance going on. The reality was that the worse the news, the more intense the hush. And now the room was deathly quiet.

The screens had multiplied, with still more being carted in. On them were maps and CCTV feeds from various sites, too numerous for any one officer to keep up with. Another clutch of officers were plugged into headphones, monitoring the traffic between the Bronze Commands and their burgeoning Silvers before relaying the information on.

The map of Rockham stood centre stage, the disturbances there being, thus far, the worst. And growing ever more dangerous. Although Billy was the best in the business, his earlier previous requests for reinforcements had turned, as the night wore on, into staccato demands to 'Send more men. Send more men.'

Trouble was they just didn't have any more men to send.

The previous week's forty-eight-hour marathon of separating the participants of an EDL sit-in outside the Home Office from the counter demonstrators meant many of London's Level 2 trained officers had taken this weekend as time in lieu. In another room, a handful of officers was rousting this lot out of bed, checking that they weren't too inebriated to be of any use. The early heatwave had also prompted members of the TSG, knowing how hard pressed they'd be at the start of the world cricket series in which Pakistan and India, currently on the brink of war, were due to play, to take their annual leave. Most of these had had the good sense to leave London, and many of them were also sensible enough to turn off their phones at night.

If the disorder continued, as it looked set to do, the NPCC would soon take over the coordination of mutual aid. But for the moment it was Joshua's job to hit the phones. Which opened its own can of worms. Gone were the days when a Met commissioner could phone a chief constable in Avon or in Manchester, or any other of the forty-three authorities, and find himself talking to somebody with whom he had probably at some point in his career worked and after they had weighed up the situation, policeman to policeman, cohorts of riot police would be dispatched to London. But because of the election (so-called – the numbers voting being so minimal as to make the word 'election' laughable) of police and crime commissioners, Joshua now had to walk the gangplank of phone calls to pumped-up PCCs who had little experience of policing and even less of reacting well when woken in the dead of the night. So unproductive had been his first few conversations, he'd decided to continue his ring-round in the morning once the chief officers had had the time to tell their commissioners in words of no more than two syllables, and preferably less, how the prospect of London going pear-shaped was not in their best interests.

And while all this was going on, the number of troublemakers on the streets kept increasing. Oh, for the days when people, and by people Joshua included the under-twenty-fives, actually slept at night. Now, six hours in, clubbers, fired by drugs and drink, had come out to join those already recruited by BBM, with the result that the convulsions were radiating through the entirety of south London.

It didn't help that the beast of the twenty-four-hour news cycle was getting all the red meat it had ever dreamt of. Reporters who'd fantasised about going to war could now stand happily in front of marauding crowds, burning buses and buildings, and youths using golf clubs to break through windows, to tell tales of fire engines and ambulances queuing, and not a policeman in sight. All Joshua had to do was look across at the TV, on silently in one corner, and, as often as not, he would catch that looping image – a woman with a small child in her arms, leaping from a burning building – and that would tell him, as if he needed to be told, how bad it was and also to know how much worse it might soon be.

And now this new FWIN, warning of trouble in the Lovelace.

3.20 a.m.

A hand shaking Cathy. So roughly that her bed in Casualty seemed also to be shaking. Another symptom, she supposed, of the terror that had gripped her even as she'd slept. But then a voice: 'Mum.' Lyndall's voice. 'Mum, are you okay?'

She opened her eyes to find Lyndall bending over her. 'I told you not to leave the flat,' she said.

'And I told you never to run into a burning building.' Lyndall wrapped her arms around her mother, hugging so hard that Cathy couldn't help but wince. She slackened her grip. 'I'm sorry.'

'I'm just a bit bruised is all. How did you know I was here?'

'The hospital phoned Pius.'

'And you came. After you agreed to stay put.'

'I didn't come on my own, Mum. Pius brought me. They said your lungs are clear of smoke. We've come to take you home.'

3.21 a.m.

Before Billy had the chance to discover what fresh delight the new Force Wide Incident Number was warning of, his minder yelled, 'Duck,' an instruction he reinforced by raising his shield and simultaneously pushing down on Billy's head.

Just in time. The skirmishers had re-armed and returned, and now a fusillade of pavement fragments pelted down on the line of officers and beyond. This bombardment was accompanied by a set of Roman candles, one of which passed over the front ranks to hit the tarmac within a foot of where Billy was crouched. He watched as it bounced, once, twice and a third time, until it ended up in the area below his protective shield.

With his minder still pressing down on him, he could only continue to watch the show unfold. A bang and a blaze of white and then, almost, it seemed, in slow motion, a stream of stars shot out of the candle to hit the left-most underside of the shield, before ricocheting to the right and then rebounding. The candle was now a crazy fizzing thing, his only protection from it the arm he held over his eyes in such a way that he could still see and thus have a chance of dodging the sparks. Its emissions continued to batter the shield until at last – and it seemed to take an age although it must only have been a few seconds – the candle burnt itself out. He stamped down where he thought it had landed, although he couldn't be sure: the glare had blinded him.

135

'Are you receiving?' A voice sounded over the high-pitched whine that seemed to slice through his ears. 'Billy, are you receiving?'

Oh, right: they'd been wanting to tell him something. 'Yes.' So overwhelming was the buzzing in his ears, he couldn't tell if he was shouting. 'I'm receiving you.' Bright striations of light were all he could see, and beyond them, black.

'It's the Lovelace,' he heard. 'We're picking up rumours of a hostile build-up inside the estate.'

The Lovelace was a no man's land for the police on a normal day. In this situation, it was every policeman's worst nightmare.

'We can't have a repeat of '85 . . .' which Billy knew was shorthand for the horror of PC Keith Blakelock's death at the hands of a mob in Broadwater Farm '. . . but we do need you to check this out so we can either dismiss or confirm the rumour.'

And if it was confirmed, he thought, then what? But this thought he kept to himself, saying only, 'No problem. I'll have India 95 do a full heat survey – see if there are any legs to the FWIN.'

3.25 a.m.
More than anything, where Jayden wanted to be was home. Not immediately – first he'd knock at Lyndall's to make sure she was safe.

Her mother wouldn't like him knocking in the early hours, but her mother was not like his: she'd know that he had only done it out of concern. She'd probably be up anyway: not easy to sleep in this racket.

And after he found Lyndall was safe – she would be, wouldn't she? – he'd cross the landing and let himself into his flat. Quietly, so his mother wouldn't hear. Good chance of that. Of all the people in the Lovelace, she'd be the only one flat on her back and snoring loud enough to shake the windows. And even if she was awake, then even she, who got so angry when she was frightened, couldn't blame him for being late. Could she?

First, though, he had to get home. He'd been trying, but every corner he'd turned had been blocked either by rioters or the police. He didn't know which was more dangerous: probably both. And now again, he cut off left, meaning to go down a shortcut he knew, but saw something burning at its end. He couldn't go near. Couldn't risk getting involved. Or arrested.

No choice but to find somewhere out of the way where he could wait until the path was clear. Turning away from the site of the riots, he sloped off down the road.

3.30 a.m.

Pius was hunched so far over the steering wheel that his nose was almost touching the windscreen. Lyndall was in the back and also leaning forward, in her case so she could lay a hand on her mother's shoulder and keep it there.

The hand felt hot and oppressively heavy. Cathy had to use willpower not to move away from it. Her nerve ends were thrumming, making the confinement of the car almost too much to bear; it was all she could do to stop herself from wrenching open the door and jumping out. If she had, she wouldn't have been hurt: the car was crawling along so slowly a brisk walker could have overtaken it.

The night was inky black, not from clouds but from smoke. She could see the swirls it made around the street lights and how layers of it kept drifting through the car's full beam. She dreaded to think about the lives that might have been lost in the fires that had made that smoke.

She wouldn't think of it.

She would keep her mind occupied by planning what she was going to do when they eventually did reach home.

She'd have a shower, she decided, even before a cup of tea. She'd stay in the shower for as long as it took to get rid of the stink of smoke that seemed to have saturated not only her clothes but also her skin. And after that, she'd throw her clothes into the washing machine. No – she wasn't going to wash them; she was going to chuck them out. Not in the kitchen waste – too close. She'd take them downstairs to the communal bins. And then? Banji, she thought, I'll ask him to come over. In fact, she reached into her pocket, why not ask him now?

Her phone was so black it didn't even look like hers. She wiped the soot on the skirt she was planning to throw out and tried to switch the phone on. But either the fire had damaged it or else its battery was dead. She thought about asking Lyndall for hers, but she didn't think

Lyndall had Banji's number. And besides, she now remembered, Banji had lost his phone. He'd told her so what felt like weeks ago but was probably only yesterday.

'What day is it?'

'Sunday,' Pius said, adding absently, 'I must remember to prepare my sermon,' as if this were something he often forgot. He had moved even closer to the steering wheel and also turned on the windscreen wipers.

It isn't raining, she nearly said, but then she realised that he was using the wipers to sweep away a film of grey ash that was obscuring his vision. 'How many buildings have they set light to?'

'Two when last I was there. And cars as well. And tyres as . . .oh dear.' Pius braked so abruptly that she was thrown forward and would have hit the windscreen if not for the dual restraint of her seat belt and Lyndall's hand. 'What on earth?' His exclamation was more an expression of disbelief than a question.

Something had stepped into the road in front of their car and then had stopped.

Not something. Someone. A tall, thin white man.

A tall, thin, naked white man.

'A streaker!' Lyndall lifted herself out of her seat to get a better view.

The man raised both arms up, high, in a V, his fingers splayed as if he were trying to touch the sky. His mouth was open, his lips stretched to inscribe an O, although the scream he seemed about to let loose was never delivered. He stood like this, motionless for a while, making sure, presumably, that they took in the whole sight of him, before dropping his arms, closing his mouth and ambling the rest of the way across the road, over the pavement and to a low wall. He put his hands on the wall and pushed down, leaping up and over, treating them to a last glimpse of a pale bottom before he vanished from sight.

'Needs to spend more time in the sun,' was Lyndall's comment.

'Poor man.' Pius, who had turned the engine off, now sparked it back on. But instead of driving off he steered the car over to the kerb. 'We're close to the trouble,' he said, 'and the church can't afford to lose this car. I'll walk you the rest of the way home.'

PRIVATE AND CONFIDENTIAL
FOR INQUIRY USE ONLY

Submission to the internal inquiry of the Metropolitan Police into Operation Bedrock

Submission 9992/D/67: photographic evidence gathered by Air Support Unit 27AWZ, call sign India 95, between 03:23:14 and 03:28:18 on ███████████████

Camera stills D/67/a–t

location: Rockham police station and Rockham High Street

subject: demonstration

Images 67 a) to c) show a number of fires that had been set in the vicinity of the police station and Rockham High Street. As can be seen from the dark shadows caused by the fires, burning tyres were involved. Images 67 d) to h) show a crowd gathered around the fires.

At the request of Bronze Leader Chief Inspector B. Ridgerton, the Air Support Unit then took a series of thermal images over the Lovelace estate.

The images l) to t) show a temporary build-up of people on the outskirts of the estate who, over the course of several minutes, began to disperse. At 03:26:43, Air Support Unit 27AWZ, having transmitted to Bronze Leader the assessment that the Lovelace was calm, passed, on further instructions, over the estate before heading in a north-easterly direction towards the solvent refinery and then northwards to trace the spreading disruption.

3.30 a.m.

When Lyndall asked 'What's that?', Cathy followed her pointing finger over the burning barricade to see something moving in the dark. Her first thought was that the air had turned to inky water along which waves were travelling. But what she was looking at was too fragmented to be waves; it now seemed more like the beating of wings. Birds, she thought, except these shapes were smaller than any bird. Bats then? No, not bats either. This fluttering was weightless and inanimate, dark flecks twisting like leaves on a rising current of air. As they flickered past a street light, she saw that these leaves were black. Like leaves of a nuclear winter, she thought, or a volcano. 'It's ash,' she said.

Which now floated down, feathery specks settling on their heads and shoulders and fragmenting in their hands when they tried to brush them off.

'I want to go home.' As soft as Lyndall's voice was, her unease was unmistakeable.

'We're not far,' came Pius's equally tense reply.

3.30 a.m.

From the dark stillness of the city viewed through Peter's office window, it was almost impossible to credit the reports that other parts of London were going up in flames. But should he glance over at the flat screen on the wall behind the conference table he would be bound to catch another glimpse of a woman so desperate that she had pitched herself and her young child out of the window of her third-floor flat. It was a miracle that neither of them was badly hurt. Given the reports coming in, it would be another miracle if they managed to get through the next few days without fatalities.

That the thin veneer of civilisation could be so easily ruptured was alarming, Peter thought. And then that equally alarming follow-through

140

thought that, with the PM away, it fell on him to try to patch it all back together again.

He glanced at his watch: 3.30 a.m. The PM would soon be ringing back. He sighed – so loudly that the three male members of his staff who were working at the conference table all looked up. Not so Patricia – more accustomed to his noises, he supposed, as he registered the intensity of her concentration while she tracked the progress of the disturbances through social media on three separate screens.

He looked away.

What to do? That was the question: what to do?

He breathed in, about to let out another deep sigh, but instead he sniffed the air. He smelt coffee and not the over-brewed office muck that they tried to pass off as coffee: real coffee, as sweet and nutty as he liked it. What he wouldn't do for a cup, so much so that his imagination must have conjured up its scent.

'Coffee?'

He turned to find Frances standing in the doorway.

She'd insisted on coming with him to the office. When he'd told her he'd be tied up, she'd said she'd be sure to find some way of making herself useful. He'd been vaguely conscious of her bustling about in the background but had been too preoccupied by the ghastly news filtering in to worry about what she was up to. Now, seeing her holding a tray that contained not only a steaming cafetière and some cups but also sandwiches, he realised that the huge bag she had carried into the car must have been stuffed with goodies.

How magnificent she was, especially in a crisis.

'Darling!' He was about to go over and kiss her when he saw her gaze concentrated on the members of his staff. 'The Minister could do with a break,' she said.

That's all it took for them obediently to rise.

'I've laid coffee and sandwiches for you on the table outside,' she said. 'Do help yourselves. And let me know if there's anything else you'd like.'

By the enthusiastic chorus of thanks and the speed with which they made a beeline for the door, he wasn't the only one who'd been desperate for something decent to eat and drink.

141

Patricia had also got up and was leaving with the others, but as she came abreast of Frances, Frances said, 'I've got three cups. Why don't you stay here with us?'

So fleeting was the uncertainty that crossed Patricia's expression, only somebody who knew her as well as he did would have noticed it. 'Thank you, Mrs Whiteley.'

'Please, call me Frances.' Frances threw a quick glance back at the three men who were piling sandwiches onto plates: 'Napoleon was only able to say that it was an army that marches on its stomach,' she kicked the door shut with her foot, 'because he'd never come across our civil service.' She then laid down her tray. 'We need to work out how you're going to play things with the PM.'

3.35 a.m.
They were almost home.

Almost home and dry is how Cathy thought of it. She wanted so much to be inside the flat with all the doors and windows locked. Which is how they would remain despite the heat.

The estate was hushed, especially when compared to the pandemonium they had just passed through. They walked in silence. As they drew abreast of the community centre, they stopped – again without a word – and stood silently in front of the bank of flowers badly wilted by the heat.

A lonely sight. It made Cathy realise afresh that she would never see Ruben shambling across the road or be warmed by one of the smiles that were so much more rewarding for being so rare. She swallowed, overcome by a legion of feelings distant from the ructions in the High Street.

When eventually Pius broke the silence to say, 'His parents will be terribly upset,' they knew he wasn't talking about the dead flowers. 'They wanted answers,' he said. 'Not this.' He waved his hand in the direction of the High Street from which the sound of police sirens, swelling and dying away, was intercut by shouting. 'And look what they've done there.' He meant the abandoned building beside the community centre whose brick walls, formerly clear, were now covered in ugly black scrawls. 'How could Rockham do this to itself?'

Lyndall, who had moved over to look more closely at the graffiti, said, 'It's not Rockham. These are the tags of the Zed7s whose base is two miles away. Wouldn't usually risk being in Lovelace territory.'

'So this is what we've come to,' Pius said. 'A lawless free-for-all bringing the gangs together.' He blinked away a tear that was not provoked by smoke. 'It's a travesty of everything we ever hoped for.'

3.39 a.m.

Joshua hoped that Billy's opinion, backed by the heat survey, that the Lovelace was peaceful and likely to remain so, was correct. Because if it wasn't, and the Lovelace went up, the casualties would be horrific. But Billy was one of the best, and he had prior knowledge of the area, so they had taken his word for it and diverted India 95 towards the solvent factory – what idiot had given permission for that? – and beyond, following the trail of spreading trouble.

It had swept across the river and was moving north, and as it did, the incoming reports grew ever more diverse: of a rave raided, for example, not in order to steal from the ravers but to recruit them into the looting from nearby shops; or of the burning of another police car – what the fuck had they been thinking of to leave it unattended? – which had forced the evacuation of an apartment block in St John's Wood; or of the sprinklers set off in a major department store after some rioters decided to have a barbecue in the food hall. Meanwhile, word from outside London was just as bad. The phones requesting aid were ringing off their hooks.

One call, though, was conspicuous by its absence. The PM's call, which Joshua had long expected to receive.

And all the while Rockham continued to burn.

3.40 a.m.

'Yes, Prime Minister. Of course I will. Goodnight.' Peter put down the receiver.

'Not coming?' Frances was smiling widely.

'He thinks it would be better not to break off negotiations if it can be avoided. I am to chair the first COBRA meeting.'

'Good.'

'Is it, though?' Peter had been thrown by how readily the PM had agreed to his strategy. Had he, he wondered, been outmanoeuvred? 'The country's going up in flames, and he's not flying back? What's he playing at?'

'At politics, my dear.' Frances smiled. 'He's done a risk analysis – just as we did – but come to a different conclusion. He thinks that if you're in the hot seat and you calm things down, he can spin it as never having been as bad as you've said it is. That's the risk he's taking. But if things go pear-shaped, he reckons he can come riding in on his white charger to sort the country out. That's the risk we're taking. I'm going to keep betting on us, especially given the PM's tin ear for what's really going on.'

Patricia nodded enthusiastically at Frances's every word.

His two women working together. Interesting, if a little disconcerting. But not something he had time to worry about. They could advise him, and they could examine and develop each other's theories to their hearts' content, but he was the one who had to prepare himself to chair COBRA.

3.50 a.m.
Pius left them at the bottom of the walkway. Pressed by them, he promised to go directly home, thus provoking Lyndall to remark, as he walked off, that 'Even pastors sometimes lie.'

The barriers that lined the walkway had also been newly covered in graffiti. And would remain so, Cathy thought, until the Lovelace was no more. She reached out for Lyndall's hand.

The walkway was quiet. Eerily so. Now and then she caught a glimpse of a face in one or other of the darkened windows, but either she was imagining these or else the occupants of the flats shrank out of sight as soon as she as much as glanced in their direction. They're as afraid as I am, she thought, forcing herself to say, and in a cheerful voice, 'Almost there.'

Only one more ramp to go. Up they went and rounded the last bend. Already imagining herself in that shower, Cathy was just feeling the tension drain away when the people who must have been watching them from the shadows stepped out.

They had handkerchiefs obscuring their faces so that the only visible sign that they were human was their glinting eyes. They were young men – that's all she could tell. They stood unmoving, and they stood in the way.

She acted instinctively, pushing Lyndall behind her: 'What do you want?'

'Mum.' This from Lyndall.

Cathy raised her voice. 'I don't have much money,' she told the trio of highwaymen, 'but you can have what there is.'

'Mum!'

She tightened her grip on Lyndall's wrist, half twisting her away so that if it came to running, Lyndall would have a head start. The other hand she pushed into her pocket. No money. Only her blackened phone.

'Here,' she offered it to the leader of the threesome.

He backed off, saying, 'We don't want your phone, Mrs Mason,' and untied his handkerchief to reveal a familiar face. 'Or your money. The Zed7s are about. We're making sure they don't cause no more trouble on our turf.'

'I told you, Mum.' In the half-light of the landing Cathy could see that Lyndall had turned beet-red.

'Oh.' She felt so foolish.

'Come on.' Lyndall put her arm around Cathy. 'Let's go in.'

10 a.m.

The streets of central London were quiet. Not unusual for a Sunday. And yet as Joshua's Range Rover, its lights flashing but its siren off, raced to Whitehall, there was something about the quality of the silence that seemed to speak of breaths in-held.

Last night's disturbances had petered out around dawn, but from what they'd gleaned via BBM chatter and the Twitter-sphere there was every likelihood of the disorder returning – and country-wide – once darkness fell. Thus the COBRA meeting to be chaired, in the PM's absence, by the Home Secretary.

Not a meeting Joshua was looking forward to. His job was to keep a city and – given that where London went others often followed – a whole country calm. In contrast, Whiteley seemed to be using the riots to further his bid for power. This he had demonstrated in a series of early-morning interviews whose running thread had been his barely concealed criticisms of the police and therefore, by inference, of the PM's choice of Commissioner. Having already claimed the scalp of one head of the Met, Whiteley was out for another. While he had no intention of providing his, Joshua's first priority was to stop the riots, and for this he had to find a way of working with Whiteley.

There were so many factors that militated against success, not least the weather. A heat haze was already hovering over Whitehall, some of it brown smog. It was going to be even hotter today than yesterday; by nightfall, anybody who didn't have a garden would be out in the streets.

So much to keep tabs on, although at least Chahda had relieved him by going ahead to the Cabinet Briefing Office room to set up communications in the suite in which they'd sometimes need to hunker down in the event that the area of upheaval kept expanding.

Chahda was a good officer and, as last night had demonstrated,

146

solidly dependable. Still, Joshua thought, there was something out of kilter, some dragging of feet when it came, for example, to pulling the records of the officers who'd been witnesses to the death in Rockham. Perhaps it was a reluctance to single out any officer for blame: a position with which Joshua had some sympathy, especially at this early stage when passions were inflamed. But you didn't get to be Commissioner without knowing that the thing you most wanted to hide from public scrutiny would end up as the next day's banner headline. They needed, therefore, to cover all eventualities. Chahda, who'd spent so long as deputy, should know this.

'We're here, sir. And so's the press.'

Already! He sighed and pulled up the knot of his tie, and placed his peaked hat on his head, feeling for the straight brim. A breath in, a direction to self to say nothing but to say it pleasantly, before he opened the door and stepped out.

The press pack didn't take any notice of him. Corralled behind a set of barriers, they were all too busy straining to hear what Home Secretary Peter Whiteley had to say.

A set-up. Must be, because this many hacks would not have turned up by chance, and on a Sunday morning well before the meeting started, especially when most of them were probably nursing riot hangovers. Someone must have tipped them off. Whiteley's wife, perhaps, whose clear ambition, according to the PM, was to ring in another change of decor in Downing Street. Or Whiteley's Special Adviser, Patsy or Patricia something or other, whose short skirts drew attention to her long legs and who always seemed to be hanging on her boss's every word. The PM had dropped a hint that there might be something special, and he didn't mean Special Advice, going on there. Not that Joshua gave a toss how many women Whiteley, or any other politician, bedded: not as long as they all left Joshua alone to get on with the job.

He walked round the car towards the entrance, where a functionary was waiting to lead him to the Cabinet Briefing Office in the cellar between Parliament and Trafalgar Square. As he handed over his phone, and before he passed through the door, he turned for a last glance at the Home Secretary.

Whiteley was in full spate, banging his right fist against the palm of his left.

Probably promising to personally raid the houses of every single rioter and clap them all in irons, Joshua thought, and then he went in.

10.15 a.m.
Banging and a woman's voice – 'Open this door' – followed by more banging.

Cathy grabbed for her dressing gown.

'Open up.'

'I'm on my way.' She ran to the door and wrenched it open.

Jayden's mother, also still in her dressing gown and looking worse than ever, said, 'What have you done with him?' as soon as she saw Cathy.

'Done with who?'

'My son. Jayden. What have you done with him?'

'Isn't he back?'

'No, and Lyndall said you'd gone to find him.' In Elsie's paranoid world, anyone prepared to go to the trouble to look for her son was as likely to chop him into little pieces and throw them in the river as bring him safely home. 'Where is he?' The top of her dressing gown opened to give Cathy a glimpse of the lace of a nightie that, once white, had turned a muddied grey. 'What the fuck did you do with him?'

If anybody else had talked to her like that, especially after the night she'd had, Cathy would have closed the door on them. But she made allowances for Elsie, who, she suspected, had a severe case of agoraphobia on top of the belligerence she never could restrain.

'I didn't find him,' she said. 'But that doesn't mean he wasn't there. I got diverted.'

'Well, why isn't he home?' Elsie was gnawing at the edges of an already bloodied fingernail. 'He's dead, isn't he?'

'He can't be dead. We would have heard if he was. And,' remembering how quickly Pius had been contacted about her, 'if he was hurt we'd also have heard.'

A series of staggered inhalations had the effect of robbing Elsie of almost all her breath: 'So where is he?'

'Maybe he slept the night elsewhere?'

'He wouldn't. He doesn't. Not unless I have one of my turns.' She meant one of her explosive rages during which she would break any object that came to hand. It sounded ugly, but Cathy, who often took Jayden in during these episodes, knew that his mother never threw anything directly at him, the only collateral damage being the crockery he had taken to acquiring in bulk from the pound shop he worked in.

Elsie's jagged breaths transitioned into a wailed-out 'What am I going to do?'

Such a pathetic sight. Cathy felt like hugging Elsie, but she knew better than to touch her or even verbally to sympathise – two of the many things that Elsie could not abide. So instead she said, 'It was chaos last night. There were barricades everywhere. He might not have been able to get home. He might have stayed with someone.'

'Who? Lyndall's his only friend.'

Surprised that his mother had actually noticed this, Cathy thought, should I? And then she thought, yes, she had to, to prepare Elsie. 'The only other thing I can think,' she said, 'is that he could have been arrested.' And, quickly, before Elsie could react, 'It's unlikely. Jayden never makes trouble. But give me a couple of hours and if he's not back I'll go check with the police.'

'He has to come back,' Elsie said, which Cathy took as agreement to her plan.

Poor Jayden, she thought, as she closed the door. It wasn't Elsie's fault that she was such a liability, but it must be a terrible strain on him.

10.20 a.m.

The underground briefing room was packed. As if the PM himself was chairing, Peter thought. All the players had pitched up: the police, of course, and the head of the NPCC, and there were video links to many other police authorities. But more importantly from Peter's point of view, every one of the major secretaries of state had been willing to sacrifice what was probably their only morning off in order to attend the meeting. A sign, he knew, not so much of the gravity of the situation

– it wasn't yet clear how grave it really was – but of the seriousness with which they viewed his bid for the top spot.

For or against him, they wanted to watch his play. And if it went well, he thought, they'd give him good reviews.

He was in his element as a chairman, a conductor orchestrating a collective conversation, bringing in the strings here and the wood there to make the music sound as he wanted it to sound. To do this properly, one must know one's orchestra, their vanities and their concerns, and the things that they didn't do so well, and these he had spent a long time studying. As a result, things were going swimmingly. The only possible fly in the ointment was the Commissioner, but Yares had so far played along. Probably intimidated by the serried rank of politicians.

Well, if he changed his mind and decided to step out of line, Peter was ready for him.

On the other side of the table, Joshua kept his own counsel. Someone had to, what with the monstrous collection of egos in this room. Forget the newbie police commissioners, who were having a marvellous time being beamed into COBRA to guff on endlessly about what they could and couldn't do while the Home Secretary nodded his encouragement – they could be forgiven for being star-struck and anxious to impress. He had less patience for the behaviour of the politicians: the Foreign Secretary, who, oddly, hadn't gone with the PM, wittered on about how this was going to play abroad, his real point being how good he was at reassuring Johnny foreigner; the Justice Minister, whose second double chin puffed up as he vowed that, with him in charge, magistrates would understand the need to impose the most draconian of sentences; Defence, who continuously interrupted everybody to offer military support should it be needed; and as for the man in charge of Work and Pensions – well, he wasted precious time outlining his many measures to combat gang culture, although what had happened in Rockham and then spread had nothing whatsoever to do with any gang. In short, they were all blowing their own trumpets, as politicians were wont to do. Or auditioning to keep their jobs, Joshua thought, as Whiteley moved them on to the next topic, namely police leave, which, he now informed them, he had 'ordered cancelled'.

He had said the same thing on the BBC. Joshua could not, would not, let it go unchallenged. He leant forward. 'Sorry to interrupt, Home Secretary, but I am sure that what you meant to communicate here, and in your interviews this early morning, was that leave has been cancelled. Which it has been. By me – it being an operational matter that falls within the remit of the Office of the Commissioner of the Metropolitan Police.'

Whiteley smiled. 'Thank you, Commissioner.'

Was that menace in his smile?

'A slip of the tongue,' Whiteley continued. 'That is of course what I meant to say.'

And, yes, it was menace, because when he added,

'I am confident that . . .'

the stress he afterwards placed on his repetition of Joshua's phrase:

'. . . the Office of the Commissioner . . .'

was meant to ridicule, and when he continued:

'. . . has done everything it can to counter the dreadful scenes we saw on our streets last night . . .'

his sarcastic tone belied his words.

A beat. A moment for Joshua to realise that the conflict he'd hoped to avoid was upon them, a reality made visible by the way the other occupants of the room looked everywhere but at the two antagonists. Even the PCCs on their video links sensed something brewing and were looking first at Whitley and then at Joshua, as if at a tennis match.

'But is it not true, Commissioner,' Whiteley continued, 'that what happened in Rockham was a replay of Tottenham 2011? Did the Met not learn those lessons? Could you not have contained the situation?'

'Yes, we could have,' Joshua said. 'At least we could have once. But there is now a solvent factory in Rockham, and its existence played havoc with our contingency plans. If it had gone up, we would now be dealing with a raging fire and multiple casualties. So we had to divert some of our best-trained officers to guard this factory. This, combined with the cuts to the force, meant we just didn't have enough officers on the ground to contain the Rockham disturbances.'

'Clearly you did not.' A brief smug smile. 'But there is also another

151

matter to be discussed. You would agree, I expect, that the best policing is preventative?'

A typical politician's trick: to state the obvious. Joshua nodded.

'Pity then that you and your "office" seemed to have absolutely no intelligence that any of this was going to unfold.'

'Don't you think it's a big mental leap,' Joshua kept his voice calm, 'to assume that because one man died in unfortunate circumstances, rioting was going to break out?'

'A leap?' Whiteley's tone was even calmer. 'Perhaps so from your point of view. But from where I sit I have been disheartened . . .' he looked down at his briefing notes for longer than could realistically have been necessary, 'to discover that,' he used a finger to tap twice at the sheet of paper in front of him, 'fifteen people have died in London in police presence – that means out on the streets or in custody suites – during the last year. And that not a single charge has arisen from these deaths. Knowing this, one might be forgiven for assuming that there would be a build-up of hostility towards the police, which was bound to come to a head. Especially in a place like Rockham, where there is no love lost between the community and the force.' His emphasis on that word *force* seemed to crack the air.

Joshua could feel Anil Chahda shifting in the seat beside him. Probably wanting Joshua to shut this conversation down. 'I think you will find, Home Secretary,' Joshua said, 'that this number is lower than in previous years.'

A pointed furrowing of his brow. 'And therefore acceptable?'

'We do everything we can to prevent such deaths. But our officers are on the sharp end. We have to deal with people suffering from alcohol or drug abuse, or from mental-health problems – especially given the cuts in social services – or with people who are just ill and don't know it, on a daily, an hourly, basis. In this climate, there are bound to be accidents.'

One eyebrow nearly touched the other. An extended pause and then, 'Don't you think we should leave it to the appropriate authorities, in this case the IPCC, to judge whether this particular death was an accident?'

Oh, he was good, this politician, at playing Joshua at his own game. If it had been a tennis match, he would definitely have won.

And he knew it. 'We have a full agenda,' he said. 'Rather than pre-judging the results of an ongoing IPCC investigation, I suggest we move on.' His gaze shifted from Joshua. 'Deputy Commissioner Chahda, now would be a good time for your report on the measures that you have put in place to combat further unrest in Rockham.'

1.50 p.m.

When he couldn't find a way to get home without encountering further trouble, Jayden had headed in the opposite direction. He ended up by the canal, where he waited until the sun began to rise. He could still hear noises coming from Rockham. He was so tired. He curled up in a dip in the bank, close to the bridge where the alkies usually congregated, and closed his eyes.

He hadn't meant to fall asleep, but he woke up later, hot, thirsty and covered in soot. He had no idea what time it was; all he knew was that his mother would be wild. He hurried along the edge of the canal.

It was quiet now. So quiet he almost managed to convince himself the whole thing had been a dream. But the closer he got to the Lovelace, the greater was the visible destruction. At one corner he saw firemen arcing up their hoses to damp down a smouldering pile of bricks and cookers and fridges and some pieces of furniture, which, apart from the building's metallic skeleton, was all that was left.

On the High Street, security grilles had been levered off and windows punched out, the whirlwind of destruction leaving behind empty boxes, unwanted remains and dazed shopkeepers who were trying to bang in wood and steel to cover the breaches. Others lined up shovels and spades in case 'those bastards come again', as one of them shouted to his neighbour.

He thought of Mr Hashi. There wasn't much of value in his shop that would have attracted any looter, but Mr Hashi and his mother always kept themselves quiet. They must have been terrified by the noise and the destruction. He'd drop by on his way home, check that they were okay.

When he got to the shop, he saw that it had been hit, its grilles levered off and glass shattered. And while the shop might not have been looted, it had been trashed. Where once had been shelves now were only holes in the wall, with pottery dogs and china pigs and crockery that no one ever bought broken amongst the plastic buckets and splintered brooms.

The place stank as well. He couldn't tell of what, but it made him gag.

Mr Hashi was by the counter with his back to the door. He must have heard Jayden coming in, but he didn't turn.

'Mr Hashi.'

'Go away.' A voice that didn't sound like Mr Hashi's.

'It's me, Mr Hashi.'

Mr Hashi whirled round. 'Get off my property.'

'I came to see if I could help.'

'You have done enough, Mr Jay Don. You and your kind. Look.' Mr Hashi swept out a hand. 'Everything broken. Not because it was desired but because what they wanted to do was break me. Look there.' He was pointing at a wall on which somebody had painted 'Go Home'. 'The message is plain, is it not? And they passed their water on the wall. One of them, he did not stop there. Look again.' Mr Hashi was now pointing at the floor. 'Come on, Jay Don. If you are so brave, come and look.'

Even from where he was standing, he could see the sticky brown mess and he could tell what it was from the smell. He didn't move.

'Animals,' Mr Hashi said. 'To call them so is an affront to animals.'

'I'm sorry, Mr Hashi. Let me help you clear it up.'

'I saw you, Jay Don.' Mr Hashi bent down to pick up one of the broken brooms. 'I saw you with them.'

'I wasn't with them.'

'I saw your face. I know what was going through your mind. You think this comfortable life is all the life that I have lived? You think I have not known how it is to be carried by a crowd? I saw that this had happened to you.'

Nothing Jayden could say to deny it. He shuffled his feet. Looked down at them moving in the mess.

'I, in my own time,' he heard Mr Hashi saying, 'I resisted such a crowd. You did not. I saw you, and the dirt on your face is the mark of your guilt.'

'I didn't take anything. Honest, Mr Hashi, I didn't.'

155

'I didna.' Mr Hashi jabbed the broom at him. 'I didna . . . You do not even know how to speak your own language.' He began to move towards Jayden. 'It may be that you did not do your business on my floor, but you let them do it. That is all it takes: for people like you to stand to one side. Do so now. Get off my property. Or I will hurt you.'

The fury in his expression showed that he meant every word. Jayden turned to go. He heard a loud 'Aaaaaaahhhh.' He looked over his shoulder. Mr Hashi, broom held above his head, was running at him.

He also ran. Out of the shop, his vision blurred by tears he didn't know he was shedding. And when he heard someone shouting, 'Stop,' he ran faster, and faster still at the shout, 'Police: stop where you are,' rounding the corner, his feet pounding in an effort to get as far away from Mr Hashi's shop and from the Lovelace as he could.

2 p.m.

Jayden was still not back.

When Cathy walked to the police station, to check whether they had him, she found it ringed by uniforms. The new sign had been demolished – concrete couldn't have set in time – and the only way of getting in was to pass through a narrow corridor between two police lines.

As she made her way towards it, a familiar figure emerged.

'Banji.'

He kept walking away from her.

'Banji.' She started running.

He had a head start and he was moving so fast that he rounded the corner before she had time to catch up with him. She kept running – 'Banji' – her sandals slapping against the road. 'Banji.'

He must have heard her, he couldn't not have, but he neither stopped nor turned. At the same time he didn't seem that serious about getting away from her. If he had run, she would have lost him, but he didn't run. And when she came abreast of him, and when she grabbed his arm, although he still didn't turn he did stop moving.

She scooted round to stand in front of him. He looked a wreck, his clothes messed up by what looked like oil and his eyes bloodshot. And cold as well. Like a stranger's, and when he said, 'What a sight you are,' his icy voice showed that he didn't mean a sight for sore eyes.

She didn't know whether he was referring to the sweat pouring down her face or her badly singed hair. It didn't matter: what she registered was his hostility.

Part of her wanted to ask why he hadn't bothered checking on her and Lyndall. What she said instead was, 'What were you doing in the police station?'

'I went to tell them what I saw on Friday,' he said. 'Not that it's any of your fucking business.' He narrowed his eyes. 'And why the fuck are you following me?'

'I wasn't.'

'A coincidence, is it, that everywhere I turn, I bump into your lard arse?'

It was as if he'd hit her. She took a step back.

'You haven't changed, have you?' He closed the space between them. 'All those years ago, you clung on like a limpet. You're fatter now – I'll give you that – but you're still the same fucking drag. Who never could take a hint.'

As she stood, reeling from the impact of his words, he flicked out an arm. She stood her ground. He wouldn't hit her. Surely not.

He did. He hit her in the stomach. The blow was not hard enough to cause her to double over, even though this is what she did. Because of shock that he had hit her.

'Get away from me,' she heard him saying. 'And stay away. I'm warning you. Stay away.'

And then he went.

There was a small park – more a green enclosure and children's playground, really – nearby. She made her way to it.

This oasis, surrounded by council blocks, had once been gardened to within an inch of its life, with primroses and marigolds planted in strict rows and anything more luxuriant severely pruned. Scorched-earth gardening, Lyndall used to call it. Now, as Cathy pushed open the squeaking gate, she saw that the earth had been, quite literally, scorched. Not a single flower had survived the water ban, while what grass remained was brown and so full of thistles that no one would ever dream of trying to sit on it.

This had once been a place where mothers could let their young children run free. Now half the slats on the bench that Cathy went to sit on had been broken off, and under the section that was still useable lay used syringes.

He had hit her.

She kicked the syringes. Pushed them further back under the bench.

Actually hit her. And for no reason. The shock of it hurt more than the actual blow.

She disgusted him. He'd made that clear.

A voice inside of her protested. She had not been following him. And she had not done anything wrong. And yet this voice was soon drowned out by a much louder one. A voice that said that he was right. That she was fat. That she was slow. And that she couldn't see a hint, never mind take one, even if it slapped her in the face. If she had been able to, she never would have let him back into her life.

All these years since Lyndall's birth that she told herself she had changed. Grown up. Become a different person.

Ridiculous. She was the same fool she'd always been. Who – and however hard she tried to keep the sentence at bay, it still came bursting out – who had loved a monstrous man.

Who still loved him.

That was the worst of it. The things she had told herself. That she was over him; that he was nothing to her; that it was better he had gone. All lies. That's why, when she'd bumped into him after all those many years, she had invited him into her home. Because she could not bear to lose sight of him again.

As if this had ever been her choice.

Last night she had not cried. Not in relief when she'd escaped the burning building. Not when she had heard that the woman she had rescued might never recover from the effects of the fumes she'd inhaled. Not when Lyndall and Pius had been moved to tears by the unfolding mayhem. But now her tears were splashing her neck, soaking her blouse.

She made no attempt to wipe them away. She sat and went on crying as if her tears would never stop. And all because a man she had trusted and loved had once again abandoned her.

11.55 p.m.

The call came just before midnight, Joshua's home phone ringing. He picked it up to hear someone say, 'Hold for the Prime Minister.'

At long last.

A lucky coincidence that the PM had caught him at home. He'd only just dropped in to pick up fresh shirts, his intention being to return to work.

He could have sent his driver for the shirts, but he hadn't fancied those big boots plodding through his private space. And it was helpful to leave the pressure of the control room, if only for a short time. Time to think. Which, come to think of it, he was getting a lot of as he kept holding for the Prime Minister. Seconds turned into minutes. He looked impatiently at his watch.

'Joshua.' That familiar voice. 'Sorry to have kept you waiting.'

'Not a problem. Are you on your way back?'

'I shouldn't walk out on the negotiations.' A pause, while Joshua wondered how the negotiations could be more important than the country going up in flames. 'I trusted you to deal with this,' the PM continued. 'How could things have got so out of control?'

'There have been cuts,' Joshua said.

'Cuts . . . the perennial excuse when anything goes wrong. It won't wash, Joshua. Not when everybody has had to pull their belts in.'

'There have been other factors,' Joshua said, 'that affected our ability to respond. We had to divert valuable manpower into guarding the solvent factory in Rockham. If it had gone up, all hell would have been let loose. If we hadn't had that to contend with, we might have had enough men to stop the rioting in its tracks.'

'I see.' The doubt in the PM's voice suggested that even if he saw, he didn't believe it, a suspicion confirmed when he followed up with: 'I understand you clashed with the Home Secretary at COBRA.'

'He was spoiling for a fight.'

'Probably not the best idea to give him one.'

Pot, kettle, black, Joshua thought, but before he could frame this thought into a coherent sentence, the PM shifted the terrain. 'Look, I know you've got a lot on your plate, and I am confident that you will resolve the problem asap. I'll let you get on with it. But before you go, have you had time to look into that matter I mentioned the other day?'

What was he talking about?

'When you came to Downing Street.'

Oh. That.

'Yes, Prime Minister,' Joshua said. 'I did look into it.'

'And?'

'And there is no record of Teddy having been picked up.'

Another pause followed by: 'Good. Well, I'm sure you're busy. I'll leave you to it. Goodnight.'

11.55 p.m.

Cathy could hear the din of riot issuing from the television, cutting through the similar noises that were reverberating through the Lovelace. In every living room in all the land, she knew people must be sitting on the edges of their sofa, mouths agape as they watched the riots spreading. Not her.

Banji's blow had felled her. She had come home and gone straight to bed, where she lay for hours staring up at the ceiling, looking at nothing as darkness fell.

He had done it to her twice. That's the thought that kept recurring. Twice.

The first time she'd been young and desperately in need of love. He'd been everything that she was not: streetwise, sure of himself and enigmatic. Even his ability to stomach drugs and alcohol had seemed exotic to her then. But when he'd left her, she'd persuaded herself that it was for the best.

Fine. Good. We make mistakes and move on.

She had spent years making herself feel better by pretending that she'd never really loved him. Now she knew that for the lie it was, and now, as well, she knew the truth. Which was that he had never really loved her.

160

She could forgive the girl she once had been; she didn't know if she'd ever be able to forgive the adult.

The sound of running feet. She shut her eyes.

The door burst open. 'You've got to come and see this, Mum.'

'I'm tired.'

'But you've got to.'

All she wanted was to be left alone.

'Come on.' It was clear from Lyndall's stance, feet planted and hands on hips, that she was determined to get her way.

Easier to follow her to the living room than to resist, so that's what Cathy did. 'What's so interesting?'

Lyndall pointed at the television. 'Keep watching. It'll be on again in a minute.'

The screen showed one of those loops they used when everything is happening at once and they didn't have sufficient cameras to cover it. Footage, already familiar, of fires burning, and policemen in retreat, and a woman jumping with her child from a building.

'I've already seen this.' She made to turn away.

'Wait. It's coming.'

A new sequence. The skeleton of the building she had run into yesterday. Still smouldering but with no roof and no outside walls.

'Yes, I've seen that as well.'

'Not that,' Lyndall said. 'Wait.'

The camera panned away from the shafts of metal that had once been a building to the street below and towards a barricade that hadn't previously been there. Flames rising, youths throwing more fuel on a bonfire. Another pan but this time with a change of angle, coming as it did from behind the police lines and towards the barricade. The camera stayed on a man who had separated himself from the group and, as the camera stayed on him, looked straight at it.

'See who it is.' This from Lyndall.

Unlike his fellows, this man did not bother to hide his face. He looked, dead centre, at the camera, smiled and raised an arm. And before the camera tilted down, the cameraman presumably scrambling out of the way, the man smiled again and threw a burning bottle. And that man was Banji.

Monday

PRIVATE AND CONFIDENTIAL
FOR INQUIRY USE ONLY

Submission to the internal inquiry of the Metropolitan Police into Operation Bedrock

Submission 1051/W: camera stills 6473–6503 gathered by Support Unit 31AXZ, call sign India 97, taken between 0:55 and 02:05 on ▮▮▮▮▮▮▮▮▮▮▮▮

location: Rockham High Street

subject: continuation of disturbances and community response

Photographs W6473–79 indicate an apparent stand-off on Rockham High Street between alleged looters and Rockham residents, who, it is assumed, are shopkeepers guarding their premises. A variety of weapons – steel poles, sticks, bricks – can be seen in the hands of both opposing sections. A man, IC3, can be seen to the left of the photograph apparently arguing with the alleged rioters.

Photographs W6480–85, show the putative looters dispersing after the ASU hovered directly above them. Photographs W96–98 show the man, IC3, also running away.

Photographs W6499–6503 show the Rockham High Street now calm. The ASU was given instruction to proceed to a location outside of Rockham following reports of new disturbances.

8 a.m.

The line of Joshua Yares's lips tightened as he sped-read his way through that morning's newspapers.

The red-tops had all gone for alliteration, with headlines such as 'England Explodes' competing with a more punitive 'Dixon's Disgrace' and what was probably an early edition's 'Rockham's Ruin'. What the papers also shared, and this included the broadsheets, is that they read like comics, their terse prose outgunned by photographs of buildings burning, people panicking, rioters rioting and crowds of police apparently doing nothing but looking on.

Joshua's lips tightened some more when he saw that, despite the huge variety of available images, every editor had opted to include the identical two: the first was the woman, child in arms, plunging down three floors to escape her burning home; the second was a close-up of the man all the tabloids had nicknamed 'Molotov Man'.

A rap on his door. He shifted the papers aside. 'Come,' and then, 'Come in, Anil. Take a seat,' watching as his deputy plodded over to the desk and gingerly lowered himself into the chair opposite. 'How are you holding up?'

A weary shrug. 'I'm afraid it's still an uphill battle, sir. The NPCC organised a couple of TAU coachloads for us – sorely needed. They were on their way when word came that it's about to kick off in Salford, so they had to turn back. We're getting them from further north instead – the Durham and the Scottish chiefs have been helpful – but it's all going to take time.'

'Until we've got enough bodies to push back, we'll just have to exert as strong a hold as we can,' Joshua said. 'Meanwhile, did you find a moment to glance through the papers?'

'I did, sir. Grim reading.'

'That it is.' Joshua picked up the topmost tabloid, opening it to its centre spread where an oversize picture of the Molotov-throwing man

166

was surrounded by smaller photos of other kinds of mayhem. 'You must have seen this.'

'Couldn't miss it.'

'Once the press picks its face of evil, they never let go. If we don't find this man, they will – and then they'll throw him in our faces. We need to know everything that can be known about him and then we need to find him.'

'Yes, sir.'

'No more surprises. Everything.'

'I've already put an officer on it.'

'Put on more if that's what it takes. I want this man found.'

'Should I issue an APW?'

'Not at this juncture. We have to assume he's still in Rockham – it's where he'll feel safest – but gone to ground. Tell CS Wright to leave no stone unturned.'

'Even if it inflames the situation?'

'I want this man and I want him here, on my carpet, as soon as he is picked up. Is that clear?'

'Crystal, sir.' Chahda levered himself out of the chair. 'I'll get on to it right away.'

10 a.m.

Come the hour of the emergency debate, MPs who'd gathered in the Members' corridors to swap horror stories from their constituencies piled into the Chamber, squeezing close on the benches, latecomers jostling each other in their efforts to stay within the lines to give themselves a chance to have their say.

The Prime Minster, who was still in Switzerland, had asked Peter to lead his government's response. Another political miscalculation, Peter thought, and, given that all eyes were now on Parliament, another chance for him to shine.

The Speaker gave him the nod: 'Home Secretary.'

He got up, slowly, from the front bench and in the same languorous pace stepped forward to lay his notes on the dispatch box, taking a moment then to look around. He could feel the weight of expectation on him, and he felt it not as a burden (the House being for once united) but as an embrace. He took a deep breath in. 'I am confident that I speak for the House,' and then, conscious that the suspended microphones were picking up his every word and relaying them out to a wider than usual audience, he added, 'and that I also speak for the nation when I condemn the criminality of the past thirty-six hours. There can be no excuse for the burning of homes, the raiding of shops, the robbery of members of the public and the attack on police officers.' He waited for the rumble of agreement to pass through both front benches and around the House, and even after it was over he let the silence stretch before lowering his voice. 'We will restore order,' he said. 'And we will punish the offenders. Make no mistake about it, we stand united in our determination to preserve our way of life.'

As a fresh tide of 'Hear, hears' died away, he let his voice drop another notch.

'The police,' he said . . .

'The police,' Joshua heard, and pumped up the volume on his TV.

'. . . and especially individual officers, have shown considerable courage against the odds. Twenty-five police officers have so far been treated for their injuries, and we fear that there are likely to be further casualties. I know the House will join me in thanking them, and their fellow officers, for their courage and in wishing the injured a speedy recovery.'

As agreement once again reverberated, Joshua, now watching intently, waited for the 'but' he knew had to be on its way. And sure enough, after a pause for emphasis followed by a further lowering of the voice (if he went on this way he'd soon be whispering), Whiteley continued: 'But those at the top of the command structure of the Metropolitan Police bear considerable responsibility for what has happened. They treated the initial flare-up in Rockham as a public-order issue rather than what it was: the starting gun for mass criminality. There were simply not enough officers on the streets. They lost the initiative and because of this they lost control.'

The front bench was all a-nod, their response mirrored by their opponents across the aisle. Having joined them so nicely together, Whiteley ratcheted up his attack.

'I expected, and I'm sure you did as well, that the lessons of 2011 would have been learnt. I will make it my mission to find out why they were not. I have already begun this process. During the COBRA meeting I yesterday chaired, I informed Metropolitan Commissioner Joshua Yares of my concerns. Among the measures we agreed is the recall from leave of all serving police officers . . .'

The cheek of it, to claim credit for this again, and after Joshua had called him on it yesterday.

'. . . and that requests for mutual aid be coordinated by the Association of Chief Police Officers . . .'

Another routine step that Whiteley was stealing credit for.

'I expect to see as well an increase in numbers of officers deployed at all points of disruption or potential disruption.'

As if after all the recent cuts – pushed through by this same Home Secretary – they had the personnel to do this.

'To this effect, I have offered to the Commissioner each and every measure in our possession, including the deployment of baton rounds, tear gas and water cannon. I am sure the House will join me in urging the Commissioner to give this offer the serious consideration it merits . . .'

Another dig because yesterday Joshua had explained why none of these measures, and especially water cannons, were currently appropriate. But why let a few facts get in the way of a rousing speech, especially when the bastard of a Home Secretary was on a roll?

'The justice system will play its part in punishing these criminals in the most rigorous manner. Anyone charged with riot-related offences will be kept in custody. Those convicted – and the courts will continue to sit through the night for as long as it takes – will find themselves in jail. I will be reviewing statutory provisions to ensure that the courts have powers appropriate to the scale of this lawlessness. If needs be, I will raise sentencing tariffs. For the present, however . . .'

And now a pause as Whiteley let his gaze travel the full length of the Chamber and once again dropped his voice.

Joshua Yares turned the volume up another notch.

'. . . we expect the police to ensure security in our streets in every city, in every town, in every village, throughout the land.'

Damaging but not fatal. Joshua breathed some of his tension out.

Prematurely, because . . .

'Many Members are anxious to raise their constituents' concerns,' Whiteley continued, 'and so I will give way to my Honourable Friend,' he turned to look up at the ranks of his own backbenchers, 'the Member for Brancombe Forest, who has been popping up and down like a jack-in-the-box in a bid to attract my attention.'

Not that Yares had noticed.

He was instantly on high alert.

It was a trap.

It had to be. The clue was that the Member for Brancombe Forest was Albion Hind, whose tawdry sex life had been exposed in the press only after he had failed to persuade his local police to arrest a particularly persistent reporter. Since then he had used what little influence remained to him to try to hound his Chief Constable from office. No good could come from any question he asked, especially given that, by the way he now rose to his feet, someone must have made a concerted attempt to sober him up.

His TV being on so loud it was distorting, Joshua turned down the volume.

'I am grateful to the Home Secretary for giving way,' Hind was saying, 'and I join him in condemning the criminality of the past few days. There is much to be said and I would like to be the one to say it. But I know that many of my Honourable Friends will also want to have their say, and so I will restrict myself to a single question: would the Home Secretary comment on rumours that the unrest in Rockham was triggered by rogue elements within the Metropolitan Police Service?'

Not something the Minister should comment on. Not when the IPCC had taken on the investigation. 'IPCC,' Joshua mouthed at the TV, 'IPCC . . .' and for a moment it seemed as if Whiteley could hear him and was going to do the right thing because . . .

'Given that the Independent Police Complaints Commission is investigating the death in Rockham,' he said, 'the House will understand why my answer must be circumspect.'

Not yet the time to relax, since this was Whiteley, who had his eyes on another prize.

'What I can say,' Whiteley continued, 'and I can assure the House that I am not here using privileged information, is that I too have heard the rumours that some of the officers involved in the originating incident have been subjected to internal inquiries into possible previous misconduct. As to the content or result of these inquiries I cannot speak, but what I can say . . .'

Joshua Yares did not get to find out, at least not then, what Home Secretary Whiteley felt he could or couldn't say. He was already out of his chair, and past his desk, and at his door, and pushing his head out, and bellowing, 'Get Deputy Commissioner Chahda back in my office double quick,' before stepping back and closing the door so hard that people on the ground floor must have heard the bang.

10.45 a.m.
Banging and a woman shouting, 'Open up.'

Cathy, who was sitting on the floor beside a smouldering wastepaper bin, froze.

More banging. 'Open up. Now.'

If she stayed on the floor and out of sight, Elsie would eventually get bored and go away. She fed the last of the photographs of Banji into the fire.

'Mrs Mason.'

Elsie never used her surname. Probably didn't even know it.

'It's the police. Open the door.'

The police?

Lyndall's school, which had also been targeted during the attacks, was closed for repair. And Lyndall was out – she'd needed air, she'd said. Throwing the contents of a glass of water into the bin to make the embers safe, Cathy ran to the front door and wrenched it open.

There were two uniformed officers, a man and a woman, on her doorstep.

'Mrs Mason?' This from the man, who pressed forward to put his boot inside the door. 'Mrs Cathy Mason?'

'Has something happened to my daughter?', thinking that they always sent a woman to break bad news.

'We're not here about your daughter, Mrs Mason.' The man was holding up a piece of paper. 'I have here a warrant to search your premises.'

171

Only now did she see that behind the front two were three men who also looked to be policemen, but in plain clothes. 'Why would you want to search my place?'

'You have to let us in, Mrs Mason.' He pushed the door so hard she had no choice but to back away. She ended up jammed against the wall as the four men filed in.

'What's going on?'

The female officer who had waited as her colleagues entered now stepped in. 'The sooner they are left to get on with the job, the sooner it will be over,' she said, closing the door behind her. 'I think that's your lounge over there. That's a good place for us to be.'

10.50 a.m.

'What the fuck, Anil?' Joshua, who'd been standing at the window, wheeled round when he heard Anil Chahda's tentative knock followed by his even more tentative entrance. 'What the fuck?'

'I'm not sure what you mean, sir.'

Joshua pointed at the silent television. 'I mean this,' and then, as the camera focused on Peter Whiteley, 'I mean him.'

'The Home Secretary?'

'Yes, the Home Secretary. Who has just used Parliamentary privilege to impugn this force.'

'I'm sorry to hear that, sir.'

I'll give you sorry, Joshua thought. 'Is it true?'

'I wasn't listening to the debate. Is what true?'

'That officers of the Rockham police force have previously been subjected to internal inquiry. Is it true?'

'Yes, sir, it is true. Not all of them, of course.'

'And why didn't I know?'

'I beg your pardon, sir?'

'Are you deaf? I am asking you why it is that I didn't know the answer to a question that I had asked you on more than one occasion.'

'I can't answer that, sir.'

Such insubordination. So much so that he wondered whether Chahda was entirely well.

He saw how the skin of Chahda's brown face was blotched with red, and he saw sweat beading his brow. Must have run to get here. 'For heaven's sake, man, sit. Sit.' He reinforced this command by striding over to his desk.

Having seated himself, Chahda withdrew a large white handkerchief with which he mopped his brow.

Such a great lump of a man, Joshua thought, and said more quietly, 'Okay. Let's start again. And this time, let's try to understand each other. Question: did I ask you for the record of any past disciplinary action taken against members of the Rockham lot?'

'Yes, sir, you did.'

'And did you supply me with such information?'

'Yes, sir, I did.'

'I see.' Was it possible that Chahda's mutiny could stretch to the telling of an outright lie? 'In what form did you supply this information?'

'I know you don't like everything online, sir, so I copied the relevant documents for you.'

'Which you put where?'

'Why, there. By your desk.'

Joshua looked down at the desk, as tidy as it always was, save for the pile of that day's newspapers. 'There's nothing here.'

'In your in-tray, sir. Where I always used to put your predecessor's papers.'

His in-tray. Of course. The one he'd been promising himself to look at ever since stepping into the office, and the one he'd had no time for. It stood, neatly, on a side table. He pulled it to him and rifled through. Sure enough, halfway down was a folder on which 'Records of Rockham Police Officers' had been written on the tab in Anil Chahda's minuscule script.

He should have known it was there. 'Is what Whiteley said correct?' And he shouldn't have shouted at his deputy. 'Have any of the Rockham officers been disciplined for misconduct?'

'A few of them have. Usual infractions. Lack of diligence. Failure to present evidence. Insubordination. Traffic irregularities. A couple of written warnings but none serious enough to warrant further action, except in one case: an officer who was sent for race-awareness training after a number of complaints.'

'And did this officer take an active part in restraining the unfortunate man who died?'

'No, sir. But he was present at the earlier stop and search. Nothing untoward as far as we can tell. The report of the officer who was with him at the time matches his in every respect.'

'I bet it does.' Something to think about at another time. For the moment: 'How did the Home Secretary know about the Rockham officers?'

'Beats me, sir. Except . . .' Chahda swallowed and looked down at the floor.

'Except what? Come on, man, spit it out.'

Chahda lifted his head. 'Well, as you said yourself, sir, you did raise the issue on a number of occasions, once within the hearing of other officers. It is within the bounds of possibility that the information was passed on by them.'

'Why would one of our own do that?'

'Perhaps because they thought you were being overly harsh on others of our own? You know how loyal they can be.'

To expose a fellow officer in order to get at the top command – what was Chahda on? Joshua was so flabbergasted that all he could say was, 'I see.' What he saw, clearly and for the first time, although he had previously suspected it, was that Chahda's loyalty did not lie with him.

'Would you like me to investigate further, sir?'

He could just imagine how a witch-hunt would go down at this moment of highest pressure. 'No. Not at the moment. Any news of Molotov Man?'

'No definite leads. But they have located the girlfriend. They're searching her place as we speak,' Chahda said. 'Hopefully that will help us find him.'

11.45 a.m.

They'd been in her flat for an hour, and they were still there.

They'd torn the place apart. Neatly enough – they put back everything they'd pulled out – but it was awful to watch them prying into her private places, and Lyndall's. She felt herself exposed. Stripped bare. They'd even rooted through her malfunctioning fridge and the kitchen

174

cupboards she'd been meaning to spring-clean. And still they wouldn't tell her what they were looking for.

Then at last they were done. The men filed out. The woman, who had followed Cathy everywhere, even to the toilet, didn't move.

'Aren't you going to go with them?'

The woman smiled. 'In a bit.' She was sitting at the edge of a chair, but at the sound of footsteps she jumped up to poke her head round the door. 'We're in here, ma'am,' stepping aside then standing to attention as a petite blonde with red-bowed lips entered.

From the patch on her collar – two crossed batons that looked like electronic cigarettes – Cathy guessed this newcomer must be a senior officer, a thought confirmed when, in a surprisingly deep voice, the woman said, 'Mrs Mason? I'm Rockham's Acting Commander, Chief Superintendent Gaby Wright. Would you mind if I asked you a few questions?'

'And if I do?' The petulance of her tone, combined with the woman's raising of one perfectly groomed eyebrow, made Cathy feel like a badly behaved child. She bit back on the feeling: 'Who gave you the right to search my flat?'

'A search warrant, legally obtained, gave us the right. I trust my officers showed it to you?'

Cathy nodded.

'And did they put everything back, neatly, where they'd found it?'

Another nod.

'Good.' CS Wright nudged the wastepaper bin with her foot. 'Tell me about this.'

'It's a bin,' Cathy said. 'I bought it in the market. Cost a fiver.'

A quick smile devoid of warmth. 'It has been a long night. You won't mind if I sit, will you?' She sat. 'Look, I know you want us out of your hair, and we will soon be gone, but before that . . .' She used one hand to pull the bin closer while simultaneously holding out the other to receive the pair of blue plastic gloves that her subordinate had produced. She pulled on one of the gloves – a tight fit despite her small hands – and reached into the bin, rooting through the ashes. 'I want to know about the things you burnt.' From the generalised mush she pulled out a fragment that was half intact. She held it up. 'Why did you burn this?'

'To get rid of it. Is that a crime?'

'No.' This time her smile was a little warmer. 'It is not a crime. And in case my putting on a glove gave you the wrong impression, it was to stop my hand getting dirty, not to protect evidence. Still, I'd like to know what it is you burnt.'

What would be wrong with telling this ice maiden that she'd torn up everything – photos, letters and other mementoes – she'd ever got from Banji? That after she'd torn them up she'd been still so full of rage she'd decided to reduce them to ash?

She would have said all this had Lyndall not just at that moment come running in. 'Mum. There's police crawling all over the L . . .' She stopped. 'What the hell?' She looked to Cathy and then to the standing constable, until her gaze came to a rest on CS Wright.

Who stood up. 'And you are?'

'Her name is Lyndall. She's my daughter.'

'Pleased to meet you, Lyndall.' Having peeled off the glove and dropped it in the bin, she stuck out her hand: 'I'm Chief Superintendent Gaby Wright.'

Lyndall averted her gaze.

'We're looking for someone.' Gaby Wright kept her eyes fixed on Lyndall. 'A man. Friend of yours and your mum's. Name of Banji. Do you know where he is?'

So that's what this was about. That bastard and his stupid prank with the petrol bomb.

But how had they known to come looking for him here?

'Do you?'

'No, we don't know where he is,' Cathy said.

It was as if she wasn't there. 'How about you, Lyndall? Do you know?'

Lyndall shook her head.

'You may think that your silence is protecting a friend from harm, Lyndall, but you couldn't be more wrong. Banji is in serious trouble, and if he doesn't give himself up it will get even worse.'

'What?' Lyndall rolled her eyes. 'Worse like it went worse for Ruben?'

'Do you know where Banji is?'

'Why would I know where he is?'

Watching from the sidelines, Cathy registered the defiance in Lyndall's expression and that contrary sign, the wavering of Lyndall's voice. She interposed herself between the two: 'She's fourteen years old. You can't interrogate her. Not without my permission, which I'm not prepared to give,' wondering where she had found the courage to be so defiant while turning her head to say, 'Lyndall, go to your room.'

With uncharacteristic alacrity, Lyndall fled the room, banging the door on her way out as she said something that sounded distinctly like, 'Fuck you, you killers.'

'Well.' Another rise of that arched eyebrow.

'She's upset. We all are. Ruben was loved.'

'A most unfortunate death, which will, I can assure you, be thoroughly investigated. But Banji's a whole different kettle of fish. We need your help to find him.'

She didn't know where he was. That's what she could have said, and that would have been the truth. But something about the way this woman had come in, uninvited, and assumed she owned the room, and something about the way she had tried to pump Lyndall – as if she would know anything – had turned Cathy's stomach. She closed her mouth. Shook her head.

A sigh. 'If you don't tell me everything you know about this man,' Gaby Wright's gaze hardened, 'you will leave me no choice but to arrest you on suspicion of conspiracy to commit arson in relation to the throwing of a bottle of burning petrol.'

'I wasn't anywhere near when he did that.'

Another sigh. 'Conspiracy does not require physical presence.' And a third. 'Let me tell you what is going to happen, Mrs Mason, if you don't answer my questions. I will have no choice other than to formally arrest you. Once we have you in the station – where you will be given access to a solicitor, should you want one – we will take a statement from you. If your alibi and other factors bear out your innocence, we will release you. But you do know, don't you, that anybody charged with a riot-related offence is to be kept in custody? And that, given the threat to chemical facilities in the vicinity of Rockham, Parliament has agreed to the extension to suspected rioters of the pre-charge detention rules under Section 41 and Schedule 8 of the Terrorism Act 2002, as extended by the Terrorism Act 2006. What this means is that we can now keep suspected rioters for up to twenty-eight days. So while we are waiting for the appropriate checks to be made, and with the backlog building up these could take up to the full twenty-eight days, we'd have a duty of care to your daughter. We'd have to call in social services.'

2.15 p.m.

It was more than two hours after the police had left and Lyndall was still in her room. Twice Cathy had gone to stand outside her door but, having pressed her ear against the door and hearing nothing, not even any music, had gone away. She had also left a sandwich by the door, but half an hour later the tomato had made a soggy mess of the ham that, in the heat of the flat, was beginning to smell.

She took the sandwich back into the kitchen and threw it out.

When she opened the tea cupboard, she couldn't help seeing the mess through the eyes of the policeman who had searched it. It was a disgrace. In urgent need of cleaning. As were all the others.

She set to work. First, she scrubbed the kitchen counters and then she emptied the cupboards before scouring the shelves, trying at the same time to scour out the memory of the policeman's disapproval.

What she couldn't rid herself of, however, were the things that she had said.

That humiliating admission: *he hit me* . . . pointing then as extra proof . . . *in the stomach*. And that denial, *no*, that she'd been forced to make: *no, I don't know where he lives, I never went to his place*, and, *no, I don't know who else he's friends with*, repeating it until the disbelief on that bloodless face turned into believing contempt. And even after that, the probing had continued: what Banji meant to her, what she meant to him, a relentless drip of increasingly personal questions that laid bare her own stupidity.

And at one point when all this was going on she'd thought she'd heard somebody in the corridor. It must have been Lyndall, who wouldn't have known that Cathy was only answering the police-woman's questions so as to protect her. She'd be furious – and knowing Lyndall she'd convert that fury into sullen withdrawal.

She had finished wiping down the shelves. A satisfying process but now, although the cupboards were clean, every surface, including those she'd already wiped, were covered in jars and tins, some of which needed throwing out while others were so sticky she couldn't possibly put them back.

She filled the sink with hot soapy water. She was really getting somewhere. Lyndall would be thrilled. She grabbed for a jar, but it was so sticky it slipped out of her hand. In that moment, all the frustration that she'd been suppressing seemed to fire up her leg so that when she kicked the jar, it hit the wall, cracked and rebounded with such force that parts of it hit the wall opposite.

It left a sticky trail of glass and green gunge on the floor. Could it have been greengage jam, she wondered, or something else that had turned green with age? Most likely the latter – it stank. She fetched some newspaper, which she used to trap the glass, then got down on her hands and knees and, with a bucket of soapy water at her side, washed the lino.

By the time the floor was clean enough to pass temporary muster, she was boiling hot. The floor was clean, but the rest of the kitchen was a disaster zone. She would see to it later. For now she needed to talk to Lyndall.

She went down the corridor and knocked on Lyndall's door. No answer. She turned the handle. It didn't budge. She knocked again. 'Lyndall.'

Silence. She gave another knock. 'Lyndall.'

Some shuffling followed by the grating of a key, and when she turned the handle again the door opened.

Lyndall was on her bed, stretched out on her side to face the wall. She didn't move when Cathy entered.

'What's wrong?'

No answer.

When Cathy went over, Lyndall shuffled closer to the wall, but at least she did nothing to stop Cathy sitting on the bed.

'Come on, honey, tell me what's wrong.'

At last an answer, but, delivered as it was into the pillow into which Lyndall's face was squashed, Cathy couldn't make out a word. 'I'm sorry, I didn't hear that. Say it again.'

Lyndall spun round. 'You. Know. What's. Wrong.'

She must have been in the corridor; she must have heard everything.

'You promised,' Lyndall said. 'You promised me and you promised her.'

'Her?' Cathy had given the policewoman no promises.

'Jayden's mum.'

Cathy's exhalation was so intense she felt her chest deflate.

'You promised her that if he didn't come back, you'd look for him.'

She sighed again, not from guilt for having forgotten a boy whom everybody except Lyndall always forgot, but more from relief. 'Yes, I did. And with everything that's happened, I didn't do it. I'm sorry.'

'It's not me you need to say sorry to.' Lyndall did another flip to face the wall again. When Cathy touched her, she shrugged the hand away.

There was no talking to her, not when she was in a mood. Cathy got up and, relief still coursing through her, left the room.

6.10 p.m.

'Home Secretary,' Patricia's voice was icy, 'you have put the blame for the failure to contain the disturbances onto the police. But there has been a 10 per cent year-on-year cut in funding of the Met during your time in office. Don't you think that the cuts may have affected their capacity to respond to what was after all a series of extraordinary events?'

'I don't think . . .'

'Yes, you do, you always think. What you don't do is consider.'

'You're right. I don't *consider* the events to be in any way extraordinary. A man died in Rockham. We will know exactly what happened there only after the IPCC has completed its investigation. Our current concern is with the demonstration that followed. I would have been the first to defend it if it had been orderly. But it was not orderly.' A pause.

'Slow it down.'

'The police should have come down hard' – he took care to separate each word from the one that followed. 'If they had, they would have contained the situation.'

'But the cuts?'

'You asked a two-part question; allow me the opportunity to address the second part.' Peter looked to the place where a camera would be. 'We came into office promising no further cuts in front-line services, and we have kept this promise.' His words came out smoothly, leaving him free to concentrate on preventing the tell of his boredom – that slight twitching of his left eyelid, which Patricia would be sure to pounce on – from displaying itself. 'It is true that we have encouraged the outsourcing of clerical work, custody arrangements and the transfer and care of prisoners, but this is so as to streamline the service and free up police officers to carry out the jobs for which they were trained. And as well . . . he took a deep

182

breath, about to deliver that quick one-two of falling crime stats that always did the job, but he was distracted by the sight of the Minister for Work and Pensions holding forth on the real news on the television behind Patricia. 'Save us,' he said. Despite that the sound was off, Work and Pensions' wild gaze told him that his Cabinet colleague, an incompetent bore at the best of times, was making a complete hash of the interview.

'You were saying?'

He straightened up. 'And as well,' he said, but then he slumped back down, 'and blah, bloody blah. I can do this bit in my sleep.' Another glance at the screen: 'Are you sure I shouldn't have said yes to the six?'

'Don't worry. The six is just picking over yesterday's events. Come dark, the trouble's going to kick off again. Then everybody who isn't out destroying stuff will be at home glued to their TVs. That's why the ten – and they're already planning to extend it – is the right slot for you.'

6.30 p.m.

'Come.' Joshua Yares looked up from the memo he was drafting.

'The file you requested, sir.'

He laid down his pen. 'What took so long?'

'It had been mislabelled, sir, and sent mistakenly for destruction. We only just saved it.'

Destruction? What the hell was going on? 'Thank you, sergeant. Put it over there, will you.' He pointed at the low table that stood beside the sofa at the other end of his office.

'Anything else, sir?'

'No, thank you. That will be all.' Joshua got up and instead of immediately going over to the table, he went to stand by the window. He stretched his arms up high above his head, afterwards dropping them and moving his head round in circles, hearing how his neck creaked, granulated knots audibly resisting his attempt to ease the stiffness from his shoulders. He straightened up. He could see the dark water of a waning Thames, and beyond the river the pods of the London Eye through the milky white of an early summer sky. From the cool of his air-conditioned office, it was hard to imagine just how unpleasant it was out there. But he knew that it was and that it was going to get even more unpleasant once the disorder that BBM and the Twitter-sphere were planning exploded. He turned away from the window and went over to the sofa.

He reached for the folder that the sergeant had laid on the table. On the cover was a name: Julius Jibola. He opened the file to a picture of a man who stared, unsmiling, at the camera. Another page turned and, sighing, he began to read.

7.30 p.m.
One more politician on the TV banging on about feral youth and feckless fathers and Cathy was going to scream. She switched the TV off.

What to do now?

The radiator was on full blast and the room, despite every window being wide open, was as hot as an oven. She downed another glass of tepid water.

Lyndall had at last emerged – driven, no doubt, by hunger. She had gone into the kitchen, presumably to fix herself something to eat (Cathy didn't dare go in with her), and then, seeing the mess, must have stayed, by the sounds of the clattering, to clear it up.

The heat was too much to bear.

And it wasn't just the heat.

The clattering had turned into actual banging. Okay, Lyndall was prone to melodrama, but this was going way over the top. Couldn't just be that she was missing Jayden, could it?

Only way to find out was ask, but at this moment Cathy did not have the strength. She clicked on the television. Saw Banji with his Molotov. Turned the television off. Thought, is this how it's always going to be? Punished my whole life for something I did when I was too young to know any better?

From the pocket of her skirt she took out the crumpled pack of Marlboros she'd found nestling at the back of one of the kitchen cupboards.

She'd given up years ago, soon after they'd moved into the Lovelace and after she'd caught the three-year-old Lyndall pretending to smoke. She must have hidden this pack with its one remaining cigarette then. Just in case. Now the sight of it drove her from her seat and out.

A blast of heat, underscored by pollution, and while dusk had not yet properly taken over, the sky was a strange brackish colour. It was so hot, the estate was weighed down by lassitude despite all the open doors, with the only closed one being, as ever, Jayden's mother's.

Cathy took the lone fag out of its pack, as well the box of matches she'd also stashed away. She stared at them. Longingly. Thought, why not? Reminded herself about the agony of giving up. But then another voice: one can't do any harm. She would reward herself, she decided, after bearding Elsie's lair.

She made her way over to knock at Elsie's door. No answer. She knocked again – and again – standing there long enough to confirm her suspicion that Elsie was never going to open up.

Mission if not accomplished then at least attempted. She could indulge herself. Not outside her own flat, however.

She stepped over to the wall by Elsie's flat. Put the cigarette in her mouth. Felt the unfamiliarity of it. The guilt. And the excitement. Lit a match. Brought it up to her mouth, her hand hovering, but before she touched the match to the cigarette she was distracted by the sight of a score of police, all in riot gear, who were standing around the entrance to the community centre.

They'd already set aside the tributes to Ruben, piling the flowers and cards and teddy bears into one messy heap some feet away. Now one of their number who was close to the door and holding something red pulled back both arms before thrusting them forward and against the door. There was a bang followed by a series of other bangs as he used what she now realised must be a battering ram to break the door down. And he wasn't the only one: another policeman began pounding at the bricks that blocked access to the vacant building next door.

Ouch – she dropped the match as it burnt her finger. And saw she wasn't the only one to be watching. All over the Lovelace, lethargy was transmuted into action, with people hurrying down the gangways.

The door to the community centre caved in almost at the same time as the bricked-up building was breached. Police surged through both openings as the first of the Lovelace residents appeared at ground level.

Leading the charge was a young man who, fists raised, dreadlocks flying, was running at the police. A helicopter was buzzing low. So low Cathy thought it might be going to land inside the Lovelace. And then she saw something else: more policemen, ranks and ranks of them, who must have been waiting around both corners and who now snaked in from either end, blue helmets glinting as they converged in a pincer movement. The helicopter lifted up to pass through the murky sky before beginning its circled return just as a boot shot out in front of the running man and tripped him up. He flew forward, sprawling down. Which is all they saw of him for a while, as a clutch of policemen had soon surrounded him while the rest formed a line, waiting for the next of the Lovelace runners.

7.45 p.m.
As Joshua made his way towards the control room, he heard the sounds of a commotion. He quickened his pace. Other officers, in uniform and plain clothes, and clerks were already crowding the doorway.

They were so busy trying to see what was going on, they didn't register his approach. He took hold of the shoulders of the two at the rear and hauled them backwards. That made a space big enough for him to pass through, which widened when the others saw that it was him.

'Ah, there you are, sir.' This from Anil Chahda. 'I was just coming to fetch you. There's been another flare-up in Rockham.'

The biggest screen in the room was running a loop that must have been taken from one of the Air Support Units. A huge concentration of riot officers, who by their helmets' MP codes 01 and 02 were members of the Met, had formed a double line, while a further line was advancing, batons flailing, to push a crowd away. No need to ask where and when: someone had punched that information onto the screen.

A near riot – this one before night had even fallen. 'Is it still ongoing?'

'No, sir. They managed to disperse the crowd.'

Thank Christ for that. 'How did it start?'

'We thought our suspect might be hiding in the community centre. When our officers tried to gain access, the crowd reacted. We had to send in reinforcements.'

'Why didn't they use a key?'

'They didn't have one, sir. The IPCC has one but they failed to return our calls. The only other person known to possess one was a Lovelace resident, name of Marcus Garcant, known to us. On being asked to produce the key, he swallowed it. We have him in custody. But it was the judgement of the officer on the ground that she couldn't waste further time by waiting for the key to come out the other end.'

Marcus Garcant: he'd read that name. Community leader. Anti-police but well loved in Rockham. Was Chahda trying to provoke more trouble? 'What have you charged Garcant with?'

'We're holding him under suspicion of riotous assembly.'

'Any evidence of that?'

'Not so far, sir. But reports are that Garcant was everywhere on the first night. We've got a lot of CCTV footage to get through. We'll find him on it eventually.'

'Release him.'

A flaring in Chahda's eyes. Was he going to refuse?

Bring it on, Joshua thought, bring it on. 'And get somebody to apologise for the inconvenience.'

'If you say so, sir,' came Chahda's reply.

'I do say so. They're angry enough in Rockham without us picking on their leaders.'

They were looping the same footage, so when he looked over Chahda's head, he was in time to see again the flash of light against the dipping score of police helmets. The loop seemed to be passing at double speed; soon he saw that raising of police arms. 'Did we at least find our man?'

'I'm afraid not, sir.'

So the people of Rockham, who already had a grievance against the police, had witnessed such heavy-handed tactics and all with no result.

'What's the latest intel on the availability of guns in the area?'

'A small group of gang leaders are known to carry them, sir. We've picked them up as a precaution.'

More doors kicked in. In this case necessary, but still: 'We're going to have to pour full resources into the Lovelace tonight,' which meant that the rest of London would then be starved of them. 'Contact the

TFC with a view to having some armed officers in reserve. Just in case.'

'Already set in motion, sir.'

There was something menacing in this man despite his efficiency.

As soon as this emergency was over, Joshua was going to seriously consider getting rid of him. 'If this latest hits the Twitter-sphere, we'll be in for a rocky night. Issue an order city-wide and make sure it is properly distributed. Our aim is, and must be, to contain the trouble and not to stoke it up. No water cannon, no tear gas. Not without my express permission.'

'Yes, sir. Anything else?'

'Not at this moment. The Home Secretary asked to be kept in touch with developments. I'll ring and let him know about this.'

And after that, he thought, I had better go and see a man about a Molotov.

8 p.m.

'I see, Commissioner.' Peter glanced at Patricia, who was listening on another receiver and writing down every word. 'What happened to provoke it?'

As Commissioner Yares tediously went into the details behind this latest Rockham flare-up, Peter heard his mobile ringing. It was Frances's ringtone.

She had, he now remembered, previously called the office and asked that he call her back. 'Get that, will you,' he mouthed at Patricia, who, bless her, stretched out for his mobile and spoke softly into it while continuing to note down what Joshua Yares was saying. Which at long last came to an end.

'Thank you for keeping me informed, Commissioner. I trust your news, when we next speak, will be more positive.' Peter hung up. 'The man's a peacock. All that glamour display of his about policing by consent just hides that he is too lily-livered to stop trouble in its tracks. And now his men provoke a riot before it's even dark – and all for no reason that I can comprehend. He yawned and thought, if he had his way, Yares would soon be gone. 'What did Frances want?'

'All she would say was that it was urgent and that you need to come home.'

Could something have happened to Charlie? 'You sure she didn't say anything else?'

'Only that you should come home.'

Couldn't be Charlie, then.

'Do you want me to call her and tell her when you'll be able to?'

'Yes.' And then, 'No. On second thoughts, I better make the call myself. Hand me my mobile, will you?'

She gave it to him and, saying 'I'll fetch some more ice', left the room.

For which he was grateful, it being easier to talk to Frances when he was on his own.

He dialled her phone. Engaged. He tried the home number. It rang and rang but nobody picked up. She must be busy on the mobile.

He'd try again in a few minutes; in the meantime, preparing for the impending interview had taken so much time, he now had an enormous amount to get through.

8.50 p.m.

The estate was quiet. Much quieter than she had ever heard it, especially so early in the night. Not that it was empty. If she stood on the balcony and looked down, she could see, through the fading light, knots of people gathered all around.

They weren't Lovelace residents; they were the police.

A group of them were guarding the community centre: as if it was the people of Rockham, rather than their own colleagues, who had broken into it. Another group was watching as a workman bricked up the building next door. And there were more as well, strolling about, not in the usual twos but in groups of five or six. Which didn't count the ones who were sitting, she'd heard, in the vans around the corner. Waiting. For something that, by the sounds of a burst of laughter that reached her ears, they might quite enjoy.

9 p.m.

Head down, knowing that it would soon be time to leave, Peter kept ploughing through his piles of paperwork.

He had tried Frances three or four times, but each time it had gone straight to answerphone. Couldn't be that urgent or else she would have found a way to get in touch. When she switched her phone back on, she would see how many times he'd tried to reach her. Still, a vague worry lurked, and it prompted him to bring to the surface other odd things he'd recently observed. The way he'd caught her frowning, for example, just the other morning, when she thought he wasn't looking, or the uncharacteristic recent lapses in her concentration. Not like her – she was usually so on the ball.

She couldn't know, could she?

No, of course she couldn't. Of course she didn't.

He picked up the mobile and tried again. Again without result.

Time for him to go and do the first of what would probably turn out to be a round of interviews. He packed papers into his box – he'd have to read them in the car – and yawned. He wasn't tired; he was nervous. Not about speaking to the press per se, but for this one interview that might turn out to be the most important of his life. He yawned again.

His mobile vibrated. A text.

From Frances and it read: 'Come home.'

He dialled her mobile.

Straight to answerphone. Odd.

Another buzz. Another text: 'Come home.'

What was she playing at?

He texted – he hated the form, made him feel so clumsy: 'Am on the ten. See you after.'

To which he got an immediate response: 'Come home. Now. Or else.'

9.25 p.m.

Or else what, he wondered, as they drew up outside the house.

'Wait here,' he said to Patricia. 'I won't be long.'

She nodded. 'You're all right. We can reach the studio in fifteen.'

Fifteen minutes should do it. Whatever *it* was. He stepped out of the car and stood a moment, looking around.

Night had finally covered an outlandish dusk, and now his street was dark and quiet, with only an occasional glimmer of light peaking through drawn curtains. As he walked towards his house, the shadows of trees loomed large. Despite an absence of wind, they seemed to be leaning in on him. Something not right: he could feel it. He looked at his house. It was dark.

As soon as he slipped his key into the lock, Patsy started barking and when he opened up, she kept on. 'Out of my way.' He pushed her with his foot. This stopped her noise, although she persisted in sniffing at him as if he were a stranger. He called out, 'Darling?'

No answer. He clicked on the hall light.

The door to the living room was open. He switched on the light. The room, he saw, was empty. Perhaps the snug? He walked to the end of the hall and opened the door to her snug: 'Darling?' It too was quiet and dark. Through the window he could see the outline of unmoving shrubs. She wasn't in the garden. Not that he could see.

Upstairs then. He mounted the stairs. 'Hello? Frances? Where have you got to, darling?'

She wasn't in the bedroom. Or in any of the other rooms. She couldn't have gone out: if she had, one of their guards would have mentioned it. He had switched on every light he passed so that the house was now ablaze. He glanced at his watch. Seven minutes gone.

The only room he hadn't tried was the kitchen, because he had seen that it, too, was dark. Now he made his way back downstairs. She wasn't in the kitchen – of course she wasn't – but the door to the garden was open. He moved, in darkness, only to trip over something that turned out to be the dog. It yelped and got up. He could see its baleful yellow eyes staring up at him. 'Why are you always in the way?'

'She's only ever in your way. She doesn't like you.'

He whirled round to find Frances seated at the table.

'What are you doing in the dark?'

'Thinking.' She sounded eerily calm.

'You didn't fancy the garden?'

'It's no cooler there. And the air stinks of pollution.'

Something in her tone. 'Are you all right, darling?'

'You tell me.'

'I'm due to be interviewed on the ten,' he said. 'In fact,' a quick glance at his watch, 'I need to go.'

'If that's what you want to do, then go.' She sounded sweet. As sweet as toothache. 'But if you do,' she said, 'don't bother coming back.'

She knows, he thought. 'What's this all about?'

'About?' Not only calm but almost serene as she picked up her phone and held it up. 'It's about this.'

She made no move to bring it to him, so, heart hammering, he went to her. When he took the phone, his fingers brushed hers. After she let go, he saw her wipe those fingers down her skirt. She does know, he thought. He glanced at the phone.

He was looking at a photo of him and Patricia.

'Where did you get this?'

'It was texted to my phone. Number Unknown. Signed "A Friend". Clearly no friend of yours.'

He looked again. They were only standing together on a pavement. Side by side, yes, but they could have been talking business. 'I see,' he said. 'And?'

'Scroll on.'

More of them, then. He swiped across the screen. It went black. 'It's gone.'

'Oh, for God's sake, Peter.' She snatched the phone back. 'Can't you do anything for yourself?' She pushed a few buttons and then, without yielding it to him, began to swipe through a series of photographs.

It was like watching his own execution, these pictures flicking past at Frances's command. He saw him and Patricia laughing. Him and Patricia, arms swinging as they walked through an entrance. The back of him and Patricia, his arm now going up as if to put it round her. The two of them standing close, his arm around hers as he said something in her ear.

He couldn't breathe. But had to.

He breathed.

He had imagined this, of course he had, but this was nothing like he had imagined it would be. That had involved his telling one or the other that it was over. When he had made up his mind. This fright was something other. A frozen thing that kept him from figuring out what he was going to say.

Buy time, he told himself, buy time. 'What is it that you think is going on here?' Wondering, could she have more? More intimate than this?

'What I know is going on here,' Frances scrolled back to the first of the photos, 'is . . .' she separated her fingers to magnify the first of the images before moving it down so he could see the name of the hotel that he and Patricia had last been in '. . . you and your mistress strolling side by side into a posh fuck-pad.'

The swear word was so out of place, coming as it did from her genteel mouth, he almost smiled. 'She's not my mistress.' If she had more incriminating photos, she would surely have said so. 'And it's not a fuck-pad. It's a respectable hotel.'

'You haven't forgotten, have you, Peter darling, that my father made me an expert at this sort of thing?'

She wasn't calm, he realised; she was enraged. He could feel it radiating off her as heat.

Her fury that theoretically should frighten him was having the opposite effect of making her seem strangely attractive. He pushed that to one side to say, 'I am not your father. And, yes, as you can see, we were walking into a hotel. And, yes, we were discussing something confidential. No reason to leap to a filthy conclusion.'

'Just discussing? So where are your bodyguards?'

Not the time to tell her how splendid she looked. But he had to say something. Lie, he told himself, while sticking closely to the truth. Or at least as close to the truth as was possible. 'If you must know,' he said, 'I was meeting Chahda.'

'Who?'

'Anil Chahda. Deputy Commissioner of the Metropolitan Police Service. I was trying to get him to dish the dirt on his boss. That's why I asked my protective officers to stay back. Couldn't have them knowing what I was up to.'

She blinked. A chink in her composure. He must capitalise on it.

'I'm convinced that the PM's great saint of a Commissioner has been a naughty boy,' he said. 'And that Chahda's on the brink of spilling the beans.'

At which point, and he didn't know whether to be relieved or angry, the doorbell rang.

He glanced at his watch. Shit. It would soon be ten. 'I'm sorry, darling.' The news would just have to push him back. 'I must go and tell them . . .' he was already on his way, striding down the corridor and wrenching open the door.

Patricia. It would be her, wouldn't it? Coming to get him. When he had expressly instructed her to wait for him in the car.

'I'm busy,' he said.

'We just got a message from Number 10. The PM's back. And he's going to do the news.'

All he needed.

'Not now,' he said. 'I'm busy.' And shut the door in her face.

10.20 p.m.

Wires snaked past Joshua's polished shoes as he stood behind a hardboard panel that hid him from the cameras. From this place, even though he could clearly hear what was being said, his only vision was via a tiny monitor over which a man with earphones and a clipboard was coiled.

He could have sat out the PM's interview from the comfort of the Green Room. He had started there. But as word spread through the building, he was inundated by producers of increasing seniority, all of them trying to persuade him to appear on their programmes. Even here, inside the studio, someone had sidled up to whisper in his ear that he was the man of the hour and that the nation needed to hear what he had to say. Next time I come, he thought, as he tried to sugar his refusal with a smile, I'm going to bring a bodyguard.

He concentrated on listening to the PM, who, without hesitation or the slightest raising of his voice, dismissed the suggestion that he had disappeared just as England started to burn, slapping his interviewer down pleasantly enough by outlining the success of the negotiations that would lead to the creation of a slew of new British jobs. Then to the riots, where he mixed grave concern at what had happened – and what was happening (they were playing the footage behind him) – with a vow to show no mercy to the malfeasants.

It was a good performance. While Whiteley's pugnaciousness seemed to hint at insecurity, the PM oozed unwavering self-assurance. A difference in class confidence, Joshua wondered, or was Whiteley just more duplicitous than your average politician?

The interview was drawing to a close. On the monitor, Joshua could see that the pictures of people gathering that night had been replaced by one huge still of Molotov Man. Perhaps the PM had asked for this. Now he turned and pointed at the picture. 'Make no mistake,' he said. 'We will find this man. And we will punish him.'

10.25 p.m.
'He did well,' Peter said, as the newsreader moved on to describe the latest disturbances in a score of city streets. 'Sounded convincing.'

'It's what he's good at.' Frances used the remote to kill the sound. 'It's how he got the top spot.'

Was this a dig? He looked at her – a quick glance so she wouldn't catch him looking.

Despite that she'd said she believed him, she was still sitting at the other end of the sofa, as far away from him as she could get. But then, he thought, they often sat like this, and at this moment she was bound to be shaken up by the shock delivered to her by whatever bastard had sent those photographs. And listen to how calm she sounded as she said, 'Easy enough to feign confidence when he's only just come on the scene. But if they don't stop the rioting, and by the looks of it they won't, he'll start seeming much less credible. Fortunate, really, for you that he decided to come back.'

She couldn't be so calm, could she, or have this conversation, if she thought he was lying?

'We're going to be all right,' she said.

The 'we' confirmed it. She did believe him.

It was over. And soon – and thinking that she had never looked as attractive as she did now – he'd make sure it was properly over.

He shifted along the sofa, at the same time stretching one arm across its back.

She rested her head on his arm, briefly, before yawning and straightening up. 'I'm going to call it a day.'

The dog, who'd been sleeping at her feet, also sprang to its feet. If he were to rise now, it was bound to bark at him.

'Some things I need to work on,' he said.

'Of course.' Another smile. 'Come up when you're done.' Passing him, she reached out a hand and ruffled his hair. 'Goodnight,' she yawned again, and then, dog close at heel, she left.

Leaving him alone to breathe out the relief he felt.

10.27 p.m.

'All quiet in Rockham,' Billy heard over the radio that linked him to Silver.

And, yes, he thought, bet it bloody well is quiet there, what with half of the Met having a knees-up on the streets. What they were doing there was not his to ask; he couldn't help wondering, though, when, heading off to this front line, he saw a gang of them having a brew-up in lieu of anything more pressing to do. They'd offered him a cup and he'd been tempted, but then Silver had told him to hurry because all hell was breaking loose in an adjacent borough.

'Duck.'

He ducked without thinking, as he had been doing, he felt, for days, for weeks, for his whole life almost.

That cry again: 'Duck,' and the thud of something soft landing on the line of shields.

This lot they were facing were throwing sanitary towels covered in ketchup, both of which they'd probably just looted. Taking the piss. What had started in Rockham as a serious protest had turned into a vicious carnival of the unfunny. There'd even been racist attacks, he'd heard, under the guise of a reaction to the death of a man that most of the newcomers to the disturbances hadn't known and didn't care about.

'Duck,' he heard.

What else could he do? He ducked.

10.30 p.m.

The PM plucked off his microphone and handed it over as he said, to Joshua, 'What provoked the second Rockham incident?'

'Someone they were searching for.'

The PM made a tutting sound. 'Not my place to interfere, but you do understand, don't you, that your job is to get control of the streets, not to stir it up? If that means taking up the suggestions Peter made . . .'

Peter, was it? Not Home Secretary, or that arsehole who's after my job, but Peter.

'. . . then I suggest you give them every consideration. It's up to you, of course. You're my choice as Commissioner, and I'll back you all the way. But we can't have anarchy, especially with the economy in such a fragile state.' He glanced ahead to where one of his men was tapping his watch. 'If that's all . . .'

'There is something else, Prime Minister. I need to tell you something.' Seeing the man with the microphone still hovering: 'For your ears only.'

Another tut. 'I have to get this slap off. Come with me to the make-up room.'

He strode away with Joshua following. Once in the room he asked for privacy. He grabbed a bunch of tissues onto which he slathered cold cream and began wiping the heavy layer of slap from his forehead and his cheeks. 'What's so urgent?'

'It's Molotov Man.'

'You've picked him up, have you? Now that is good news.'

'We haven't picked him up, Prime Minister. Not yet. Although we are pulling out all the stops.'

'Keep pulling them. The sooner you find him, and the sooner you lock him up – or, even better, put him on a public pillory, which is what the tabloids are after – the better.' Having wiped away the thick layer they'd used to cover up the sun damage on the right side of his face, the PM began to work on the left.

'But we have a problem, Prime Minister. Banji, the name by which this man is known in Rockham, is his cover—'

'His cover?' The PM used the mirror to fix Joshua with a stare.

'Afraid so. His real name is Julius Jibola.'

The Prime Minister let the tissues fall and turned to look at Joshua. 'Are you saying what I think you're saying?'

'I am, Prime Minister. Molotov Man, aka Banji, real name Julius Jibola, is one of our undercovers. And he's missing.'

Tuesday

STRICTLY PRIVATE AND CONFIDENTIAL

Submission to the internal inquiry of the Metropolitan Police into Operation Bedrock pertaining to the Rockham disturbances and related matters

Submission OB/MPS/CC/28

To: The Office of the Inquiry into Operation Bedrock

From: The Office of the Commissioner of the Metropolitan Police Service

The chairman of the inquiry into Operation Bedrock requested the minutes of a meeting concerning DC Julius Jibola that took place at the Office of the Commissioner of the Metropolitan Police on ███████████████

On investigation, no minutes were found, nor any summary of the discussion. Both the then Commissioner and the then Deputy Commissioner have confirmed that there was no minute-taker present.

On further investigation, the diaries of both men confirmed the meeting as having commenced at 7 a.m. The logbook of the staff of the Commissioner recorded those present as:

Metropolitan Police Commissioner Joshua Yares, chairing.

Deputy Commissioner Anil Chahda, also present as Acting Head of SO15.

Detective Chief Inspector Derek Blackstone, in command of the formerly named National Domestic Extremism and Disorder Intelligence Unit, NDEDIU.

Chief Superintendent Gaby Wright, acting officer in command of Rockham.

There are no available notes from any of the participants on the discussion points of the meeting.

7.05 a.m.

CS Gaby Wright was on her feet in front of a screen and now, at a nod from Joshua, she clicked the mouse to produce a blurred black and white image. 'This is the reception room of the Rockham nick, two days ago at 13.55. This,' she pointed at the screen, 'is the man we now know to be DC Julius Jibola.' Another click and the man began moving towards a glassed-in desk. He was clearly speaking, although the picture was mute.

'Turn the sound on.'

'I can't.' A quick curt smile. 'The recording facilities malfunctioned and with the station besieged it wasn't safe to bring in anybody to fix the problem. We have picture but no sound.'

The man's mouth was open, his hands moving in wild gesticulations.

'Did the desk sergeant at least take down what he was saying?'

'I'm afraid not, sir. The station was hard-pressed with people either reporting damage to property or enquiring about missing relatives. All other active officers being out on patrol, or guarding the exterior of the station, the desk sergeant had little support.' She pointed at the screen where the man, still talking, had stopped some feet away from the desk. 'Jibola anyway never reached the desk.'

'He looks angry.'

'Angry and also, according to the desk sergeant, largely incoherent. From drink, the sergeant assumed. He was raving about a murder, which my sergeant only later pieced together must have been a reference to the unfortunate death in the Lovelace community centre. As you can see,' the pointer indicated a line of people, 'there was a queue. When Jibola was told he'd have to wait his turn, he threatened to access the interior of the station by barging through the security doors. The sergeant said that in that case he would have Jibola arrested. Jibola's response was to exit the police station.' She fast-forwarded to the man turning and walking out. 'Assuming he was just another drunk, and with no support, the desk sergeant let him go. He was later caught on CCTV heading south-west away from Rockham High Street.'

'Hold on a minute.' It was all Joshua could do not to let his jaw rest where it had dropped. 'Are you telling me that one of our own entered your station with the intention of reporting an incident in which your officers had been involved, an incident that ended in the death of a member of the public, and your desk sergeant failed either to take a statement or refer him to you?'

'Unfortunate, I grant you.' Another one of those quick smiles.

'Unfortunate?' He was going to wipe that smile off her face. Preferably after he'd ripped the insignia from her neatly turned-out uniform. 'It's not unfortunate; it's disastrous. Especially when we know that DC Jibola was telling the truth about having been at the community centre. And this we know because, as you have just informed us, he was handcuffed after remonstrating with your officers, before being let go with a caution. But when he comes into your station with the clear intention of reporting what he saw, your desk sergeant first ignores him and then threatens him with arrest.'

What a catalogue of incompetence, and all in his first week.

'It beggars belief.'

Out of the corner of his eye, he could see Chahda leaning forward as if about to leap to Gaby Wright's defence. Do it, he thought, I dare you. And then I'll have you, too.

'Do you have any idea what this is going to look like if it gets out?'

'I know what it looks like, sir.' An unruffled Gaby Wright now demonstrated how capable she was of defending herself. 'But it isn't like that. There was no earthly way that the desk sergeant, a capable and experienced officer, could have guessed that a man he had never met, or heard about, and who was behaving in an erratic and threatening manner, was one of ours. If he had known, he would have acted differently. But he didn't know. None of us did.' Another of those humourless smiles.

'Okay.' Joshua breathed in and on the out-breath said, 'Let's move on. How close are you to finding Jibola?'

'We've got nothing concrete, sir, at least thus far. We searched the rooms he was renting. They were bare: no trace that he'd ever even been there. We're continuing to search the Lovelace, and we're also doing a sweep of the empty buildings by the canal. If we don't find him in any of these locations, we may have to conclude that he has left Rockham.'

Thus shifting the problem off her patch. Joshua glanced down at Jibola's file. 'This woman,' pointing at a photograph, 'Cathy Mason. Might she know where he is?'

'I talked to her at some length, sir, and I don't think that she does. She's a credible witness who said that DC Jibola, who she knows only as Banji, had recently turned nasty. Apparently he hit her. She was so upset she burnt everything she'd ever had from him. He appears to have successfully hidden his true identity and his position as a police officer – she still thinks he's a van driver. She never visited his rooms and didn't know where they were.'

'A Molotov-throwing undercover agent who manages to maintain cover. Wonders will never cease.'

'If you say so, sir.' Another quick tweak up of those red lips. 'But while I believe Mrs Mason to have been telling the truth, and that Jibola has successfully kept her in the dark, I suspect her daughter, Lyndall, of knowing something. Perhaps even Jibola's whereabouts. Take a look at this.'

Another click of her mouse, another black and white image. 'This was captured yesterday at 10.51 a.m. by fixed CCTV camera 4947, which is on the southernmost corner of Rockham High Street at the intersection with Berkshire Road. This,' she set the picture moving and pointed at a young woman walking away from the camera, 'we believe to be Lyndall Mason. She progressed along Rockham High Street to be captured on CCTV here,' she fast-forwarded before pausing the footage, 'here,' and then again, 'here. As you can see, in two of these three moments she is looking around, which could indicate that she is checking to see that she is not being followed.' She set the images rolling again. 'At 11.03, Lyndall Mason was caught on CCTV turning the corner here,' another click, 'into Pringle's Yard, a dead end with no operational surveillance cameras.'

'DC Jibola would have had good knowledge of any visual black spots in the area.' This from Anil Chahda.

'We assume so. And now if I fast-forward,' another series of rapid mouse movements brought up a succession of CCTV photographs, 'these were taken by the same camera at the intersection of Pringle's Yard and Rockham High Street over a period of thirty minutes. You will see from the timeline that runs under them that Lyndall Mason did not come out of Pringle's Yard. The first CCTV re-sighting of her was over forty-three minutes later, here,' a still of the figure walking towards the camera, 'on Rockham High Street at 11.47, shortly before she arrived back in the Lovelace, where I was speaking with her mother. Scrutiny of CCTV cameras in the area yielded no further information on her route. She must have circled round to the High Street avoiding all the cameras.'

'So what was she up to?'

'That's what we wanted to know, and so early this morning,' she closed down the screen and replaced it with another on which was a fresh picture of the deserted dead end, 'I sent an officer to examine Pringle's Yard. As you can see, one end of the yard, here, appears to be blocked by a substantial fence. On closer examination, however, my officer detected an unevenness in the fence poles.' She tapped her laptop and the image was magnified. 'This pole, here, has been worked free of its top mooring. It can be pushed aside to create a space wide enough for a slim figure to squeeze through. We can't prove that this is what Lyndall Mason did, but there is one further piece of available evidence,' another click, which brought up an aerial photograph of what looked like wasteland, bordered in the distance by a canal. 'This was captured by India 95 during routine surveillance. It shows the area beyond Pringle's Yard. We think that this,' she pointed at the screen, at a distant dot which, when she enlarged it, might have been a person, 'is Lyndall Mason. The times fit. And if you look at her right-hand side, you will see that this young woman appears to be carrying something, just as Lyndall Mason was.' More clicks and they were back to the CCTV where a plastic carrier bag was hooked over the girl's right arm. 'If it is Lyndall Mason, she was heading for the canal. This is why we've expanded our search to include the buildings, some of them abandoned, that line its banks.'

'Why don't you just ask the girl where she went?' This from Chahda, a question that earned him a quick glance that looked close to a rebuke, and when Gaby Wright said, 'I did start to question her,' her smile was undeniably chilly, 'but her mother would not allow me to continue. Lyndall Mason is a minor. Given DC Jibola's relationship with Mrs Mason, I thought it better not to push it. Not until I had taken advice.'

DCI Blackstone, a big man and overweight, who'd been slumped back in his chair as if none of this had anything to do with him, now sat bolt upright. 'It's not possible, is it, that DC Jibola is Lyndall Mason's father?'

'It is possible, yes. The dates of the first liaison between Cathy Mason and DC Jibola make it so. But when I asked Mrs Mason, she denied it.'

'Thank fuck for small mercies.'

'As an extra precaution, we obtained sight of Lyndall Mason's birth certificate,' Gaby Wright said. 'The mother is given as Cathy Mason. There is no mention of any father. But I still think the girl knows something.'

'Then pull her in.' Again roughly from Anil Chahda, which earned him another sharp look.

Gaby Wright kept her eyes focused on Joshua rather than his deputy. 'Can do, sir. If you think that's what I should do?'

'Hmm.' Hers was a careful move that made him responsible for any mistake. 'Leave the girl alone,' he said. 'At least for the time being,' ignoring Chahda's grimace to get to his feet. 'Thank you, CS Wright. You must be anxious to get back to your beat. Let me show you to the lift.' And then to the two men: 'Wait here for me, will you?'

7.20 a.m.

Peter hefted the tray onto his wife's bedside table. 'Here you are, darling.'

Frances surveyed the orange juice he had freshly squeezed, the two boiled eggs (three and a half perfect minutes), the sourdough toast and a pot of tea – strong, as she liked it. 'My, you have gone to town.' She picked up the glass and took a tiny sip of juice before putting it back on the tray. 'Pity I'm not that hungry.'

'Thought you'd be ravenous.'

She broke off a bit of toast and fed it to the dog, which was lying beside her on the bed. 'How so?'

'Well, you know, after last night.' As soon as he said it, he knew he shouldn't have, this realisation confirmed by the onset of her deep frown.

Stupid of him. He must take it slower. Be more mindful of her feelings. She was bound to be bruised, if not by his behaviour – her performance in bed showed that she had believed him – then by the fact that someone had been malicious enough to send those pictures. He leant across to kiss her, lightly, on the lips. 'Can I get you anything else, darling?'

'No, thank you.' A pause and then, 'Did someone ring while you were downstairs?'

'Yes.' So she was still a bit suspicious. 'The PM did. He wanted to thank me for being – how did he put it? – oh yes, a proficient caretaker while he'd been tied up in the negotiations. He said he was going to take over the chairing of COBRA and that I, of course, am welcome to attend.' And then, seeing Frances laughing: 'What's so funny?'

'Oh, you know.' She patted the dog's silky head.

'Not sure that I do.'

'I was just thinking that you politicians are a bit like dogs.' She puckered her lips to bless the dog's head with a kiss. 'Especially of the male variety.' Which she followed by more butterfly kisses. 'Aren't they, Patsy-watsy?'

'Frances!'

Frances lifted her head. 'The PM was leaving his scent on your patch.'

Something rather gleeful in the way she delivered this sentence. He almost called her on it but then, seeing her smile turn to a frown, and recognising this to be her thinking frown, he held his tongue. And held it some more as she continued to be lost in thought.

There followed an extended silence through which he could hear the tick of his bedside alarm and the soft snuffling of the dog, who settled herself in Frances's lap and went back to sleep.

Tick, tick.

He looked down at his bare feet.

Thought, soon time to cut my toenails again.

He looked up again and at his wife. The straps of her cream negligee had slipped off one shoulder to expose that paler cream of her breast.

Tick, tick.

He contemplated stretching out to slip the strap off the other shoulder, but he knew better than to dare, especially when she was thinking.

Tick, tick.

And then, at long last, her gaze came back into focus.

'The PM thinks,' she said, 'or at least wants you to think, that it's still all to play for. We know he's a weak leader at the best of times, and that these aren't the best of times. He's likely to handle the situation badly. But if by some miracle the riots help rather than harm him, you're going to have to up your game. You've not got much time left: the Party will never countenance a new leader too close to the election. We need a plan of attack.' She hiked the strap of her negligee into place. 'You've already gone a long way to convincing the public that police failures helped stoke the disturbances. Your best bet is to continue to hit the PM's Commissioner. Chahda's the key: by promising him the top job, you've got him on side. But it's not enough for him to hint that he has the ammunition to topple Yares. You need to find out what it is.'

'He's so cautious. He told us about the misconduct of the Rockham police, but that's a matter of record. I bet there's something else – I know there is. What I don't know is how I am ever going to get him to spill the beans.'

'Well,' she shrugged, 'either you've got to be more persuasive. Or' – a beat – 'you will have to trap him into telling you what he knows.'

'Trap him? How?'

'He has a reputation as a lady's man. Why not exploit that?' Another drawn-out pause and then, 'Patricia's charming, isn't she? And from what I've seen of her, I reckon she's game. Why not set her on Chahda?'

7.35 a.m.

As Joshua opened the door, the two men's heads sprang apart.

Probably getting their story right, he thought, and said, 'Sorry to have kept you waiting. I had to take a call from Number 10.' He went to join them at the table. 'The PM has now had time to consider his response. In light of the likely danger to DC Jibola's person should it be made public that he is a serving police officer, the Prime Minister has agreed, reluctantly, to keep the information under wraps. No one else is to be told, at least until we locate Jibola and find out what the hell he's up to.' He opened up Jibola's file. 'What was he doing in Rockham anyway? It doesn't say.'

'That's a bit of a puzzle, sir.' As big as he was, DCI Blackstone gave every appearance of wanting to dissolve into the wood of the conference table.

'Which I need you to untangle. Now, if you wouldn't mind.'

'I'll do my best, sir.' Blackstone took in a deep breath, sucking in his stomach. 'As you know, Jibola's file had been mistakenly put in the pile for destruction. As soon as we rescued it, I followed the thread of his Rockham-related history. It appears that the former commander in charge of Rockham, CS Wright's predecessor, requested assistance with a particularly violent gang in north Rockham a couple of months ago. Jibola was seconded to this task. It was a short operation at the conclusion of which Jibola would normally have been posted elsewhere. But my predecessor, in consultation with MI5, decided that there was a case for further surveillance of the community in Rockham and specifically around the Lovelace.' A deep breath in and then: 'In light of the imminent demolition of the estate, several vacant units were given over by the council as temporary accommodation to new immigrants, many of whom originated in the Horn of Africa. It was my predecessor's opinion that because of the hold that al-Queda-affiliated groups have in some of these countries, particularly Somalia, these newcomers warranted further scrutiny. DC Jibola was tasked, by my predecessor, with establishing himself in south Rockham and getting to know this community.'

'I see.' What he really saw was that, by emphasising Rockham's previous Commander, and his own predecessor, Blackstone was making sure to slough off responsibility for what had happened. And he would get away with it because he was relatively new in the job and everybody knew that the last regime had overseen an absolute fuck-up in all departments but especially in his. Cleaning these particular stables was in fact a central part of Joshua's brief – and the reason that the PM had championed him in preference to Anil Chahda – and it was clearly going to be difficult. After a decade of lethal exposures about the misdeeds of their undercover ops, SO15 had been buffeted by such a multiplicity of root-and-branch changes it was a wonder the tree was still standing. By the time the merry-go-round had slowed sufficiently to let anybody new on, none of the previous senior management had managed to keep their seats. Which meant a loss of institutional memory. And a lack of anyone to blame.

Anyone, Joshua thought, except me. He glanced over to his desk, where the photograph of him beside the Queen stood in pride of place. If this isn't resolved and soon, he thought, I'll be packing it up and taking it home again.

'Did anybody keep an eye on Jibola? Anybody at all?'

'One of our operators did,' Blackstone said. 'He was supposed to ring in at set times, and he did so until recently. But then he stopped. When his operator tried to reach him, she couldn't. She tried to track his safe mobile, but it had gone off air. She assumed it was a system failure, a consequence of signal overload in Rockham due to the riots. If she'd been a trained officer, she might have raised the alarm earlier, but you know we have had to outsource technical jobs. We just don't have the quality of staff any more.'

And, yes, it was true what Blackstone was saying, but it was also true, as the PM had said the other night, that they had to stop blaming their failures on the cuts. 'You need do something about your scrutiny systems as a matter of urgency,' he said. 'But for the moment, let me sum up where we've got to.' He held up his right fist. 'One,' raising his thumb, 'one of your agents has gone rogue on British television. Two,' his index finger joined the thumb, pointing at Blackstone as if he were about to shoot him, 'having mislaid his file, you didn't even know he was in Rockham. Three,' he unfurled his middle finger, 'you have no idea where he's got to. Four,' he let go of the fourth finger, 'and five,' and his little finger, 'you don't know why he did what he did, or what he's planning to do next.' Hearing himself laying it out so baldly made him realise that, never mind having to take the picture home, if this wasn't resolved, he'd be the first Commissioner of the Met never to pick up a knighthood.

He bunched the fist again. 'And there is the not insignificant matter of Jibola's liaison with Cathy Mason waiting to blow up in our faces. How that could have been allowed is beyond my comprehension.'

'The deployment of undercover is inherently risky.' This from Chahda. 'Under RIPA . . .'

'Yes, Anil, thank you. Being familiar with the RIPA rules of engagement, I know all about the get-out clause of collateral intrusion. But the key word is 'proportionality'. This particular intrusion happened twice and over many years, which is neither necessary nor proportionate. Jibola should have been kept miles away from the Masons, not sent, unsupervised, back to Cathy Mason's bed.'

'This was Jibola's first mission in Rockham, sir,' Blackstone said. 'His meeting Mrs Mason must have either been an unfortunate coincidence or a manoeuvre by him.'

'Is it not your job to ensure that such coincidences or manoeuvres cannot occur?'

'Perhaps it is, sir, but the only way my predecessors could have known that Jibola had had a liaison with Cathy Mason is if he had informed them, which, it appears from the files, he did not.'

Joshua held up a hand to stop Blackstone from going on. 'I'm glad you mentioned the files,' he said, 'because they bring us to another astonishing oversight. Jibola's last meeting with a psychologist was more than two years ago. He should have been re-seen.'

'It happens,' DCI Blackstone said, 'especially when an officer is in the field.'

'Yes, it happens,' Joshua said. 'But it should not have happened to Jibola. The psychologist who last saw him said,' he leafed through the folder until he found the page he was looking for, 'and I quote: "*Although DC Jibola does did not want to be reassigned to a regular beat, it is my opinion that the man is not psychologically equipped to withstand the stresses of undercover work. If it is not possible to remove him, careful and regular scrutiny of his state of mind is advised.*" Which,' Joshua looked up, 'never happened. And please don't waste more of my time with tales of lost files and changing S015 command structures. It is your job to keep track of your files, just as it is your job to keep track of what your agents are up to.' He closed the file with a bang. 'CS Wright is doing her best to clear up this mess. If she needs more officers, give them to her. In the meantime, find out who in the force Jibola might have confided in. I suggest you start with his IC3 colleagues. Ask them what they know, but for God's sake keep a lid on this.' He pushed the file away in disgust. 'Jibola was once married. Has it occurred to you that his former wife might know something?'

'Should I interview her?'

'Thank you, DCI Blackstone, but . . .' thinking that he didn't want to hear about the failure of any more surveillance cameras or of files going missing, 'I'll see to it myself. I'll let you know what I find. Thank you, gentlemen.'

'But, sir?'

'Yes, Anil?'

'What about the girl?'

'What about her?'

'Wright should be tasked to pick her up. Squeeze out what she knows.'

'We can't start detaining minors on fishing expeditions.'

'From what I hear, police stations within a ten-mile radius of Rockham are overflowing with minors courtesy of Wright's snatch squads.'

'Wright is, if you forgive the pun, right. If the girl turns out to be Jibola's daughter, detaining her could look vindictive. Leave her alone. Do not attempt to dig up any dirt either on her or on her mother. If a future FOI request ever exposes that we spent public money investigating something as innocuous as who Lyndall Mason fancies on her Facebook page, or how many people liked Cathy Mason's tweeted cookery tips, heads will roll.'

9 a.m.

Heat blasted down, bouncing off the buildings, and especially any shiny surface, before rising back up from tarmac that these days had to be gritted to stop the roads from melting. Cathy fanned out her loose top, trying to cool herself but without result: the air was just too dry and too hot. But as she made her way round towards the front of the imposing Magistrates' Court she felt a drop of water landing on the back of her neck. And another, this time on her head.

Rain: what a relief. She looked up. Only to find that the sky was the same cloudless blue as it had been for days. For weeks. For getting on a month now. She sighed. The water must have dropped out of the air-conditioning unit in the wall above her. She moved out of range and around the corner, weaving past knots of people congregating outside the court. She went up the steps and through the revolving doors into a grand wood-lined entrance hall that was also heaving with people.

A voice saying, 'What are you?' sounded in her ear. She turned to see a man in a blue guard's uniform who, having sidled up to her, was waiting for her reply. When she didn't give him one, he repeated the question, 'What are you?' adding, when she still did not respond: 'Solicitor? Solicitor's Clerk? Accused? Relative? Journalist? Sightseer?'

'I'm looking for a probation officer I know.'

He grimaced. 'Good luck with that. Probations' rooms have been given over for solicitor interviews, so probation will be either in the holding cells, where you can't go, or they're in the magistrates' chambers, ditto as before, or in court. Try the courts. Solicitors might be able to point you in the right direction.' And then, as the revolving doors disgorged a fresh batch of newcomers: 'Bag on the conveyor, through the security arch. Courts One and Two up the stairs and to the left. Three and Four, same thing but to the right. All in session. Have been for the last forty-six hours,' he lifted a hand to wipe a brow beaded with sweat, 'and counting.'

She put her bag on the conveyor and stepped through the security arch. On the other side, a security guard asked her to open the bag, subjecting it to a quick rummage before dismissing her. She was still zipping the bag up when he added, 'Keep moving,' underlining the instruction by waving her on.

'Don't block the way. Keep moving.'

She pushed through the crowd and up the stairs.

Both courts to the left were full, but when she crossed the landing and opened the door to Court Four no one stopped her from going in.

The room at least was cool. And quiet save for the burbling air conditioner that was undercut by quiet sobs. She stood a moment, getting her bearings. She saw two young men seated in the wood-enclosed dock, both with their heads bowed. To the side and slightly in front of them was a raised table backed by the same dark wood panelling that lined the rest of the courtroom. Behind this table were three people locked in muted conversation. On a desk in front of them, and also facing into the room, was a lone man: must be the clerk of the court. Then there were a couple more tables, for lawyers she presumed – she'd have had to cross a rope to reach them – and after those, benches that must be for the public.

There was only one unoccupied seat in the public section. To reach it, Cathy had to push past the weeping woman. She sat down hurriedly beside her as the magistrate in the middle of the three turned to address the men in the dock.

'Hodan Sharif and Steven Chapman, you have pleaded guilty to burglary and handling stolen goods.' The magistrate looked across at the men, one of whom was gripping the wooden rail so tightly that the stretched skin of his knuckles was almost white. 'In deciding your sentences, we have given full credit for these guilty pleas and we have taken reports as to your circumstances into account. But, in reaching our decision, we have also paid heed to His Honour Judge George Mullholland's recent guidance when he said that in the face of civil disorder, the judiciary's job is to pass sentence on behalf of a justifiably terrified public. It is for this reason that, although we recognise the part that rehabilitation plays in any sentence, we have in your case placed emphasis on the need to punish and thus deter others from committing similar offences. Please rise.'

As the two got to their feet, the woman sobbed louder.

'Hodan Sharif,' the magistrate continued, 'you have pleaded guilty to the charge of handling stolen goods. Although you weren't amongst those who broke into the Carphone Warehouse, you said that as you were passing the premises one of the looters handed you two cases for the iPhone8 worth £34.99 each and asked you to keep them for him. You said that you took the cases as a favour and that you planned to hand them back later. When you were arrested, the cases were still in your possession. You are of good character, having no record of any previous offence. Yours is a tragic case in that your father is recently deceased and you have become the breadwinner for your mother and younger brother.'

The woman beside Cathy began to wail.

'In any other circumstance,' the magistrate raised her voice, 'you might have been eligible for a non-custodial sentence. But because you went, voluntarily, to the scene of great disorder and participated in a manner in which no law-abiding citizen would have, we hereby sentence you to six months' imprisonment.' And then, looking straight at the wailing woman, 'Madam, please.'

The woman was so lost in her grief that she didn't seem to register that the magistrate was addressing her.

'I can see how distressed you are,' the magistrate said. 'But you need to leave this court. If you don't, I will have to ask the usher to remove you.'

When the woman continued to wail, Cathy leant over to say into her ear, 'If you don't go, they'll drag you out.'

At which the woman seemed suddenly to snap to. She got up, pushed through to the end of the row and made her way to the door. There was an agonising silence, everybody watching while pretending not to.

When she got to the door, she stopped. She turned, slowly, to look at the dock. Tears to match hers were streaming silently down a face that was quite clearly her son's. The woman shook her head and left.

'Steven Chapman,' the magistrate said, 'you have been found guilty of the burglary of six mobile phones, an Android tablet, batteries, chargers and a USB cable to the value of £940. Your probation report indicates that your life has also not been without difficulty, and this has led you into crime. According to the report, you have recently shown a willingness to turn your life to better purpose by volunteering in a day facility for learning-disabled adults, something which we applaud. You have four previous convictions, three of which are more than five years old, so we will not consider them. Your latest conviction, however, was only two months ago when you were arrested for travelling on a bus without having paid the fare, a sign of your continuing refusal to obey the laws of the land. Given the seriousness of your offence, your previous convictions and the constraint on this court that prevents us from imposing sentences longer than six months, we are referring you up to the Crown Court for sentencing. You are remanded in custody until such time as a judge can consider your case.'

As the policeman behind the dock began to lead the two away, the magistrate glanced at her watch. 'We have been sitting since 5 a.m. This court is now adjourned. We'll resume at 11.15 a.m.'

9.30 a.m.
Patricia looked scrumptious, Peter thought. Like a sunbeam in her short orange skirt, a pair of strapped yellow sandals and a yellow top over which she had layered some kind of off-white chiffony affair. Watching her sashay over, he felt the regret of having to end it with her, even as he knew that this is what he had to do.

Not here, though. Not in the office. And not now either.

Soon.

She said, 'Sorry to bother you, Home Secretary,' his PPS being in the room, 'but the Home Affairs Select Committee has requested your presence this afternoon.'

'For what?'

'They want to ask you about a solvent factory. I assume it bears some relationship to your time in Environment.'

Solvent factory: it rang no bell other than as a recent potential flash-point in Rockham. But then Environment, his first step up the ministerial ladder before his meteoric rise, was political pre-history as far as he was concerned.

'I've called up the files so we can work out what it's about but, if you'd rather, I can tell them that you're tied up and will speak with them at a later date.'

He nodded. No reason for him to jump when the pompous arse of the select committee cracked the whip. 'What time are they sitting?' He glanced down at the list of his day's appointments.

'Two to four.'

Which, Patricia would also know, was scheduled for discussions with her. And there were things to talk about. As well as . . .

No. He must not think of that. He had made up his mind. It was over. Or would be when he told her.

'What should I tell them?'

Such short notice: he could easily cry off. But hold on a moment. Think hard. Even though he normally would have excused himself, he had to keep in mind that these were not normal times. He needed to demonstrate how cooperative he was. And he needed to be seen.

Should he phone Frances, he wondered, and ask her opinion – something that he would normally do.

The thought of lifting the phone and speaking to her seemed to weigh him down. No need, he told himself, to keep running back to Mummy. He would, and he did, make his own decisions. Which in this case was that, because his enemies might use a no-show to start a rumour that he had something to hide, he would attend. 'Fit them in at 3.30,' he told Patricia. 'That'll give us time to catch up on what they might want. And also on those other issues.'

9.35 a.m.

Although the sign said 'Cleaning Materials', Cathy's knock was met by an immediate 'Come in.'

She opened the door and stepped into what clearly was still a cupboard, except that someone had squeezed a desk and two chairs under a teetering shelf of cleaning materials and between pails and mops and brooms.

Gavin Jenkins was sitting behind this desk. As she squeezed her way in, he lifted his head to say 'Cathy?' He got up, hurriedly, and hit his head on the shelf above him. 'Damn. Every time.' He steadied the shelf with one hand, using the other to catch the bottle that came rolling off. 'My mother always said I'd come to a bad end, but even she wasn't witch enough to know that I'd end up being brained,' he glanced at the bottle, 'by bleach.' He put the bottle back on the shelf before squeezing around the desk and coming over to kiss her on the cheek. 'What brings you here?'

'Coffee.' She handed him the paper cup.

'You're a lifesaver.' He took off the lid and breathed in the aroma. 'And a genius.' He took a sip. 'It even tastes like coffee. Where did you find it?'

'A cafe a few blocks away. All the nearest had run out.'

'Some many hours ago.' He took another long swig. 'Caffs without coffee. Courts without justice. That's how it goes these days.' He gave a wry smile. 'Have a seat – take the client one, it's safer.' A quick glance at his watch. 'I'm due another in less than ten, but you can help balance my sanity by keeping me company until then.' He walked back behind the desk, ducking his head to avoid the shelf. 'Lyndall's not in trouble, is she?'

'Not her, no. But a friend of hers could be. A neighbour of ours, Jayden – I think you met him the last time you came to tea?'

'Thin, quiet, besotted by Lyndall?'

'That's the one. He went out on the first day of the Rockham riot and hasn't been home since. I asked at the police station and at various hospitals. It's like he's disappeared off the face of the earth.'

'How old is Jayden? Fourteen? fifteen? If he's under sixteen, they ought to have processed him at a young offender unit rather than at a police station, and if he was picked up on the first night there might still have been available space. I'm not surprised that you've lost him: it's chaos out there.'

'Not so orderly in here either.' Cathy pointed at the teetering piles of files beside his desk.

'It's a fucking nightmare, if you'll excuse my language. The private guys haven't got the stamina for this kind of work, and there's just not enough of us left in the state system. I'm fast-processing scores of kids from difficult backgrounds, kids with records, kids that just went mad for the first time in their lives, most of whom should get a community sentence. But the politicians have stoked up a lynch mob, and it's turned the magistrates jail crazy.'

'And here I am, giving you more work.'

His smile lit up his face. 'You know I'd do anything for you.'

Which was also part of the reason she had hesitated before asking for his help.

'Look,' another quick glance at his watch, 'if I take Jayden's details now, I'm bound to lose them. Email me his full name, address, date of birth, any previous record, last known sighting and I'll see if I can pull in some favours.'

'That would be great.' She got to her feet. 'Thank you, Gavin.'

'Anything. Especially after this coffee.' He took another long swig, smiling as he looked up at her. His smile faded. 'Are you okay?'

'Yes, I'm fine.' Even as she tried to return his smile, she found herself blindsided by misery that she tried to conceal behind a quick, 'I'll let you get back to work.'

'How's that man of yours?'

She was glad she had already turned away, so that all he would see was the tightening of her shoulders and all he would hear would be her one word, 'Gone.'

'Oh.' It didn't matter that he couldn't see her face. He knew her well enough to hear it in her voice. He got up, came behind her and, putting his hands on her shoulders, turned her round until she was facing him. 'I'm sorry.'

She nodded.

'I know how much he means to you.'

It was all she could do to nod again.

'What happened?'

She shrugged. That was the worst of it. That she didn't know. 'He's just so . . .' thinking then of the viciousness of Banji's blow and of his expression caught and endlessly repeated on screen, 'so angry.'

'Held in, I would have said.' A pause. 'But I'm sorry to hear it. You're a great woman. You deserve better.'

He pulled her closer, hugging her to him, and although her resolve had been not to lead him on, she didn't have the strength to resist. So good to be held. She could feel his hand resting lightly on her head, and she could feel the heat of him, and in that moment of utter stillness she could even hear the beating of his heart. He is so safe, she thought. And could once have been her long-term safety; he'd certainly offered that. Why couldn't she have settled for somebody as solid and as gentle as him?

'I'm such a fool.'

'Not a fool.' He continued stroking her hair. 'You're just a feeling person in an unfeeling world.' He seemed about to say something else when a rap on the door caused him to drop his hands and jump away. 'Sorry.'

'Don't be.' She leant over to kiss him lightly on the cheek. 'Thanks,

Gavin.' Then she turned and made her way out, squeezing past a young man on his way in.

'You know what, man,' she heard as she closed the door, 'you're a fucking cliché, doing it with your girlfriend in a cupboard.'

2.30 p.m.

(For this once) Peter stayed in bed as Patricia showered, then to watch (for this last time) as she got dressed.

She did so slowly and with a complete lack of self-consciousness – sitting, naked apart from her suspenders, on the edge of the chair opposite the bed and rolling up her stockings.

Remembering the falling strap of Frances's cream negligée, he found himself wondering what Patricia wore in bed when she was at home and alone. His guess would be pyjamas, although, on second thoughts, she probably slept in the buff, especially in this heat, as she always did with him. Not that he would (now) ever know.

She smiled. 'A penny for your thoughts.'

Tell her, he had to, *tell her now*, while what he actually heard himself saying was, 'Do you think there could be someone following you?'

'People are always following me.' Her smile got wider.

'I'm serious,' he said. 'Have you noticed anything different? Especially recently?'

'Why?' Her smile faded. 'What happened?'

'Frances was sent some photographs.'

'Photographs?' She was frowning as she reached for her bra. 'What kind of photographs?'

'Of us. Two days ago. Going into that hotel.'

'Just going in?' Her hands reached behind her back to snap the clasp with an ease that always amazed him. 'Or something more?'

'Nothing more, thank goodness.'

She got up. Walked over to her bag. Took out a fresh pair of knickers and put them on. 'Did she freak?'

A question that showed her age as well as how little she knew Frances.

'She was distressed,' he said, 'in her own way. But she calmed down when I filled her in on our meeting with Chahda.'

'You told her that we were there for Chahda, did you?'

221

'Well, it was true.'

'True?' She sighed. 'I guess if it's half-truths she's after, then it is true.' She had brought a fresh blouse as well, a red blouse, which she now unrolled and pulled over her head.

Only the orange skirt to go and then she would be completely ablaze.

'So do you think someone could have been following us?'

'Not that I noticed,' she said. 'Not then. Not since.' When she shook her head, the light seemed to flare yellow amongst the strands of her brown hair. 'Probably a coincidence – someone who happened to be passing, someone who doesn't particularly like you, who saw us together and decided to flip your wife out by snapping us on their phone.'

If only that were true.

'Couldn't have been more serious,' she said, 'or else they would have come in after us and got something more incriminating, wouldn't they?'

A good point: the photos were innocuous and vague enough. 'Still,' he said, 'it is worrying.'

'Poor Peter,' she said, 'so many things to worry about.' She smiled – she had such a lovely open smile – as she came over to the bed, there to stand gazing down on him.

He breathed in – *Tell her. And tell her now,* he had to, it was only fair – and on the out-breath said, 'Maybe we should cool it.'

'Cool it?'

It was hard to read her expression. 'Just for a while.'

He knew he should go further, should put an end to it. But he couldn't bear to. Not now. Not so abruptly.

A slow tailing-off would be kinder. He reached up for her hand. 'I hope you understand?'

She gave the hand to him, and she stood, letting him squeeze it, although otherwise not responding.

She was so quiet, he didn't dare move.

He continued to lie there, holding on to her hand, for such an extended period that he began to think he could hear that same sound – tick, tick, tick, tick – a metronome that had seized hold of him this morning and was holding him prisoner.

She took back her hand, her expression still unreadable. His best guess was that she was angry, that she would now put on her skirt and leave the room, something, he realised, that he did not want her to do.

A beat. And then, 'Budge up.' She nudged his shoulder. When he shifted further into the middle of the bed, she laid herself down next to him, facing but not touching him.

He blinked away an unexpected tear. 'I don't want to lose you.'

'You don't have to,' she said. She touched him lightly on the cheek. 'I can wait.' And ran her finger down it. 'If you mean it when you say you will tell her.'

'I can't. Not now.'

'But you will?'

He said, 'Yes,' even though he knew he couldn't, that he shouldn't, promise this. But it was still a yes, not just from cowardice but because he really wanted to say yes, and because he remembered Frances feeding the breakfast he'd made for her to her dog.

A light switched on, a thought not previously countenanced, that he could make his yes a reality. Other politicians had been trailblazers in this respect, and it hadn't done them much harm. The world had changed: everybody knew that the best-intentioned marriages could end. He said it again: 'Yes.' And felt pleasure in saying, and believing, it.

She was smiling as she kissed him. Her breath so sweet. Not like Frances's.

'Okay, then, let's take it easy for a bit.'

'I'll miss you.' He swept out an arm to encompass the room. 'And I'll miss this.'

'You'll still have me in the office.' She got off the bed and fetched her skirt, which she pulled on. 'Let's start right now.' Up went the side zip. 'I won't come back with you in the car; I'll take the bus. Will you be needing me later, for the committee?'

'I think I had better go with my PPS,' he said. 'It'll be expected.'

'Sure thing.' She was taking this so well. 'Anything else I can do?'

'Anything?' And when she nodded, 'Well, actually, there is something that you might be able to do for me.'

3 p.m.

There were only two customers in the restaurant, both of them staring despondently at the few remaining plates of sushi drifting past them on the belt. Two further men were behind the counter, cleaning it, with the only other occupant of the place a woman who was cashing up.

Joshua approached the till. 'Mrs Jibola?'

She looked up, briefly, took in the sight of him and said, 'Had to come in the full regalia, did you?' before returning her attention to the piling up of coins.

'Are you Mrs Jibola?'

Her gaze stayed down. 'I don't use that name no more.'

'I'm Police Commissioner Joshua Yares.'

'Yes, I know who you are.' A quick glance up. 'And if I didn't, your fancy stripes, shiny shoes and the fuck-off Rover outside on a yellow line would have been a giveaway. Only thing I don't know is why you think you have the right to come waltzing in here.'

'I'd like to talk to you.' He saw both the customers and the kitchen workers were watching. 'Is there somewhere private we can go?'

She gave an unamused little snort. 'What I saw Julius up to on the news was hardly private. That's what's blown you in here, isn't it?'

'Please, Mrs Jibola.'

'I already told you.' She swept the coins into her hand. 'I don't answer to that name.' She threw them into the till, shoved the notes in after them and banged the drawer shut before saying to the men behind the counter, 'I'm outside for a smoke.' She stood on tiptoes to slide open the top bolt on a metal door near the till and, without looking back at Joshua, walked through.

He followed to find himself in a narrow alleyway at the end of which stood a couple of high metal bins. As good a place as any for a chat, even if it was stiflingly hot. He pulled the door shut. The area around the door was littered by cigarette stubs, and to avoid them he took a giant step forward. Straight into a pool of muddy water that, given the drought, was unexpected. He pulled his shoe out quickly but not quickly enough to stop his sock from getting wet.

Did they throw their washing-up water out here, he wondered, or was this condensation from steam that was hissing out of the vent above him, adding even more humidity to an already sweltering day. He took out a handkerchief and wiped his face, seeing how across from the vent and on the opposing wall was a camera that was angled down on him.

'It's to make sure we're not stealing anything,' she said. 'I bet whoever's watching is trying to work out what you're after in your doorman's uniform.' She took a pack of cigarettes from her pocket, flicked one out, put it in her mouth, swapping the pack for a lighter, taking one quick puff of the lit cigarette and blowing out the smoke. Another inhalation, longer this time, and then she dropped the cigarette into the water. 'That's all I'm allowed. I'm giving up.' She watched, greedily, as the cigarette fizzed out. 'So what's all this about? Julius did a runner, did he, after his pyrotechnics?'

'Something like that.'

'He always was a bit of a coward.'

'Do you know where he might have run to?'

'Why would I? I haven't seen him for at least a year.' She lit another cigarette. 'And if I did know, why would I tell you?'

'Because I'm not Julius's enemy, because I'm trying to help.'

'Help?' A laugh so dry it could scorch. 'You?' She let the second cigarette drop to the ground, this time in the dry, and mashed it out with her foot. 'Let me tell you how you and your lot have so far helped Julius. He was a good man when I married him. Soft. Wanted to be of service. So when the Met decided to buff up its image by letting a few black faces hang about the place, he swallowed your shit about new brooms and diversification and joined up. His first year on the job, trying to ignore the abuse from his colleagues and pretending to be one of the lads, diversified him into being a drunk. His second helped him branch out into coke. His third, and he still hadn't been promoted, he almost had the sense to walk. But your lot came at him again, flattering him, telling him he was a natural for undercover. I could tell, anybody who didn't want to please like Julius did could have told, that what they really were after was his black face. He couldn't see it. Said he loved the job. He loved it all right. So much he stopped coming home. Stopped wanting to have sex – must have had another woman. He said he didn't, but you lot, with your identities in suitcases, you teach them how to lie, don't you? He was a quick learner, was Julius, but it cost him. Not that any of you noticed, or if you did, you didn't give a shit.'

'But I do,' Joshua said. 'And it sounds like you do, too. Help me find him and I'll do my best for him.'

'Are you not listening or are you just slow?' She reached into her pocket and pulled out another cigarette. 'I already told you: I have no idea where he is.' She took out her lighter, which she clicked on, holding it close to her cigarette but not close enough to light it. Her hand wavered, as if she were making up her mind. Then she clicked the lighter shut and put it back in her pocket. 'The man I married is gone.' She spat the cigarette out into her hand and began to grind it between her thumb and first two fingers. 'Only thing I heard since is that he straightened up: stopped drinking, stopped taking drugs.' She flicked away the threads of paper and tobacco she'd just made. 'By the looks of what I saw on TV, that didn't last.' She glared at him, reminding him of the fury on Julius Jibola's face as he had thrown the Molotov. But perhaps he had imagined this, for now he saw that she was smiling. 'Look at that.' She was pointing down.

Following her gaze, he saw how the shreds of her tobacco had floated down to stick to his wet shoes.

'I heard you on the box,' she said, 'when you got the job. You went on about how you were going to reform the Met. Make it more representative. More egalitarian. That's a laugh. Even if you meant it, I bet you've found yourself wading through more shit than you will ever cop to. Don't stress, though,' she gave a quick bark of what was meant to be amusement but sounded more like scorn. 'It won't stink you up. You bright white ones, you lot in charge, you'll get somebody else to clean up your mess. People like Julius, people with dark skins or no money: they're the ones who suffer. And me as well. Since he left, times have been hard. Which, speaking of, if I want to keep my job, I have got to get back to work.'

She turned and saw that the door was shut. 'Are you stupid or what? Couldn't you see that there's no handle on this side?' She slammed her hands against the metal, repeatedly, the banging ricocheting between the two high walls until at last the door swung open. 'About time.' She marched through and slammed the door behind her.

3.40 p.m.

With his PPS beside him and the horseshoe of members of the Home Affairs select committee arrayed in front, Peter stifled a yawn. 'We appreciate your coming here,' the chairman said (this the second time in as many minutes that he'd said this), 'at such short notice, and of course in the face of the ongoing disturbances, which must be taking up a lot of your time. If you would just bear with us.' There were papers passing along their table, and had been since Peter had taken the hot seat, adding to his sense of something cobbled together at the very last minute.

'I'm not sure I understand why you want to talk to me,' he said.

'Bear with us.' More furious paper passing.

'It might help if you could at least tell me how this session fits in with your ongoing inquiries.'

The chairman looked up. 'It doesn't.' And smiled. 'This is an exploratory session. We're considering an investigation into the citing of industrial facilities in inner cities.'

'I see,' he said, remembering how, at COBRA, Yares had used the solvent factory as his excuse for not containing the Rockham riots. Yares, or his puppet the PM, must have put the committee up to getting the issue on record.

'In light of the impact that the solvent plant in Rockham has had on the security of the whole borough,' the chairman was saying, 'it seemed like a good place to start.'

'What is it you want to know?'

'To the point as ever, Home Secretary.' Another unfolding of that smarmy smile. 'Which is why we value you.' He let this glance skitter from one member of his committee to the next, saying, 'Ready?' and then, addressing himself it seemed to the document in front of him, he said, 'Can you confirm that permission to site the solvent factory in the built-up area of south Rockham was granted while you were at Environment?'

'Yes, I can confirm that.'

'And that permission was signed off by the then Parliamentary Under Secretary of State for the Environment? By you?'

'Yes, I was the Under Secretary. And, yes, I did sign it. But that's not as simple as it seems.'

227

'How so?'

'My signature was the rubber stamp required at the end of a long process that did not involve me in any way whatsoever.'

'Are you saying that you signed it without knowing what it was?'

'What I'm saying is that that diligence was carried out by my predecessor. He, I'm sure you will recall, tragically died in office. Mine was a sudden appointment. When I came in, the papers concerning the Rockham factory were in his in-tray. I consulted the civil servants who had overseen the process and, of course, I also talked to the Minister about it. I was told that everything had been properly carried out, the i's dotted, the t's crossed, and that only my predecessor's heart attack had prevented him from signing. All that was required – and the paper trail makes this clear – was that I add my signature to a preapproved and scrutinised decision. Which I did.'

'Thank you, Home Secretary.' Head down, the chairman was writing furiously, which, given the presence of two stenographers, was either a trick to belittle the people before him or, and this was Peter's bet, his way of stretching time to let his thinking catch up with his mouth.

Tick, tick – the sound of his bedroom clock – tick, tick. 'Is there anything else?' He looked at his watch and then, again, at the clock on the wall.

'I know you're busy, Home Secretary.' Head still down, the chairman continued writing. 'And again I'd like to underline how much we appreciate your being here. I can assure you that it won't take much more time.' Only now did he raise his gaze. 'Can you tell us if you know any of the following: Nigel Harris, Frank Morris, Brendan Sonderland, John Wilson?'

'Know them?' Peter looked at his PPS, whose expression mirrored his own bewilderment. 'In what capacity?'

'I beg your pardon, I should have spoken with more clarity. I mean know them socially. Are any of them part of your social circle, for example. Do your wives know each other? Do your children play together? Could you have dined with them on more than one occasion? That kind of thing.'

With his PPS now rifling through his sheaf of papers, Peter said, 'Run through those names again.'

'Yes, of course. Probably wiser to take them one by one. Nigel Harris: do you know him or have you ever met him socially?'

The name meant nothing to him. 'No.'

'Frank Morris? Do you know him or have you ever met him socially?'

Not this one either. He said 'No' at the same time as his PPS leant over to whisper in his ear, 'Take a look, Home Secretary.' He was pointing at a list of the members of the board of the company that owned the solvent factory. Heading the list was Nigel Harris, with Frank Morris second in line.

'Brendan Sonderland?

Did the name seem familiar because he'd just seen it? Or was there another reason why it rang a bell? Best to play safe. 'Not to my knowledge, no.'

'Not to your knowledge?'

The cheek of that incredulous tone. Peter drew himself upright. 'In my capacity of Home Secretary, I meet scores of people every day. That name, Brendan S . . . S . . .'

'Sonderland.'

'. . . sounds vaguely familiar. If you're asking me do I know him well enough to remember meeting him, then my answer is that I do not. But if you're asking me whether I have ever met him, all I can say is I might have, but, if so, I cannot remember the occasion.'

'I see.' A supercilious curl of the lips now accompanied his follow-up. 'How about John Wilson? Do you know him or have you ever met him socially?'

Another name he had just read. And a common enough name. 'I've probably met one or two John Wilsons in my time.'

'Well, do you know the John Wilson who is on the board of the Rockham solvent factory?'

'Not to my knowledge.' This is a stitch-up, he thought, a McCarthyite interrogation, and the members of the committee are sitting there like monkeys, letting this farce unfold.

Well, he wasn't going to make it easy for them. He looked at each and every one of them in turn and was pleased to see that this eyeballing caused most of them to drop their gaze. They were embarrassed. As well they should be. They should also be ashamed to have let their committee – one of the most important of the checks and balances of a great parliamentary democracy – be used in this fashion by his enemies.

He'd had nothing, other than his scrawled signature, to do with the original decision. If they wanted to charge anybody, they'd have to dig up his Environment predecessor, who, come to think of it, had been cremated.

Tick, tick.

He glanced down at his watch and then looked up. Pointedly.

'Thank you again, Home Secretary, for answering our questions.' A quick glance round the horseshoe. 'If there's nothing anybody would like to ask?' A question from which the men and women of his committee kept their eyes averted, allowing the chairman to nod and say to Peter, 'And thank you so much for sparing the time to talk to us. We won't detain you any further.'

9.30 p.m.

If Cathy had not come out of the kitchen just then she'd have missed Lyndall. But coming out, she saw her standing by the front door.

At the sight of her mother, Lyndall, who'd kept to her room the entire day, seemed to shrink against the door.

'What are you up to?'

'I'm going out.' Lyndall dropped her gaze.

'Out? Can't you hear what's happening out there?'

'All I can hear is your TV. Which is blaringly loud. As usual.'

'Well then . . .' Cathy pushed past Lyndall to double lock the door before removing the key and taking it to the sitting room, where she also muted the TV. Lyndall was right. It had been on very loud. Now the banging and the shouts that had been ringing through the Lovelace for hours could clearly be heard.

She went back to the corridor to find Lyndall still standing at the door. 'Can you hear now?'

Lyndall nodded. 'What is it?'

'The police are out in force breaking down doors all over the estate. Must be trawling for rioters. And by the sounds of it, people are kicking back. It's been going on for hours. How come you didn't hear anything?'

Lyndall pointed to the earphones around her neck.

'Is that all you've done all day?'

Another nod.

Despite having told herself to keep her cool, Cathy felt exasperation bubbling up. But then, noticing Lyndall's red-rimmed eyes, she swallowed it down. She went up to Lyndall and, meaning to comfort her, put her arms around her.

The first thing she registered was the rigidity in Lyndall's shoulders, the second how they further solidified at her touch. Not quite a flinching away, but near enough. She let go. Stepped back. 'Come on,' keeping her voice as soft as she was able, 'tell me what the matter is.'

231

'Nothing's the matter.' As Lyndall bit her bottom lip, Cathy saw the glint of tears in those dark eyes.

'But there is. I can see there is.'

Lyndall shook her head and backed away. There was the sound of something hard hitting the door.

'What's that?'

Lyndall backed away some more, so that she ended up jammed against the door. Another clink.

'Show me.' Cathy could feel her anger rising, and it was further stoked by the stubborn shaking of Lyndall's head. She slipped a hand round Lyndall's waist. 'Come on. Let me see.'

She tugged at the handle of the plastic bag Lyndall was holding. When Lyndall pulled back, she tightened her hold and twisted.

'Mum,' she heard, but distantly.

An hour before, she had found herself staring at a sunset so red that even after she had shut her eyes the redness had pursued her into darkness and now she saw that same red mist as, despite Lyndall's cry of, 'Mum, you're hurting me,' she continued to twist Lyndall's arm.

The two of them were locked together in a struggle for the bag until, saying 'Mum' once more, Lyndall let go so suddenly that the bag shot up and hit her in the face before dropping back to the floor.

What did I do, Cathy thought, as Lyndall lifted up a hand to touch the blood that trickled from the cut on her cheek, red turning to pink as it mingled with her tears.

She never hit Lyndall. Never. 'I'm so sorry.'

'What's the point of being sorry?' delivered on a ferocious glare.

'I didn't mean to hurt you.'

'Don't you dare touch me again.' Lyndall was more angry than hurt. She pushed past Cathy and down the corridor to the bathroom. She opened the door, shut it, opened it again to poke out her head and say, 'And, yes, I will clean the cut,' before slamming the door shut.

There was the sound of the bolt being drawn, and after that Cathy could hear her own jagged breaths – as if she had been running – and to punctuate them the sound of someone really running outside on the landing. Someone being chased. Shouts of 'Stop!', which she ignored.

She looked down.

When the bag had fallen, it had also broken, and everything had spilt out. She saw a tin of condensed milk, a can of cola, half a loaf of sliced white, a tin of baked beans and a can opener. For what? she wondered, and then, refocusing the question, for who?

9.40 p.m.
That it had come to this, Billy thought. That they were actually contemplating using water cannons on the streets of London. I mean, yeah, they had them, but they'd had them in storage for years and every previous Home Secretary had, with the backing of most of the good guys in the service, refused to give them the green light. This Home Secretary had seemed no different from his successors: they all talked up law and order while cutting resources, but they also took their lead on operational matters from senior management. And yet this Home Secretary and his boss the Prime Minister were outdoing themselves in their promises of the methods they would use to quash the rioters, methods that the Commissioner had gone on record rejecting.

Something was going on behind the scenes. And, Billy thought, as he kept plodding forward, one foot in front of the next, when politicians manoeuvre it's the police who end up picking up the pieces. Once the public got used to water cannons, there would no putting the genie back into the bottle. Before anybody knew it, every plod would be carrying a gun.

He caught this uncharacteristically gloomy thought. Told himself it was fatigue talking. Forget your average tour of duty, he'd been on his feet, with only the occasional half an hour of shut-eye, for over eighty hours. And counting, given he was on his way back to base in Rockham.

He should have been there already but had chosen to walk rather than be driven, and also to take the long way round, by the canal. It was a whim of his to breathe some air, although in this heat, and with smoke still hanging low, there didn't feel to be much air around. But at least he was on his own, if only for this moment.

As this thought occurred, he realised that he wasn't going to be alone for much longer. Ahead some fifty yards, two men were standing. They were facing each other and their voices were raised, although he couldn't make out what they were saying. As he moved closer, he realised that only one of them, male IC3, was talking, at the same time jabbing his finger into the other's chest.

Billy sighed. His minder was right: he should not be out here on his own. Not so close to angry Rockham and dressed in the full kit. He could so easily become a target.

The two men were caught up in their row; they hadn't even noticed him. He could turn away. Leave them to it.

'You're a bastard,' he heard. 'You and all the rest.'

A falling out amongst thieves?

'He wasn't a danger,' he heard. 'Hit first, ask later: that's your way, isn't it?' Another jab that pushed the second man backwards. 'You were supposed to help him. Not kill him.' More jabs, and the other man visibly staggering under their impact, which is when Billy saw that he couldn't get away because his attacker had hold of him.

'Bastard police.'

That's when Billy saw that the victim, also IC3, was in uniform.

Stupid bloody plod, out here on his own. Even as he registered the irony of this judgement, Billy was already running towards the two, shouting, 'Break it up.'

Adrenaline, and stupidity, had driven him thus far. Now, as he came upon them, he realised that the man in uniform was no policeman.

Billy's baton was already in his hand. With a flick of his wrist, he expanded it to its fullest length. 'Break it up.'

He pushed the presumed victim out of the way and flicked his baton so that the presumed attacker was forced back and against a fence.

'Fuck off.' The man shook his head wildly, as if that might be enough to shake Billy off.

'Calm down,' and, as the man tried to move forwards, he said it again, 'Calm down,' and poked the baton into the man's clavicle.

The man went still.

'That's better. Now what's all this about?'

The white of the man's eyes were suffused with red and his breath stank of over-stewed onions and stale alcohol. He tried to turn away, but Billy held him speared. 'I asked you a question. What's going on?'

'They killed a man who did no harm.'

'So you thought you'd take that out on a traffic warden, did you?'

The man's mouth opened. His jaw agape. Comical really. He twisted his head and looked. And what he saw made his fists unfurl.

This one under control. Out of the corner of his eye, Billy saw the other beginning to back away.

'Oi, you. Come and stand where I can see you properly.'

The man shuffled into vision.

'That's better. Now, from what I saw, this man here,' he jabbed with his truncheon, just enough to make sure he kept quiet, 'looked to be in the process of assaulting you. Do you want to press charges?'

'No, sir.'

'Are you sure?'

'I don't want trouble.'

'Okay. Go on home, then.'

That's all he needed to say for the man to turn tail and, head down, begin to almost run.

'Slow down,' Billy called after him. 'Stay calm. Use the back streets. And for pity's sake, don't wear your uniform after dark, not with the streets as restive as they are.'

As the man walked more slowly, Billy turned back to the other. 'What are we going to do with you?'

No answer.

Billy didn't have one either. On the one hand, he had seen enough to arrest the man. He'd clearly been drinking and, by the wild redness of his eyes, staying up all hours. Probable rioter. If they kept him in, they'd likely find him on the footage.

On the other hand, that could tie Billy up doing the paperwork, and the Rockham officers would hardly thank him for adding another body to the overcrowded nick, and . . . Well, that was the puzzling thing. Something about this man. How immediately he had stilled himself when the baton went up to his neck: as if he knew what would happen if he didn't. How horrified he had been when he realised he'd attacked a traffic warden. How he met Billy's gaze now rather than look away. How he held himself quietly but not because he was cowed. On the contrary, his expression showed defiance. As if he were daring Billy to take him in. And all this, despite having the look and the smell of a down-and-out.

If Billy did arrest him, he'd have to frogmarch the man along the bank until a squad car could get to them. He thought about the chaos, not only in the Rockham nick but in every station within a radius of ten miles. He thought about his minder, who'd be wanting him back, and about the men who'd think he'd sneaked in a rest they weren't allowed. And then he thought about the water cannon, and the military men who were being parachuted into the higher ranks, and the way the politicians were talking, and he thought that soon the discretion that even the lowliest bobby was allowed and had been since the beginning of the force would be history.

Which was the clincher. He let his baton drop and telescoped it in.

'Go on,' he said. 'Go home.'

The man didn't move.

'Hop it.' And when the man still didn't make a move, it was Billy who chose to walk away.

9.45 p.m.

A rap on his office door. A head poked round. 'Excuse me, Home Secretary.' Some junior from the outer office.

'Can't you see I'm in the middle of something?' Usually enough to rid himself of unwanted interruptions.

Not this time. 'Home Secretary?'

'Yes?' When he jerked his head up, he was revisited by the wash of the sunset that had bloodied the sky. 'What is it?'

'Your wife.'

Again he seemed to hear that unrelenting ticking of a clock that had punctuated his day. 'What about her?'

'She's here.'

His first thought was that he'd forgotten something they were supposed to be doing together, although he couldn't think what that might be. His second thought, as he stretched across for his diary, was that she had come to spy on him.

'Should I . . . ?'

'Yes, yes. Show her in. But before you do,' he pointed at the wall clock, 'Take that out, will you?'

He pushed away the document he'd been working on as the junior

236

rose up on tiptoes to hook the clock off the wall and carried it away.

Clock gone. Merciful silence.

Which didn't last, as he should have known it wouldn't, because the ticking was in his head, and here it came again as Frances was practically bowed in – she had this effect on all his staff. As he made his way over to her, he couldn't help thinking of a recent nature programme he'd half caught in which whichever Attenborough looka-like they were trying out had said that the spider commonly known as the blonde, otherwise called the yellow sac, was responsible for most bad domestic bites.

'Darling.' He kissed her proffered cheek, impressed as always that she had managed to keep so cool in the heat. 'Didn't they ring to tell you I was working late? I did ask them to.'

'Yes, they rang. But I was in town having a drink with Amanda and we were passing by. So I thought I'd drop in.' She continued on with her 360-degree examination of his office.

Yes, he almost said, it is big, but there's still nowhere that I could have hidden Patricia. 'It's sweltering out there,' he said and, assuming her full search must naturally include his bathroom, 'Would you like to wash up?'

'No, thank you. I'm fine.' Her gaze had been snagged by the wall-mounted TV, on which the riots were silently playing. 'Where's that?'

'Rockham again. It was calm earlier, but now it's got so bad they've had to wheel out the water cannon – the old ones Boris got conned into buying years ago. I'm surprised they still work.'

That look, her thinking look again, which produced: 'That might cook the PM's goose.'

His thought as well.

Did she think like him, he wondered, or had she taught him to think like her?

'Trouble is,' she said, 'it might also cook the government's goose. Questions are already being asked as to what you've done to fuel such rage.'

She was always so critical. So ready to point the finger. It was getting on his nerves.

But then he told himself he was only tired. And overworked. Which, speaking of: 'I'd love to come home with you but . . .' he pointed at the piles of papers on his desk.

'It's fine,' she said. 'Amanda's waiting for me downstairs.'

'Well then . . .'

That would normally be sufficient to get her out. Not this time. Instead: 'About your appearance at the committee.'

'You watched?'

'Naturally.'

He knew what she was going to say next: that he should have warned her he was going before the committee. That he usually did. But with one thing and another . . .

'We should have talked about it beforehand,' she said.

'I would have consulted you, darling.' Did the endearment sound as awkward to her as it was beginning to sound to him? 'You know that I normally do. But I had such a lot on today, including watching the PM throwing his weight about at COBRA. And what I told the committee was true: it was my first day at Environment. I signed an already approved document. The decision had nothing to do with me.'

'I see.' She blinked.

'Is there something I'm missing here?'

'I'm not sure.' She frowned. 'Something about some of those names. I think we might actually have . . .' And then her expression cleared. 'No, perhaps I've got it wrong.' She nodded in that definite way she had. 'I have. And it's totally correct: permission for the factory had nothing to do with you. Well,' she was smiling, 'I can see you have a lot on. I'll leave you to it.' She turned, treating him to a last sweep of her straight blonde hair, this way and that, tick, tick, exiting his office while he continued to stand there wondering what her visit had really been about.

10 p.m.

Joshua had buffed his shoes and shined them twice, so it was unlikely that the slightest strand of tobacco or smear of mud remained. Even so, his eyes kept straying down.

Nothing to do with the shoes, this he knew, and everything to do with the fact that they'd left him in that alleyway, ignoring his bangs, until he'd been forced to phone his driver to come and pull him out. With the likely result that he'd soon be the laughing stock of every bobby in London. The only reason that an exaggerated account of the incident might not be circulating in the evening paper is that the explosion of violence in Rockham – and elsewhere – was all anybody was currently interested in.

The situation was at crisis point.

A few days is all he needed. By then he'd have most of his men back from leave and enough bodies in mutual aid to get a proper hold on the situation. But he might not get those few days. Wheeling out the big guns, namely water cannon, for the first time in mainland Britain, and also the increasingly talked-about strategy of using tear gas and baton rounds, might satisfy the hangers and floggers, but anybody who had ever tried to police a disturbance in which unrelated groups of troublemakers came together to create anarchy would know how ineffective such methods of mass control could turn out to be. Never mind that their going in heavy risked provoking even more people out onto the streets, something that was already taking place in Rockham.

And there was the added headache of a maverick cop on the loose. If that got out, all kinds of hell would land on his head. If only, he couldn't help thinking, Detective Constable Julius Jibola would go chuck himself off the nearest available cliff – after having sent a postcard to say that this is what he was planning to do.

His gaze again on his shoes. He sighed. Although Jibola's ex-wife had been childish in her vengefulness, there was a lot of truth in what she'd had to say. Men like Jibola had been used by the old Met as cannon fodder and without regard for their well-being. And she was right as well in that many of these same officers hailed from ethnic minorities.

The Met had badly needed a new broom. Trouble was the past and too many young people in the city with nothing to lose were threatening to overwhelm his ever-thinning blue line. Never mind the unrelenting heat.

They'd had to switch off the air conditioning to help prevent an electrical blackout being created by a combination of the condition-ocracy (those lucky, or rich, enough to have air conditioning) and the boiling of kettles as people all over the capital settled down to watch the made-for-TV horror fest of the riots.

A knock. 'Come.' He turned to get his jacket from behind his chair. But seeing who it was who had poked his head around the door, he said, 'Oh, it's you, Blackstone, do come in,' while letting the jacket lie.

'Excuse me, sir.' Blackstone was still peering through a crack in the door. 'I'm after Deputy Commissioner Chahda. I thought he might be in here with you?'

'He had to go out.' Which, when Chahda had told him that there was someone he had to see, and that he was leaving his assistant in charge, had come as some surprise given the rising disorder. 'Can I be of assistance?'

'No . . .' A hesitation and then, 'Well, perhaps, sir. Something odd that I, something . . .'

'Come on in. Take a seat. Tell me what's bothering you.'

'Thank you, sir.' As Blackstone made his way over to the desk, Joshua saw how damp his shirt was, the heat being an added burden for the weightier officers. 'I don't know if it's important, sir.'

'Why not let me be the judge of that?'

'Yes, sir. Thank you sir.' A pause and then, 'I did talk to some of the officers, sir, who were known to have associated with Detective Constable Jibola.'

'Yes, the Deputy Commissioner informed me that you had. I gather none of them had much to offer in the way of assistance.'

'Afraid not, sir. They all told the same story that Jibola had dropped out of circulation. None of them had seen him for quite a while – years in some cases.'

A pause.

'But?'

'But the thing is, sir, something odd happened just now when I was talking to the last of them. You know how, given the pressure on the Rockham force, we have been pitching in to supply the IPCC with the relevant documentation for their inquiry into the death?'

'Yes, I know.'

'Well, the thing is, sir, while I was talking to the officer who knew

Jibola, one of my colleagues was checking the quality of the 999 call that triggered the police visit to the community centre.'

'The one the community leaders say would not have been made?'

'That's the one, sir. They're wrong. The call was made, logged and recorded. And I have heard it. I heard a male voice expressing concern about a male IC3 behaving in an erratic manner on the Lovelace. The caller asked the police to attend in case the man needed assistance.'

'Why is that of concern?'

'Because, sir. Because the thing is, the officer I was talking to, the one who knew Julius Jibola, also heard the recording, and he recognised the voice. I questioned him carefully and got him to listen a couple of times: he was insistent that the caller was DC Julius Jibola.'

Wednesday

STRICTLY PRIVATE AND CONFIDENTIAL

Submission to the internal inquiry of the Metropolitan Police into Operation Bedrock

Submission OB/MPS/CC/29

To: The Office of the Inquiry into Operation Bedrock

From: The Office of the Commissioner of the Metropolitan Police Service

At the request of the chairman of the Inquiry Panel into Operation Bedrock, the Office of the Commissioner of the Metropolitan Police Service has subjected a telephone call made to the emergency services on ███████████ to further scrutiny.

The call logged at 20:45:35 was to report a man behaving erratically in the area of the Lovelace estate in Rockham.

The IPCC, which is ongoing with its inquiry into the death in Rockham, agreed to release a copy of the recording to the Office of the Commissioner on the condition that no details of the call should be made public until the conclusion of the IPCC investigation.

Light equalization was used to enhance the recording by removing background interference. The call was then subjected to audio forensic analysis.

The report is attached.

In summary of its conclusions:

The 999 recording was compared with a sample of DC Julius Jibola speaking into a tape recorder during his training.

On the IAFPA consistent/distinctiveness scale, the two recordings scored a 4: i.e. that they were highly distinctive. Had not enhancement been used to isolate the voice in the 999 call, they would most likely have scored a 5: i.e. exceptionally distinctive with the possibility of these features being shared by two different speakers as remote.

It is therefore our conclusion that DC Julius Jibola did place the 999 call.

A transcript of the call is appended.

In summary:

The caller informed the emergency service operator of the erratic behaviour of a male IC3 on the Lovelace estate in Rockham. The caller was calm and provided details of location and time clearly and with patience. In his words, 'the man, IC3, is waving a stick about and officers should attend as soon as possible to stop him hurting himself'.

The caller, who added, 'I am currently following him to try and keep him safe,' would not give the operator his name.

The mobile phone number of the caller was shortly thereafter rendered non-operational.

We can confirm that the mobile telephone had been supplied by SC&O10 for use by DC Julius Jibola in pursuance of his undercover activities.

This document is for the internal inquiry only and on no account should be released to the public.

5 a.m.

'There has to be a connection if only in Jibola's mind,' Joshua said, 'between his witnessing the death in the Lovelace and his taking part in the criminality. I interviewed the officer who knew him. His description matched the psychologist's – i.e. that Jibola had been emotionally unstable for some time and that his particular sore point was what he perceived as a bias within the force against ethnic minorities.'

This statement was met, initially, by silence. Taking his eyes off his two companions, he looked around. After eighty hours of riding the tempest, energy levels tended to peak at night, with first light bringing a fall off in numbers in the streets and a corresponding decline in officers in the room. Five a.m. then became the time when least was done and the army of cleaners moved in. They were usually deployed throughout the building but these days they gave first priority to the clearing away of stained tea cups, wastepaper baskets overflowing with the detritus of fast food, and papers to be shredded in this room. Seeing both the Commissioner and his deputy present, the cleaners now quietly swept past the legs of men whose heads had slumped on their desks, before hauling the rubbish out. Soon officers of the day shift would start filtering in, along with the Bronze Commanders come to deliver their reports, re-stoking the urgency that would subside again after orders had been given to be carried out elsewhere in the Met.

For now, however, there was quiet, which Gaby Wright eventually broke. 'If you don't mind me saying, sir' – despite that she must have been working round the clock, she was as tidy and as well turned out as ever – 'we have no way of knowing what is going on in Jibola's mind.'

'That's right. We don't.' Anil Chahda's uniform was in contrast crumpled, as if he'd slept in it, and this despite him having taken half the night off.

'You may both be correct. But the fact remains that if people were to find out that Jibola is one of ours – and that he was a witness at the community centre – they'd leap to the conclusion that his participation in the riots had something to do with what he witnessed. Matters are finely enough balanced without one of our officers seeming to accuse his fellows of murder. We have to neutralise Jibola before the media get their claws into him.' Out of the corner of his eye, Joshua saw Anil Chahda yawning – what, he wondered, was the matter with the man? He concentrated his gaze on CS Wright: 'You've done what you can with the resources available. What we now must do,' seeing his deputy still yawning he raised his voice, 'with your agreement of course, Anil, is step up officer numbers in Rockham. We've got to search every inch of the borough.'

One further enormous yawn before Chahda said, 'That's all very well, sir, but where are we going to get the men from?'

'From here.' Joshua used a pointer to indicate the boroughs surrounding Rockham, 'and from here. As well as aid coming from elsewhere.'

'That is going to leave us dangerously exposed throughout the rest of London.'

'Well, then, we'll have to be quick about it, won't we? I want an observational cordon around Rockham, mobile CCTV, the lot. We have to clock anybody in and anybody out.'

'It's going to cause trouble.'

'If it does, so be it. If it means bringing out water cannon, if it means deploying baton rounds' – hearing himself say this, he thought how far he had travelled in such a short time, and then, putting steel into his voice – 'well then, that's what we will have to do. We have to find this man.'

7 a.m.

At the sound of his Commons' door opening, Peter looked crossly up. First a call from Anil Chahda to warn of more trouble coming to Rockham and now somebody marching into his office without the courtesy of a knock. His irritation intensified when he saw that it was Patricia. What on earth did she think she was doing coming to his Commons room, and so early?

'I've been missing you.' She gave a smile and a cute wrinkle of her nose but, seeing him frown, added, 'Only kidding.'

'Come on, Patricia.' He had no time for games. 'We agreed to cool it.'

She raised her hand in a salute, 'Yes, sir,' hitting her forehead so hard it jerked her head back. 'I'm on board with that.'

Could she be drunk?

She certainly looked more tousled than usual, with her dark hair frizzed out as it only ever was in bed. Come to think of it, she was wearing the same clothes she'd had on yesterday: had she actually been to bed? 'So what exactly,' he said, hardening his voice, 'are you doing here?'

She took a step back. Pouted.

He dropped his gaze deliberately down to the papers on his desk. And heard her saying in that wheedling voice she also only ever used in bed, 'Come on now, Petey-weetie, don't be such a cross patch.'

She must be drunk. All he needed. He looked behind her and at the door.

She turned and, he was thankful to see, made her way towards it. He picked up his pen.

He heard the key turning in the lock.

'What are you doing?'

She came back to stand so close to his desk that he could smell that floral scent he knew so well, and some other strange musky smell that was underlaid by the stink of stale alcohol.

He sighed and got up, the better to tell her that she had to go.

She tilted up her head. Smiling.

In that moment he remembered the manner in which Frances had covered her mouth with a sheet that early morning when he had made to kiss her. Patricia lifted a hand and stroked his cheek.

He shouldn't. He couldn't.

But the door was locked.

To hell with it. He kissed her. For the longest time, feeling how she responded.

How different it would be, and he couldn't stop the thought from forming, to wake up beside her. If only, he thought, if only, and held her more tightly.

When finally he let go, and when he took a step back the better to look at her, he saw how her eyes had welled with tears. 'What's wrong?'

She swallowed, opened her mouth and swallowed again. Something she wanted to say to him but couldn't quite. Something he wouldn't want to hear? In the silence that stretched between them, it occurred to him that she was about to tell him that she was pregnant, this thought striking a blow to his gut that made him want to unsay his question and unthink this thought.

'Not enough sleep, that's all.' She gave a wan smile. 'And it feels weird sneaking round like this.'

Relief made him reject his first response – that they'd been sneaking around for at least eighteen months – and choose instead a reassuring: 'It won't be for long.'

'Won't it?' She looked as if she were about to cry again.

He sighed. He had such a lot of work to get through, never mind that he must ready himself for the Chamber.

Her teeth were beginning to work at her bottom lip, a giveaway tell of her distress. He let out another sigh. 'Come on, Patricia. You know what we agreed.'

'What you made me agree to, you mean.'

Like that, was it?

Like Frances, actually. Well, bugger them both.

He opened his mouth to say so.

She got in first. 'You asked me to do something,' she said. 'And I did it. And what I found out is going to make your year.' Her brown gaze was afire. 'I've had very little sleep, so if you don't want to hear what it is, I'd be just as happy to go back to bed.'

Was she teasing him so as to reel him back? His first impulse was to call her bluff. Tell her to go and sleep off whatever hangover she was clearly warming up to.

Except: what if she really did know something?

'I'm sorry,' he said. 'Didn't mean to be so curt.'

So easy to turn her round. She smiled. 'I got Anil Chahda to spill the beans,' she said. 'And what he told me is better than we could ever have dreamt.'

11 a.m.

A staccato ping, someone prodding at Cathy's doorbell, was immediately followed by the sound of a key turning in the lock. Lyndall's school, which had only just reopened, must have shut again. A pity. She'd been enjoying the break from Lyndall's sulky presence. She called out, 'Lyndall?'

'No, it's not Lyndall.' Gavin's voice. 'Sorry, I assumed you'd be at work.'

She pulled on her skirt. What was Gavin doing there? And, as well, how come he'd kept her key? 'I'm on the late shift.' She came out of her bedroom to see him at the end of the corridor, standing by the door. 'What are you doing here?'

'I brought you a present.' He stepped to one side, to reveal someone standing directly behind him.

'Jayden!' She saw him, head lowered, shifting from one foot to the other, and even from the other end of the corridor she could see how filthy he was. 'How great to have you back, safe and sound.' She hurried down the corridor. 'Lyndall's going to be over the moon.' She hugged him as best she could given he still wouldn't raise his head. 'Where have you been?' He smelt awful.

No reply.

'I tracked him down in Feltham,' Gavin said. 'They were holding him for alleged damage to a shop window. When I threatened to blow the whistle on them for keeping an underage boy without either informing his parents or giving him anywhere to wash, they got somebody to look at the CCTV footage. And guess what: the youth with face obscured who was caught on camera throwing a brick through a JD Sports window was wearing a black T-shirt, not a blue one like Jayden's. So they let him out.'

'Poor you. And they kept you without letting you call anyone?' When Jayden still didn't speak, she said, 'Your mum will be so happy to have you back.'

Now at last he lifted his head. 'I didn't . . .' he said. 'I won't . . .' before dropping it again. He was trembling.

'It's okay, Jayden.' This from Gavin, who gave the boy's head a fatherly pat. 'Go and have a shower. I'll fill Cathy in.'

251

Having deposited a set of Lyndall's clothes outside the bathroom, Cathy went to join Gavin in the lounge. He was standing in front of the open window, trying to cool himself in the breeze. 'Except it's like a hot fan,' he said. 'Apparently carrying in sand from the Sahara. That's why our sunsets have been so spectacular.' He touched the radiator below the window. 'I see you finally got them to switch the heating off.'

'I think the boiler just gave up the ghost,' she said. 'So what's up with Jayden and his mother?'

'They let him have two phone calls while he was inside. The first time, when he told her where he was, she said it served him right and hung up. The second time she slammed the phone down as soon as she heard him say hello. He's furious. The closer we got to the Lovelace, the louder he kept insisting that he wouldn't go back to her. Said if I made him, he really would pick up a brick and throw it through the nearest shop window. I would have taken him elsewhere, but he's in a terrible state and there are roadblocks all over Rockham. I didn't think he could have survived the tension of being questioned by the police on the way out as well in. So I brought him here. Hope that's okay?'

'Of course it is.' The last thing she needed was someone else to worry about, but she knew Lyndall would never forgive her if she turned Jayden away. And, besides, she thought, given Lyndall's continuing silence, it might be a relief to have Jayden as a buffer. 'But we do have to let Elsie know he's safe.'

'I'll do it. I'll also threaten her with some of the things he told me about her behaviour – that should keep her away for a bit and buy him time to catch up on sleep. He was dropping off in the car.'

'I'll put him in Lyndall's room. But I have to go to work this afternoon.'

'Late shift? Not like you.'

'All the others were too frightened to go home after dark.'

'You're a brave woman, Cathy Mason, living as you do in Riot Central.'

She smiled, thinking that she'd probably volunteered less out of bravery and more to buy some space between her and Lyndall. 'And you're a kind man, Gavin, to bother with Jayden.'

He said, 'For you, Cathy . . .'

She shook her head and tapped him twice on the lips to stop him going on.

He gave a rueful smile.

'I'm sorry,' she said, thinking that she would have to tell him what she had finally understood.

Which was the realisation that, despite Banji abandoning her, not once but twice, he was, and had always been, the only man for her.

11.35 a.m.

On any normal sunny day, St James's Park would have been packed with Whitehall insiders crossing from one appointment to the next, and tourists meandering between Horse Guards Parade and Buckingham Palace, and pensioners lined up in rows of white deckchairs, heads tilted back the better to catch the sun. But now those who were brave enough to even face the outside were all cleaving to the shade. Which is why Peter and Frances had chosen one of the benches near the Blue Bridge overlooking the lake. That way they could be sure that nobody would come close enough to hear what they were saying.

'Good of you to come out.'

'Don't be silly, Peter. Of course I would. I *am* your wife.'

He didn't like the way she was looking at him. He averted his gaze, looking away from her and towards the lake. As he did so, one of the park's white pelicans that had been by the water's edge, seemingly asleep with its head folded under its wings, suddenly snapped to and, as he continued watching it, unrolled its neck to use its hooked bill to snatch up a pigeon that was just then passing by.

He'd heard of this happening, but in all his years in Parliament had never seen it.

'Look at that.'

Although the pigeon was firmly clamped in the pelican's beak, its grey feathers fluttered out of both edges of the bill as it struggled to get out.

The pelican lifted up its head and beak, and shook them, wobbling its neck, trying to force the pigeon further down the sac of its throat. The pigeon was still very much alive; its fight-back stretched the skin

253

of the pelican's gullet until it was almost translucent, with the dark outline of the smaller bird clearly visible. It was a ferocious fighter, and a horrified Peter found he couldn't tear his gaze away as the pigeon succeeded in struggling back up the pelican's gullet and into its beak, and for a moment it looked as if it might manage to get free. But as the pigeon's wings quivered – it was trying to fly out – the pelican began to clap the two edges of its beak together, battering the pigeon. Having done this for a while, it shook its head, shaking its still living prey and pushing it down its gullet, this time far enough down so that the pelican could twist back its neck, resting it on its back feathers, which stopped the pigeon from climbing up. Having entrapped the pigeon in this fleshy U-bend, the pelican began to swallow convulsively, each jagged gulp forcing the pigeon, now unmoving, further down and, at last, into its stomach.

Peter was so hot, conscious of the sweat trickling down his back – he'd have to change his shirt again.

'So why am I here?' Frances's voice pulled him back to the bench they were sharing. 'What is it that you couldn't tell me on the phone?'

He told her everything then that Patricia had told him. She listened with her gaze focused on the middle distance, across the water and towards the Eye. But when he had finished, she turned to face him full on. 'It's good.' Her eyes were shining. 'No, it isn't just good. It's great. Exactly what we were after. He's finished.'

'I'll feed it to one of the lobby bods, then.'

A reproving shake of her head. 'What? And let the world know that it was you who shopped him?'

'Unattributed, of course.'

'Come off it, Peter, you surely know that "unattributed",' hooking manicured fingers in the air to make quote signs, 'is only for the public. It will take less than two hours for the entire Westminster village to know it was you. The Party will never forgive you.' She looked away again, across the water and at the stationary Eye: 'Why isn't it moving?'

'They had two mid-air collapses from heat exhaustion yesterday. They closed it to monitor the temperature in the pods.'

She turned back. Looked at him full on. 'You're going to have to talk to the PM. Make him see that he can't wriggle out of this.'

He kicked himself for having let her say it before he could own up to himself that this, of course, is what he had to do.

He looked at the lake again where the pelican – he was sure it was the same one – was floating. As he watched, it lifted its wings, once, twice and then spread them, beating them against the air, and this had the effect of lifting its body, not far at first – its feet kept hitting the water, kicking up spray – but gradually gaining height until it was airborne and flying away across the water.

'Hardly a pelican in all her piety,' Frances said.

So she'd also seen the massacre of the pigeon.

'Why couldn't it have been satisfied with the fish the keepers give them?'

Frances shrugged. 'Some animals prefer their food fresh.' A pause and then: 'I thought Patricia was only good for trying to get into your pants. Turns out she can also make it with a dead weight like Anil Chahda. Wonder how she managed to squeeze the ammunition out of him.' She smiled. 'Better get going for PMQs,' she said. 'His office will be in maximum flutter just beforehand: make your appointment then.'

12.10 p.m.

The PM as man of the hour.

Or so he clearly thought. He'd recently suffered a dismal set of PMQs but that was now reversed as the opposition competed with his own backbenchers to demonstrate their support and their approval. Look at him, this bullish man, who had recently seemed aged by office and the threats to his position, now standing straight and proud as he used the bass force of a growling voice to promise: 'Not only will we support the police in using water cannons, if they need to, but this government has today suggested to the police authorities that the water be mixed with indelible chemicals that will later identify the wrongdoers. Our message is clear: anyone who goes out onto our streets with the intention of breaking the law will be marked by us and can expect to experience the full force of the law.'

'Hear hear' – that rumbled agreement – and Peter's voice as enthusiastically supportive, 'Hear, hear,' and in accompaniment he nodded grimly, so that no one in the House or watching on TV would ever have guessed that inside he was beaming.

The metronome that had been plaguing him for the past few days now proved itself to be the countdown to the Prime Minister's demise. Frances was right: with what Patricia had found out, the PM would have no option but to resign. I've got you, he thought, I've got you, even as he watched the Prime Minister riding happily at the head of a House in full cry.

'As to the suggestion by my Honourable Friend,' the PM was saying, 'that to resolve the overcrowding in our police stations we corral rioters in Wembley Stadium, I say that although I, along with all my Honourable Friends, would prefer to see our great sportsmen and women in the stadium, I will, if needs be, give serious consideration to this suggestion.'

'Hear, hear,' and Peter as well calling it loudly, 'Hear, hear,' and nodding to emphasise his agreement and in time to the internal ticking of that clock, as he thought, time's up, Prime Minister, time's up.

When the PM sat down beside him, he could feel heat radiating off the man.

Tick, tick, while one of their backbenchers responded to his name by keeping on his feet and asking, 'Could the Prime Minister tell us what plans he has to hold errant parents of underage minors to account for their children's behaviour?'

Well done, Peter thought, couldn't be better. He'd remember the favour and repay it once he was in charge.

When the PM went to the box, standing with his back to Peter, Peter almost seemed to see a noose drawing round the strained sinews of that bullish neck.

'My Honourable Friend,' the PM was saying, 'is correct in saying that parents whose children threaten to bring this great nation to its knees should be held to account. We cannot tolerate a culture of neglect that glorifies thuggish behaviour and disrespects the rule of law. It is for this reason that we are drafting regulations that will allow magistrates to impose fines and, if necessary in extreme cases, prison sentences on parents who should be, and will be, held responsible for the behaviour of their underage children.'

Noose tightened, which was almost evident in the PM's heightened colour as, accompanied by a chorus of agreement, he sat down again, turning to Peter, a smile on his face as if to say, see, I can do it, and better than you – in response to which Peter fed a hearty 'Well done, Prime Minister' into his leader's ear while all the time thinking, come two o'clock at Downing Street and you will discover just how thoroughly you have cooked your own goose.

2.35 p.m.

In the time that Peter had been sitting outside the Cabinet Office he had heard the clip of footsteps passing along the many corridors of Downing Street, and he'd heard doors opening and doors closing and snatches of conversation in between. Big Ben, which had tolled the hour as he'd climbed the stairs, had also rung out the fifteen and thirty minutes past the hour, this forward movement of time reinforced by the ticking of the grandfather clock that stood in the lobby. But now everything, save for the sound of the clock and the beating of his heart, was quiet.

The cheek of the PM to keep his Home Secretary waiting so long – a power play, no doubt, which demonstrated, if any further demonstration were needed, how bad things were between them. So petty, though – unworthy of a man in power.

Well, at least if Peter had been nursing doubts about what he was about to do, this helped dispose of them. Thirty-five minutes and counting was designed to drive him into a rage. Not that he would be so driven. He would bide his time. Think of something else.

He thought about Patricia, outside in the car (she'd earned that privilege). He wondered how she was finding the wait. And then, without meaning to, he found himself thinking about Frances's question as to how Patricia had managed to get the ammunition that he needed.

No – don't think of that.

He heard a voice raised, presumably in jest because the response was laughter.

So long since he had laughed with Frances. With Patricia on the other hand . . .

'Home Secretary?'

'Yes?' When had this functionary of the PM's office appeared?

'The PM will see you now.'

Time. Head high, he walked through the now open door.

The Prime Minister was at his usual place in the Cabinet room with his chair at its usual angle to the table to distinguish it from the other chairs, even though there was no one else sitting there. Hearing Peter coming in, he raised his bullish head, and said, 'Peter,' without a smile or a hint of an apology for having kept him waiting. 'I hear you came in through the back door?' And now a sly grin. 'Not like you to miss a photo opportunity.'

'70 Whitehall seemed the more appropriate entry point.' He stood, because the Prime Minister hadn't offered him a seat, and looked down the room, beyond the columns to the other end where the PM's Press Secretary was standing, arms akimbo, glowering, his thin face looking even thinner and full of menace.

'So?' The Prime Minister's voice drew him back. 'Have you come to tell me to my face what is already public – that you're launching a challenge?' The Prime Minister narrowed his hooded eyes.

'No.' Peter shook his head. 'That's not why I'm here.'

He might as well not have said anything.

'Your disloyalty takes the breath away,' the Prime Minister went on. 'I gave you the Home Office against the advice of almost everybody in the Party. Some of your Cabinet colleagues said you weren't ready, some said you didn't know what loyalty was, and others just hate your guts. Well, turns out they had reason. I helped you to grow into the role, backed you when you needed backing. I made you, and you have paid me back by trying to unseat me. Well, let me warn you,' one finger wagged in the air as if he were a school teacher, 'I might have made you, but I can also break you.'

To hector like this and in front of his malevolent Press Secretary – it was unconscionable.

And simultaneously fortunate, because it cleared Peter of any last vestiges of conscience at what he was about to do.

'Step out of line one more time,' the Prime Minister said, 'and I'll fuck you up, good and proper.'

The cheek of the man. And the hubris. 'I don't think you're in a position to do that, Prime Minister. Not after the public find out what you've been up to.'

'What the hell is that supposed to mean?'

'Actually, Prime Minister,' he looked pointedly at the glowering Press Secretary, 'this is for your ears only.'

A flickering exchange of glances between the PM and his Press Secretary, who shook his head almost imperceptibly, a signal that either Peter had misread or his boss decided to ignore. In one of those lightning changes of moods for which the Prime Minister was renowned, he got to his feet and said, 'Let's go out onto the terrace. I could do with some air. And if you wouldn't mind, Martin,' another quick glance in his Press Secretary's direction, 'ask someone to rustle us up some tea.'

The walled half acre at the back of Number 10 was a sorry sight, with the box hedge that lined the terrace so spiked and yellowed it looked dead, and the lawn so dry that it blended into the paths that ran through the garden and up to trees whose leaves were wilting.

'Met Office keeps promising rain.' The Prime Minister sipped at his tea. 'But at this point, it's difficult to place much trust in anything they say.' He put down his cup so firmly it rattled the saucer. 'Impossible in your case as well. You know I was planning to stand down after the election. If you'd played your cards right, you might have been my heir apparent. But you've pushed and pushed and driven the Party into disarray.'

'What I've done,' Peter said, 'has been out of loyalty to the Party.'

'Oh, give me a break.' A hollow laugh. 'You wouldn't know what loyalty was if it came and slapped you in the face. If you had even an ounce of it in your body, you'd have got your allies to pull together with the rest of the Party. That's what's needed more than anything in a time of heat and riot, never mind the coming election.'

'I couldn't agree more, Prime Minister.' He was suddenly parched. He took up his cup and gulped at his tea. 'There's a year to go before the election, and we need to unify. But we can't do it with you at our head. Not after what you've done.'

'Enough, Peter. I'm bored with this. Spit out what you've come to say and then leave me in peace to get on with the real work of governing the country.'

Peter set his cup carefully down. 'If we lose the next election, we could end up in the cold for a decade or more. That's why I challenged you.' He swallowed – why couldn't they have brought water with the tea? 'I would have preferred a clean contest. Given how many of our parliamentarians are frightened for their seats, I was confident of my chances. I certainly had enough support to trigger an election, something which your campaign managers must also have told you.' He licked his lips, feeling how shredded they were with dried skin. 'But,' he said, sitting back, 'we can no longer afford a contest. You cannot continue in office. You have to go. For the sake of the Party. And for your own sake.'

'Have to, do I?' His mocking smile stretched from ear to ear. 'Why is that?'

'Because of your son. Because of Teddy.'

A blink, just one, as the PM held himself otherwise perfectly still. 'Go on.' Softly said.

'This is what I know. What everybody might soon know. Teddy was recently stopped by the police for driving under the influence. A breathalyser showed him to be over the legal limit. He was also in possession of a small quantity of marijuana. I assume you know all about this?'

Nothing. Not even a blink this time. As if this man was made of stone.

'He was arrested and taken to the police station, where he was given a blood test that confirmed the breathalyser result. He was cautioned and let go. A report was made with a view to charging him.'

Another 'Go on,' even softer.

'The paperwork concerning Teddy's arrest should have been passed on to the CPS, who would have charged him – as they always do in cases of drink driving.'

'So Teddy got himself into trouble. It happens.'

'Yes, it happens. But what doesn't usually happen is that the arrest record then goes missing.'

'Has Teddy's?'

He nodded. Said, 'It has, Prime Minister,' thinking, as you know full well.

'Are you suggesting that I disposed of a police file?'

'I'm only telling you what I know. And what I know is that the Commissioner of the Metropolitan Police, Joshua Yares, asked his deputy, Anil Chahda, to pull the records that covered the evening when and the area where Teddy was arrested. Deputy Commissioner Chahda did as he was instructed and, curious as to why a new Commissioner would bother himself with such an ordinary log of arrests, examined it before forwarding it on. Teddy's name leapt out at him, as of course it would. The Deputy Commissioner assumed that Yares had asked for the log so that he could deal with this delicate situation himself, and he expected soon to be informed of the matter. But when Commissioner Yares returned the log, without comment, Chahda saw that the record of Teddy's arrest had been excised.'

'He saw that, did he?' The Prime Minister stretched an arm across the fence that lined the terrace and snapped a twig off the box hedge. He broke it in half before dropping the pieces into his tea, which he then set aside. 'And what does this have to do with me?'

'Well, that's where things become a little muddy. From where I'm standing, and having been informed of Yares's recent secret visit to Number 10 – he came in through the back door just like me – I would hazard a guess that you told Yares about Teddy's arrest and asked him to destroy the file.'

'And if I were to assure you that I did not?'

'Then, Prime Minister, I would have to believe you. But that wouldn't disappear your problem. Commissioner Yares was chosen by you and in the face of my strong opposition. He is also known to be a personal friend of yours. He's an intimate of your wife. He's Teddy's godfather. And now, after less than a week in office, he has used his position to break the law so as to benefit your family. Whether the commission of inquiry – I'm sure there will have to be one – or, for that matter, the man in the street, decides that Yares acted on your orders or destroyed the record off his own bat, Yares still remains your man and Teddy your son. I cannot see how you can survive this. Especially after your homily on parental responsibility at this morning's PMQs, never mind your recent and rather odd take on the legalisation of street drugs.'

Another reptilian blink. Rumour had it that the third was a sign that he was preparing to eat you. 'So is it your idea now to throw me to the wolves?'

'Not me, Prime Minister. But the situation will.'

'I won't go down without a fight. You know that, don't you?'

'You've had a shock. You'll need to think about this. But from where I stand, this is what it looks like: although you may end up exonerating yourself in the short and medium term, the headlines will be punitive. The press will bleed you, and they will bleed your family, digging up any and every piece of dirt they can find and twisting it to make it seem worse. It will wound you, and there isn't a political party that will keep on a wounded leader – remember Thatcher and Blair – especially in the run-up to a poll.'

'You may be right.' The Prime Minister nodded as if this was a minor point he was acceding to. 'It might finish me. But it will finish you as well. Nobody likes an assassin.'

Frances's point as well. Peter nodded.

Which seemed to invigorate the PM. 'Especially one who operates with such blatant self-interest,' he said. 'Once the faithful find out that it's your doing, any chance of your becoming leader will vanish.'

'Perhaps it will.' Peter shrugged.

That sound again.

Tick, tick.

'I'm willing to take that risk.'

Tick, tick.

'If, that is, you choose to play hard ball.'

'I see.' And there, that third blink. 'Am I right in supposing that you have a different game plan?'

'I have a proposal, yes' – the bait laid – 'that would spare the Party and spare you.'

'How very loyal of you.'

His turn to respond with a blink. Tick, tick. And if the Prime Minister didn't take the bait?

'So what is this proposal?'

Bait taken. Now to close the trap. 'You step down.' He was still extremely thirsty. He eyed the pot. But the tea would by now be over-brewed and cold. And besides, it wouldn't do to have a trembling hand picking it up. 'Give family reasons: everybody knows your wife hates this life and that your son needs you.'

'Bit trite, don't you think?'

'We could come up with an illness, if you'd rather. Something recoverable from but which would prevent you leading the country in the run-up to the election.'

'I see. And then?'

'Whatever happens, Yares has to go. Better to off him now, before anybody gets wind of the scandal.'

'Another illness? You think anybody would buy that?'

'No, not an illness. A resignation. Perhaps the riots – which he has clearly not controlled – which have brought to his attention that this is not the job for him. Since he won't want anybody to find out the real reason he has to go, we'll have his silence. We could sugar the pill with a knighthood – rumours are that this is the main reason he took the job.'

The Prime Minister nodded. 'He does want that K.'

'We then make Chahda Acting Commissioner, with the guarantee that if he continues to perform we will confirm the appointment as permanent. I know Anil a little and so I know how loyal he is to the police service and to the government of the day. I'm confident he can be persuaded, for the sake of the Met, not to pursue the business of the altered record.'

'Meanwhile you step into the breach and into Number 10?'

'That would be for the Party to decide.'

'But if I were to go quietly, and if we were to publicly bury the hatchet, that wouldn't harm your chances, would it?'

'That of course is entirely up to you, Prime Minister.'

'I see.' The PM, who had rested his right hand on the table, now began to drum his fingers rapidly against the hard surface. It was something he would do at moments of high tension during Cabinet meetings and which Peter had learnt to ignore, for to look at those fingers was to see how fast they moved and to be mesmerised by them.

A pause.

'How many people know about this?' before the drum roll started up again.

'Apart from myself, only Chahda.' No point in complicating things by bringing Patricia into this. 'And Frances, naturally, but she is discretion itself.'

The hand lifted off to hover above the surface of the table. 'I guess she learnt that from her father.' The hand dropped down and, as if to balance it, the Prime Minister drew himself up until he was ramrod straight: 'You suggested I think about this. I'd like to. I propose twenty-four hours to sound out my wife and so forth. Does that seem fair?'

Which would give time for Peter to get more of his ducks in a row. 'Yes, Prime Minister.'

For a man facing the imminent end of a political career, the Prime Minister was surprisingly nimble. Now he jumped up, saying, 'Our work here is done,' and went over to the glass doors to pull them open and say to someone in the room, 'Show the Home Secretary out, will you? And get my office to liaise with his to fix an appointment for his return,' glancing at his watch, 'at around 2.55 p.m. tomorrow. And, tomorrow, let's not keep him waiting. After you, Peter.'

As Peter stepped through the doorway, the PM continued barking out instructions. 'Get someone to make an appointment for the Commissioner of the Metropolitan Police to come and see me. Not now. Later. I'm feeling rather queasy. Probably the endless burgers the President insists on. Cancel my appointments for today; the urgent ones I'll do by phone. I'll go to Chequers, where my wife is, and work from there.'

The contrast between the dark interior and the bright blaze of sunlight as Peter stepped through the back door was so great that his vision blurred. As he paused, waiting for it to clear, he heard a car door opening and then someone running towards him.

Patricia was almost upon him before he realised that it was her. What was she doing, running, practically into his arms, in public and in the full light of day?

She shoved a mobile phone at him. 'Put it to your ear. Anybody watching will assume it's an urgent call.'

The thought of someone watching made him look up. In time to see a curtain that had been shifted aside, shifted back. Too quickly for him to be sure, but he thought it might have been the Prime Minister.

'How did it go? I'm dying to know.'

He took the phone and at the same time took a few steps back. 'You've got to be more careful.'

She was still smiling. 'I will,' she said, 'I promise. But aren't you going to tell me?'

He owed her: his victory was hers as well. (What had she done?) He lifted the phone to his ear.

'Tell me, tell me.' She was almost jumping up and down in her excitement.

What a child she was. 'I've given him a day before I go public. He's going to crumble. I could see it in his blinking face.' He lowered his hand.

'Well done, Peter. Well done.' When she came closer to take the phone, he smelt that unfamiliar scent again. (What had she done?)

'I need to get back to work,' he said. 'Why don't you take the rest of the afternoon off?'

10 p.m.

Rockham seemed abnormally subdued as Cathy began her walk home from the station. At least this time she hadn't had to answer questions – where are you going? Where have you come from? Who have you seen? – as she had done when she had left the area. Perhaps that's why it was so quiet: although the roadblocks had been removed, everybody was probably still too frightened to show their faces. A relief, therefore, that Jayden was keeping Lyndall company at home.

Her route took her past the back entrance of the police station where a double line of riot police stood, their faces paled by fluorescent light and blued by a rising moon. Their numbers had increased since she'd been at work, for there were also vans parked along the street – most of them full of police. Behind the vans were a couple of what at first she mistook for builders' trucks.

Eyes on her as she passed by and burning into her back as she kept on. She could hear voices too soft for her to figure out what was being said, and then she heard doors opening and doors closing and footsteps. She stopped and looked behind her.

A group of police, there must have been at least twenty of them, had formed themselves into two snaking lines and were making their way up the middle of the road, straight towards her. They were coming fast. She backed herself against a wall.

A disturbance in the air, a hot dry wind created by the thudding past of the phalanx of police. Each was carrying a shield in one hand while using the other to whip the air with a baton. There was the burble of a radio, abruptly cut off as they ran. Behind them trundled the small trucks, which, she now saw, did not belong to any builder. The one in front had a nozzle sticking out of its white metallic roof – it must be a water cannon – while the other had two attachments: an excavator's scoop instead of a bumper and what looked like a mobile crane behind its cab. As it went by, she saw the logo of the

Metropolitan Police painted on its side, and then it rounded the corner onto the High Street.

It was very dark. And quiet save for the footfalls of the police and the trundling forward of the vehicles.

This wasn't her business. She should go home via the back streets. Watch whatever it was that was about to kick off from the safety of her sofa.

She did not go back.

Rounding the corner, she could see a flash of red that she took for the brake lights of one of the trucks. As she was trying to figure out why it had stopped, she tripped. She was pitched forwards, grabbing for the burglar bars of a shop window to stop herself from falling.

Upright again, she looked back to see what had tripped her up. She could just about make out the outline of an empty crate that someone must have left outside the shop. She hadn't seen it before because, although the rising moon was by now high enough to soften the night, the street was unlit.

A power cut? She peered through the darkness to where the police were regrouping. Such military precision and all in silence. She must get out of there.

She turned; she must go back. But then she saw how a fresh contingent of police had rounded the corner and were heading straight for her. If she didn't get out of the way, she'd end up sandwiched between the two.

Just ahead and to the right there was a side street. She'd go there, she decided, find sanctuary in one of the flats above the shops. But when she drew abreast of the side street she found that it was blocked by a further line of police. They held their shields up and so close packed that there was no space for her to slip through.

She was trapped. She approached the line. 'I live in the Lovelace,' she said. 'I'm on my way home from work. Could you let me through?'

The policeman whom she'd addressed stared straight ahead. As if she wasn't there.

'Could you?'

'I'm sorry, madam,' he was speaking softly and out of the side of his mouth. 'You'll have to wait.'

Wait. For what?

No sooner had the question occurred than the dark was lifted by the simultaneous switching on of the street lights and a blaze of something much brighter than any street light could ever be. She turned to look.

The first police had formed themselves into a line that stretched the width of the High Street and blocked it. Ahead, an unoccupied section of the road was lit by a dazzling beam from the top of one of the trucks. One hundred yards further on was a different barricade, this one forged not from uniforms but from shopping trolleys, old doors and bricks and pieces of wood. Behind this barricade were knots of young people. Quiet and still. Expectant. Waiting for the next move.

It came in the form of a policeman in a peaked hat, who detached himself from the line-up of his colleagues and began to move towards the barricades. He was met by a barrage of stones, all dropping to the ground in the area in front of him. He stopped and raised his megaphone: 'This is a final warning. Go home or we will arrest you for obstruction of the public highway.'

Another barrage that also fell short.

The policeman turned and made his way back towards the line of his shielded colleagues, who parted to let him through. Or at least that's what Cathy thought they were doing, but the gap they had created was much wider than one man would ever have needed and, besides, he had already stepped onto the pavement.

Engines started up, and then both trucks began moving through the gap and beyond it, heading for the crowd. Behind them the line of police re-formed and started walking forward, slowly, in their wake.

A fresh bombardment from behind the barricade, lit now by the bright light. As the trucks moved forward, more projectiles flew, a hard rain that thudded down on the metallic scoop on the truck in front. The truck stopped, engine still revving. The second truck lined up beside it. A moment's pause and then a powerful jet of water shot through the nozzle of the water cannon to hit the barricade, sending pieces of masonry and wood flying.

There was a further inching forward of both trucks, so that the next shooting jet of water reached the crowd. One man in front took the full force of the water that pushed him over, and spun him round, and kept tossing him as he scrabbled, arms out, trying to find something to hold on to. Seeing what was happening to him, his companions ran from the hard spray that still kept hitting out, at the same time as both trucks were moving forward until they reached the barricade and, with the water cannon still firing onto what now looked like an empty section of the road, the shovel of the companion lorry smashed straight through the line of shopping trolleys.

11.30 p.m.

Joshua's car crunched around the Chequers' driveway and drew up outside the house, which looked to be in total darkness. But as he got out of the car, the door opened and the Prime Minister himself emerged. Another sign as to the urgency of the summons, now reinforced by an accusatory 'You took your time' from the Prime Minister.

'There was trouble in Rockham,' Joshua said.

'When isn't there?' The PM's frown turned into a glower. 'You've got to get a grip, you know.'

Yes, I know, Joshua thought and said: 'I trust you're feeling better, Prime Minister?'

'Better?'

'I heard that you were ill.'

'Oh that.' The Prime Minister sighed. 'No, I'm not ill. But, no, I am also not feeling better.' He looked at Joshua's driver: 'Take the car round the back. Someone will show you where to wait,' and then, to Joshua: 'Let's walk.'

He turned on his heel, leading Joshua away from the house and the formal gardens, striding down the long drive and through the gates, all the time remaining silent. His only words, 'We're fine on our own,' were addressed to the policeman who made a move to accompany them. He continued on, briskly, over a field and up by the side of an electrified fence, his shoes crunching against the parched ground as he made for Coombe Hill.

The moon was full and it lit the ploughed fields around them, the nearest of which, Joshua could see, had almost turned to dust. The night had brought with it little relief, hot air seeming to rise up, so it was almost as if they were walking over a thin crust of volcanic earth.

Not that the Prime Minister seemed to notice. He kept up a brisk pace, still without a word, his bullish head down and his shoulders rounded as if he were trying to shield himself from something unpleasant. And then, abruptly, and for no apparent reason, he stopped.

'Look at that.' He was pointing above Coombe Hill and at a full moon over which layers of red and orange mist seemed to be drifting. 'Eerie, isn't it?' the Prime Minister said. 'They say it's an optical illusion caused by the light passing through the Saharan dust in our atmosphere. Given that there is not even a puff of wind to blow in a single cloud, it's a mystery how half of the Sahara managed to make its way here. A red moon: a sign of strife to come. Which, speaking of,' and only now did he look at Joshua, 'what the hell is going on in Rockham?'

'We had to go in hard,' Joshua said, 'to find the missing officer, and this has inflamed an already tense situation. Come nightfall, gangs of youths, many of them from outside the area, set up roadblocks. We couldn't let them turn Rockham into a no-go area, so we had to go in even harder. We used water cannon – not something I wanted to do, but we had no choice. It was a well-planned and properly executed operation, and it worked. Rockham is quiet and the blockages have been removed. But we had to deploy so many resources to the area, other parts of London have suffered. It's a setback. It's going to take another couple of days to fully restore order.'

'Did you at least find your man?'

'Afraid not.'

'Jesus, Joshua. If you don't get control soon, we're going to have to call in the army.'

'Before it comes to that, every single police officer, no matter what their rank, up to and including me, will be out on the streets.'

'Every other officer maybe.' In the pause that followed, Joshua saw how the Prime Minister's gaze seemed to catch fire, the whites of his eyes turning almost as red as the moon. 'But as for you . . .' Another pause and then, 'You know you were my choice for Commissioner, Joshua, and you know I fought with my Home Secretary, who was spoiling for a public ruck, to get you in. But no sooner did you take up the post than the whole bloody world explodes.' The Prime Minister, who had almost been spitting in his fury, swallowed, stood silent for a moment, blinked once and then continued, in a quieter voice, 'Let me correct that last: it's not the whole world, just the world that you are supposed to be in command of. While the copycats in other cities have been subdued, London is still in uproar. Instead of restoring order, your men are stirring up even more trouble by looking for a bastard who clearly should never have been in the police force, never mind running around on his own.'

Was this why he'd been summoned all the way to Chequers – so that the Prime Minister could read him the riot act? Something he could easily have done on the phone?

He didn't think it could be, not in the middle of a riot.

Silence, into which the Prime Minister blinked again, and after that Joshua heard rustling that he at first took to be the wind. But the night was hot and still, and a series of high mewling whistles soon told him that the sound was birds.

'Red kites,' the Prime Minister said. 'There are scores of them roosting in the woods over there.' He sighed.

'Something you want to tell me, Simon?'

The use of his Christian name brought back the Prime Minister's gaze. A series of blinks: once, twice and for a third time. No anger in his expression now, only a sort of sad neutrality as he shook his head. 'It will have to wait. Just a warning: look to your own, Joshua. Not all of them are on your side. Come on, let's get going.' And with that, and not another word, the Prime Minister led the way back.

Thursday

3 a.m.

Peter lay on his back listening to the soft rise and fall of Frances's breaths and wishing he was likewise asleep. But every time he closed his eyes, an image of the death struggle of the pigeon combined with another that he would rather not imagine filled his mind's eye.

Enough. Counting the plaster flowers that spiralled through the ceiling architraves, lovingly restored under Frances's supervision when they had first moved in, might lull him to sleep. He'd give it a try, starting at the opposite corner of the room and working his way round.

He looked towards the right-hand corner. It was too far away for him to make out many details. Come to think of it, the only reason he could see even as much as he could was because there was a street light glinting through a gap in the heavy curtains. Not that this was stopping him from going to sleep, but now that he was aware of it, he'd not be able to let it pass.

He slipped from the bed and padded quietly over to the window.

As he reached up to pull the curtains to, he caught a glimpse of something red, and when he parted the curtains to try to work out what it was, he saw a full moon over whose surface floated a bloodshot mist. He snapped the curtains tight shut and made his way through the darkness into bed.

He waited for his breath to calm before he carefully pulled at the sheet that Frances had wound around herself, at which point she spoke.

'What are you going to do if he calls your bluff?'

'I'm sorry, darling. Did I wake you?'

'I wasn't asleep. What will we do?'

'He won't. He can't. Chahda's solid.'

(Hoping this was true, and on the wings of this hope, seeing that same distasteful image. Stop it. Enough. Answer Frances.)

'The PM can disown Yares,' he said. 'I'm pretty sure he already has.'

(Chahda must be solid: hadn't he told Patricia of Yares's abrupt departure for Chequers?)

'But that won't let the PM off the hook,' he said.

'Don't underestimate him. He's a doughty fighter.'

Not like her to have misgivings. 'Don't worry, darling.' He reached out a hand, which she took.

He squeezed her hand, and she squeezed his back. And yawned.

'Tired?'

'Mmm.' She yawned again.

'I'm so sorry. I'm disturbing you.'

She muttered something that he couldn't quite make out. 'I beg your pardon?'

She said, more clearly, 'Sleeping pills in the cabinet. Or brandy might help.'

'Thanks, darling.' And he did need sleep. 'I'll try one or both. And so that I don't keep you up, I'll sleep elsewhere.'

Another inaudible comment as she wound the sheet more completely around herself.

He took the sleeping pills from the bathroom cabinet and then downstairs, belt and braces, poured himself a large brandy.

There were other bedrooms in the house, but on the occasions when he couldn't sleep, he always liked to go to Charles's. Something comforting about the almost monastic feel of the room, combined with its dinosaur curtains (which Frances really should soon change).

He was tired. He needed sleep. He chased a sleeping pill down with a slug of brandy. Squeezed himself into the bottom bunk. Closed his eyes. And saw those two images again: the first of the pigeon struggling to free itself from the pelican beak and, superimposed on that, a great bear of a man crying out as he entered Patricia.

7 a.m.

The light filtering through the thin curtains told Peter that he must have overslept, although, without his watch, he had no idea of the time. His head was hurting. Looking forward to clearing it with a long cold shower, he climbed out of the narrow bunk and made his way back to the master bedroom. There the drawn curtains had kept the room dark. And quiet. Frances must still be sleeping to the sound of someone outside who was clipping a hedge.

Except, he realised, the sound was coming not from outside but from inside the room. Odd. He peered through the gloom. And saw Frances not only awake but also out of bed. She was sitting on the carpet surrounded by what seemed to be a heap of clothes. He clicked on the light.

They were clothes – his clothes – and the sound that he could still hear was Frances, who, head bent, was cutting them.

'What are you up to?'

She held up a pair of his trousers. One of his black pairs.

'They don't need repairing.'

'They didn't,' she poked one hand through the hole she must have just made in the crotch, 'but they do now.'

Had she gone mad? He crossed the room, intending to take the scissors from her, but before he could get close, she was on her feet and stabbing the scissors in his direction.

She knows, he thought. Said, 'Frances. Darling.'

'Fuck you.' Her blue eyes blazed from a face that normally pale was dark red as, still jabbing the scissors, she advanced on him. 'I warned you.'

He was slowed down by sleep. At the very least, he was going to end up badly cut.

'I told you what I would do.'

He was closer to the bathroom than to the landing. He backed away and then, when she began to run at him, the dog now yapping at her heels, he turned and also ran, straight into the bathroom. He caught a glimpse of the scissors stabbing down as he banged the door shut. When he drew the bolt, they hit the door so hard they made it shake.

She wouldn't have enough strength to stab through the wood. Would she? He stepped away from the door.

Silence. He checked that the bolt was securely in place.

She must know, he thought, but who could have told her? And then he thought that the Frances he knew so well would never have threatened violence. This had to be a dream. He glanced at the bath and saw that it was blue.

Definitely a dream from which he would soon awake. In the meantime, he was sweating. He went over to the basin to wet his face, after which he held his wrists under the running water.

The sound of something being dragged.

Back at the door, he pressed his ear against the wood. He thought he could hear Frances's hard-won breaths, but they might have been his.

Footsteps – and her voice, 'Come on girl,' and then he assumed that the soft click he heard was the door being closed.

He stood, quietly.

No further sound, or at least none that he could hear. He switched off the tap and went back to put an ear against the door. Still nothing. He started counting and only after he had got to fifty did he call out, 'Frances?'

No answer.

He tried again: 'Frances?'

It was possible that she was still there and if he came out she'd launch a fresh attack. But he was properly awake by now (this was no dream), and if she did he would close the door on her arm.

Holding his breath, he used his left hand to carefully draw back the bolt while with his right he held the door against the door jamb. Then slowly, slowly and inch by inch he opened the door.

She wasn't there, not that he could see. But something else was. He opened the door a fraction wider and saw that she had dragged her dressing table across the room so as to stop him coming out. He called again: 'Frances?'

When still she did not reply, he decided to risk the room.

He'd either have to push the dressing table out of the way, which would be noisy and might fetch her back, or else he needed to crouch down and climb under. Not very dignified, but in this situation to hell with dignity. Having said 'Frances' one more time – although by now he was pretty sure she wasn't there – he widened the opening of the door before getting down onto his hands and knees and crawling through.

The room was empty.

Thank heavens for small mercies.

He looked at the devastation she had left behind, with what appeared to be his entire wardrobe scattered about. When he picked through the pieces, he saw that she had attacked every one of his trousers, in some cases severing the legs, while his shirts were splattered with blue ink that was now beginning to leak onto the carpet.

For the house-proud Frances to have done that, she had to know. Someone must have told her.

His dressing gown was hanging in its usual place on the back of the door. When he tried to put it on, however, he discovered that it had also been shredded. Turned into a tattered shawl. No other option but to go down in his pyjamas.

What if she were waiting for him on the landing? And what if she attacked again? He cast around for something with which to defend himself. He could only see her hairbrush, so he grabbed that.

No one on the landing. He tiptoed across and to the stairs. Nothing. And down. Still nothing.

But he could soon hear the burble of a radio coming from the kitchen. No other choice but to brave her there. Big breath in and then he strode across the hall and wrenched open the door.

What he saw almost convinced him that this must be a dream.

She was at the table drinking tea – a familiar sight of many years duration – with a neat pile of newspapers awaiting his perusal. She was dressed in her pale-blue frock, the one he particularly liked and which showed off her figure to best advantage. Her hair was coiffed and smooth.

She clicked the radio off. Looked up. Said, 'What are you doing with my brush?'

And a weird dream as well. He put the brush down on the nearest counter. 'What time is it?'

'Time for you to see the PM,' she said. 'His office has been ringing.'

He looked to the counter where the phone usually was.

'They were so annoyingly persistent,' she said, 'that I threw the house phone into the garden. Do apologise, when you have the chance, to the policeman I almost brained. Not that turfing it out gave me much peace,' she continued, 'because they then kept trying your mobile. And so,' she shrugged, 'I fear I was a little rough.' She glanced down to where his phone, back off, glass smashed, was lying at her feet. The dog, who was also there, raised her head and barked.

'Shhh.' She pushed the dog's head down.

The dog convinced him: he was awake. 'What's going on?'

'And still he keeps on with the charade.' She said this not to him but past him, as if there was somebody behind him.

He whirled round. There was no one there.

'Try the papers,' she said.

They were on the table, just by her right elbow. He didn't trust that she wouldn't pounce, so he stood away from the table as he snatched them up. In doing so, he knocked her cup over.

She sat and watched it fall. 'That's not going to do your phone much good,' she said as the cup broke, spilling tea.

She got up.

He flinched.

She gave a derisive little sniff. 'You're not worth it.' And went to put the kettle on.

He didn't trust his legs, so he sank down to the floor. Picked up a paper.

Not a dream. A nightmare. The front page, which for the last six days had been filled with images of rioting, now consisted of a banner headline – 'Home Affairs' – and two photographs. The first featured him and Patricia walking side by side out of his office, while in the second their heads were close together, unmistakeably moving in for a kiss. No further text save for an instruction to turn to a centrefold, which, when he pulled the pages apart, he saw was filled with more of the same, including a photo of his hand on Patricia's bottom.

'They say they also have you in flagrante,' Frances said, 'although they haven't printed those. Saving them for the net, I expect.'

'Home Secretary Plays Away', he read on the next paper in the pile.

'Congratulations,' she said. 'Your dream of making it to every front page has finally come true.'

He felt heat rising. And nausea, which he swallowed down. He was ruined. And by his wife. 'How could you?'

'How could,' she paused so as better to stress her final, '*I*?'

'You sent those pictures to the gutter press.'

'And have my humiliation played out in public? Why would I do that?'

'To get revenge.'

'If you think that I, of all people, would do that publicly, then you understand me even less than I thought. So listen to me: I did not send those photographs to the tabloids. I hadn't even seen them before Ann phoned to warn me.'

'You saw them the other day.'

'I saw some. I showed those to you. These are different: proof that you lied even when you could have, when you should have, told me the truth.' She got a cup out of the cupboard above the kettle and put it down on the counter so roughly it was a wonder that it didn't break. She turned her head to pin him with a fearsome glare. 'But why not go on worrying about who did this to you rather than what you've done to me? And to your son.'

His breath caught in his throat. 'Does Charlie know?'

'I have told the school to hide the papers and block the web. But some kind soul is bound to find a way to fill him in.'

He winced, thinking about the sniggers that poor Charlie would have to endure. But no time for that right now. 'So you didn't send them?'

'Is that all you can think about?'

He remembered then that gaze from Downing Street. 'This must be the PM's doing.'

'Forced you into bed with her, did he?' She poured out water from the kettle into a cup.

'He did it to ruin me.'

281

'Whereas you, you whiner,' she pulled the tea bag out and dropped it on the counter, 'you did it just to get your leg over.'

When she picked up the cup, he saw that she was trembling. So much so that when she lifted it, she didn't manage to get it anywhere near her mouth. In her juddered breaths he could hear her effort to keep her composure. She put the cup down.

Seeing her head lowered, he felt the first twinges of a terrible regret. 'I'm so sorry.'

She stood, head bent.

'If I could undo it.'

She was as still as a statue.

He went up to her. Put his arms around her.

She did not reject the move but neither did she relax into his embrace.

He knew her so well he could feel the effort it cost her not to.

'I'm sorry.' He stroked her forehead, pushing soft strands of hair behind her ear.

She reached up, grabbed the hand and twisted back his thumb.

'Ouch.'

She kept on twisting it.

'Stop it, Frances.' His effort to get away had him almost on his knees. 'Stop it. You're hurting me.'

She let go so abruptly that he did drop down.

'For God's sake.' As he raised himself up, he spotted a face at the window. It was a policeman peering in to see what the noise was about. He waved his hand, and the face disappeared.

He said, 'You have to stop, Frances, there are people watching.'

'They certainly are. Including a full pack of paparazzi out front.'

How strange that only then did it dawn on him how thoroughly he was finished. Not only in his leadership bid but as anything in the government. Or even as an MP.

'I expect they're waiting for the two of us to come out arm in arm,' Frances said, 'my role to look wronged but supportive, yours to tell them what a mistake you made and how much you love me.'

Was she offering him a way out? 'Would you?'

She looked at him. No expression. In that moment it occurred to him that all was not lost. That he could make this better.

She lowered her head.

He stood and waited – what else could he do? – for her to look up again. He saw her shoulders begin to shake. She was crying. He wanted to console her but didn't dare go close.

When she stopped shaking and lifted her head, he saw that her expression was clear. 'I want you out.'

'I will go,' he said. 'If that's what you really want. Once the paps have cleared off.'

'You're so slow, Peter.' He had never heard her voice so cold. 'Always have been. You're a godsend – front-page material just as the riots are trailing off. The last thing they're going to do is clear off.'

'I need time.'

'I told you, Peter, infidelity is the one thing I would not tolerate. Which sin you have compounded by lying about it.'

'She doesn't mean anything to me.'

'I suggest you tell her that. It no longer interests me. I'm asking you to leave, and I will not ask you again.'

He glanced down. 'I've got nothing to wear.'

She shrugged. 'Not my problem.'

He said, 'Come on, Frances, be reasonable.'

'If you're not gone in five minutes,' she said, 'I'll denounce you on the doorstep.'

8 a.m.

Moving up against the tide of people on their way down the Tube steps, Billy was finally on his way home. He stepped out of the entrance, refusing the proffered newspaper after a quick glance told him that rioting's pole position had now been taken by the Home Secretary's marital ructions. And so the world spins, he thought, as he walked wearily through streets that, after what he'd recently witnessed, seemed preternaturally calm.

He was so tired. Sleep beckoned as he slipped the key into the lock. But though the door opened easily enough, when he tried to widen the gap he couldn't. He craned his head in and saw that the post and the papers that had been delivered in his absence had jammed the door. If he hadn't been so tired – too tired to even work out whether it was three, four or five days since he'd last been home – he would have expected this. He pulled the door closed and then shoved it so hard that it passed over the blockage.

Once in, he collected up the post – mostly catalogues over which Angie loved to pore – and piled it on the hall table for her return. He was glad he'd advised her to keep the girls at her parents' until the trouble died down. Not that there'd been any around their area, but you never could tell. And this way none of them would have to smell him until after he'd had a shower.

He lifted an arm to sniff his armpit, and it almost choked him. He had managed occasionally to wash, but even a scrub down with carbolic would have been of little help since he afterwards had to put on the same kit, day after day, and in this heat. Lucky his men were in the same position. If not, he would have driven even the most hardy away from any line he was in.

The men had been magnificent, surpassing all expectations. So much so that senior management – who normally looked down on them, thinking of them as a necessary evil and the hooligan end of the service – were these days flocking to shake them by the hand and have their photos taken doing so. Which was the only silver lining in the disaster of the last five days.

The rest was just such a waste. Of livelihoods, of homes, and more importantly of lives: those idiots who had got caught up in an orgy of destruction would now find themselves jailed for rioting, thus making themselves forever unemployable. The only good thing was that nobody had been badly hurt, and with the Lovelace already scheduled for replacement, those shopkeepers who'd been burnt out would most likely have been the ones soon driven out by rising rents. An irony that: that the rioters had done the dirty work of the speculators they abhorred.

He really did stink. He must have a shower.

But first a cup of tea. He picked up the newspapers – he would have cancelled them if it hadn't taken so long for it to dawn on the muppets at Silver that something serious was kicking off – and took them to the kitchen.

He put the kettle on. While he was waiting for it to boil, he realised that either he was smelling worse than he'd originally assumed or something else was. He opened the fridge: almost empty but, apart from a pint of milk that might be on the turn, nothing bad. He sniffed his way to the pedal bin. He kicked it open and was nearly knocked back by the stink. Must have thrown some meat in – it was covered in so much green slime he couldn't tell what it was – and without first putting in a liner. If he didn't clear it away before Angie's return it would confirm her (he thought ill-founded) opinion as to his lack of house training.

He took one of the newspapers from the pile and laid it, Home Secretary's ugly mug face down, on the tiled floor. The stuff in the bin was noxious – more paper needed. He grabbed for another one and, as he was smoothing it down, he read the headline: 'Where is he?' underneath which was a close-up of a man's face and, under that, another equally large: 'Reward offered'.

Oh great. The hacks putting a price on the head of a rioter was really going to help community relations, wasn't it? He smoothed the paper out and picked up the bin, meaning to empty it. But before he did, he glanced again at the photo. A rabid expression – that's why they must have chosen it – on a male IC3 who, he saw, the paper called Molotov Man. He blinked and looked again. He was tired, deadly tired if the truth be told, but he couldn't help thinking that he had seen this face, and recently.

But where? He sat back on his heels, breathing through his mouth, as he let his mind range free, which worked for him when he was trying to put a name or a place to a suspect.

Had he seen this face rearing close (which would mean that the man would have been one of the ones leading the attack)?

No, that wasn't it. Somewhere else, then. And recently.

He scrolled backwards through the last few days. Not an easy task when one moment had spilt into the next. It had been dark, that he remembered, but then most of what had happened had happened after dark. Not in a street, he thought. Somewhere else.

And then – gotcha – it came to him. This was the man he'd seen by the canal ranting at the traffic warden. Whom Billy had taken to be a drunk not worth arresting. Who, it turned out, was top of the riot's most-wanted list, at least according to the red-tops.

Shit. He sighed. More than anything he wanted to take a shower, bag up his uniform and go to sleep. Now, instead, he knew he had to phone the Rockham station and report what he had seen. Try to help them find this man before some avaricious member of the public decided to take the law into his own hands.

10 a.m.
'Using the back door again, Home Secretary?' The PM's Press Secretary's gaunt face was set to sneer. 'It's getting to be a habit.'

Fuck off, Peter thought, although he held his tongue.

'He's upstairs in the flat.' The Press Secretary turned on his heels.

They could have gone the back way rather than through the main building and up the winding staircase, a route presumably chosen so that he would have to endure the sneaked side-glances and theatrical double-takes of those whose paths they crossed. And also, he thought, so that he could pass the succession of photographs of previous prime ministers that lined the wall and know that he now had no chance of ever being included in this honour guard.

The Prime Minister had seen to that. Well, Peter would return the compliment and pull the PM down.

They moved through Number 10 and up the last flight of stairs to the Prime Minister's flat. 'He's expecting you.' Having rapped on the door, the Press Secretary opened it to practically push Peter in before closing the door.

'Peter. At last.' What a contrast from their last meeting. The PM jumped up and came over to shake him by the hand. 'What a time you've had of it.' He stepped away and stood a moment, looking Peter up and down. 'What on earth are you wearing?'

'Tracksuit bottoms. And a pyjama top. All I could lay my hands on.'

'Frances took it that badly, did she?' The PM moved past Peter to open the door and shout, 'Martin, are you still there?' and on receiving a faint, 'Yes, sir, I am,' continued, 'find the Home Secretary something decent to wear. And make sure that it fits.' He closed the door. Swallowed. Said, 'Martin knows about the affair, of course' – as if anybody in Britain wouldn't – 'and is available to help you work out how best to play this in public. But first I think you and I should have a chat. Come. Take a seat. Can I get you something to eat?'

From betrayer to genial host: well, the PM always did have a reputation for Machiavellian twists. 'No, thanks. I'm fine.'

'Not even a coffee? You look as if you need one.'

If he didn't agree to one, the PM would only find another way to extend his crowing. 'Why not?'

'Good.' The PM raised his voice: 'Darling, would you mind making Peter a coffee?'

To which came the instantaneous reply: 'Tell him to make his own,' followed by the slamming of a door.

'Sorry about that.' The PM gave a small tight smile. 'Afraid you might have to put up with quite a bit of that kind of thing.' He went over to the kitchen counter. 'Not that our wives have much liking for each other, but when it comes to sexual infidelity, women always tend to back each other up.' He busied himself putting on the kettle, measuring grinds into a pot and placing cups and a milk jug on a tray.

Standing and waiting for the axe to fall, all Peter could do was look around this garish room with its clashing textiles. Frances would have imposed style on this mess, he thought.

'No matter how supportive our wives are, they can never really understand the pressures on us.' The Prime Minister poured water into the pot. 'And, besides,' looking up, 'that business about Teddy hardly endeared you to her.'

So the PM was trying to downgrade his own corruption into the (presumably now irrelevant) business about Teddy. Well, he wasn't going to get away with it. 'Sacking me will not make the problem disappear, Prime Minister.'

'Who said anything about sacking you?' The Prime Minister carried the tray over and laid it down on a side table. He pushed down the plunger of the coffee pot, against obvious resistance, and poured. 'You do take milk, don't you?' He poured in milk. 'And no sugar?' handing the cup over without waiting for a reply.

Peter looked down to where dark grounds were floating on the surface of the liquid.

'It's dreadful what the hacks have done,' the Prime Minister said. 'I feel for you.'

'I bet you do.' He stretched across and, taking up the sugar bowl, ladled in two heaped teaspoons.

'It is my belief,' the PM said, 'that what goes on inside a marriage is – if you will forgive the pun – a private affair.'

'Didn't stop you from having me followed.'

A frown. 'You think I had you followed?'

'I know you did.' Even sugared the coffee had no taste. 'And asked them to photograph what they saw.'

The PM leant forward. 'I am going to stop you right there, Peter.' His voice though soft was full of menace. 'Before you say something both of us will regret. You have had a shock, I understand this, but you should think long and hard about accusing me of obtaining and/or distributing any photographs of you. I had nothing to do with it.'

Yes, Peter thought, just like he'd had nothing to do with the burying of Teddy's arrest report. 'You knew about me and Patricia.'

'Of course I knew. Along with the whole Westminster village. I'm surprised you managed to keep it from Frances as long as you have. I would have thought she'd have been more alert. But just because I knew doesn't mean I leaked it.'

He didn't need to: he had minions for that.

'Or that anyone in my office did. If you're looking for a scapegoat, you'll have to look elsewhere. I suggest you start with those you have hurt.'

Did the PM want to strip him of all dignity by telling him that he knew Frances had released the photographs? He put his undrunk coffee down and got up. 'I don't think we need to play out this farce any longer, Prime Minister. I am quite capable of writing my own resignation letter.'

'Sit down, man. To repeat: I have not asked for your resignation, and I do not intend to. I will not let the red-tops dictate who I do and do not have in my Cabinet. And I will not have my people hounded out for the things they do in the privacy – as long as it's legal – of the bedroom. I could also do without a reshuffle given the impending election. You've made a fairly decent fist of the job so far and, once we have settled our differences, we can pull together. For all these reasons, I propose to keep you on as my Home Secretary.'

Despite himself, Peter felt hope flare. He sank back into the sofa and thought, it can't be that easy. 'And in exchange?'

The Prime Minister took a sip of his coffee, grimaced and scraped his teeth against his tongue. 'What awful swill. It's full of grounds. She's right: I never do brew it long enough.' He put down his cup. 'And, yes, you're also right, there is a quid pro quo – or three of them. For starters: I assume that in light of the adverse publicity you will no longer be standing against me?'

Peter nodded.

'In that case, my first condition is that you do not actively support another candidate. In exchange, and when the time comes for me to retire, I will consider backing you.'

And if you believe that, Peter thought, you'd believe the proverbial anything. But what he said was, 'And your other conditions?'

'The second is that you leave the Teddy business with me. Rest assured I will pursue it – and if Yares is the rotten apple, as you think he is, I will get rid of him. But I will do this at the right time, and not in the middle of a riot when the last thing we want to do is undermine the Met.'

'I'll think about that. After I've heard your third condition.'

'Of course.' The Prime Minister sighed. 'This one is rather personal, I'm afraid, but I can see no other way round it. I cannot have my Home Secretary hounded by the press, which is what will happen if you don't act decisively. So my third condition is that you either stay with Frances, and for this you need to get her active and vocal support, and give up Patricia Diaz, or you publicly declare your marriage to be over. I've discussed both options with Martin. He agrees that we can weather either, as long as there's no further shilly-shallying.' The Prime Minister sighed again as he got to his feet. 'I know this is a big ask, but if you want to stay in post, this is the only way we can see to make it work. Think about it, but not for too long. I'd like an answer,' he glanced at his watch, 'within the hour. And best not go running around town until you've decided. I would let you stay here, but,' a glance at the interior of the flat, 'you may not be entirely welcome. Martin will be waiting for you downstairs, hopefully with some decent clothes. He'll find you somewhere you can sit and consider your options. We could fetch

Frances, if that would help. Or if you'd rather talk it over with Ms Diaz, I believe she is somewhere in the building.'

'What's she doing here?'

'Frances has your security detail to protect her from intrusion, but Patricia Diaz is on her own. As soon as we saw the early editions, we offered her protection. Given the pressure that will be on her, not least to sell her story, we didn't want to give the press easy access to her. And she was keen. She would like to see you. Understandably.'

10.15 a.m.

What had the Prime Minister been trying to tell him? That's the question that preoccupied Joshua on the journey back from Chequers. He'd been so busy trying to figure out an answer that his driver had had to point out that he was still sitting in the car after they had arrived at his home. And what followed was a night broken by the hammering of that question: what had the Prime Minster been trying to tell him?

How was it possible that the Prime Minister had been questioning his ability on the day before his first week's anniversary in the job? Yes, the riots. But they could hardly be laid at his door. And the water cannon had driven the rioters off the streets of Rockham, while the ploy of keeping the press away (for their own protection) combined with newspaper riot fatigue and the huge splash of Whiteley's affair had kept the incident off the front pages. The gamble that he had taken – that his legacy would be of a liberal policeman who had lowered the bar for illiberal measures – might have paid off. And if the Met Office could this time be believed, the storm that was on its way would be furious enough to put an end to any further rioting.

None of this mattered, though, if the intrigue that the PM had intimated was brewing was about to blow up in his face.

It couldn't be Jibola. They'd kept a wrap on that: the only person outside of Scotland Yard who knew about it was the Prime Minister, and he wasn't about to betray Joshua, was he? No, of course he wasn't: he'd stuck his neck out to ensure that the head of the Met was somebody he trusted. And he would know that Joshua had nothing to do with the disaster of Jibola. If the blame could be laid at any one officer's door, that officer would have to be Anil Chahda.

And the PM had warned him about somebody on his staff.

It came back to Joshua then how broad had been Chahda's greeting smile that morning. Joshua had registered it at the time and wondered what it was that could have made Chahda, who wasn't normally much given to smiling and who had been on duty all night, so happy. And now he thought back to that moment, he thought there might have been an edge of triumphalism in that smile.

Could Chahda have found a way to slough off the blame for Jibola onto Joshua? Could that be what the Prime Minister had been warning of?

'Commissioner?'

The sergeant down the corridor must be wondering what Joshua Yares was doing stopped rather than striding as he normally did. And the sergeant would be right to wonder: not like Joshua to worry about things before they happened. He stirred himself into motion and, saying 'Have you checked we have all the papers for the meeting?', swept past the sergeant and into the meeting room.

10.25 a.m.

Peter's mood picked up as soon as he put on the clothes Martin gave him (all perfect fits: was it part of the Press Secretary's job to know the inside leg and neck measurements of the entire Cabinet?) and as he ate the breakfast they brought to him. He put aside all thought of his decision while he ate. But after he had used the last piece of toast (how did they also know that he preferred sliced white?) to soak up the eggy residue on his plate, he set the plate aside and replayed, in his mind, the PM's conditions.

Number one: that he would not give his support to any other leadership candidate. A condition that, given there was no one else he would dream of supporting, he easily conceded.

Number two: that he let the Teddy business lie. Understandable that the PM would only support Peter if he wasn't going to find himself shafted. And the 'business' had had an effect: despite his sanctimonious declarations of principle, the PM's generosity to Peter was a result of

291

knowing that Peter could easily destroy him. So, yes, Peter could agree to this condition.

Which left number three: that he choose between Frances and Patricia. How to make that choice? Eyes closed, he thought about them both.

Frances first. Which immediately conjured up memories of her reddened fury and of her contrasting white chill as she had ordered him out, and of her final words: 'You'll be hearing from my lawyer.'

She was so enraged she might not take him back.

That left him with a question: would he want her to?

'Be logical.' Those words said aloud to make him think.

Logically and on the plus side, he and Frances had a life together, a house, a set of friends, a history and a son. Divorce would be to throw all of this away, although Charlie would surely not take sides.

A lot to lose.

In the minus column was the falling away of mutual passion. Not something he could easily repair because, yes, although he'd done wrong to cheat on her, it was a wrong for which he was prepared to take responsibility. He could pretty much bet she would be unwilling to even consider the part that her lack of libido had played in the strain within their marriage.

Once his desire for her had been strong, but after her repeated rejections led him into Patricia's arms, this desire had waned. He still admired her beauty but no longer really fancied her.

Or was he just telling himself that because he thought he couldn't have her?

Patricia, on the other hand, was available. And fun. She was young. Being with her made him feel young again. And her youth meant that she looked up to him. Not that she didn't also care for him. Look what she had done for him.

(No, don't think of that.)

He didn't have to fight for space with her. He was infinitely better established, and she accepted that without needing to flaunt her superior knowledge, or her contacts, or her strategic brain. (On the other hand, she certainly had less of all three.)

If only he could have both.

The one provided security, the other excitement; the one knew the rules, the other cared nothing for them; the one was ambitious, while – and as this thought occurred, he recognised it as the killer blow – the other was ambitious for him.

The balance weighed, the decision, which was no real decision, made, he stretched across the desk and pressed the intercom. 'I'm ready now,' he said. 'Could you show Patricia Diaz in?'

6.30 p.m.

It had been three days since Jayden had been anywhere near the market. Head down, he made his way along the empty street, and the closer he got to his destination, the slower he moved. The only thing that kept him going forwards was the promise he'd made to Cathy although what made him want to run away was the fear that she had got it wrong. He was sure they would still hate him; he only kept going because he knew that Cathy would ask him how it had gone, and he always had been a bad liar.

He could see before he reached the shop that it was all boarded up. They might have gone away. The thought brought a sigh of relief even though he knew in his heart that they had nowhere else to go and he could anyway see an open door-wide gap in the boarding.

He walked quietly now so they wouldn't hear his approach, although how this was going to help he couldn't have said. And then, because he couldn't slow himself down any more, he reached the gap. He looked into the darkness.

'There you are, Jay Don.' Mr Hashi stepped forward.

He had a broom in his hand. Like the last time.

But this was not like the last time. Mr Hashi was smiling. 'Have you come to help in the clear-up?'

Jayden nodded.

'You know I cannot pay you. I have no business.'

'I don't want money,' he said. 'I want to help.'

Another smile, although this time Mr Hashi laid down the broom before sweeping the top of one arm across his face as if wiping something away. 'I spoke wrongly,' he said, 'when we met. I was upset. Even then I knew it wasn't you who attacked my shop. But I was upset.'

Jayden nodded. Looked down at his feet. Shuffled from one to the next. Didn't know what else to do or where else to look.

'Mrs Mason, she told me what happened to you,' he heard Mr Hashi

294

saying. 'She told me how they locked you away for what they think you are. Just like those others destroyed my shop for what they think I am.'

Jayden swallowed. Wondered what words to offer in reply. Felt Mr Hashi's hand lightly placed on one of his.

'I forgot that life is also difficult for you,' Mr Hashi said. 'My mother, she did not forget. She, how do you say, offered me the hell for what I said to you.'

'Gave you hell.'

'Thank you, Jay Don. I need you also for language guidance.'

Mr Hashi's hand was still on his.

Telling himself that in Mr Hashi's world it didn't mean anything when men held hands, Jayden did not pull away.

'Mrs Mason, she is a good woman,' Mr Hashi said. 'A truth-sayer. They are precious.'

Jayden nodded.

'My mother also,' Mr Hashi said. 'But we are not all so fortunate.' Which was the closest Mr Hashi had ever got to showing that he knew how difficult Jayden's mother was.

'Still, we must try to do our best,' Mr Hashi said. 'And to keep to the true path.'

It was all right for Mr Hashi to speak like this, but how was Jayden supposed to know where the true path was?

'Mrs Mason helped me find it. That is what friends are for.'

He thought about his one true friend, Lyndall.

'It is not always easy,' Mr Hashi said.

And then he knew where his path led. He had to help Lyndall do what she needed to do. Before it was too late. He said, 'Can I come tomorrow, Mr Hashi? There's something I've got to do.' And when Mr Hashi nodded and dropped his hand, Jayden smiled, saying, 'See you tomorrow,' and walked quickly away.

7.05 p.m.

'Of course I am standing by my Home Secretary,' the Prime Minister was saying. 'He's doing an excellent job. That's what matters to me, and that's what matters to the country.'

Cut to footage of Peter Whiteley arm in arm with a young woman, confirmation of his marriage break-up, which had headlined the evening news.

'Given the recent tension between the two men and rumours that the Home Secretary was about to challenge the Prime Minister,' the announcer was saying, 'it is intriguing that the Prime Minister has gone out of his way to support Peter Whiteley.'

'Who cares?' Cathy asked the empty room.

'The Prime Minister's Press Secretary has denied rumours that there was a backroom deal between the two men.'

She aimed the remote at the TV and tried to click it off.

'Perhaps the unrest in the streets has convinced them to settle their differences.'

The batteries were dead; she kept forgetting to buy more.

'Frances Whiteley, the Home Secretary's wife, was unavailable for comment.'

She got up and switched it off.

It was blisteringly hot in the lounge. Dark as well, which, given the hour, was odd. She padded, barefoot, to her open front door and stepped out.

Almost as dark and the air so heavy it was like breathing water. She looked up and saw clouds, and not those white puffs that had floated in recently only to dissolve into the blue. This was a solid mass of black storm clouds that was sweeping in over the estate. To the east, where the covering was less complete, shafts of yellow streaked across the sky, making the incoming storm loom even more ominously.

She looked across the balcony to Elsie's house. Door shut as it had been for days. Elsie must be in a bad way what with Jayden still refusing to have anything to do with her. Cathy thought about going over. But she was too weary to withstand the accusations she knew would be forthcoming.

Poor Jayden, she thought, although at least by the smile on his face on his return from the market she knew he must have made it up with Mr Hashi. One good outcome she'd facilitated. If only she could be as effective with her own daughter, who was still basically not talking to her.

She drew herself up. She'd try a fresh tack, she decided: be a better mother by fixing the kids a meal.

Back in the kitchen, she clicked on the radio.

'For all of you who've seen the fire and, if the weathermen have finally got it right, are about to see the rain, that was James Taylor *Fire and Rain*,' the DJ was saying. 'Next *Let it Rain* – any excuse to re-play Eric Clapton – but before that, in the news, the Home Secretary, Peter Whiteley . . .'

She turned the radio off.

She went to the fridge that had become their makeshift larder. But one for the cultivation of bacteria, it seemed, with everything going off. What a terrible housekeeper she was, to add to her other faults. She set herself to emptying the fridge, separating the rotten from the still vaguely edible. She ended up with a pile to throw away and some limp salad leaves – and she'd recently eaten enough salad to last a lifetime.

She should go shopping. But it was getting late and she no longer felt like cooking. Which did not mean she could not provide.

She went down the corridor, knocked on Lyndall's door and immediately went in.

Lyndall and Jayden had been sitting close together on the floor, although at her appearance they jumped apart.

'I'm going to order in. What do you fancy? Pizza? Chicken? Curry? Come out and tell me when you've decided and,' looking at Lyndall, 'there's also something I need to talk to you about.'

They joined her in the lounge, Jayden still smiling and Lyndall sloping in with that sulky expression of hers.

'So what's it going to be?' Cathy kept her voice deliberately light.

'Chicken,' Jayden said.

'Good choice.' She reached for her mobile but then another thought occurred. 'It's still light. If anything's going to kick off, it'll happen later – if it doesn't rain. Why don't we eat out?'

They both nodded.

'But before we do,' she said. 'Something I wanted to say . . .' She paused. She had to find a way of talking to Lyndall but didn't know how she was going to. She tried again. 'It's about Banji.'

'I told you.' Jayden was looking not at Cathy but at Lyndall.

Who shook her head.

'You promised you'd tell her.'

Another silent refusal.

'What's this about?'

'Go on. Tell her.'

Lyndall swallowed.

'Go on. Or I will.'

She'd never seen Jayden this assertive.

Was there something between them, she wondered, and then, this thought driving her to sink down into the nearest seat, could Lyndall, history repeating itself, be pregnant? She wanted and needed to know, and simultaneously did not. She sat trying to calm herself. Waiting.

'Thing is, Mum.'

She looked down at her lap.

'Thing is, I know where Banji is.'

7.30 p.m.

A rap at Joshua's door, which opened to reveal a grinning Anil Chahda. 'We've got him, sir.'

'Jibola?'

Chahda nodded.

Problem solved – and the coming storm, which was already darkening the sky, might well resolve the rest. 'Did he give himself up?'

'We haven't actually laid hands on him yet, sir. But we do know where he is, and we're getting ready to extract him. I sent you an audio file. It should be with you by now.'

There was indeed an email waiting for Joshua with a file attached. He clicked it open and turned up the volume on his laptop.

'*Thing is, Mum,*' he heard. '*I know where Banji is.*'

'That's Lyndall Mason's voice,' Chahda said. 'Gaby Wright confirmed it.'

'*How could you know?*'

'And that's Mrs Cathy Mason.'

'*He had to find a hiding place, so I showed him the warehouse by the canal. The last one they closed. Jayden and I used to play there. I knew about an attic room that's hard to find.*'

298

'We've identified the warehouse,' Chahda said. 'Gaby's lot had already searched that building, but we've now got hold of the owner and the plans. There is indeed such a room, which the first search must have missed. And we have added confirmation: CI Ridgerton phoned the Rockham station this morning to report a sighting of the man near the canal.'

This morning, Joshua thought, and you didn't tell me, as he heard Lyndall Mason saying, '*I wanted to tell you, Mum. But he made me promise not to. Said you wouldn't understand.*'

'*Understand what?*' Lyndall's mother's voice was raised in anger.

'*Why he did what he did. That's all he'd say.*'

Joshua pressed pause. 'How did you get hold of this?'

'We installed a listening device.' Another grin, this one triumphant. 'It was the only way.'

A gamble by Chahda that had paid off but which his boss had expressly forbidden. Chahda must be the rotten apple the PM had been warning of. When this is over, Joshua thought, I'll pack him off in a tumbrel. He pressed play.

'*I took him food. But today the trapdoor was shut and he wouldn't answer. I'm worried, Mum. He kept saying how there's people after him.*'

He stopped the recording. 'Are there officers already on their way to extract him?'

'Not yet, sir. We've alerted SC&O19, but, given the disturbances, there's a shortage of trained officers. And of ballistic vests.'

'You're planning to go in armed?'

'A precaution, sir, after what we've seen of Jibola's behaviour. And, reading into what Lyndall Mason said, he's also paranoid.'

It's not paranoia, Joshua thought, if people really are after you. 'Let me know when you're ready to roll.'

8.30 p.m.

The cafe was crowded, the air thick with the aroma of home cooking, and the windows misted by the moisture and from the bubbling pots of food. Not that Lyndall and Jayden seemed to notice. They polished off every morsel of jerk chicken and rice and peas that had been piled on their plates and then shared a third portion, seeming almost to inhale the food like only the truly starving or the adolescent ever did. And then at last Lyndall's 'Thanks, Mum' was delivered on an open smile. 'Sorry I've been such a pig,' followed by a more tentative, 'Can we go see him now?'

Cathy nodded. She didn't want to, but seeing him, and warning him off Lyndall, was the only way she could think of breaking them both free. She glanced out to where the sky had blackened with the threat of the incoming storm. 'Let's have some tea,' she said. 'And wait to see if the rain will pass.'

8.40 p.m.

A rumbling – the heavens growling – and then the clouds that had turned an evening sky into night were cracked open by a blaze of light.

'Jesus, did you see that?'

That same sound and almost immediately afterwards (the storm must be right above them) a sheet of yellow light seemed to set the sky afire.

'It's like the Northern Lights.'

Rain had begun to drum down on the roof of their van so that when the sergeant said, 'Except the Northern Lights won't electrocute you,' he had to shout to be heard. 'This lot could. When the signal comes, run at a crouch. Heads low and keep a good grip on your weapons.'

More thunder followed by a jagged lightning that seemed to sizzle through the air.

'That was close.' Joshua was sitting with Anil Chahda in the back of his car as the rain thundered down.

'It'll work in our favour,' Chahda said. 'No way Jibola will hear us coming.'

Joshua peered out into the thick darkness. 'Do the men know that Jibola is one of us?'

'No, sir.' As thunder rolled again, Chahda, smelling of the musk aftershave he used, leant over to shout, 'We've kept that information on a strict need-to-know basis.'

'That'll make them more trigger happy.'

'They're well trained, sir.'

'Even so, I don't want Jibola hurt.'

'Course not, sir. If it can be avoided.' Chahda pressed his watch to light up the dial. 'Thirty seconds.' He looked across to Joshua. 'No point in all of us getting soaked. Why not stay here until it's over?'

'Oh, I reckon I can withstand a bit of rain.'

'As you wish, sir.' Chahda opened the door and the rain came blasting in. 'They're off.'

Ahead, the van doors had been rolled open to let out a line of men who, crouching low, ran towards the warehouse door. The rain was so thick that the darkness had soon sucked them in.

'Come on.' Joshua was also out and also running. Within seconds he was soaked through.

Another crack of thunder and the sky split, the lightning sending a jagged streak over the running line of men, who, having reached the door, formed themselves into two lines on either side of it. A thud, this time an earthly one, as a battering ram was slammed against the door, which splintered and gave way, so that soon Joshua could see the wraiths of sodden men disappearing into the dark interior.

He followed, registering the hard puffing of Chahda's breath beside him, watching the flash trace of torchlight flitting up the stairs.

'Watch your step, sir.' This from the officer who'd been posted at the bottom of the stairs. 'Some of them are really rotten.'

Above them soft voices could be heard calling out, 'Clear.'

By the time they reached the first floor, the flicker of torches was already on the way up again.

A flash of sheet lightning lit up the cavernous space, illuminating broken windows and a floor littered with crates and bits of furniture, all of them covered with what looked like oil. Joshua wiped a finger over the balustrade, feeling how sticky it was and then, holding the finger up to his nose, smelt not oil but something stickier and more viscous that stank of something rotten. An awful place to hole up in. If Jibola had been in a bad way when he'd got here, he would be much worse now.

Darkness as the lightning faded and those soft calls: 'Clear.'

'We think he's up a trapdoor on the floor above,' Chahda said in his ear.

They climbed the last flight of stairs up to the top floor, where they found the men grouped along one wall. One of their number was standing away from them and using his torch to illuminate what was clearly a trapdoor in the wooden ceiling. At a nod from his sergeant, another pulled at the latch of the door, which opened, letting down a ladder which the officer caught and gently lowered so that it didn't bang, the torch illuminating what should have been a space but wasn't.

'He's dragged something over the area,' Chahda whispered. 'That must be what Lyndall Mason meant.'

A moment's confab – how were they going to get up there without alerting Jibola?

'We'll go in fast,' the sergeant kept his voice so low they had to crowd round him to hear what he was saying, 'in the hope that the element of surprise will prevent any counterstrike. We need something solid to stand on – the battering ram – and the carbon arc searchlight should blind him for a moment. I will go in first with that; Wilson, you'll be following with your weapon cocked. You others after. Careful if you have to fire: we don't want to lose any of our own.'

No sooner said than prepared. One of the officers got onto the platform they'd built out of crates and stood, waiting. When the next blast of thunder began to roll, he lifted the battering ram, banging at whatever was blocking the opening and shifting it out of the way. As soon as that was done he jumped to one side while his sergeant, light upheld, climbed up the ladder, followed by his second. There was a queue behind, the men waiting to go up, with the first one already halfway when the sergeant's face appeared in space of the open trapdoor. 'You better come and see this, sir,' he said to Joshua, and then, to his men, 'Stand down, lads. Stand down.'

8.50 p.m.

With the storm showing no signs of letting up, they decided to brave it. The rain was sheeting down so hard that within minutes of coming out of the cafe all three were soaked. Since no coat any of them possessed would have withstood such a deluge, there wasn't any point in going home and drying off before venturing out again and, besides, since the rain was warm, the wet felt almost welcome.

'Although if it goes on much longer,' Cathy said, 'it's going to be as black as pitch.'

Such a quantity of rain had already fallen that the gutters were bubbling with it, and the roads awash. At first they hugged the far sides of the pavements to avoid being splashed, but soon they were so wet it didn't matter. Walking turned into a game of hopscotch as they dodged the vegetables and plastic bags and other detritus that bobbed along with the rivulets of rain that were soon so deep that they took off their shoes and walked on carrying them. Past the High Street, which was empty – no pedestrian in their right mind or, for that matter, rioter would venture out in this unless driven to.

Which Cathy was. 'No,' Lyndall kept saying and shaking her head when Cathy suggested aborting the expedition. 'No' and 'No' again. 'He needs us.' And so on they went, soaked to the skin and making their way towards the canal. Which, when they got to it, was inky black and heaving with rain.

They crossed the bridge, normally a resting place for drunks who wanted to be left alone to drink, and on to the opposite bank.

'It's there.' Lyndall's pointing arm was washed in rain. 'The third in that row.'

Cathy thought she saw something – a dark shadow, moving. 'Is that . . .?' But no, nobody there: probably just an illusion of the rain. 'Come on,' she said. 'Let's go and get him.'

There being so much mud churned up on either side of the gravel path, they walked in single file with Cathy in front. Water dropped off her chin and splashed down the ends of her bedraggled hair, and it got into her eyes, so she kept on having to shake her head to clear her vision. She was grateful for the distraction. When she finally did come face to face with Banji, what was she going to say?

The brooding outline of the building Lyndall had pointed to was coming closer.

'It's the one after this,' she heard Lyndall saying.

Somebody there. She saw them now as a dark outline. 'Who's there?' she called.

The faint beam of their torch lit up the shafting rain. 'What are you up to?' The man – a policeman, she saw – was peering anxiously at them. 'Identify yourselves.' He raised something – a whistle – to his lips.

'I'm Cathy Mason.' She stepped up to make sure he saw her empty hands. 'And this is my daughter Lyndall and Jayden, a friend.'

'What are you doing here?'

'We're . . .'

'Taking a walk,' Lyndall piped up.

'Funny time for a walk.' The policeman let his whistle drop and swiped his face, wiping away the rain. 'But you can't keep on this path. It's blocked. You need to go back the way you came and cross the bridge, and then you can walk along the opposite bank. Although if I were you on such a filthy night, I'd just go home.'

Over his head Cathy thought she saw lights flickering high up in the warehouse. 'What's going on, officer?' She was right: there were lights there.

'Police operation,' he said. 'Nothing that . . .'

Lyndall's loud 'You told them' stopped him from finishing his sentence.

'No, I did not.'

Lyndall's voice even louder: 'You did. You fucking well told them.'

'Now, now.' The policeman shone his torch in Lyndall's face.

Her eyes were ablaze and focused on her mother: 'That's why you were acting so nice, buying us supper and all. Waiting for the rain to end. You told them and then you slowed us down so we couldn't go and warn him.'

'Him?' The policeman took a step closer. 'Who's him?'

'Oh, go fuck yourself.' Lyndall turned on her heel and marched off.

8.55 p.m.

It had been a filthy day and the beginnings of a night that wasn't turning out to be much better. Peter rolled off Patricia to lie beside her on his back: 'I'm such a cliché.'

'It's okay.' Patricia stretched out a consoling hand. 'It's only because you had such a hard day.'

Which – given that he'd lost his wife, his home, the possibility of ever becoming Leader – was an understatement that nearly made him laugh out loud. He breathed in, registering that same slightly musty odour he had smelt on her earlier. 'Have you changed your perfume?'

'No.' She frowned. 'Why?'

'Just something I keep smelling.'

'Really?' She lifted up an arm and (something Frances would never in a million years have done) sniffed under an armpit. 'Seems okay to me.'

Leave it, he told himself. And said, 'Perhaps a shower?'

He saw the hurt in her expression, but all she said was, 'Okay, then' before getting out of bed and closing the door of the en-suite behind her.

As soon as she had gone, he felt the relief of being on his own.

Despite the air conditioning, the room felt stuffy. Enclosed. Claustrophobic. It was the change, he supposed. Because although he'd been with her in many a hotel room, these had always been fleeting visits, a step out of their separate lives. But now he had no home to go to and, with the press camped on her doorstep, they couldn't go to hers.

So here they must stay.

For better or for worse.

He sighed, got up and went over to the windows that ran the length of one wall. Not their usual choice of hotel: this one was corporate with many rooms stacked, each one of the same size and same inoffensive decor as its neighbour.

He pulled the cord and the curtains swished open to expose a dark night. He thought that the storm, whose thunder could be heard even through the double glazing, and whose lightning had flashed in like a warning, must have moved on, but as soon as he pulled open the slotted casement at the top of the window, rain came sheeting in. He pushed it closed, thinking, drought over, flood on the way.

'Shall we go out to eat?' Patricia called.

Eat at a restaurant with his face and hers on every media outlet: what was she thinking of? 'We'd better use room service.'

'Okay.' Her faint reply was followed by the sound of singing.

She was happy.

Of course she was. She'd got what she'd always wanted: him.

He'd order a nice bottle of red with supper, he thought, and if there wasn't one that suited his fancy, he would send the concierge out with full instructions. In the meantime, what he needed most was a stiff drink.

He went over to the minibar and broke the seal. Didn't like the look of the whisky so got out a mini bottle of gin to which he added tonic. Took a sip. Grimaced. Why anybody ever used slimline tonic was beyond him. Thought, maybe more gin would drive that plastic taste away, and poured another in.

9.04 p.m.

As soon as Joshua surmounted the final rung and hauled himself up into the room, he saw the body.

It was hanging off a beam in the ceiling. A male, IC3, dangling with his back to the trapdoor as if he were looking through a window in the eaves.

'He's dead?'

The sergeant nodded. 'Sure is. And by the ligature mark on his neck looks like he's been dead for a while.'

The low-roofed space was messy with empty cartons of food littered about and dust so thick that Joshua could see where rain had dripped off the sergeant and also the marks left by his feet when he had approached the body.

'Do we have any paper shoes?' Joshua was shouting at the people below so as to be heard above the drumming rain, and on receiving a reply in the negative he said to the sergeant, 'Go and find me two plastic bags. Clean as you can get them. Get the Deputy Commissioner to bring them up – but not to step past the door. And ask an FME to attend urgently. Tell them I'm here: that should hurry them up. The rest of your men are to wait in the van until such time as we have secured the scene.'

'Yes, sir.' The sergeant made his way down the ladder.

Not wanting to cause any further disruption to the room, Joshua just stood and looked at the dangling body.

He had watched the footage of Jibola throwing the Molotov over and over again. He had also read his record, interviewed his wife and begun to understand how beleaguered Jibola must have been feeling in order to do what he had done. Now, taking in that awful, lonely sight, he thought again about how very desperate Jibola must have been. Unless of course he hadn't hanged himself.

He looked through the dust, trying to see if he could make out any tracks that might indicate the dragging of a body.

'Sir.' Anil Chahda's head had appeared in the trapdoor 'Is it Jibola?'

'Seems like it, but I'm going to go over just to be sure.' He took the bags from Chahda, wrapped them round his shoes and used the handles to tie them on. Then, taking care to trace the sergeant's foot-prints in the dust, he made his way over to the body. The head was hanging, swollen, at an angle, the eyes bulging, the skin paler than he expected but even so: 'Yes,' he called to the waiting Chahda. 'It is Julius Jibola.'

11.55 p.m.

The rain was pelting down, soaking her. She was cold. She needed more clothes. She looked down.

Blood – that was the colour of the rain: blood that was now dripping off her summer frock. She cried out.

Heard Lyndall shouting, 'Mum.'

Lyndall mustn't see this. She couldn't know.

'Mum. Wake up.'

She opened her eyes to find Lyndall leaning over her.

She blinked. Sat up. 'I was dreaming.'

'Yes, and shouting the place down.' Lyndall's glare was ferocious. 'Something you feel guilty about perhaps?' Without waiting for an answer, she turned away.

'I didn't tell them,' Cathy said.

'I don't believe you.'

'But it's true.'

'How did they know, then?' Lyndall kept her back to Cathy.

'I don't know how.' She could hear great torrents of rain cascading from the landing. And the night so dark. 'They could have followed you – ever thought of that?' Which was mean of her. 'Or somebody might have seen something and reported it. Or maybe they just decided to search the building again. All I know is that I didn't tell them. And that I wouldn't have.'

'Why not?' At least Lyndall turned back, although she was still frowning and her fists were clenched. 'I know he hit you. He told me that he did. And I know you can't forgive him. He told me that as well. So why wouldn't you have got your revenge by betraying him to the police?'

'I wouldn't,' Cathy said.

'Why not?' That hammering demand. 'Why not? Why not?'

'Because I loved him, no matter what he did.' She had to say more: to tell Lyndall the whole truth. She took in a deep breath and then, before she could change her mind, she burst out with the information she'd held back for so many years. 'I also wouldn't have told the police because there was no way I could do that to your father,' she said and then, seeing Lyndall pale, her honeyed skin losing its colour, immediately regretted what she'd said.

'Banji is my father?'

Too late now to take it back. She nodded.

'I knew it.' As if her legs had given way, Lyndall sank down onto the floor. When Cathy reached down, Lyndall flinched away from the touch. 'I knew it.'

'I'm sorry.'

'What for?' Lyndall's eyes had filled with tears. 'Did you stop him from seeing me when I was a baby?'

'No, I didn't stop him.'

'Did he reject me?' Lyndall's voice quivered.

'No, that isn't right either.' She tried to put all the warmth in her voice that a hug, which she knew would not be allowed, would have delivered. 'He never even met you. He left after I told him I was pregnant. I never told him in so many words that you were his, and he never asked. Just disappeared without a word. It wasn't you he rejected, it was me.'

'Why didn't you tell me?'

'Because what he did was to do with me, not you.'

'But I've been asking you for years.'

'It wasn't to do with you.'

'Oh yes it was.' Lyndall got up and stood a moment, looking at her mother. 'If Banji is my father, it has everything to do with me.' Without another word, she left the room.

Friday

5.30 a.m.

Although the storm seemed to have blown itself out, the clouds were still so thick that dawn was a mere glimmer, struggling to assert itself.

At least the storm had driven away the rioters, Joshua thought, as he looked out at the dark churning of the Thames. Behind him, Anil Chahda was talking on his mobile.

'Thanks,' Chahda said. 'Let us know when you do.' He hung up and said to Joshua's back, 'Her initial assessment is that the cause of death was asphyxia combined with venous congestion.'

'I.e. hanging.'

'Exactly. The high ambient temperature means she can't be precise about the post-mortem interval. Her rough reckoning is some time in the past eighteen to twenty-four hours. She'll know more after an entomologist has had a look.'

The river was so swelled by the recent downpour that waves were lapping against its banks. 'Does she think suicide?' He could hear the buzzing of his mobile on his desk – a text coming through.

'That's her view at the moment, but the site was too messy for her to come to a reliable judgement on the probability of a struggle prior to death. There are injuries visible on Jibola's face and on his torso that might indicate such a struggle, but we also know he was present and active during the disturbances, which is another more likely explanation for this bruising. She'll test for the presence of rope fibres on his hands. If they're there it would point more strongly to suicide.'

Something any policeman would know, Joshua thought. And, turning, said, 'I gather that the Masons attempted to gain access to the warehouse?'

'Yes, and were turned away.'

'If he did kill himself, Lyndall Mason would most likely have been the last person to see him. We'll need to talk to her about his state of

311

mind. But prior to that, we need to figure out how much it's safe to tell them both,' thinking that someone would also have to go and tell Jibola's ex-wife.

'Yes, sir. But I'm afraid there is a further matter which relates to both mother and daughter. If I may access your computer?' At a nod from Joshua, Anil went to the desk.

He leant over the computer and soon the room was filled by the sound of a woman crying out.

'Someone in trouble?'

'I think it's a nightmare, sir,' Chahda said, as a voice that Joshua recognised as Lyndall Mason's called out, *'Mum.'*

As that *'Mum'* was repeated, Joshua strode over. *'Mum,'* he heard, *'wake up,'* before he had time to stretch past Chahda and cut off the sound. 'When was this recorded?'

Chahda peered at the screen: 'Commencement of activated sound this morning at 2:05:17.'

'Hours after we found Jibola. Why are you still listening in on them?'

'The trace had remained active. This recording was forwarded to me as a matter of routine.'

'Deactivate it. Do that asap.' He saw his mobile blinking on his desk. So early for someone to message in. He picked it up. 'Seal the recordings and stop anybody from listening in.' As early as it was, he saw that there were two new messages. They'd been sent in quick succession, both of them giving the same number and containing the same three words: 'Call Mr Switch.'

'Will do, sir, but I still think you need to hear this.'

'I have an urgent call to make,' Joshua said. 'If you wouldn't mind giving me some privacy.' He waited as Anil Chahda walked to the door. 'I'll shout when I'm done.' As soon as the door had closed, he clicked on the number to return the call.

'Downing Street switchboard.'

'Joshua Yares here. Were you trying to get hold of me?'

'Ah, yes, Commissioner, I'm glad we tracked you down. The Prime Minister asks that you attend him at Number 10. As soon as you can.'

5.35 a.m.

Peter's head was pounding so badly that he hoped that the clicking shut of the door that had wrenched him from an uneasy sleep was Patricia with painkillers.

He gingerly cracked open an eye, only the tiniest bit.

The room was dark. Thank God for that.

He couldn't see her, not without moving his head, which he was disinclined to do. But a rustling of paper told him she was by the door.

What could she be up to, he thought, although what did it matter? He closed his eyes.

'You have to see this.' Her voice was unbearably loud.

'I've got a bastard of a hangover.' The effort of producing even those few words was enough to make him groan. 'I have to get more sleep.'

'You can't.'

Who was she to tell him what he could and couldn't do? He'd make sure to ask her that – when, that is, he could summon up sufficient energy. In the meantime, all he managed was a yawn.

The act of opening his mouth sent a shaft of pain through his jaw and up into his temples that was so intense he almost shouted out.

Note to self: do not do that again. Which thought provoked a second agonising yawn.

Her footsteps were like drumbeats. When she sat down on the bed, the world seemed to tip.

'Wake up.'

He felt her breath close to his ear. I must stink, he thought.

'Come on, Peter, up you get.' She put her hands under his armpits and heaved. 'You've got to look at the papers.'

'Not more of that nonsense? Just ignore it. They'll soon get bored.' Another groan as she heaved again. 'Let go of me.'

He was too heavy for her. She did let go. 'They're calling for your resignation.'

'Well, they can't have it. He turned, gingerly, away from her. 'None of their business who I sleep with.' If he lay quite still, with his back to her, maybe she'd take the hint.

'This is not about who you sleep with. It's something else. You have to see it.'

She wasn't going to give up. Groaning, he turned, pushed down on his elbows and that way managed to lever himself up into a seated position. He sank back into the pillow that she put behind him. 'Okay, what is it that's so urgent?'

'They're calling you a liar,' she said. 'On every single front page, or at least on every front page that matters.'

'A liar? For leaving my wife?'

'No, not for leaving your wife. For telling the parliamentary committee that you didn't know the board members of the company that runs the solvent factory. It's not true. You met two of them on more than one occasion. They even had dinner at your house, and the papers say they can prove it.'

5.40 a.m.

As Joshua made his way through Parliament Square and down Whitehall towards Downing Street, he could hear the bleeping of the street-sweeping trucks and the hum of their brushes. They were sweeping up the hangovers – the leaves and plastic bags and mashed-up papers – of the storm, returning Whitehall to its usual pristine state, although it was going to be difficult to get rid of the Saharan sand that, having been precipitated by the storm, covered most visible surfaces. So much so, Joshua thought, it was like wading through rust. Or dried blood.

A memory of the sight of the dead Julius Jibola assailed him, followed by this morning's troubling revelation that Jibola, who'd been posted twice into Cathy Mason's bed, had turned out to be Lyndall Mason's father. And now he'd killed himself, or been murdered, within a mile of where the Masons lived, and his daughter, who hadn't until that point realised she was the daughter, was his last known contact.

It was one thing if he had committed suicide, but if he'd been killed, and if Lyndall Mason had seen anything that might identify the killer – well, this was a complication that could bring the Met down.

He had reached the gate. He nodded to the officer who opened up for him. He walked through and to the door of Number 10, which opened as he arrived, and soon after he was led up the stairs and to the flat.

The Prime Minister, still in pyjamas, said by way of greeting, 'We've got a major problem,' and after that, 'You look like shit. Come in. Sit down.'

He hadn't realised how tired he was until he sank into the soft embrace of a garish sofa.

'Rough night?'

'Rough week. But at least we found our man.'

'Your missing undercover? That's good news.'

'Not really. He's dead. Most likely suicide.'

'I'm sorry to hear it.' The Prime Minister lowered himself down into the sofa opposite Joshua and sighed. 'I assume you've read the latest on our errant Home Secretary?'

'I had a quick glance. And wondered who leaked his schedule to the press.'

'My bet would be on the vengeful wife. Kind of behind-the-scenes thing she would do. She was also the one who would know who ate at their table. And if you'd ever met the father, you'd know that striking back is the kind of thing Frances would do.' The PM sighed. 'Awful that it has come to this, but isn't that always the way? Men like Whiteley may be brilliant political manipulators, but when it comes to dealing with people, especially it seems their intimates, they've got a lot to learn. In Whiteley's case, he should have kept hold of Frances instead of running off with the mistress.'

'Maybe it's love.'

'Maybe – if, and I somehow doubt it, the man is capable of loving anybody other than himself. I hope for his sake that it is love: that will be consolation for the end of his political career. Which is what he's facing. Once you get caught lying to Parliament, you're finished.' The Prime Minister fixed Joshua's gaze with his own. 'It's a bad business. I'm going to have to ask for his resignation, and if he refuses, I'm going to have to sack him.'

It wasn't yet six o'clock in the morning. The PM was not even dressed. He was a man who usually played his political cards close to his hand.

Surely he had not summoned Joshua here on some uncharacteristic whim? 'Am I missing something, Prime Minster?'

Another weighty sigh. 'Peter's exit is going to trigger a major problem for you.'

'How so?'

A long pause before the Prime Minister leant forward: 'When we met here – what was it, only a week ago? Yes, I think it was – I told you that Teddy had given me a garbled account of having been stopped by the police. I couldn't get much sense out of him – just his insistence that he'd been scapegoated – and so I asked you to investigate. Is that how you also remember our conversation?'

'Yes, Prime Minister,' his mouth moving as he held himself deathly still.

'When I phoned you at home the following Sunday – when I was out of the country – you told me that there was no record of Teddy having been arrested. Is that correct?'

'Yes, Prime Minister.'

'Well, that's where the problem lies. Peter Whiteley insists that he has proof that Teddy *was* arrested and that a breathalyser, followed by a blood test, confirmed that he had been driving over the limit. Whiteley also says that Teddy has not been charged because the record was tampered with. And he fingers you as the person who did the tampering.'

'I don't know where he got that from. It's not true.'

'I didn't think it could be.' There was a pause, with the Prime Minister's normally steady gaze fractured by a series of blinks, which came to an end as he said, 'The problem is that Whiteley has been talking to someone under your command who not only supports this version but who, he says, can prove it. And who is prepared to do so in public.'

Chahda: it had to be. 'I assume you're talking about my deputy?'

'I'm not at liberty to say. I'm sure you'll understand.'

A nod.

'When Whiteley first came to me with this accusation, I was able to contain it. But the man is paranoid and vengeful. Despite the fact that he can now no longer hope to be Leader, he'll want me, and my family, to suffer. As soon as he loses his Cabinet post, he'll go public with what

316

he knows. Since I had nothing to do with the expunging of the record
– you've just confirmed that – you'll bear the brunt of his accusation.
I cannot afford a protracted investigation that would cast doubt on the
integrity of the Met. If the finger points at you and you can't turn it
away, I'll have no choice but to sack you. I hope you understand?'

What else could he do but give another nod?

'Well then.' The Prime Minister got to his feet. 'I'm sorry it has come
to this. I did my utmost to steer Whiteley away, not out of friendship
to you but because I remain convinced that you're our best chance to
clear out the rotten apples that have eroded the authority of the Met.
But you now need to prepare yourself for what's to come. Whiteley's
due here at ten. As soon as the meeting is over, he's bound to want to
detonate his ticking bomb. I'll talk to you at half nine to discuss next
steps.'

10 a.m.

This is what it must have felt like to be led to the guillotine, Peter
thought, as he concentrated on putting one foot in front of the other
and on staying upright once he had reached the Prime Minister's study.

His enemies had done for him.

His political career was over.

His only consolation was that, by the day's end, his would not be
the only severed head lying in the bloodied basket.

I'm going to take you down with me, he thought as he sat opposite
the Prime Minister.

'Thank you for coming, Peter.'

As if he had a choice.

'Just get on with it, will you?'

'Sure, if that's what you prefer. First up, I know you had nothing to
do with the decision to site the solvent factory in Rockham . . .'

Which hadn't stopped him stealing and releasing Peter's diaries.

'Unfortunately,' the Prime Minister continued, 'it is no longer a question of who took the decision. What your enemies . . .'

As if those enemies had nothing to with him.

'. . . and the press will hold against you is that you lied to the House.
They will not let this go.'

317

And if they did, you'd find another way to get me.

'I can't have a lame-duck Home Secretary, especially given the riots and in the run-up to next year's election. For this reason, I have to ask—'

'Don't bother.' Peter took an envelope out of his otherwise empty briefcase and passed it over.

The Prime Minister laid the envelope down on his desk. He looked across at Peter. 'I would have seen your challenge off. You know that, don't you?'

'I know nothing of the sort. But it's too late for all that now. So do me a favour, spare me the platitudes and get on with it.'

The Prime Minister picked up a paper knife and used it to slit the envelope open. He pulled out the single sheet of paper, put on his reading glasses and skimmed through the letter. 'Is this really all you want to say?'

'At this particular juncture, yes.'

'All right, then.' The Prime Minister laid the paper down on his blotter and smoothed it out before setting it aside. 'We'll release it along with my reply thanking you for your hard and effective work in government.'

'Your time might be better spent drafting your own resignation letter.'

The Prime Minister pushed his glasses to the end of his nose. 'You're determined to get your pound of flesh?'

'You've left me no other choice.'

'You know it wasn't I who released your diaries?'

'So you say. Just as you played the innocent in relation to those photographs. I hope you understand why I can no longer be bothered to keep up a pretence of believing you.'

'Have it your own way.' The Prime Minister set his reading glasses aside. In doing so he must also have pressed some hidden button because there came an immediate knock on the door. Just one knock, which brought the Prime Minister up onto his feet. 'Somewhere I need to be,' he said. 'So if you'll excuse me.'

'Of course, Prime Minister.' Peter got up. 'You'll forgive me if I don't shake your hand.'

'Again, have it your own way.' The Prime Minister came out from behind his desk and moved past Peter to the door. 'Your official car and bodyguard will be withdrawn as of this moment. I suggest you wait or else risk being run down by my security and mobbed by the press. I wouldn't advise the back door either: the paps have cottoned on to your presence, and they're waiting to ambush you. Martin will help you with a more dignified exit strategy from the building. In the meantime, he'll find you somewhere to sit. While you're waiting for the all-clear, I'd suggest that you watch one of the satellite news programmes. There's going to be an item shortly that you will want to catch.'

10.15 a.m.

Was the PM about to resign?

That's the thought that kept coming at Peter after they stuck him in a poky room that adjoined the office of the Garden Room girls. He switched on the television and sat down on a rickety chair – the only one available – to watch pundits blathering on about what was assumed would be his imminent resignation.

'Whiteley has proved himself an able Home Secretary,' one of the pundits was saying, 'even though his appointment was a sop to the hardliners in the Party. But recent rumours that he was about to launch a leadership bid deepened an already wide gulf between the two men. The Prime Minister must be relieved that Whiteley has now been caught, metaphorically speaking, with his hands in the till.'

'Metafuckagorically speaking,' he told the room. If thoughtless cliché was all it took, maybe he should consider television punditry as his next career.

He switched off the sound and sat watching as the camera moved off the three talking heads and on to an item on the rising immigration figures – preparation, he assumed, for his political obituary. One relief of stepping down: he would no longer have to try to solve this particularly unsolvable problem.

The item was brought to an abrupt stop, replaced by a headshot of the programme's anchor. He unmuted the TV '. . . has scheduled an impromptu press conference,' he heard. 'We'll come back to our report of rising immigration levels later, but now we're heading over to the

319

headquarters of the Metropolitan Police, where the Prime Minister is about to make a statement.'

Cut to the Prime Minister in front of a microphone, and beside him Joshua Yares.

If he was just about to resign, why he was doing it there and next to his Commissioner? Could they be so joined at the hip that they were going to commit hara-kiri together?

Wishful thinking: it was much more likely that the coward was trying to save his own skin by throwing Yares to the lions. Not that Peter would let him get away with that. Even if Yares went, he was going to go public with the story of Teddy's arrest.

'I am here today,' the Prime Minister began, 'to share something that has caused me and my wife considerable pain.'

Hold on a minute: what was that emaciated boy, it must be Teddy, the Prime Minister's only son, doing there?

'It's a pain we share with other parents.' The Prime Minister – what a ham – lowered his head. He stood that way in silence, stretching the moment long enough to force out a clearing of someone's throat back in the studio. As if in response, the PM raised his head to looked straight at the camera. 'It has been brought to my attention that my son, Theodore, was recently arrested for driving under the influence of alcohol and under suspicion of having in his possession a small quantity of a Class C drug. In the normal course of events, he would have, and should have, been charged. But someone in the MPS, acting without consultation, buried the report of the incident. As soon as I knew of this . . .'

As soon as? What a lie.

'. . . I asked the Commissioner of the Metropolitan Police to investigate. I can assure you that the guilty party, who has now been identified, will not only lose their job but a docket will be sent to the Crown Prosecution Service with a view to charging them with perverting the course of justice. You will understand that, given the continuing investigation, I cannot provide any further information.'

Unbelievable. Peter's jaw was gaping wide.

And still the Prime Minster kept on. 'For the present, I am here to hand my son Theodore over to the police where . . .'

Even more unbelievable: the man was humiliating his own son so he could stay in power.

'. . . he will be charged with the offences of which he is accused. I regret having to do this in public – I don't want my son to suffer excessively just because of who his father is – but in the light of recent disturbances, I wanted the country to know that all those who break the law, and that includes the Prime Minister's son, must be held to account for their behaviour.' A pause and a blink that wetted his gaze. 'My wife and I will stand by Teddy during this difficult time and help him learn the error of his ways. As I am sure all of you concerned parents,' looking straight out at his audience, 'who have recently been in this same position will do.'

The clever bastard. By exposing his son, he had neutralised Peter's only weapon. And in doing so, he was also coming out as the grand conciliator. Listen to him:

'We have been through a difficult time. The dedication of our police and the refusal of the law-abiding majority to have any part in the disorder have now hopefully laid our recent troubles to rest. It is time for us to take stock and to repair our wounds.' He stretched out an arm and laid it on the jutting bones of his son's hunched shoulders.

There was one last holding of the camera's gaze, in which Peter saw a glint of victory that he knew was aimed at him, before the Prime Minister steered his son out of shot, leaving a gibbering journalist to try to sum up the emotion that he, that the whole country, must be feeling at this public exhibition of a father's pain.

'Enough.' Peter cut off the sound before throwing the remote so hard that it hit a wall, rebounded and, still travelling at speed, went straight through the window.

10.30 a.m.
'I'm sorry it has come to this,' Joshua said.

A tightening of Anil's Chahda's shoulders. 'I didn't do it.' He had his back to Joshua.

'So you say. But the record clearly indicates that it was you who pulled the arrest warrant and you who returned it in altered form.'

'I pulled it because you asked me to. I returned it when you gave it back to me.'

321

'I did not ask you to tamper with the record.'

'And I did not tamper with it.'

'We can keep going round this circle,' Joshua said, 'but we'll only end up in the exact same place. Which is that an inquiry might exonerate you, but it might equally decide that you have a case to answer. If you resign now, you will leave with your record intact.'

'But once I'm no longer around to protect myself, you'll go for me.'

'That's unfair, Anil, and you know it. Yes, if it can be proved that you changed the record, you will be charged. But it has to be so proved. If you leave now, it will be with the glowing reference of the last Commissioner – I have not been in post long enough to amend it.'

'Are you telling me to resign?' A pause before he added, still with his back to Joshua, 'Sir?'

'I'm not telling you to do anything. I'm just laying out your options. But while you're thinking about it, I think you should remember that the arrest record is not the only issue. There is also the not inconsiderable problem of Julius Jibola. You had oversight of SC&O10: the buck stops with you there as well.'

'I was given charge because the unit was malfunctioning. Blame cannot be laid at my door. Not if you're being fair.'

Until then Joshua had been sorry that Chahda was facing such an ignominious end to his career. But to use that 'fair' word! It was pathetic and it was trite – part of the undertone that many a copper had to listen to when collaring someone, or escorting them to the custody suite, or sitting opposite them in the interview room, or hearing them pleading on the stand. It was always those same types who talked about fairness, the ones who, though they broke the law, considered themselves special enough to get away with it. Kids, really, who refused to grow up. How on earth had one of them managed to climb to the top of the Met?

'Leaving aside the issue of the altered record,' Joshua said, 'if anyone was to find out that you bugged the Masons without judicial approval and against my express orders, you'd be out on your ear.'

'It's how we found our man.'

'And it's also how we know that Jibola was Lyndall Mason's father. And once we know it, we cannot un-know it. Can't you see what an impossible predicament that puts us in?'

Now at last Anil Chahda did turn round. His eyes were moist. And bloodshot. 'Are you sacking me?'

'I will.' In contrast to Chahda's slump, Joshua drew himself up. 'After due process, of course. You can try to stick it out. I wouldn't advise it. So what I'm suggesting – and it is only a suggestion – is that you go. Now. Voluntarily. It will be so much easier on you if you do.'

6.15 p.m.

'What a minging bastard that Prime Minister is,' Lyndall said as the news moved on to examining the mystery of the resignation of the Deputy Commissioner of the Metropolitan Police Service. 'How could he do that to his own son?'

Jayden shrugged. 'At least he went with him.'

Sitting on a hard chair, a little way off from where the two were snuggled together on the sofa, Cathy felt cold.

The storm that had killed four people (one by lightning, one by drowning and two from falling trees) and flooded many a house had also brought temperatures down to a seasonal low. Since the council's solution to the communal boiler problem had been to decommission it, things were likely to get very cold in the Lovelace, especially if, as they were saying it might, the temperature dropped any further.

'I bought some lamb,' she said. 'I'm going to fix us a stew.'

No response from Lyndall, which, given that she had said not a word to Cathy either before school or since coming back, was no surprise. And at least Jayden was there to favour Cathy with his open smile and his murmur of appreciation, even though Lyndall had soon cut it off by entwining her long legs around him. When he shouted at her to get off and tried to get away, she gave a whoop and launched herself at him.

Leaving the two tussling on the sofa, Cathy went to the kitchen. She could hear them laughing as she cut onions, which caused her eyes to stream – or at least that's what she told herself. She fried the onions (she'd forgotten to buy garlic, so she'd have to make do without) and then added the meat – probably too early, but experience had taught her that most stews were forgiving even of her own deficient skills. They'd eat together, she thought, by which time Lyndall might have decided to climb off her high horse, and then later they could go together to the canal (she'd go even if Lyndall tried to stop her) and see if they could find Banji.

324

And then?

A shout from the living room – 'Is something burning?' – shook her back into the present moment.

She turned down the heat and began to stir the stew vigorously. Probably a mistake, since she ended up scraping up the burnt bits and mixing them with the rest, creating an unappetising-looking gunge. It needed more liquid. She'd use water to thin it at the same time as she threw in a tin of baked beans. She reached up into the cupboard for the tin just as someone rang the doorbell. 'Get that, will you?'

She pulled the lid off the tin. The whiff of something sulphurous: could it have been spoilt by the heat? She poked a finger in. And the bell rang again.

'Please, somebody answer the door.'

She heard footsteps – Jayden's (well, she shouldn't have expected Lyndall to do anything she asked her to) – heading for the door. She licked her finger. It didn't taste great but that might be because the ketchup she'd used was so sweet. And even if the beans were a bit off, more cooking would stop them from doing any damage. She stirred the contents of the tin into the pot.

'It's the man off the telly,' Jayden said.

She glanced up to find him standing at the kitchen door. 'Which man?'

'The copper who was stood next to the Prime Minister. He says he wants to talk to you.' He was standing eyes downcast and shifting from one foot to the next.

She said, 'Don't worry. It can't have anything to do with you,' and, forgetting that she had failed to put an apron on, wiped her hands on her thighs.

Blast it – now there was a long streak of tomato. She hurried to the door.

She also would have recognised Met Commissioner Joshua Yares from the news, even if he hadn't straightaway introduced himself, which he followed with, 'Can I come in, Mrs Mason?'

'What for?'

'Something I need to talk to you about.' She looked over his shoulder where she saw several of her neighbours standing. He had seen them too. 'In private.'

She nearly told him no. She wanted to. But something about his gaze, something almost pleading, made her step aside.

He took off his peaked hat as he walked over her threshold. Which is when, she later realised, she knew. But at the time, she didn't know she knew. She led him to the sitting room.

'What do you want?' This from Lyndall, who got off the sofa to stand, feet akimbo, hands on her hips.

'If you wouldn't mind, Mrs Mason?'

'Go to your room, Lyndall.'

'Why should I?'

'I said go to your room.' Her voice was raised and her expression fierce. 'And take Jayden with you.'

Red with fury, glaring at her mother, and with the lower half of her mouth set into an ugly frown, Lyndall swept past, almost pushing Cathy out of the way, and stomped down the corridor, followed by a sheepish Jayden.

'Close the door,' Cathy called out after them.

As soon as the door banged, the policeman said, 'Why don't you take a seat, Mrs Mason?'

Another clue. She knew. And protected herself by simultaneously not knowing.

'Do you mind if I also sit?'

She shook her head.

He sat. And said, 'I'm afraid I have bad news.'

'Banji?' No one else it could be.

A nod. 'I'm sorry to tell you that your friend Banji has been found dead.'

'Did the police kill him?'

'No.' He shook his head. 'We found him hanging. It's too early to be certain, but it looks most likely that he killed himself.'

7 p.m.

They were shown into a room in the morgue. She and Lyndall together.

She hadn't wanted Lyndall there, but Lyndall said she'd never forgive her mother if she wasn't allowed to go, and much to Cathy's surprise the Commissioner – who had come with them – had weighed in on Lyndall's behalf. He said he was sure that Cathy must know that Banji had been previously married and, since the separation had never been formalised, his wife would be the one to claim the body.

'And she might not want you around,' he'd said.

She didn't ask why such a high-ranking policeman was paying so much attention to a single death, or why his wife wasn't the one to identify him, or how he knew so much about Banji, including the existence of the wife. Later she would wonder about that.

In the moment, she went into the room. It was small and narrow, with half walls painted white and glass above waist height. There was a bench in the middle of the room on which there was what must be a body. It was covered by a white sheet. No other furniture save an upright chair.

There was a man there. Pale and tall, wearing a sparkling doctor's coat and – and for some reason this detail stuck with Cathy – his mousy-brown hair had been gelled to stick up in spiky tufts.

'Take your time.' He was waiting by the body.

She felt Lyndall's hand slipping into hers and remembered those many other times when, about to cross the road, her young daughter had done the same thing. Remembered thinking – how could Banji have foregone the pleasure of knowing his child and feeling so much trust?

'Are you sure you want to do this?'

Lyndall, her eyes full of fear, nodded.

'Come on, then.' Hand in hand they made their way over to the bench.

'When you're ready, I'm going to pull back the sheet,' the man said. 'So that you can see his face. Let me know when you're ready.'

She felt the tightening of Lyndall's grip. She squeezed her hand. Said, 'We're ready.'

The sheet was withdrawn and there he was. Not the man she had known. A wax resemblance: a honey skin greyed, two brown eyes closed and bulging, a fleshy mouth that no longer had any colour and that was turned down to a forbidding line.

She said, 'Yes. It's him.' Lyndall's fingers digging into her palm. 'It's Banji.'

'Thank you.' The man made ready to pull the sheet back up.

'Don't.' This from Lyndall.

He dropped the corner of the sheet and stepped away. 'Take your time.' He went to stand in the corner of the room.

'We want to be with Banji,' Lyndall said.

'Stay as long as you want.'

'Alone.'

Cathy could feel how Lyndall was trembling.

Lyndall inclined her head in the man's direction. 'Tell him he has to go.'

He said, 'I'm sorry. I'm not allowed to.'

Was there a secret microphone in the room so that people could eavesdrop? There must have been because when Commissioner Yares opened the door, all he said, and to the man was, 'Leave them.'

'But, Commissioner.'

'I take responsibility. You can have that in writing.'

'If you say so.' The man slipped past the Commissioner and out of the room.

'Thank you.'

The Commissioner nodded. 'Just one condition. Because there will have to be a post-mortem examination, you must not touch him. Do you understand?'

When Cathy nodded, he left the room, closing the door quietly behind him.

She stood, motionless, Lyndall's hand was still in hers.

She looked down at the man she once thought she had known. He was lying there. So still. So unlike himself, if, that is, she had ever really known who he was.

It's a second death for me, she thought. The first was many years ago when she'd had no choice but to cut him from her heart.

All those years that had passed before he had reappeared and never once had it occurred to her how much Lyndall looked like him. And now, seeing her live daughter and her dead love, it was as if she could hardly tell them apart.

She said, 'I love you.' Whispered it so that neither would hear.

Lyndall's hand was limp in hers. She let it drop.

Lyndall moved forward then. Just a step until she was close to him. She raised the hand that Cathy had been holding.

Cathy readied herself to spring forward.

Lyndall kissed two fingers and then she lowered them until they came to rest just above Banji's forehead. 'Hello, my daddy,' she said.

11.30 p.m.

They were side by side on the sofa as they had been for hours. In silence. Until at last Lyndall's voice sounded out: 'Was it my fault?'

'No, darling. It wasn't.'

'But I knew he was there. I could tell he wasn't okay. I should have told you.'

'He asked you not to.'

'I shouldn't have listened to him. If we'd got to him earlier, if you'd been able to stop him . . .'

'Listen to me.' She stretched out an arm and pulled Lyndall to her. 'It is not your fault.'

She felt how Lyndall was trembling.

'But if I had . . .'

'Sshhh.' She gripped her tighter and began to rock her. And that's the way they stayed for a long time, Cathy rocking Lyndall, who shed the tears that she could not.

One day she would. She knew that. Knew how much she had loved him.

But for now she needed to face the truth. And share it with her daughter.

'That first time he left,' she said, 'had nothing to do with you.'

'It was because you were pregnant.'

'I was pregnant, but that isn't why he left. He told me why. Said he didn't love me. That he never really had.'

'But he came back.'

'Yes, he did, and it's taken me all this time to understand. I realise now it wasn't to do with me. It was to do with you. He came back because he wanted to know you.'

Saturday

One Year Later

Peter

'With only ten days to go before the election,' the reporter was saying, *'it would take something as serious as last year's riots to stop the onward march of the government. And even if rioting was to break out again, the Prime Minister has proved himself a strong leader in times of crisis.'*

'Not bad for a liar,' Peter told the air.

'Perhaps this is why he is currently polling as well as both Margaret Thatcher or Tony Blair did at the peak of their respective careers.'

'Not news,' Peter said. And it wasn't.

The Prime Minister's public humiliation of his son (who got a driving ban – big deal – and a slap on the wrist for a bit of pot) had made him the nation's favourite and put an end to any further leadership challenge. The end of the drought, and the spike in tourist revenue, had added to the feel-good factor. So now, despite his previous and oft-repeated insistences that he was planning to step down after the election, the Prime Minister had made it clear that since the country and the Party wanted him, he would serve another term.

'He seems to have become that rare thing – a politician who, having apparently moved past his sell-by-date, has a late resurgence.'

'Enough.'

Beyond enough. He clicked the radio off.

He was in shirtsleeves, alone at the kitchen table, while Patricia dozed upstairs. He could go on being in his shirtsleeves, he turned his wrist to look at the time, for at least another hour before he had to leave. He poured himself a third cup of coffee.

One year on from his fall and he had grown accustomed to this slower pace of life, which was bound to slow down even more after he gave up his seat. It suited him. Granted there were still times, mostly in the dead of night, when he would wake in a panic about how he was meant to survive this smaller life, but the sight of Patricia beside him was enough to drive such doubts away. He also had consultancies and seats on boards aplenty, which brought the added advantage of a bank balance that, despite the punitive maintenance payments, was much healthier than it had ever been.

And, of course, there was the baby to look forward to.

How wonderful to be able to spend time with this one when he came. Not like when Charles was born, when he'd been distracted by the urgent need to build a political career.

Which reminded him: Patricia had suggested he send the picture of the latest scan to Charles as a way of coaxing him round, if not to Patricia then at least to the brother who'd be with them in a couple of months.

May as well do it now.

He went to the bottom of the stairs and called, 'Where did you store that scan, darling?'

No reply. She must have dropped back to sleep.

Her laptop was on the kitchen table. He'd find the photo on his own and forward it on to Charles as a surprise to her.

He switched the laptop on. When it asked for her password, he typed in the four digits of his birthday – sweet that she had chosen these.

Easy enough after that to locate her store of photographs, although the sheer quantity of folders was daunting.

As efficient as ever, she had named each folder, although, he soon discovered, not in a way that was open to easy interpretation. When he tried the obvious one – 'Baby' – it opened to a series of photos of Patricia with her three best friends, all of them looking much the worse for wear from drink. And her folder called 'Recent' was a series of selfies she had taken in the bath. Touching to see how she was smiling, and how she had focused the camera on her growing bump. Impressive also that she had not dropped her phone in the water while taking them.

He cast his eye down the list again. There was one labelled 'BS'. Could stand for Bullshit or, equally, Baby Scan. Yes, he had a good feeling about this one. He clicked on the folder.

And nearly fell off his chair.

* * *

334

He couldn't stop himself from roughly shaking her.

She opened her eyes in fright. 'What's wrong?'

'What does "BS" stand for?'

'I'm sorry?' She blinked. 'What did you say?'

'You heard me.' He shook her again. 'You have a folder called "BS": what does it stand for?'

She swallowed.

'Answer me.'

She pushed herself up. Covered her stomach with both hands as if she was in danger of being hit.

Which he would never do. Although he felt like it. 'I'm waiting,' he said. 'What does it stand for?'

She looked at him. Said, 'Bill's Surveillance,' the first word tripping up against the second.

'Who's Bill?'

'A friend.' Then she shook her head. 'No. More like an acquaintance.' Another shake. 'Doesn't matter who he is.'

'He was following us?'

'Yes.'

'He took those photos?'

'Yes.'

'The ones of us in bed as well?'

'Yes.'

'And then he sent them to Frances?'

'Yes.'

'On your say so?'

'Yes.'

'Why?'

Silence.

'I want to know why you wrecked my marriage.'

'I didn't wreck your marriage,' she said. 'You didn't love her. You loved me. You kept on saying so. But you were never going to leave her.'

'I was,' he said. 'I told you that I was.'

'But you weren't. You didn't have the guts.'

'How dare you?'

335

'I knew it for sure when you prostituted me with that policeman – and all so she could find the ammunition to get her to Number 10. Wasn't your style to ask me to fuck another man, so I knew she was the one who had suggested it.'

'You ruined my political career.'

'You wouldn't have been happy. Not with her.'

He looked away.

'You were so under her thumb you couldn't have left her. Not unless she chucked you out.'

He said it again: 'You ruined me.'

'It wasn't me. You keep harping on about how the Prime Minister was to blame for making your private diaries public. Maybe he was. But how do you think he would have got hold of the diaries? She must have given them to him.'

'You make me sick.'

She looked at him. 'Do I?' She held his gaze so tightly that eventually he looked away.

Joshua

The last time he'd come here, she'd objected to his car outside her house. So this time he had his driver stop a block away. Then, dressed in civvies (she'd also told him to keep his uniform out of it), he walked around the corner, pushed open a gate that was half hanging off its hinges, passed along a path that badly needed weeding, and to her door where, because he knew that the bell didn't work, he knocked.

She opened the door and said, 'Oh, it's you, is it?' as if, despite his calling to tell her that he was on his way, she hadn't known he was due. She looked him up and down. 'Thought you'd be sporting the badge.'

'What badge?'

'Of your elevation. I saw they made you a proper Sir.'

'We only get to wear that on formal occasions.'

'Pity,' she said. 'Your kind like to show off all the time.'

He said, 'You asked me to come here, and here I am. You better tell me what it is you want.' And then, as she continued to block the entrance, he added, 'Do you really want to talk on the doorstep where everybody will see us?'

She stepped aside. 'The lounge,' she said.

It not being his first visit, he knew which way to go. He went down the corridor past the line-up of photographs of Julius. He walked through a doorway and into a small room that was under-furnished but newly dominated by a huge wall-hung television screen.

'Yes,' she said, following his gaze. 'I did buy it with your money. That's what you're thinking, isn't it?'

'It's not my money,' he said. 'Now tell me, why am I here?'

'That's good,' she smiled. 'I like that you don't pretend.'

'What do you want?'

'I want our deal made formal. I want it written down.'

'Don't you trust me?'

'No reason why I should. But why I want a proper document is because you lot never do last long. Take the other one – your deputy – that you did the dirty on.'

'What makes you think I did the dirty?'

'My husband was a copper. Other coppers tell me things. Especially now he's dead.'

'Coppers have been known to exaggerate.'

'Don't get me wrong: whatever you did to him, I couldn't give a shit. Why I'm bringing him up now is that he was riding high – talk was that he was after your job and nearly got it – and where is he now? Working security in Asda would be my guess. If it happened to him, it could also happen to you. Okay, you're white, so you won't fall so far – but if it happens, I'd be the loser. I want what's due to me – Julius's pension – no matter whether it's you or some other idiot in charge.'

'What you're getting is more than a constable's usual pension.'

'Yeah.' A quick bark of hollow laughter as she turned her head to look around the room, at its dowdy walls and sparse furniture. 'I'm living the life of a multimillionaire.' Her gaze was now on him and hard. 'I want our arrangement formalised.'

He reached up to straighten his cap, which, he realised at the last minute, he wasn't wearing. 'All right,' he dropped his hand back down. 'I'll ask somebody in the Federation to prepare the paperwork. They'll send it to you to approve and sign.'

'Thank you.' Swallowed. Looked away. Swallowed again.

'Is there something else?'

'No,' she wouldn't look at him. 'Nothing.'

'Well then.' He had to squeeze himself against the wall to pass her. Once out, he made his way to the front door.

And heard her saying, 'I saw them.'

He stopped. 'Saw who?'

'That fat white woman and her daughter. They paid for a rose bush in the crematorium and they go there every week. Make sure it's watered.'

'That's good of them.' He made to leave once more but she stopped him again with a question.

'The girl. Is she his?'

He shrugged.

'She is his, isn't she?'

No point in lying: it was clear she knew. 'Yes, she is.'

She nodded. 'Julius wanted children, you know. More than anything, but I couldn't have them. That's what made him turn away from me in the first place.'

'I'm sorry.' And he was. This was a decent woman hardened by what her husband had done and by what had been done to her husband.

'She looks nice,' she said. 'The girl, I mean. He must have been gutted not to get to know her.'

Something in her tone. 'You do understand, don't you, that if you were to approach her, or her mother, that would void our agreement?'

'Yes,' she said. 'I know that. But that's not why I wouldn't tell. Enough harm's been done without me adding to it.' A pause and then, 'The name – Banji – the one you said he used with them, it kind of suits him.'

'It should. He chose it.' He opened the door. Stepped out.

Her voice pursuing him down the path. 'It's dishonest, though, them not knowing. Don't you think?'

Cathy

Six months after the Lovelace had closed and they were back.

It felt nothing like going home: whole sections of the estate had been torn down and the rest was so heavily boarded there was no longer any home to go back to.

Only the community centre had been preserved and, for this occasion, given a fresh lick of paint. But to get to it they had first to pass through a checkpoint where private security officers employed by the Lovelace Development Project rifled through their bags. Once through this checkpoint they were met by the sight of two lines of police standing opposite each other and creating a corridor that was so narrow they had to walk down it in single file.

With Lyndall leading and Jayden (who was now living with them) behind, Cathy concentrated on putting one foot down and then the next, over and over again, and that way trying to control the urge to turn on her heels and run away.

It's the police, she thought, they're giving me claustrophobia. And said, 'Do they really think we're about to start throwing stones at a building site?'

'Nah,' came Lyndall's reply. 'They're here to stop us refugees making for a country which we don't belong to.'

Her words had the ring of truth: although the Lovelace looked worse than it ever had, with rubble everywhere and its walkways blocked, most of the flats in the blocks that were due to be constructed had already been bought off-plan. And although final completion was at least two years off, the High Street was already abuzz with changes, with burnt-out shops taken over and refurbished to sell the kind of goods – French baby wear, handmade frozen meals – that the old residents of the Lovelace could never have afforded.

Why couldn't she summon up the energy to feel angry about that? It would help her if she could, damning the future being so much easier than mulling over the past. And yet, while Lyndall kept muttering about the filthy rich, Cathy couldn't stop herself from remembering.

She looked up to where they once had lived and, although it was all boarded up, she seemed to see herself and Lyndall standing on the landing and looking down. She knew what they were looking at: they were watching Banji tracking Ruben along this self-same route.

That's when it began to go wrong, she thought, as memory dragged her on to that next moment: Banji handcuffed on the floor of the community centre and Ruben lying still. She saw Banji struggling to get to Ruben. As if he were trying to hold back Ruben's death, she thought.

As if the thread that had joined the two men's lives had doomed them both.

She couldn't shake the feeling that it was her fault: that Banji had only been trying to protect Ruben because she expected him to.

Stop it, she told herself: too fanciful. She squeezed her eyes shut, forcing back the tears that had begun to pool.

When she opened them again, she was surprised to see how dull and grey was the sky; then, it had been blue, she remembered, and hotter than she could now imagine.

'Mum.' Lyndall's voice, summoning her back into the present. 'Mum, are you okay?'

She nodded.

The police lines, she saw, had tapered off to let the crowd expand into the space in front of the community centre. So many people that she hadn't seen for months who had come back, on this anniversary of their first vigil, to remember Ruben and to protest the failure of the IPCC to finish its report and hold anybody to account.

As Lyndall and Jayden weaved their way through the crowd, high-fiving kids with whom they were no longer schooled, Cathy greeted her former neighbours, hugging some, nodding to others. Hard to smile and not to cry, and yet, seeing Ruben's parents by the entrance to the community centre, she told herself it wasn't her right to fall.

But when, soon afterwards, the commemoration began and Lyndall and Jayden were called to lay the flowers, her tears started to run.

Such a loss, she thought, not only for Ruben's family but for the wider family of the Lovelace. As if the wrecking ball that was demolishing their homes had first run through their lives, turning the estate, and Ruben and Banji along with it, into dust.

So little she had left of Banji. No photos to look at. No letters to read. It was as if the man she thought she once had known had never really existed.

'Mum.' She felt Lyndall's arms going round her. 'It's all right, Mum,' and then, as she turned to Lyndall and continued weeping on her shoulder, she realised that she did have something of Banji's.

She had the most precious thing of all.

Abbreviations and Police Terms

APW: All Ports Warning
BBM: BlackBerry Messenger
Bronze: responsible for the command of resources, and carrying out functional or geographical responsibilities related to the tactical plan
FME: Forensic Medical Examiner
FWIN: Force Wide Identification Number
Gold: assumes overall command
Gorget patches: insignia on the collar of a uniform
IAFPA consistent/distinctiveness scale: International Association for Forensic Phonetics and Acoustics scale that measures how consistent and distinctive is the match to any particular voice
IPCC: Independent Police Complaints Commission
LAS: London Ambulance Service
Level 2 trained officers: trained for two days every six months to deal with disorder; have access to full protective equipment
LFB: London Fire Brigade
NPCC: National Police Chiefs' Council
PCC: Police and Crime Commissioner
PSU: Police Support Unit
RIPA: Regulation of Investigatory Powers
SC&O10: specialist crime directorate responsible for covert policing
SC&O19: armed response unit that includes tactical support and firearms officers
Section 60 of the Public Order Act: relates to stop and search
Silver: coordinates the tactical response

SO1: the specialist protection branch
TAU: Tactical Aid Unit (Manchester)
TFC: Tactical Firearms Commander
TSG: Territorial Support Group

Acknowledgements

The idea for *Ten Days* grew out of my verbatim play that, commissioned by London's Tricycle Theatre, was put on in October 2011, not long after the conclusion of the 2011 riots. A special thanks to Nicolas Kent for gifting me this project and for making it happen on stage.

I have used the deep background and some of the details that I had gathered for the play in the novel, but *Ten Days* remains a work of fiction whose plot and characters have sprung entirely from my imagination. Even so, I would like to thank Martin Sylvester Brown, Sergeant Paul Evans, Mohamed Hammoudan, Sadie King, Leroy Logan MBE, Pastor Nims Obunge, Stafford Scott, Chief Inspector Graham Dean and Sir Hugh Orde for generously sharing their experiences and so helping me understand how a riot can happen. Thanks also to Clifford Stott and Martin Scothern for taking the time to talk to me about the police force, to Helena Kennedy QC for putting me right on the structure of the Ministry of Justice, to David Winnick for guiding me round the House of Commons, to Ed Miliband and his office for further inducting me into the workings of Parliament, to Giles Fraser and John Turner for showing me round their stomping grounds, and to Kamila Shamsie for reading and commenting on the manuscript just when I needed her to.

My agent, Clare Alexander, not only helped me find the idea for *Ten Days* but also gave me the courage to write it: her thoughts, and her readings, were invaluable throughout. This novel also brought me the pleasure of working with a new editor, Louisa Joyner, whose thought processes are lightning fast and just as deadly effective. I thank them both, as well as the whole of the Canongate team: it has been a pleasure.

Thanks to Cassie Metcalf-Slovo, who helped me especially in the initial stages of the book. And finally, thanks to Duncan James, who read as I wrote and whose generous feedback and love sustained me during the writing of this book.